AMERICAN FICTION

Volume Nine

AMERICAN FICTION

Volume Nine

Joyce Carol Oates, Guest Judge
Alan Davis and Michael White, Editors

New Rivers Press

1997

New Rivers Press is a nonprofit literary press dedicated to
publishing the very best emerging writers in our region, nation,
and world.

The publication of *American Fiction* has been made possible by
generous grants from the Elmer L. and Eleanor J. Andersen
Foundation, the Beim Foundation, the General Mills
Foundation, Liberty State Bank, the McKnight Foundation,
the Star Tribune/Cowles Media Company, the Tennant
Company Foundation, and the contributing members of New
Rivers Press. New Rivers is a member agency of United Arts.

New Rivers Press
420 North 5th Street, Suite 910
Minneapolis, MN 55401.
(612) 339-7114
www.mtn.org/~newrivpr

Again, for Cathy and Karen,
and for you, too,
with this book in your hands.

CONTENTS

Editor's Note

Alan Davis

This is the ninth volume in the *American Fiction* series, an annual anthology that searches out the best stories by emerging writers through an open competition. For the first six editions, co-editor Michael White and I read every submission and chose the finalists, all of whom were published. Our guest judge then chose a First, Second, and Third Prize winner and wrote an introduction. Those guest judges were Wallace Stegner, Tobias Wolff, Louise Erdrich, Anne Tyler, Ray Carver, and Ann Beattie.

By the time we moved the anthology to New Rivers Press for Volume Seven, which Tim O'Brien judged, we were receiving too many manuscripts each year to do them justice without a staff of assistant editors to screen stories. (Charles Baxter judged Volume Eight.) This year, for Volume Nine, we still have in place such a staff—Kassie Fleisher, David Pink, and Margaret Risk. All of them are writers, and their bios can be found at the end of the book. They have been enormously helpful. Deb Marquart, who was an Assistant Editor for volumes Seven and Eight, is now an Associate Editor. Her assistance has been invaluable, and her bio can also be found at the end of the book. Finally, we also have in place this year a staff of good editorial assistants, and we are very grateful for their help. They are Barb Beckman, Mark Kolstad, Megan Randall, and Karen Stensrud.

In previous Editor's Notes, we have described in more intimate detail the process of editing a typical volume. This year, we'd simply like to thank the following people: first and foremost, Joyce Carol Oates, for serving as finalist judge and for writing a discerning introduction; Dee Kruger and Betty Kucera, secretaries of English at Moorhead State University, and Irene Graves and Emily Gray, at Springfield College, for their assistance; and the various student workers at both institutions who helped make this volume possible. Moorhead State University and Springfield College have also provided assistance, either in the form of grants or release time, and we thank them. We also thank New Rivers Press, especially Bill Truesdale and Phyllis Jendro, for their support, their encouragement, and their hard work. Most importantly, of course, we want to thank everyone who submitted their stories to *American Fiction*, but especially Co-First Prize Winners Elizabeth Graver and Margo Rabb, Second Prize Winner Nancy Reisman, Third Prize Winner Dulcie Leimbach, and Honorable Mention Jim Nichols. Their bios, and those of all other finalists, appear at the end of the book.

There is nothing else to say. We have done our best, and our choices are before you. Read and enjoy. You may be meeting many of these writers here for the first time, but we have the feeling that you'll be hearing from many of them again, and often.

INTRODUCTION

———

Joyce Carol Oates

"The secret of life is in art."
Oscar Wilde

I have a story to tell. Listen!

In reading, and rereading, this gathering of wonderfully varie-gated short stories, I felt the quickening of excitement that comes with being a privileged listener. In each of these stories, and espe-cially in the stories I've singled out for the somewhat artificial dis-tinctions of "prize winners," I could sense the pulse of urgency that makes a story vivid, evocative, authentic, commanding. *Listen!* To read the opening sentences of these stories is to be drawn irre-sistibly into their worlds:

> *Three days after my mother's funeral, my father decided my sister Alex and I should go back to school.*
> (Margo Rabb, "World History")

> *In Elena's earliest memory, the neighbor's cat has come through the open kitchen door with a green snake from the garden in its mouth.*
> (Elizabeth Graver, "Islands Without Names")

> *Between spring exams her second year of college, Jessie sprawled on the chapel steps and wrote in her journal:* I flail in the vacuum, I stum-ble in the maze, led astray by false prophets.
> (Nancy Reisman, "Strays")

> *Every day I wanted to quit. My infant daughter, Mary Eloise, had a suck that could pull a hubcap off a tire.*
> (Dulcie Leimbach, "Feeding Mary E.")

What I looked for in the stories assembled here, out of approxi-mately 1,300 submissions read by the editors, isn't easy to define. Perhaps I wasn't looking for anything specific at all, perhaps I was waiting only to be surprised. I read constantly, and nearly always with pleasure; I seem always to have believed, without articulat-ing it, that, as Oscar Wilde so succinctly says, "The secret of life is in art"—or one of life's secrets, at any rate. It's my practice as a reader to put aside all theoretical expectations and to listen to the "voice" of the story at hand, to be drawn into the narrative as one is drawn to listen to any speaker; having read a story, I may be inclined to reread it, and at this point I begin to respond more critically, yet with no less pleasure and appreciation, for now I can see how, in a well-crafted piece of fiction, the opening sentences, the initial scene, the very title function in terms of the story's destination. *A story is a compact vehicle moving us from point A to point B.* As Aristotle observed in terms of ideal drama, the journey's end should be both inevitable and surprising.

It has been remarked that ours is an epoch of personal memoir and of domestic "realism." Certainly the stories in this gathering bear out such an observation. Nearly all involve themselves with personal, domestic, familial, or "romantic" life; Margo Rabb's "World History" is unusual in its depiction of familial tragedy in a context of large-scale horror—a young girl's awakening to a realization of the Holocaust, and its significance to her as the daughter of a Jewish woman with a "swastika-stamped birth certificate." Margo Rabb's story beautifully brings together the intensely personal and the historical, and rings with the authenticity of a bitter, yet illuminating truth. In school, the bereaved girl sits frozen in her seat, in one of those moments of revelation that define a lifetime:

> . . . The worst thing that could happen in the world right then, it seemed to me, was to send my book forward like everyone else, and pretend that nothing had happened, that [the photo of the Holocaust] was just a photo in a book, in World History Unit Five, and nothing else. As if the war was the kind of thing you could print in a color-coded textbook, shut at the end of the lesson, and give back.

Elizabeth Graver's "Islands Without Names" is a poignant family story, so subtly crafted that we read its conclusion in astonishment, relating it to an opening we had thought we'd understood; an immensely sympathetic portrait emerges of three individuals who are "mother," "daughter," "son" to one another, intimate yet distant, even estranged. The encroaching amnesia of senility, or Alzheimer's disease, is presented here, as so rarely elsewhere in fiction, in terms one might call metaphysical: we are all involved in amnesia, in helpless forgetting of our lives and of one another. The memory-exercise at the dramatic heart of the story draws us in with daughter's hope that it will help her failing, fading mother even as we suspect it will prove futile. How moving the story's final line, emerging out of a lost time, an era when the elderly mother was herself a daughter, confused and frightened:

> Mother? she called, but her mother had slipped away again, and she couldn't seem to find the room.

———

It's true, perhaps, I might have hoped to be surprised by an example or two of experimental writing amid so much judiciously recorded realism; I would have hoped to discover more writers dealing with social, political, historical, and moral issues, reaching beyond closely observed nuances of private life; I would have hoped to be introduced to more angles of perspective that challenge the complacency of mainstream America, as in C. Dawn O'Dell's "I Lift Mine Eyes" and Zoe Keithley's "The Second Marriage of Albert Li Wu." But the intentions of art are after all private, and in no meaningful way public; one ascends to a "public" vision only by way of the small, still voice of the individual.

In this, in what might be called the authenticity of voice, these stories excel. I was moved and utterly convinced by such narratives as Jim Nichol's "C'est la Vie," the unsentimentalized story of a young, already former football player; Lara J. K. Wilson's "Whir of Satisfaction," which reads like the opening of an energetic, episodic novel; William Luvaas's "Carpentry," with its mordant wit and unexpected ending; Rachel Simon's "The Riddle of Flesh and Blood," a remarkable account of an elderly father's relationship with his retarded daughter; Steve Featherstone's "Fire Next Door," one of the more ambitious stories in the volume; and Linda Watanabe McFerrin's "Coyote Comes Calling," which in its zestful intimacy with its protagonist reads like a first-person narration. In all these stories, I was impressed by the air of carefully constructed verisimilitude, without which the most polished fiction lacks a soul.

For what is art but the concentrated effort of making the inner a matter of "outer"—communal—dimensions? Of speaking from the maelstrom of self to the world of "selves?"—of the Other? We are mortal beings but charged, in Shakespeare's eloquent phrase, with immortal longings for both ourselves and others. Out of these longings spring art.

WORLD HISTORY

___

Margo Rabb

Three days after my mother's funeral, my father decided my sister Alex and I should go back to school. My family wasn't religious, so we didn't sit shivah; we'd just been sleeping, reading, and dazedly picking at the endless mountain of baked goods that had overtaken our kitchen since she died. She'd had a sudden pain, a tumor on her liver that turned out to be cancer, and died ten days after the diagnosis; but the doctors said the cancer had been in her, growing and developing, for years.

My sister and I were reading in bed when our father knocked on our door, peered into our room and announced, as he had all week in his usual deadpan tone, that the best thing for us to do was to keep everything as before. On Monday he would re-open his shoe repair shop, I would return to the fifth grade, and Alex to the sixth. Things had to go back to normal.

I stared up at him from my *Anne of Green Gables*. I was entranced by every orphan book I could find—*Heidi, Oliver Twist, The Secret Garden*—like they were company. After the funeral, my school friends who had stopped by had been unbearably silent and careful, afraid to get too close, as if the death was catching. Melody Bly, a religious girl in my class who'd never spoken to me before, had come bearing a card signed by our teacher, Mr. Flag, and my thirty-two classmates; it had a huge gold cross on the front. On first glance I thought it was a plus sign. She talked to me as if she was reciting from a guide to dealing with the bereaved, and gave me a book called *The Five Stages of Grief*, filled with hazy photographs of silhouettes gazing out windows. I stuck it in the plastic A & P bag where my father put all the flower-covered cards we'd received, their vague quotes and sayings in wispy, curlicue scripts I could hardly make out.

My father hovered in the doorway, gazing at Alex and me in our twin beds. He rarely came in our room, as if he was afraid of catching us undressed, and he looked around it now like he was seeing it for the first time: the mobile of satiny stars hanging above our door; the shelf of Barbies, mine scantily clad in tube tops made from old socks, and Alex's with their hair chopped off; Alex's posters of humpback whales and mine of Shawn Cassidy with lipstick marks on his bare chest. Around our beds were the menageries of stuffed animals we'd had all our lives, fur-matted, faces flat as pancakes from years of being slept on. In a sudden wash of maturity at the beginning of the school year I put half of them in the closet, but in the last two weeks I'd taken them out and stationed them around my bed, like a plush army.

My father's eyes focused on the shelf by the window. There was a Yahrzeit candle on it, beside the Barbies. It was the only really noticeable change in our room. When the funeral director had offered the candle to us my father had refused it, but as we were leaving I asked if I could have it. I hadn't known what a Yahrzeit candle was but I wanted it. I wanted everything they were giving us: the Riverside Memorial Chapel's stationery, the funeral guestbook, the Hebrew prayer cards. The only Jewish words I knew were in Yiddish, which my father spattered out in his rare moments of emotion, like when he dropped a dish on the floor: *Oy gavolt! Gottenyu!* But I liked the way the words on the prayer card sounded, anyway; at the cemetery I clutched on to it so hard it became damp in my hand.

I stared at the candle. "It's still burning," I said. The funeral director had said not to blow it out, that it would last for seven days, but I'd been blowing it out at night anyway because, I told Alex, I didn't want the house to catch on fire—though really I wanted it to last longer.

My father shrugged. He didn't care about the candle. The first night, when I blew it out and got in bed, I felt guilty for not letting it burn, for doing it all wrong—just like we were doing everything wrong—not sitting shivah, not covering the mirrors, not doing any of the things Jews were supposed to do. But my father didn't believe in any of it. He would repeat Religion is the cause of all the world's ills as often as Don't throw out the milk without letting your father sniff it first. My mother was the only one in our family who'd appreciated being Jewish at all. She wasn't religious—she shuddered at her memories of the orthodox synagogue her parents had taken her to, crowded with all the other German-Jewish refugees, but she still believed in the traditions: on

Passover we'd grind apples and cinnamon into charosis, and on Chanukah she'd light the menorah and sing *mo'at zur* while my father and sister watched from the living room couch. My sister told friends we weren't Jewish at all, and though I told people we were, I sometimes wondered if it wasn't wishful thinking: that our half-attempts at holidays didn't qualify. I wanted us to do more. Or at least we could eat the charosis on matzah, not like my father did on Wheat Thins.

My father shifted in our doorway. "If you miss any more school you'll spend forever making it up," he said.

Alex shut her book. She'd already completed the homework that Mrs. Shanefsky, her teacher, had brought by along with three boxes of raspberry hamentaschen. "I'd like to go back," Alex said, her voice in the same tone as our father's.

I didn't know what to say. I hadn't made up any homework. I couldn't imagine myself back in the classroom beside Melody Bly and Mr. Flag and my friends who wouldn't even look at me. I stared at my father. He was standing in our doorway exactly as he'd stood in the hospital. He'd hardly sat at all, letting my sister and me perch on the two plastic chairs at the foot of our mother's bed. He'd hovered half in the bright, glossy hall and half in the shadowy room—my mother kept the blinds drawn, like at home. She loved darkness. The doctors would come by and try to open the blinds, and she'd tell them No—just as she refused everything they wanted to do. She'd put off the chemo, though they told her it was her only chance, and when my father and the doctors pressured her into doing it, she threw up, stopped eating, stopped speaking until she died. I blamed my father for the chemo which only made her sicker; yet at night I inched toward him on our living room couch; I wanted to clutch on to this man I hardly knew as closely as I could.

His attitude toward us going back to school was the same practical, optimistic one he'd had toward my mother's illness. He hadn't believed she was dying. None of us did. We still spoke of her in the present tense.

He stared at the puffy stars dangling above his head and pinched one, as if testing if it was real. His glasses were as thick as storm windows, his face expressionless. Stoneface, my mother called him, in a not-so-joking tone. They'd fought endlessly: Talk back! Speak to me! she'd scream at him, and he'd slump on the couch and not respond. They even fought in the hospital: my father wanted to bring my mother's parents to see her and she refused. She'd never liked her parents and the dislike multiplied the sicker she got. One afternoon my father pulled my sister and me into the hospital corridor and said he was bringing her parents anyway; she just didn't understand Omi and Opa was the problem, he said; she never accepted all they'd been through. *All they'd been through* hung in the air above us heavily, unexplained, like everything from our mother's life: her swastika-stamped birth certificate shoved in her dresser drawer; the space on the family tree my sister drew for class, with question marks where her aunts, uncles, and cousins should be. After several phone calls to my grandparents, my sister had found out one fact about their family—the place of our great-grandparents' deaths. Bergen-Belsen. It was all my grandparents knew. My sister penciled it in on her strange and stunted drawing, half a tree with only one limb.

My mother died before her parents got a chance to see her, but my father brought them to the funeral. They sat beside me on the pew, Omi in her heaping wig, Opa steadying himself with his cane. They spoke little except for a few exchanges in German to each other. I hardly knew them but it was a comfort to sit next to them on the bench: I stared at Omi's scratched handbag and Opa's old-fashioned shoes and thought about my mother. I wanted to extract her from them, whatever part of her that they held. But the doctors had told us to watch out for them too; with the loss of their daughter, at their age, and—once again: all they'd been through—this, the doctors said, might be the last blow.

After the funeral my father drove them back to their apartment and sat with them for hours; he called them nightly, now. His own parents were long dead, his fourteen Polish aunts and uncles relocated to Yonkers; only our family remained in Queens, a block from where my father was born. He enjoyed visiting my mother's parents' tiny apartment, and spoke of it as if the few heirlooms they'd brought to America were as grand as they'd always been, no matter how cracked and tarnished they'd become. I loved my father for that vision, because a part of me saw things like that, too. It was the part of me that, even as we drove from the funeral parlor, still half-expected to see my mother walking down Broadway as always, laden down with shopping bags, her tote bag stuffed with tissues and cans of apple juice and enough food so we could survive if we were stranded anywhere, anytime. She was coming back; all I had to do was wait.

And it was that same part of me that believed I could go back to school, just as I had before. That night, as Alex and I packed our lunches, I even began to look forward to the level buzz of the lunchroom and the day packaged neatly into its seven periods. We spread peanut butter and jelly on white bread and cut the crusts off, like we did before.

———

My book bag dug into my shoulders as we walked the four blocks to P.S. 11. It was October; school had only been in session six weeks and we'd missed three of them. I'd thought I could shuffle into my seat like everyone else, but as soon as I stepped into the classroom I couldn't remember where my seat was. I stood at the door like an impostor as the thirty-two eyes scanned me over, looking for noticeable defects, like a lost arm or some huge mole sprouting on my face. Finally I spotted my old empty seat, by the window, sandwiched alphabetically between Paul Panelli and Maya Schwartz. Maya grinned stiffly as I sat down.

Mr. Flag was a new teacher at the school, and managed our over-crowded classroom with unsurpassed efficiency: the day was sectioned into seven neat fifty-minute periods—math, science, lunch, gym, art, language arts, and history—which he timed accurately, so no subject would ever run into the next. We sat in welded-down rows, beside the barred windows (were they afraid we'd steal the desks, or jump out?) and he took attendance with a meticulous Delaney card system—little pink and white cards which he marked up with a four-colored pen. I could see my card on his desk, scarred all over in red. He was as different as possible from Mrs. Shanefsky, my sister's teacher, who'd dotted the box of hamentaschen she'd brought us with the same smiley-face stickers she plastered on my sister's notebook. Mr. Flag was like a businessman who'd wandered into the classroom on his way to the office.

He taught with cards, too—he swore by the Study Skills Acquisition program, color-coded packets which required writing long answers to longer questions which none of us really understood. We used SSA cards in almost every subject; if they made them for lunch and gym, he'd have gotten those too.

As the class set to work on the math SSA's Mr. Flag called me to his desk and handed me the stack of cards I'd missed. Walking to school that morning, I'd worried that he'd single me out and make an embarrassing show of sympathy; but his distant, pained smile, without one mention of the reason for my absence, as if I'd been out with a cold, seemed worse. It was as if he was deliberately withholding sympathy; restraining it as he restrained even a bead of sweat from forming on his forehead under the hot lights. This, and my classmates' fearful looks toward me as if I had the plague, and Melody Bly's hungry gaze, like she wanted to wrap me up and take me home as her own grief specimen, all made me sink back to my seat and stare blankly at the math and science cards until lunch. I didn't answer any of the questions and Mr. Flag didn't seem to notice.

In the cafeteria I unpacked my sandwich and found a slice of pound cake, one of the things the neighbors had brought, which my father must have stuck into my lunch bag so it would get eaten before it went bad. I wasn't hungry, and threw the whole brown bag away, even though my father made us bring them home for re-use. My eyes hurt; part of me wanted to cry but couldn't—I had cried in that cafeteria too many times before, over a dropped ice-cream cone, skinned knee in kickball or a lost mood ring, and I couldn't do it now.

The periods crawled on until finally Mr. Flag had Melody, the class monitor, pass out the history SSA cards and the school-owned *History of the World* textbook for our last class. I stared back out the window, past the empty school yard toward home, where my bed and my books were waiting. Mr. Flag sent Melody to my desk with a stack of the history SSA time periods I had to make up: I'd missed the second half of World War I, and now we were on World War II. She said I hadn't missed much at all.

I watched her return to her desk and dutifully scribble out the answers to every dry question, like the rest of the class, then stared back out the window. Suddenly I heard Mr. Flag's voice. "Are you having a problem with the assignment, Miss Singer?" he asked in a formal tone.

I shook my head.

"Then you should be writing," he said, and clicked his pen.

I opened the book. *History of the World* was color-coded to go with the SSA cards. World War I was canary yellow; World War II a sky blue. I glanced over the long, thick passages on the governments, battle sites, countries' borders before and after the war, statistics of lives lost. I turned the pages to look at the pictures. There were red and yellow maps of countries' borders. F.D.R. in his wheelchair. An army plane over the Pacific. Hitler at a podium, his moustache like a mistaken flick of a magic marker, a German banner waving behind him. Then, in the bottom-right corner of the next page, the last photograph of the section: a concentration camp. Bodies, bone-thin, huddled, half-alive, limbs strewn about so that you could not tell which belonged to whom. Then the chapter ended. The following page was electric orange, the beginning of Unit Six.

Everyone was scribbling the assignment.

I stared at the page with its sky-blue border; the black-and-white photograph. I'd seen pictures of the Holocaust, of the camps before. I'd sought them out, even; I read the diary of Anne Frank and watched Holocaust movies-of-the-week on Channel 5 with hunger; I wanted to know what happened to my family in the war. The books and movies never satisfied the hunger. I couldn't substitute my family's faces for any of the actresses', and the end of Anne Frank's diary left me with the crucial question unanswered: what happened to her family after the war?

I thought of what my mother had said of Otto Frank. A friend of hers from Washington Heights, her German-Jewish neighborhood, invited her to dinner several times when Otto Frank was there. My mother was about ten years old. What was he like? I asked her, proud and envious. She had shrugged. She said he seemed nice. That was all. It was before the diary had been published. She said he was thin and quiet, like everybody else.

I kept staring at the photograph. The silence of my mother's life became even greater, right then, looking at the picture; she never spoke of what happened to her and her family during the war; she tried to shelter us from it, but couldn't, I realized now; she wanted being Jewish just to be the songs for us, the food, but it couldn't be—those couldn't be separated from everything else. Her sheltering, her silence, had told us something just the same. My back prickled, my face grew hot—I stopped seeing the picture in the book, and instead saw my family: my grandparents' eyes when they gazed at my sister and me playing, as if they'd never seen children do that before. My mother, digging her fingernails into my shoulder when she heard German spoken on the bus. Stashing her tote bag full of food and supplies—just in case. Calling the police after hearing fireworks one August night, waking my sister and me, thinking we were being bombed. My mother in the hospital, her stomach inflated with growths, saying she'd always known this would happen, that she would die; that all her life she she'd been waiting.

This tiny photograph in the book, with no names, no explanations, no descriptions of who the bodies were, how they got there, if they survived—this one chapter with its color-coded sections and corresponding questions—it wasn't what my family experienced during the war. This book was about a one-event history, the kind of disaster that begins and ends, with no after-effects, no reverberations. Not the kind of history that seeps in slowly and colors everything, like a quiet, daily kind of war, the war that my mother and my family lived through, which continued to live through them, which never ended.

And the shock was that hints of this had been dropped all my life—hadn't I read *Anne of Green Gables* and *Oliver Twist* for the first time, long before the diagnosis, with the same hunger with which I read them now? When her sickness was the early, vaguely identified allergies, asthma, colds; her days in bed, the darkness of her room, of every room in our house; her face buried in her hands; the crook of her elbow shielding her eyes. The piles and piles of notes to herself, lists, reminding herself to do everything in a frantic, uneven script. The way she hugged me, cross-legged on her lap—long, frequent, unending hugs, the kind you give someone when you're not assured there will be a next one. The "I love you's" we repeated to each other so often, because my worst fear had always been that I would come home one day and find out she'd died, and she wouldn't know I loved her. We repeated it desperately, daily; and when we fought I knew this love gave me an odd kind of power, that she'd never had this guaranteed love with anyone before. I had even been afraid that someone outside of my family would catch my mother and me in these hugs, in these desperate "I love you's"—or that I might accidentally, habitually say one to someone else. I'd even considered them superstitious—but it wasn't, I could see now—it was that I knew, even then, how fragile and uncertain her life was. That the hole my mother's death left had begun forming a long, long time ago.

I stared out the barred windows to the cement school yard. I hadn't answered one SSA question, not only on this card but on any in the stack. I hadn't even faked it, writing notes to friends like others did. My notebook lay wide-open, stark white, my pencil across the blank page.

The classroom was quiet. Mr. Flag watched me with a starched smile. "Miss Singer, if you're having problems with the Unit Five card you can go back and work on Unit Four," he said.

But I couldn't turn the page. I sat frozen in my seat, looking at the picture; I couldn't look forward or backward or do anything but stay there, staring at the bodies, unknown, intertwined, tossing, their bodies, my mother's body, me.

A bell rang, the end of the last period; books slapped shut, assignments passed forward, the tearing of notebook paper; I didn't move. I didn't know why I kept looking at the picture, but the worst thing that could happen in the world right then, it seemed to me, would be to send my book forward like everyone else, and pretend that nothing had happened, that it was just a photo in a book, in World History Unit Five, and nothing else. As if the war was the kind of thing you could print in a color-coded textbook, shut at the end of the lesson, and give back.

Mr. Flag had Melody stand at the front of each row and collect the cards and textbooks. I heard them flapping around me, moving forward.

Mr. Flag stared at me, impatient. "Miss Singer, are you going to pass your book in?"

The books lay in neat stacks on the first desk of each row, which Melody moved into piles on the windowsill. I couldn't move.

"Miss Singer, pass your book in, please," he said.

I heard him whisper to Melody and her patent-leather Mary Jane's click on the floor. I didn't know what I was going to do. I picked the book up. It felt surprisingly light in my hands. As Melody walked toward me, with Mr. Flag's stark face behind her, his fingers bent stiffly over his pink Delaney card system, each card filed into its neat compartment without a thought to who existed in each one, his face with its expression of perpetual annoyance, like we were an incurable breed of disorder, disruption, and lost causes; the last thing I could do was place that book in Melody's hand. She was smiling, the same smile she'd had when she handed me the grief book, the five distinct stages I hadn't entered or passed and it seemed now, never would.

She was still smiling when I threw the book at the window. The window was open, and it hit the metal bars with a loud clang, and clapped on top of the sill as the pages flurried open. The class flinched all at once. Mr. Flag did too; and though his features reassumed their rigid position, and his face admitted hardly a change, the sound continued to ring in the silent classroom as it would in me thereafter.

Islands Without Names

Elizabeth Graver

In Elena's earliest memory, the neighbor's cat has come through the open kitchen door with a green snake from the garden it its mouth. The snake is writhing. In frantic squiggles on each side of the cat's head, the snake is twirling, turning the black cat into a green-horned monster. When her mother saw the snake, Elena remembered, she hid behind the high chair. This is what she remembered most, her mother shrieking and running behind the chair as if her child could protect her. Even then, as a two year old strapped into her seat, Elena knew that the mother was supposed to protect the baby, not the other way around.

There had been applesauce on her tray, and a piece of toast. Elena had not cried. She watched while the cat dropped the snake, while the snake slid under the radiator and disappeared. She had turned in her chair to see her large mother backed into a corner, holding a wet wooden spoon against her chest. Elena had put a piece of toast into her mouth and coaxed it with her tongue until it grew soft. She didn't remember what happened after that, but she knew that she truly remembered the incident because it had never been told to her, not like other childhood scenes that had become, by now, simply the memory of being told.

Her mother claimed to be losing her mind, losing her memory. Elena's brother Danny told himself it was just a ploy to get attention, a good show. She's fine, he told his sister. If it ain't broke, don't fix it. He didn't tell her how he found himself praying, at odd moments, to a god he didn't believe in. Not concentrated, thought-out prayer; it was more like a tic or superstition. Please make her fine, please make her fine.

Most of the time she *was* fine. She lived alone, after all. She paid her bills, and watered her plants, and never wandered outside in her slippers in the middle of the night. It was little, trivial things—the way she kept calling up Elena because she couldn't

remember where she kept her sewing needles, and then, after
Elena told her the needles were in a tea bin in the bottom of the
bathroom closet, calling her again to say she couldn't remember
why she had wanted the needles in the first place. You had a hem
to do, or a button, Elena would tell her, and her mother would say
yes, you must be right, a hem. She would rummage through her
closet and find a hem that was falling down, or a skirt that needed
to be shortened. Yes, that was it, she'd think, smoothing the familiar fabric. And there were always buttons coming loose.

She'd call Elena back to say she had sewn the hem. The phone
rang over and over again in the social services office where Elena
worked. Jean, the secretary, signaled when it was Elena's mother
by lifting two fingers up into the air. A peace sign? A victory sign?
Elena couldn't remember how they had arrived at that two-fin-
gered flag. Half the time, she pretended she was out, then felt so
guilty she ended up calling her mother back.

When Elena was four and Danny was two, they had lived on
Lake Street South. Five years later, they had moved to Toshoga
Lane, and two years after that, to the big house on Call Street.
When Elena was thirty-five and Danny thirty-three, their father,
who was twenty years their mother's senior, had died, and their
mother had sold the house and moved into the two-room apartment where she had been living ever since. Danny had seen it as
an act of calculated martyrdom. She didn't need to live in such a
dive, he had told his sister, with the sale of the house and all that
life insurance money.

But their mother didn't complain about her quarters, though
they were dark and cramped. In the house on Call Street, they'd
had a room for everything: sewing room, playroom, laundry room,
even a walk-in closet in the basement called the jam room where
they'd put orange and apricot preserves that glowed like lamps. In
their mother's apartment, there was only the room you were in and
the other room.

"I must have left it in the other room," she'd say over the
phone, and since the cord stretched long and the phone could be
taken back and forth, Elena never knew which room her mother
was talking about.

"The bedroom?" she'd ask, hoping to help locate the lost ob-
ject, but her mother slept on the couch sometimes these days and
often used her bed as a place to dump magazines, junk mail, heaps
of mending. She'd say, "What, honey?" and pretend not to understand what Elena meant.

Danny resented his mother for her weaknesses and fears because he'd been in therapy for three years and learned that they had become his weaknesses and fears. He had, he knew, inherited her way of turning her head too many times like a frantic bird before crossing the street, her terror of plugging and unplugging appliances, her stomach, which cramped up and stopped working each time her emotions ran even slightly high. He had inherited, too, a large body which should have been sturdy but was, in fact, as fragile as a piece of glass blown too large. He had inherited her white skin prone to rashes, her teary, pink-rimmed eyes. He squirmed away from his mother when she hugged him and tried not to believe anything she said.

Elena was small and strong like her father had been, and wiry like him, and calm. She believed her mother when she said she was losing her memory because why would someone make up a thing like that? Danny thought people would make up anything if it served their purposes. That way she can call a million times a day, he said. She can get you to come over to find her things. She's lonely, Elena said, but it was easy for her to be sympathetic because she had a husband, Jeffrey, who knew exactly where her misplaced keys and glasses were, while Danny was alone and lost things forever all the time.

Elena visited their mother after work, or on Sunday mornings. She would find her sitting large and pale in a chair by the window, her hands folded in her lap, waiting: *I forget I forget I forget*. At first, Elena took out a list of doctors, but her mother refused to listen when she talked about seeking medical advice.

"Nobody can help," she said. "I'm getting old, losing my mind, that's all. It's natural, it'll happen to you. Ai-yi-yi, what can you do?"

And Elena would hear that—ai-yi-yi—and remember how when she was a girl she used to chew up Oreo cookies and spit them into her doll's diaper. Then she would lay the baby on its back, lift its legs up in the air, and open the diaper to find the dark, sweet mess. "Ai-yi-yi," she'd sigh, just like her mother, and she'd wipe her little baby clean. Even then she had been good at that—cleaning up messes, taking control (yes, but you made that mess, Danny would say. You cultivate trouble so you can save the day). It'll happen to you, her mother told her, but she knew it wouldn't, for she was a fighter and would exercise her memory the way she exercised her body on the stairmaster at the gym: *when I was two when I was five when I was ten*.

Her mother was the sort to give up, just sink into it, call when she couldn't find something, wait with her hands in her lap. But she wasn't so old, only sixty-nine, and there were ways to try. Elena checked out books from the library with titles like *How to Develop an Exceptional Memory* and *Increasing Long-Term Retention of Knowledge*. She approached her mother's problem through research, the way she approached the problems of clients at work—teenage mothers, substance abusers, elderly people without homes. Like her Grandma Elena (nine years dead; each February 7th, Elena lit the Yahrzeit candle when everyone else forgot), she was a great believer in public libraries, in telephone hot lines, and brochures put out by the National Institute of Health. There were lots of experts out there, people willing to share their knowledge. She had a whole shelf in her office for her mother's problems alone.

My mother's problem, thought Danny, is she has too goddamn much time on her hands. Her problem is she can't remember if she thought or said something because she goes too long without talking. Her problem is no one ever touches her except for hello and good-bye. Her problem is she's used to running a whole house—do this, do that—futzing over kids and men, and like an idiot she gave up all that space, that big house to lose and find yourself in, and she's too cheap even to take herself out for a nice dinner. For the grandchildren, she told them when they asked her why she was hoarding all her money, but there were no grandchildren in sight. Her problem, he thought again, and his own skin hummed angrily, is no one ever touches her.

He'd had a girlfriend a few years ago, a laughing, plump, pretty girl from Ireland; he'd met her at the chemistry lab where he was a technician and she an intern. Bronwyn, a goy name from far away, and she'd called him Daniel, lifting up the "a" in his name so that it sounded light and airy, far from the flattened nasal whine of Danny in his family's mouth. Bronwyn had been round and pleasant as a feather pillow, and together they'd built molecules out of gumdrops and toothpicks, then taken apart the molecules and fed each other gumdrops, one by one. She hadn't minded his sour humor, seemed to find him funny. She'd gone back. She'd left him. Danny had thought briefly about going to Ireland, but would she have him, and how could he leave his mother all alone? In fact he didn't visit his mother very often, maybe once a month, but he carried his guilt around him like a lucky charm.

He'd gone into therapy because it was free on his insurance plan and it gave him someone other than his smug sister to talk to. The therapist almost never said anything but he was a little in love with her, so he figured it was working. He blamed his mother for this, for that, and the therapist nodded. Sometimes he got sardonic and she smiled a tiny, hidden smile. "I'm looking for my inner child," Danny would say. Or "*Pardonnez-moi* but I neglected to mention that I slept with my mother before I was born." Once she told him he used humor as a defense to mask his pain. "No shit, Sherlock," Danny had said. "For this you charge eighty bucks an hour?" He had said it, then instantly regretted it, for she had looked wounded and in truth he dreamed of comforting her in his arms (she had to have problems, right? everyone did).

In December of the year the memory problems started, Elena decided to take action. It had been almost ten months of phone calls, of lost needles and forgotten shopping lists. But she never forgets your phone number, Danny told his sister. And she never forgets that I forgot to call. Their mother refused doctors and diagnostic tests and left the bottles of vitamins from Elena unopened on top of the bread box.

"I've got some books," Elena told Danny on the phone on the first day of Hanukkah. "Just really simple exercises. We'll try out a few when we light candles with her tomorrow. You're coming, right? There've been studies—you can make yourself remember better."

Elena arrived before sundown with candles, books, and a Scottish afghan for her mother wrapped in fuchsia tissue paper. Danny arrived an hour late. They broke the rule and lit the candles in the dark.

Baruch ata adonoi, chanted their mother, the words too old for her to forget, and she lit the shamas candle, and Elena lit the first day, and Danny lit the second.

"Why do we light candles on Hanukkah?" their mother asked them. For a second even Danny thought she might actually have forgotten, but then he realized she was speaking to them in her mother tone.

"Oil in desert seven days eight nights," he answered, and his sister smiled gratefully.

"So listen," Elena said. "I couldn't find my dreidel, but how about we play another game?"

Danny and their mother made identical peevish faces and shrugged. "Here," said Elena, pulling out her books. "I think this one will be fun. It's called *The Palace*—" She paused. "*The Memory Palace.* From an ancient Chinese custom?"

"Chinese?" their mother asked. "On Hanukkah?"

"That's our Elena," Danny mumbled.

"OK," said Elena. "Sit down. Now this is how you play."

Once, long ago, in the sixteenth century, she told them, an Italian priest came to China and brought with him a powerful memory system that has been used in Europe since the days of ancient Greece.

"Is this a game or a story?" Danny asked, but in truth he didn't mind so much sitting at the table in the dark with the candles flickering, listening to his sister speak.

The way it worked, Elena told them, was you built a palace in your head, a great big mansion or castle, and it could be based on a real place or you could make it up, or a little of both, but either way you kept it there and thought about it *all the time*—that was important—and each room housed a different memory, so when you wanted to remember something, it was simple—you just went into that room. Say you were a tax collector and needed to remember some names. You made the piano room the room with those names, and when you needed the names, you went into the piano room and there they were.

"The candles are dripping," her mother said, and Elena flew up to find a trivet.

"So let's try it," she said. "Wait—" She slid the trivet under the menorah and flicked on the table lamp, and Danny felt his pupils contract. Elena sat back down, picked up a dusty yellow book and spread it open before her.

"Okay," she said. "This'll be fun. We'll start with something really simple. I'll—" She scanned one page, flipped through some others. "Yes. I'll tell you a few facts about Chinese geography, and we'll put them in a memory palace, and afterwards we'll go back and retrieve the facts."

She looked up. Her brother was scraping wax off the table with his fingernail. Her mother was peering at her, nodding. She's listening, it's working, Elena thought, and she remembered, in a brief shard, learning how to read, how the letters first looked like dark, spiked animals on the page, and then one day, like magic, they attached themselves to sound.

"All right," Elena said. "We'll start with the obvious. China is located on what continent?"

"Umm . . . Africa?" said Danny.

"*Stop it,*" she whispered. "Mom, what continent is China on?"

"China? It's part of Asia. What is this game, Elena?"

"Okay, a harder one. Why don't rainbearing winds from the Indian subcontinent reach the regions of Tibet and Sinkiang?"

"Oh, for Christ's sake," said Danny.

"I'll tell you both the questions and the answers," said Elena. "It's not a test, it's just to give us something to remember."

Sitting there, the candles burning lower, she gave them questions and answers. The rainbearing winds are blocked by the Himalayan Mountains. What three bodies of water immediately border Mainland China? Yellow Sea, East China Sea, South China Sea. What does *Chung Kuo* mean? Middle Kingdom. What does Himalaya mean? House of Snow. China is one, two, or three— *three*—times bigger than the United States. What region is known as the roof of the world? Tibet.

Her mother nodded and listened and looked at Elena with something that might have been concentration but might have been something else. She did not look, sitting there, like an ill or even an aging woman. She looked strong, like a peasant from the Russian steppes, which was where her parents were from. I smell something burning, she said once in the middle. The candles, said Danny. No, something else, like fire, from upstairs. Toast, said Elena, though she smelled nothing. Her mother nodded, but Danny sniffed the air and looked alarmed.

"All right," Elena said when she had given them enough facts. "Now we need to make the palace. What should it look like?"

"The Trump Tower," said Danny.

"Mom's never been there."

"And you have? I thought we were allowed to make it up."

"It has to be something we can picture. Mom? Where should we set our memory palace? You pick a place."

Their mother made a small, resigned gesture out in front of her. "Here?"

"It's kind of small."

Danny snorted. "You see? You give up your palace for no good reason at all, and then where on earth do you put the names of all the people who owe you taxes?"

"Please," Elena whispered. For a moment he thought her eyes might be full of tears.

"All right," said Danny. "All right. How about we use the Call Street house? There's plenty of room."

"What do you think, Mom?" Elena asked. "The Call Street house?" Their mother looked up, her eyes blank. "Should we put the geography facts there?"

She nodded slowly. "All right."

"And we can invent more rooms if we run out. What room should we start in? We'll start with the rainbearing winds. The rainbearing winds are blocked by what mountains?"

"*What* mountains, Elena? *What* winds?" their mother sighed. "I don't know about this game."

"The winds in China." Elena looked over at Danny almost triumphantly, as if to say, *see, it's true, she can't remember.* "It's the Himalaya Mountains, but now we'll put that fact in a room in the Call Street house. You pick a room."

"Oh—the pantry."

"Great," said Elena. "So now the pantry is where we store that information, and each time we think of the pantry we think of the Himalaya Mountains, like the mountains are in there. So let's try it. What mountains are blocked by the rainbearing winds?"

"The Himalayas," said her mother.

"Yes!"

"Don't forget about the pantry," Danny mumbled, and he saw it the way it used to be, its tall white cabinets, its gleaming toaster, the way his mother, though she was not tall, always managed to keep the chocolate chips and brown sugar shoved way back on the topmost shelf, where Danny could not reach.

Elena put the bodies of water in the upstairs bathroom, the Middle Kingdom in her parents' bedroom. Her mother looked cold, so Elena put the new afghan around her shoulders. The candles had burned out and it was getting late but it didn't matter; Elena's husband was playing poker with his friends, and Danny had nowhere to go.

"All right," said Elena. "What does *Chung Kuo* mean?"

The Middle Fucking Kingdom, thought Danny. He wanted to whisper it to his mother like they were cheating at school. Even more, he wanted the words to rise unbidden from her mouth.

"Picture your bedroom," Elena said. "Picture what we put there. What does *Chung Kuo* mean?"

Their mother shook her head. "I told you," she said, her voice high and whiny. "I told you something's wrong with me. Why do you pester me like this?"

"I'm not pestering you, I'm trying to help. People have used this method for thousands of years. This will be the last one for now. Imagine your bedroom at the Call Street house. What did we put in there a few minutes ago?"

Their mother grabbed hold of her mind and pushed it back, and there was the bedroom and all that space and that huge bed for two people and her husband who told her not to worry about money, but at night with the radiators hissing, burning fuel, and her children asleep next door, and her husband who was old and would die before her, she had worried. He hadn't been a warm man; they had left wide girths around each other, which was lonelier, she realized after he died, than living all alone. The ceilings in the bedroom had been tall, and she had never quite belonged there. Sometimes Danny (never Elena, or was she just forgetting?) would cry out in his sleep, and then she'd go to him. He'd been a sad, fretful, sickly child, but these were some of her happiest memories; his needs were so simple in the middle of the night—to be soothed, held, told *shhh*. Little bear, she had called him, but in the end she couldn't soothe him well enough, and he had turned into a sad, fretful, sickly man.

This place, this two-room apartment which she kept messy as a nest, was more her size, and she was happier here. Her children didn't believe her; she knew that. They thought she had moved because of cheapness, or out of some desire to make them watch her do without. All her life she'd had people around her—her parents, her husband, her children—and that huge house with its doors and windows and so much dirt, dust always creeping past the thresholds, mud on the children's shoes, burrs on their socks and in their hair. She hadn't had a mind that could sit still with all that; she had worried and plucked, wiped and cleaned, but never enough. She remembered how her mother would visit and walk around with her nose wrinkled, as if their lives smelled slightly sour. She knew Elena thought she called her at work because she was lonely, but it wasn't that, not quite. Lately she found herself bewildered: was I here or was I there, looking for this or that, and why? Elena could tell her, even if she was wrong. You were going to the store, you need your umbrella, tea, prunes. Other times, something came over her that looked, from the outside, like sadness (it was happening now, she could feel it in her eyes and on her face) but wasn't quite—tears rising unannounced, surprising her. If it was grief, it felt so far away that she couldn't recognize it, like a person she was related to but had never met.

"What, Mom, what's wrong?" asked Elena, for their mother was sitting silently, gripping the arms of the chair, tears streaming down her cheeks.

"Jesus, Elena, don't you know when to stop?" asked Danny.

"I'm sorry, Mom. I didn't mean. . . . It's the Middle Kingdom, that's the answer. I'm sorry."

"What?" Her mother turned to her.

"The bedroom. In the bedroom is the Middle Kingdom, what

Chung Kuo means. Let's stop playing. It's getting late."

Their mother rose heavily, went into the bathroom, and shut the door. They could hear her peeing in fits and starts.

"I know, I pushed her too far," said Elena. "I shouldn't have. But don't you see, we have to get her help."

You, we have to get *you* help, Danny was thinking. He wanted to say cruel things, to tell his sister that if she wanted a child to bully, then she should have one herself, and if she couldn't have one (they must have tried, she and Jeffrey, something had to be wrong) she should go volunteer somewhere or find an orphan. Our mother is fine, he wanted to say to her. It's you who has a problem. Not her, not me. Only he wasn't so sure it was true.

What *was* his problem? If he could go far enough back, Danny thought, he might be able to follow the string of his unhappiness to its deep, deep source. If there was a source; he didn't know if he believed in that. *My daddy thought I was a sissy*, he sometimes mock-whined in therapy. *My mommy refused to breast-feed me, wah-wah.* "Cut it out," his therapist once said to him. "You're wasting both our time." Then she drew in her breath. "I'm sorry," she said. "I shouldn't have said that." "No," Danny had said, a great excitement rising up in him. "You should, I want you to." For a moment something had almost happened. *I'm just sad*, he'd almost said to her, *I'm so sad and I don't know why* . But she'd lifted up her foot from her pump, then, and he'd seen the arch in its stocking, the fragile bone of her foot, and found himself speechless with desire and anger. "I guess I'm a tough nut to crack," he'd said proudly after a minute, and she'd told him the hour was up.

Now, in the bathroom, their mother thought of the Call Street house and remembered what she could. She remembered that a baby had been born (which baby?), how they had filled her with drugs so she couldn't remember it happening, but afterwards they'd put a baby in her arms and she'd thought how now maybe her mother would respect her and she'd always have something to do. It must have been Elena, who was first. She'd named her after her mother, not as a tribute, but because she thought her mother would approve of the choice, and anyway no other name seemed right. She remembered a temporary job she'd had once when the kids were at school, keeping tabs at the Girl Scout Cookie headquarters: how many orders of peanut butter cookies, of wafer and thin mint. She'd been good at that and thought about getting a real job, but he kept saying we have enough money, we have enough, until she'd almost wished they hadn't.

She remembered walking from room to room in the Call Street house before they'd bought it, singing out, hearing her voice echo, how she'd said it was too much to spend and he'd said no, they should get it, he was doing well in his job. This was a house, she had thought, where you could put a crying baby at one end until it fell asleep and go to the other end for some peace of mind. But her babies were children by then, with clattering footsteps and shrill voices. She remembered the perfect green dress she made Elena for school photo day—out of its pocket, rick-rack daisies grew, only in the end the photo was just of Elena's face, so solemn, and the plain white collar of the dress.

She didn't care about the geography of China. Elena tried so hard, but she never really understood. Though Danny would never say so, he might understand a little better. What she was afraid of forgetting was her self. In the pantry she put her husband. In the sewing room she put Elena. In the jam room she put Danny; if someone had asked her why, she would have shrugged.

She flushed the toilet, stood, and dried the tears that she could not begin to explain. She looked and nodded; her face in the mirror was one she knew. When she came back into the room, her children were getting up to leave. Elena squeezed her hard; Danny gave her a brief, stiff hug good-bye.

"I'll call you tomorrow," he said, and for once she believed him. Sweet Danny. He was difficult and she tried to dislike him, but found she never could. Not like Elena, who did everything right but did not move her. Before she'd given birth, she had thought you loved your children the way cats seemed to love their litters, blindly and equally. When she had first learned she was pregnant, so many years ago, she had thought being a mother would make her a better person, make her selfless, but it hadn't quite worked that way. He would call her tomorrow, but what was tomorrow, how many candles? Did it mean she was losing her mind if one day without appointments bled into the next?

She sat back down at the table. In the living room she put herself, for she was living, knew she would keep on living for years and years, though her brain would separate into places she could not reach, like land breaking off from continents, becoming islands without names. Danny in the jam room. The living room for herself. *In each room, put a different fact.* It was a big, big house and she could lose herself this way, but she wasn't sure she minded. It was a lot of work, keeping track, and Elena did it better, always had.

Lily, her own name, the name of a flower, and her sisters were

Rose and Violet. Lily like a flower in the vase on the coffee table in the living room. Her Russian immigrant parents had found the names in a book called *Looking for the Flowers* and given them to their big-boned girls. Boiled linseed oil mixed with mineral spirits on the wood. A soft cloth made from a diaper. In circles, round and round at first. If she was good at anything, it was this; her furniture, when she used to care for it, had shone and smelled like lemons and cracked seeds. In circles first; her mother whose name suddenly escaped her had taught her and she'd never forget. In circles, then going with the grain. She had liked that part, though she had not liked most of keeping up a house. She might have been a woodworker in another life, or a potter, or a woman who lived alone on the Russian steppes and carved wolves and eggs from stones.

"I'll drive you home," said Elena to Danny as they left the building. Inside his mind he was weeping, but he'd never let her see it.

"She'll be all right," said Elena, meaning you and I will be all right.

She went into the kitchen of her mind and found the cat and the snake, her mother cowering. Why didn't I cry, she wondered. Why didn't I shriek and wail; I was only a baby after all, and scared. Danny tried to make a Chinese palace of his head but found himself picturing the Call Street house. This room for my mother, this room for my mother, this room for my goddamn mother.

"You've done enough damage. I'll walk," he said, wishing he could run but knowing he didn't have the body for it. He wanted to make a room for Bronwyn and Ireland, but he'd never been there. He wanted to forget about rooms and leave his mother and sister far behind.

"It was a really bright idea, to push her like that," he said, turning back to his sister as she unlocked her car.

Doors were closing in his head and in Elena's, houses shrinking into rooms. In her apartment, though, their mother stood up and began wandering from one room to the other. Both rooms are the bedroom, she thought, and laughed out loud. Both rooms are the living room. Her children had visited on the second day of Hanukkah. Buttons were coming undone, wood was gathering dust, but it didn't matter because when you lived alone you could forget to clean for weeks. The jam room was for Danny; the sewing room was for Elena. Elena who was her mother and daughter both—briefly she remembered now, her mother's thick ankles and scrubbed skin, her mother's name. Once a snake had come into the kitchen in the jaws of a cat and made Elena cry. Her mother—Elena's Grandma Elena—had been visiting and had chased the cat out the door with a broom.

The jam, she remembered, had held pulp—curled, glowing bits of orange peel—and plums the color of her monthly blood. So two rooms for the Elenas—the sewing room for the girl and—where?—for the mother. Except the Call Street house was big enough to get lost in. Tibet. The roof of the world. None of them had ever been there, none of them would ever go. Three seas, Yellow and something else and something else. It didn't matter. Mother? she called, but her mother had slipped away again, and she couldn't seem to find the room.

STRAYS

Nancy Reisman

Between spring exams her second year of college, Jessie sprawled on the chapel steps and wrote in her journal: *I flail in the vacuum, I stumble in the maze, led astray by false prophets.* It was 1981, a year of minor chaos. All across campus, forsythia blazed and blossoms of dogwood peeled open. There ought to be a metaphor for this, Jessie thought, so much anxiety, so many flowers, but she couldn't get past the maze image. She lighted a cigarette and wrote the word *maladjusted*, a term she'd been using to describe herself ever since last semester's Intro. to Psych. College was overrated, she thought. It meant nothing if you didn't know yourself. Even her better-adjusted roommate said so.

From a pay phone in the Union she called her mother in Buffalo collect. "I'm a blank page," she told her mother Elaine. "An empty shell."

"Honey, is it protein? You haven't given up fish too, have you?"

"No."

"Well, what do you mean, blank page?"

"I have no history."

"Oh. You'll feel better after that Russian final. You know, your grandfather was born in Russia. Isn't that history?"

"Mom, I have to find myself."

"Where have I heard that before?"

"I mean it. My roommate Roz thinks so too."

"Roz is a lovely girl," Elaine said. "But since when did she become the fountain of truth?"

"Fountain of truth? You mean like the fountain of youth?"

"Whatever," Elaine said.

"I want to find myself," Jessie said, "I want to find America." Just like Simon and Garfunkel in the '60s, she thought. Just like Dylan.

There was a long pause. "Jessie, honey, what is it you're saying?"

"I'm going to San Francisco," Jessie said, surprising herself.

Then, just to sound like she had an actual plan, she added, "I'm taking a bus."

"You can't be serious."

"I've always dreamed of going there, always," Jessie said. "I promise I'll write." She mumbled a fast "I love you" and hung up the phone.

———

The bit about the dream was half true. For weeks she'd seen flyers for the Rainbow Turtle bus line: Explore America! Boston-California! Eight days $199. She'd called the 800 number and gotten the mailing address in San Francisco. Land of cable cars. Jessie pictured a gleaming gold and green one, bobbing up over hilltops, the cobalt bay in the distance, women in sandals and men with goatees waving from cafes, swilling cappuccino and jotting frenzied poems on napkins and restaurant checks. Late at night, all the radio stations would play jazz; during the afternoons, the Grateful Dead. The air would smell of ocean, hibiscus, Chinese dumplings, marijuana. She could visit Abby Rosenberg, her best friend from high school, who had moved to Haight Street and become a bohemian.

Unfortunately, Abby was not popular with Jessie's mother, having shown up stoned at the house one too many times her junior year, and once, while Jessie's parents were out, getting sick from too much acid. Jessie told her mother that they'd sampled the bourbon, and that Abby was a lightweight. Her mother had been skeptical, and for weeks kept suggesting Jessie make friends with Naomi Block, a girl who was even more awkward and less popular than Jessie herself, and who never "got" the poetry they read in English class. Still, both Jessie's and Abby's families belonged to the same temple, and the mothers had graduated from high school together—that counted for something.

The evening of Jessie's announcement, her father called her back and made her promise not to get on a bus before they'd talked this thing out, and certainly not before exams ended. In return, he said, he'd call the Rosenbergs.

"I'm not asking permission, Dad," Jessie said. "I'm nineteen now. I'm legal."

He sighed on the other end of the phone and waited until she got nervous and relented. "Don't worry. I'll finish finals," she sighed back.

Two days later, Jessie's mother phoned to say she would mail extra money for Traveler's Checks and a return airline ticket to Boston, along with a list of their friends in the Midwest and in California, just in case. Also to announce that she and Dad would be visiting San Francisco themselves.

"At the end of July," Elaine said. "We'll meet you there. We'll see the sights."

"This isn't fair," Jessie said.

"We can have dinner at Fisherman's Wharf. We can visit Alcatraz."

———

Jessie spent most of June announcing her plans to Boston friends and speculating that she might never return. It was nearly July when she belted herself into her backpack and rode the subway to South Station to board the Turtle bus. The train jerked and creaked, a tinny, empty string of pods. A few other people lugged suitcases. Jessie adjusted a shoulder strap and pretended to be from Canada: she pictured Toronto, which she'd visited twice, and tried to project ennui, as if she'd been traveling for months. But other riders also looked exhausted, and just before her stop, a man in running shorts pushed past her from behind, tipping the backpack and setting her off-balance.

Outside South Station, the Turtle drivers were already loading up the bus, which was painted in rainbow-colored stripes, with an amateurish picture of a turtle sprawled across the side panel. The drivers looked like hippies and Jessie was suddenly conscious of how new her jeans were. She couldn't pass for one of them, even if she wiped off her lip gloss. The skinny, red-headed driver walked around with a clipboard and a cup of coffee: on top of the bus, a dark-haired one roped down luggage. She watched them for a few minutes, and finally walked up and asked if the redhead had her on the list. He wore a braid all the way down his back, a beard, and a gold hoop earring. He nodded and smiled and heaved her backpack up on top of the bus. Then he was on to the next piece of luggage. Jessie paced the sidewalk and stared at the trains until the driver on top of the bus called down, "You've got a half-hour. You might as well get coffee."

She waved and nodded, and started walking toward the station, stopping a few paces down to light a cigarette. She inhaled and exhaled dramatically.

Inside the Turtle, all the seats had been replaced with wide platforms, foam mats, India print covers. A loft had been built into
the rear, a refrigerator installed up front. Stereo speakers hung
from the walls, and the air smelled of sandalwood incense and
diesel and old coffee. There was no bathroom. Next to the driver's seat, in front of the yellow line, sat a beat up folding chair.
Jessie chose a spot on the front right platform, a couple of yards
back from the door, arranged her coffee and donut, and opened
her copy of *The Awakening*. She sat cross-legged and stared at the
novel's first page as other passengers began to board, glanced up
and nodded at them as they made their way past her. Most of
them looked like college students. Two women spoke rapid
French, but Jessie could only pick out the occasional *"Je sais"* and
"n'est-ce pas?" One man seemed to be a body builder—thick muscled, mustached. Older, Jessie thought. In his mid-twenties, at
least. Another woman looked like a buyer from a mall boutique,
like girls from Jessie's high school: manicured hot pink nails,
khaki shorts and a hot pink Izod shirt, a friendly face. The incon-
gruity between her preppy beauty and the Turtle made Jessie feel
bolder. A trio of scruffy college boys walked by, and behind them
a loud black-clad Brit, about Jessie's age, who claimed he'd
hitched all over the US. A couple of women with asymmetrical
haircuts held hands and didn't speak to anyone else; a green-
haired girl smirked at them. Finally, Jessie noticed a skinny ado-
lescent boy, alone, his hair almost white blond. Twelve, maybe
thirteen years old—the same age as her sister. He looked like he
should be drinking Slurpees and riding bikes, but he carried himself like a veteran passenger.

The red-headed driver introduced himself as Kurt. Rules of the
Road, he said. Respect other people. Respect other people's
things. No cigarettes, cigars, or pipes on the bus. Other burned
leaves—he winked—in fourth gear only. Let us know if you need
a bathroom stop, and give us fair warning.

Jessie responded with small, measured nods: she wanted to
seem interested but not witless or overeager. It was the sort of nod
she'd seen bicycle mechanics use when they talked about gears.

The driver she'd seen on top of the bus was shorter than Kurt—
maybe 5' 7"—and had shaggy, shoulder-length brown hair and a
red bandana tied around his forehead. He introduced himself as
Hiawatha.

"What?" The Brit said.

"Hiawatha. Hiawatha Cappellini."

"Angel hair," the manicured girl whispered to Jessie.

"If you'd rather, I answer to Andy," Hiawatha said. He explained how the drivers worked, switching shifts, one of them sleeping in the little loft while the other drove. They planned to hurry across "the boring states," slow down and camp more in the West. He made a brief speech about the need for cooperation and respect, and said that the drivers controlled the tape deck music, but would take requests. Then all the passengers had to say their names, which was how Jessie learned that the manicured girl was named Cynthia and the boy called himself Joey.

"Let's go," Hiawatha said. "Let's get on the road." Jessie glanced over at the Brit, at the drivers, at the punked-out girl on the back platform, the smiling, French-speaking French women, and the beautiful Cynthia, then gazed out at the South Station train yard. She took a deep breath of bus air, funky with experience, she thought, funky from real lives lived here, on this Rainbow bus, this once-upon-a-time city bus that had been liberated. On the road, she thought. *On the road.*

———

At the first highway stop, the smokers crowded together in the parking lot and lit up. A warm wind shot through the roadside maples and over the asphalt, and from the rest stop railing Jessie watched the highway, wheels spinning at high speeds. The boy named Joey lingered near her, and after a while he asked her for a cigarette. "Okay," she said, "sure," and gave him one, which he lighted and expertly inhaled. He was scrawny, thin arms like bony tubes, blond hair flopping in his face. When she asked him where he was going he looked her straight in the eye, but then she glanced down: his left foot jiggled. "California," he said. "My brother's there."

"That's nice," she said. She would have asked more except for the jiggling foot. Maybe there was no brother, but maybe there was. Of course there was. There must be. She could only think up inappropriate things to say: *What exactly are you doing? Where are your parents? I have a baby sister your age.* So she just stood beside him, facing the highway, hot wind and smell of exhaust mixing with the green summer smells of the roadside trees. She finished the cigarette and smiled at him and turned toward the bus.

"You don't have any candy, do you?" Joey said.

"Just mints."

"Oh." He scuffed at the gravel.

"You want some?"

"Yeah, OK," he said.

She offered up the roll and he took five, pocketing two and putting the other three in his mouth at once.

At the next highway stop, they repeated the routine, Jessie handing over cigarettes and mints, Joey avoiding eye contact and gazing off at the diesel pumps. They headed into the truck stop diner for lunch, but he complained that he had a stomachache, and ordered water.

"What about soup?" Jessie said. "Soup and ginger ale?"

He shook his head.

"Toast?"

He refused. But when Jessie had finished her grilled cheese, he shoved her leftover french fries into his mouth.

"Okay," Jessie said. "You want a burger to go?"

"No."

"You sure?"

"Yeah." He shook his hair off of his forehead, slid out of the booth and away.

At the cash register, Jessie bought a few chocolate bars, a carton of milk, and a bag of chips, which he inhaled on the bus.

———

Maybe Jessie would have struck up a conversation with Hiawatha anyway. Sooner or later, even though she hadn't made the first move since a mortifying eighth grade Sadie Hawkins dance. That evening she was thinking about Joey, not Hiawatha, when she moved to the folding chair beside the driver's seat. She wasn't even thinking "angel hair" or noticing Hiawatha's beautiful skin. Joey had finally fallen asleep on the back platform, under the body builder's extra blanket, after eating two donated ham sandwiches.

"Listen," she said. "I don't think that kid Joey has any money."

Hiawatha nodded.

She waited a minute. "Shouldn't we do something?"

"He's a tough little guy," Hiawatha said.

"Yeah. But he's hungry. I think he's running away."

Hiawatha didn't answer; he seemed entirely focused on the tail-lights of a truck. Maybe she'd chosen the wrong words, violated some Turtle code: maybe the respect rule meant not speculating about other people's lives. She wondered if she should retreat to the platform and pretend she hadn't said anything. But after a couple of minutes, Hiawatha glanced over at her and announced that he himself had been a runaway. He'd been born in eastern New York State and taken to Florida, where the cockroaches were enormous. "Palmetto bugs," he said. "Huge." The foster homes had been cold way-stations, the orphanage worse; at about fourteen he'd struck out on his own. He didn't know his real birthday, he told her. He was twenty-six, maybe twenty-five, no one knew for sure. He only knew he was half-Iroquois and half-Italian. After he'd moved to San Francisco, he'd changed his name.

"Wow," Jessie said. Her own breathing seemed unnaturally loud, and she felt almost lightheaded. "God. Wow."

———

The next morning Hiawatha set up a food fund, officially for anyone on the bus short on cash but really just for Joey. If Joey was running away, Jessie thought, he was running away for a reason. But at least he'd get cheeseburgers. Scrambled eggs. Milk. Protein, Jessie thought. He needed protein.

She couldn't picture her sister Emmy on this bus, only on the one to middle school and the one to summer camp. On the camp bus, kids sang in warbly Canadian accents, played cat's cradle, tried on each other's shoes, traded the sweets their mothers had packed for the trip. Emmy better stay on that bus, Jessie thought. If Jessie had to, she'd make Emmy stay on that bus. As the Turtle crossed the flats of Ohio, she composed a letter, asking Emmy if the lake had warmed yet, if the counselors were being nice, saying she missed Camp Timberlane. *I'm jealous, Em, you lucky thing!* she wrote. At the entrance of a 76 Truck Stop, Hiawatha sidled up to her, almost touched her, smiling enough to show one dimple, and offered to mail the letter.

———

Just because Jessie wanted, more than anything, to find herself, didn't mean she couldn't find someone else too. She told herself this in a women's bathroom in Wisconsin, as she brushed her teeth and washed, then checked her face for signs of change. She told herself this as she watched Hiawatha pay a diner cashier for his breakfast and refill his coffee thermos: the burnt olive color of his forearms, the way his hair licked the back of his neck. *Stay centered*, Jessie thought, *no ideas but in things*, like William Carlos Williams said. She was having a last smoke before reboarding the bus; Hiawatha stopped beside her to talk, *a wild pony in the sunlight*, and she offered him a cigarette.

"I can't smoke anything," he said. "I only have one lung."

"One lung?"

"I was in an accident. A semi went out of control on a mountain curve. I was coming the other way, on my motorcycle."

"Oh my god," Jessie said.

He nodded and ran his hands through his hair, lifting it up off his neck. "You know what they say about the bright light you see at death? I saw it. I saw that light. A tunnel spiraling into a light."

"And then you came back."

He nodded again, and paused, as if in deference to the power of experience. "Of course, rehab took a long time. Half of my ribs were broken." He lifted his T-shirt to show her his scars. His chest was flat and smooth but there were long strips of whitish scar tissue on his left side. She touched one with her index finger. Lightly, as if it still hurt him.

With her other hand, she waved her cigarette. "Should I put this out?"

"You should quit," he said. "You would if you lost a lung."

She nodded solemnly. "I'll do it soon," she said, and took another drag.

In her travel journal she wrote *Hiawatha has really lived*.

That night while Kurt drove and Hiawatha slept, Jessie imagined Hiawatha as a small, coppery-skinned boy kicking at the pavement. No mother. And no father either. She pictured her own parents evaporating into ghosts and started to cry. Such a lonely life. Such a lonely boy. Where did he belong? After no boyhood, he'd turned into a driver on the Turtle bus, crossing the country for work, for adventure after adventure—wasn't that what drew her here to begin with, adventure? But it would be better for Hiawatha to stay in one place. With a *lover*, she thought. It was a word she'd recently started to use. Hiawatha needed a lover, needed stability and care. Hiawatha needed a home.

She sighed and watched the dark plains rush past the window, dense wheat fields, the sky huge and heavy with clouds. Most of the other passengers were asleep, head to toe in sleeping bags on the huge padded platforms. Soon heat lightning began, crackling down to the horizon, wild jagged lines and brilliant flashes. The air itself seemed green, and Kurt said they weren't far from Wounded Knee. Even if they'd had time they wouldn't be stopping: it was inappropriate and disrespectful to bring a bus full of travelers there—he didn't say tourists, Turtle passengers weren't tourists—but Jessie got the point.

In the flashes of light, Kurt's face seemed shockingly pale, and Jessie crossed her fingers to keep the bus from breaking down. She'd read about spirits in the land, but she'd never felt it before: the ones outside the bus were real. Haunted spirits. No other cars passed for an hour, and then an ambulance sped by in the opposite direction. It was a hard world, Jessie thought. This electric storm, this night of green clouds and wild wind, this land of the massacred Sioux could break her in half. Hiawatha knew it. Kurt probably did too, but not in the same way: he was just as much an Anglo outsider as she was. She felt too shy to ask him, but Kurt must have sensed her emotion, because he touched her shoulder then rested his hand on her leg. This calmed her. Suddenly there was shelter.

———

The next morning, when Kurt's driving shift was up, after they'd all had breakfast and he was climbing to the driver's loft at the back of the platform, Kurt asked Jessie to nap there with him. "There's more room up here," he said. "Come on." But something in his face said *sex* and it startled her. "No thanks," she said, and he smiled and narrowed his eyes and said, "You're just a little cock tease, aren't you?" A few feet away, the Brit raised his eyebrows. The greenhaired girl smirked, then shrugged. Jessie made her way over the platforms to the front of the bus, blinking her eyes and pressing her lips together.

She didn't mean to be a cock tease. Maybe she'd somehow been unfair; maybe her flaws were worse than she'd imagined. Maybe this meant Hiawatha wouldn't be so friendly, just when she'd started thinking about kissing him on the mouth. All day she sat on the middle platform reading *The Awakening* and playing magnetic backgammon with Joey. Hiawatha was preoccupied with camping arrangements for Colorado, the locations of state cops, and with the body builder's drunken, maudlin attentions to an un-

interested Cynthia. *Love is never equal,* Jessie wrote in her j
Love is always unrequited. Art is more important than roman
told herself, and avoided the folding chair next to the driver's seat.

But that night after dinner at a campground, Hiawatha followed
Jessie back onto the bus. He took a bottle of Burgundy from his
pack, uncorked it and poured wine into two plastic cups. Here, he
said. It's been a long day. They sat on the middle platform and he
told her about some of his other trips, the ones to Baja, how he was
learning Spanish by living on the beach there. She'd like Baja, he
said. She should take the Turtle there. He rolled his shoulders and
neck, as if to loosen them. The wine tasted good and Jessie's fingers began to tingle. She wanted to touch his skin, to rub up
against him, but held back and hugged her knees. After the second cup of wine, she stretched out and offered to give Hiawatha a
back rub, a common practice on the bus. "Thanks," he said, and
lifted off his T-shirt and lay on his belly. She could see those white
scars again, she could see where that semi had taken his lung and
damaged his body, which was otherwise compact and muscular.
She petted his head then rubbed his back with her fingers and
palms—*electricity,* she thought, *the world is electric and so are we*—
and he continued to talk and to give her wine until Kurt made a
campfire and someone started to play a guitar, and the French girls
started to sing with lovely accents, a little off-key.

———

After that, Jessie's attention strayed to Hiawatha so often she
thought she might be spiritually possessed, and decided to let herself go with the experience. She caught his scent from a few feet
away, dropped out of conversations mid-sentence: was that pull
what dogs felt, those tame golden retrievers who suddenly yank at
the leash? A dog. Dog metaphors, Jessie thought. Oh god. That's
what men always came up with. In sixth grade Artie Eldridge
called her a dog, which was the worst thing you could be, worse
than a slut, worse than a prude. *Worse than a cock tease?* A dog.

The green-haired, punked-out girl named Amy passed Jessie a
joint; after she'd taken a long hit and exhaled, Jessie wondered if
it was time to accept her dog-self. Wasn't that how healing
worked? She was a golden retriever. She was a Labrador. When
Hiawatha glanced over at her, she grinned.

The important thing was *pleasure,* Jessie thought. She fell
asleep on the bus repeating the word. The next morning, as the

bus pulled into a truck stop, she awoke grateful, and wrote in her journal that 1984—only a few years away—would be a year of renaissance, not a year of doom. *The renaissance has already begun,* she wrote, then wandered off the bus. Outside the air was chilly, and coffee from the diner warmed her, steam rising up into her face. She liked the steam. She liked the deep wrinkles in her clothes, the slick softness of her dirty jeans. The bus was deep into the Rockies now. She liked the word Rockies, rolled it around in her mouth. A little like lemon. A little like salt. Hiawatha told her they were heading for another campground, this one with showers, a park full of aspens. He squeezed her shoulder. Everything was fluttering and green, she thought. Everything fluttered.

———

Jessie had had sex exactly ten times in her life, all of them during the previous year. She'd never made love on a mountain though. If there were no wind, and enough heat and shelter, she would have chosen a mountain peak; she imagined that would be like making love in the sky. Instead, she and Hiawatha left the others for a clearing off a hiking trail. The evening sky had turned indigo and the moon was rising. The temperatures were mild. Jessie and Hiawatha kissed, big open-mouthed kisses. *I'm Kissing Hiawatha Cappellini,* she thought. The idea of the kiss and the kiss itself melted together, the thrills blurring. Pretty soon they'd peeled off their clothes and lay on top of an unzipped sleeping bag. "You're on the pill, right?" Hiawatha said.

"No," she said. "That's bad for your body." Plus it makes you gain weight, she thought. She had a diaphragm in her day pack. For a moment she forced herself to consider the bad things sex can do: pregnancy. Syphilis. Herpes. The previous year, a girl in her dorm had caught herpes; the girl's roommate whispered this to Jessie in the hall, how it hurt, how the girl who got it cried all the time and broke up with her boyfriend.

"What about you?" Jessie said, and Hiawatha frowned.

The frown was all it took to convince her to put in the diaphragm. She opened her pack, turned away from Hiawatha and smeared the cool spermicide into the rubber cup, trying to avoid pine needles and dirt, then folded the cup and maneuvered it up inside her vagina. It started to slip out of place, and she had to try again, sticky gel coating her hands. By the time she had the diaphragm positioned right, her excitement had vanished, but she pretended and tried to work up another thrill. Hiawatha quickly pushed inside her, moved against her long enough to get a rhythm going, and then stopped still, telling her not to move. Behind his head she could see a crescent moon, the silhouettes of aspen leaves, spikes of evergreen. After several seconds she tried to move again but he made a sound as if this hurt, and she didn't want to hurt him, that's the last thing she wanted—this was Hiawatha Cappellini—and she pressed her face into his neck and kissed him below the ear. Finally he moved once, twice, fast and made a low moan so she knew he was coming inside her, even though she couldn't exactly feel it.

"You're really something," he said, and kissed her mouth and rolled off her.

She wanted to put his hands back on her breasts. She wanted to put his hands between her legs. But he was pointing at the sky, the crescent moon; he seemed to like staring up through the trees. He mentioned the stars in Baja. "You should definitely come along next time," he said. How about this time? she thought, but then he yawned and his eyes drifted shut and he slept. She was left with the stars and a cool wetness leaking down her thigh. Eventually she fell asleep too and woke near dawn, pulling closer to his body for warmth. The air smelled of mountains and Hiawatha. She could, she thought, fall in love.

———

For the two remaining days of the trip, Jessie was Hiawatha's bus girlfriend, which meant light kisses of greeting, passionate kisses in more private moments, a night during which Jessie managed to place Hiawatha's hand between her legs, his mouth on her breast, and to stay interested most of the time he was inside her. It meant that Cynthia, who had decided after all to sleep with the body builder, talked to Jessie woman-to-woman about men and hidden places to have sex. It meant that Kurt stopped talking to Jessie altogether. The Brit took to slapping Hiawatha on the back. The French girls smiled at Jessie more often. And Joey, runaway Joey, stuck to Hiawatha and Jessie every minute they weren't off fooling around, asking Jessie if she and Hiawatha were going to live together now, if they might live together in San Francisco, what sort of place she thought they would get. He asked how many bedrooms they'd have. He asked about extra beds.

The third time Joey brought up the subject, Jessie said,

"Where's your brother's place?"

"In the city. He's married. He's got a huge house."

"Do you guys get along?" she said.

"Oh yeah. He's cool."

"That's great."

"Yeah. So do you think you'll live in the city too?"

———

As the bus approached San Francisco, Hiawatha listed off the beaches Jessie should visit. Maybe he'd get some time off, he said. Kurt raised his eyebrows and frowned, but Jessie ignored him. She was already envisioning herself with Hiawatha, crossing the Golden Gate Bridge for a picnic in Marin: the images of blue ocean, Hiawatha on a beach, and shrimp and avocado sandwiches were so compelling she forgot that the bus riders were leaving each other as well as the Turtle. She didn't get Joey's phone number. She didn't get Cynthia's, or punked-out Amy's. When the bus pulled up along Embarcadero, the afternoon was damp with fog, rush hour about to begin. Clumps of people waited on the sidewalk; there were backpacks and boxes to unload, and suddenly, a scattering of bus passengers. A guy with a dirty blond ponytail and a beard tapped Joey's shoulder and picked up his duffel. He wore a torn jean jacket and a wrecked pair of sneakers, and he didn't seem brotherly at all. Maybe she should take Joey to Abby's. Or maybe he could stay at Turtle headquarters. *"Joey,"* Jessie called, and Joey waved without glancing up; he stared at the ground and followed the ponytailed guy toward the B.A.R.T. station.

When she collected her backpack from Hiawatha, he kissed her and she gave him Abby's number, written on the back of a Turtle flyer. "Thanks," he said, and climbed back up on top of the bus to retrieve more packs. Then Abby appeared wearing something like a sari, her walnut hair in dozens of tiny braids. Jessie heaved her pack into Abby's little Toyota and hesitated. Hiawatha threw more duffels down to Kurt. "Hey," Jessie called, and waved, and Hiawatha waved back. "I'll talk to you later," she said.

He nodded and waved again, then pulled down another duffel bag.

———

Jessie didn't cry at all on the car ride to Abby's place, but she did smoke a couple of cigarettes. The bay was gray green, the city a dizzy sequence of figures and lights. Abby smelled like patchouli, like she had her whole last year of high school, and Jessie wanted simply to lean against her and sleep. On the radio, a couple of local activists discussed the housing crisis, and Abby popped in a tape of a ska band. The bright jerky beat helped Jessie to sit up and tell Abby her hair looked beautiful. Also to say, "That guy, the one on top of the bus?" and wait for Abby's nod, and then continue, "when I was traveling, we became lovers. He lives here."

"Good for you, Jess," Abby said. She smiled and held her hand out for Jessie's cigarette. "I thought there was something about him. You going to see him here?"

"Yeah," Jessie said. "Of course. This sounds like the English Beat."

"It is," Abby said.

"You know, I've never met anyone like him."

———

Abby's apartment was a mess, but one of the roommates had gone to Nepal, so Jessie got her own room, and for the first two days she mostly slept and ate and heard stories about Abby's whirlwind life. Abby, who had cut whole semesters of high school to hang out, now was almost never home: she took art and philosophy classes at San Francisco State, worked in a cafe called the Funky Monkey, spent an hour a day at yoga, and had just joined a small theater group. Plus she had a part-time boyfriend named Shane, who worked in a treatment center for disturbed kids and played twelve-string guitar. Sometimes Shane talked about wanting a more serious relationship: he was part-time because Abby didn't want anyone "tying her down."

"Why not?" Jessie said.

"What do you think the women's movement is for?" Abby said. "So you can do poetry instead of housework."

Jessie didn't respond. She didn't want to be a retrograde dupe of the patriarchy, but love—domestic bliss—could only help her poetry. Also, it wouldn't hurt Abby to do a little housework: the apartment seemed even worse than all-male college dorms. The other roommates showed up only to sleep, and the bathroom was a pit. Her second day there, Jessie began cleaning. No one mentioned the newly scrubbed, deodorized bathroom, but a day later a note appeared, taped to the mirror. *I pray to the goddess, I thank the women, my soul is clean.*

That week she smoked pot and read books of poetry and repeatedly dialed the Rainbow Turtle local number. For a while, no one picked up, but eventually a woman answered. When Jessie asked if Hiawatha were around, the woman said he was out, something about an engine repair, so Jessie left her name and Abby's number. But he didn't call back that day, or the next one. Finally Jessie called again and the answering voice sounded like Kurt. She asked for Hiawatha. "Not here," the voice said, and she gave her name.

Then the voice seemed smug. "He's on the north route, in Seattle. But I'll give him the message."

Sour grapes, Jessie thought. That's what Kurt's problem was. Hiawatha wouldn't be gone long: Seattle wasn't so far. That afternoon, at a cafe on Haight street, she began a poem called "Northern Passage."

————

While Jessie waited for Hiawatha's return, she rode streetcars and buses around the city, stopping off at Golden Gate Park, little ethnic restaurants, bookstores. She bought sunglasses and spent hours in the poetry sections of City Lights Books, half-reading Baudelaire, half-hoping another browser would take note, a poet, for instance, a male poet, a straight, attractive one—but of course Hiawatha would be back soon and she was in no position to start something else. Maybe she'd never return to Boston; she could cash in her plane ticket and find her own apartment. A light-filled Victorian in Pacific Heights, or near the Marina. She'd figure out the money issues later. On postcards of the bay, she wrote *What a perfect city . There is art and beauty everywhere and I might be falling in love;* she sent them to her friends back east.

But for long moments she wished Abby would skip a class or call in sick to work: sometimes on the subway, the city's strangeness overwhelmed her and she felt invisible, the only person for miles without a solid, opaque body. She was as inconsequential as a fish. She worried about Joey, and she looked for him in the park, where people seemed to be living, and on the sidewalks downtown. She'd seen kids near the seamy strip clubs off Broadway, loitering on Powell in the Tenderloin. Some of them were skinny. Some of them were blond. After she'd reassured herself that he wasn't among them, she'd retreat to another black-and-white tiled cafe. Every couple of days, she checked a city map to see the location of Turtle headquarters: it seemed far away, but seeing it on the map comforted her, as if Hiawatha were already there, sleeping.

One night the second week, Jessie and Abby killed a bottle of Chianti and got deep into the subject of men, the strange distance one can feel from lovers, what it is that draws you in in the first place.

"Shane is like the earth," Abby said. "It's like gravity, being with him. He's a very solid presence. I think he may have a young soul, but he's a Taurus."

"I bet Hiawatha's an earth sign too," Jessie said. "It's just something I sense." She reached over the table for Abby's Drum tobacco and rolled cigarettes for both of them. "I might just stay here," she said. "I'm thinking about it."

"Fantastic." Abby lighted up, held the match for Jessie's cigarette, and waited until she had Jessie's full attention again. "Men aren't for everyone," she said. "You know? Out here a lot of women love women. But I've always really liked men. Some of my lesbian friends don't approve."

Jessie had no answer for this. "To each her own," she said. "Live and let live."

Abby cracked a toothy smile. "God, you sound just like your mother," she said, which made Jessie blush.

"It's OK," Abby said. "I like your mother."

Almost nightly, while Jessie pretended not to be waiting for Hiawatha's call, her parents phoned from Buffalo. They wanted to know if she had enough money, if she was healthy, if Abby's roommates were trustworthy, if Shane seemed to be a responsible guy. There were plane schedules to discuss. There were theater and museum schedules to investigate, restaurant reservations to make, and also the matter of Jessie's sister Emmy, whom her parents had decided to bring along.

"We booked a room for the two of you," Elaine said. "We're staying at the St. Francis."

Jessie had ridden the glass elevators in the St. Francis, just to get a view of the city; afterward she sneaked into the posh women's bathroom. The hotel had the kind of velvet-lined glamour she associated with Rita Hayworth.

"I'm not staying at a hotel," she said. But there was no conviction in her voice. She wondered if she could wear a strapless, black velvet dress and still be a bohemian. If hotels were inherently anti-bohemian. That morning she'd seen a baby cockroach in

Abby's kitchen and killed it with a saucepan.

————

Just before Jessie's parents arrived, she found a note from one of the roommates on Abby's kitchen table: *Hiawatha (?) called. At Turtle house.* For a moment, she was truly breathless, and then she picked up the phone and dialed. It rang, but kept on, and she waited for five minutes, letting the Turtle phone ring and ring. Then she showered and dressed in a skirt and blouse, dabbed her neck with Abby's patchouli. She tried the Turtle house again, and then each hour through the afternoon, but she didn't reach him that day, and ended up sitting at a corner table of the Funky Monkey drinking ordinary coffee and reading apocalyptic sci-fi stories, while Abby worked her shift.

————

Her mother smelled like washed laundry and perfume, her father his dense man-smell mixed with talcum and lemon drops and menthol from shaving. They kissed her in the hotel lobby and promised her things: a day trip up the coast, a dance performance, dinners, desserts. Fat brown curls sprang off Emmy's head, she was tan from camp, skinny and bold. She gave Jessie a hug and a macramé bracelet she'd made at the crafts center.

"Let's get you squared away," her father said. He smiled and kissed Jessie on the forehead, then flagged down a bellboy to carry her backpack. Murmuring couples crossed the lobby and somewhere a piano played jazz standards. Jessie's father ushered the family into a glass elevator, and they glided up to their rooms.

Clean, Jessie thought. The hotel room was the cleanest place she'd been since the last time she visited her parents' house, and it probably was cleaner than that. Thick bedspreads, thick carpets, gauzy white sheers filtering the window light. Emmy fell on the bed closest to the TV and began to flip the channels; Jessie unpacked her things, carefully hanging her dress and skirt, arranging the jeans and T-shirts in wide dresser drawers. Then she stretched out on the second bed and thumbed a copy of *Bury My Heart at Wounded Knee* she'd picked up at City Lights. She made it through two paragraphs, then set down the book and called the Turtle number. Hiawatha would be back later, a man told her. When Jessie hung up the receiver, Emmy turned off the TV sound.

"What's that about?" Emmy said.

Jessie hesitated. Emmy wasn't a geeky kid—not nearly as geeky as Jessie had been—she was likable, smart, but also loud-mouthed and indiscreet.

"You have to promise not to tell," Jessie said.

"Promise," Emmy said.

"Really, Emmy, I mean it."

"I said I promise."

"*OK,*" Jessie said. "I met a guy I like. A man I could love. He lives here, in San Francisco."

"Wow," Emmy said. "Does Mom know?"

"No. And you can't tell her, OK? Emmy? I'm trusting you on this one. I know you like to be the one to tell but this one is secret."

"Okay," Emmy said. "You know, I French-kissed a boy this summer. Jimmy Klein. Once he stuck his hand under my shirt."

"God, Emmy, you're only twelve."

"I hate that," Emmy said. "I'm not a baby. And it's not like we were doing it."

"Well, you shouldn't be. Really, Em. Did you get your period yet?"

"You know, I'm not a slut or anything."

Slut, Jessie thought. Dog. Prude. She remembered her dog-self, and grabbed a note pad off the night table. Meanings of *slut*, she wrote, potential poem: on being a slut.

"I don't even know what *slut* means," Jessie said. "Just a name insecure guys have for girls who like sex."

"Do you?"

"It's very emotional."

Emmy paused. "Jimmy Klein's hand up my shirt wasn't emotional. It was clammy."

"Sometimes it's like that too," Jessie said. "But not with every-one." Cappellini, she thought. *Angel hair.*

Emmy shrugged. "By the way," she said, "my period's none of your business." Which meant, no, it hadn't started, and had been an issue at camp.

"You're right," Jessie said. "I just hope you don't get bad cramps. You tell Mom if you need to take something for them, OK?"

"Yeah."

Jessie slipped the *slut* note into her pocketbook and pulled out a package of Drum tobacco. "Can I smoke in here?"

"No problem," Emmy said. "I'll get us some Cokes."

———

Later, her mother breezed in with a list of art galleries; her father sniffed the air and frowned. Then he picked up *Bury My Heart at Wounded Knee.*

"You're reading this?" he said.

"I just started," Jessie said.

"That's great, Jess," he said. He knew a few things because of being an epidemiologist, and also a big reader. He mentioned some of the different clans and tribes that had been lumped together. He told her Jews and Native Americans have a lot in common.

"Cuisine, for example," her mother said.

"Elaine, I'm serious," her father said.

"You mean both being targets of genocide," Jessie said.

"Yes, Jessie, that's exactly what I mean."

"Just don't make everyone Jewish," Elaine said. "It isn't fair."

Jessie measured her words. "I know what you're saying Mom," she said. "But underneath it all, underneath history, we're really all one. You should read Jung sometime."

"That's fine," Elaine said. She stuck the gallery listing into her bag and opened the door. "I'm going to see art."

———

When Hiawatha at last called Jessie back, he said "You're at a hotel? Good going. I'll meet you there."

"Here?" Jessie said. Emmy was here. *Her parents* were next door. Even if he showed up while they were off in North Beach, it was like bringing him to her parents' house. She couldn't make love with anyone in her parents' house.

"That doesn't really work," she said, "It's a little complicated." She asked him to meet her at the Palace of Art, then told her parents she was off to meet a friend of Abby's.

"That Shane friend?" her mother said.

"Somebody else," Jessie said. "A girl. Someone Abby goes to school with."

———

She brought her diaphragm with her. She took a cab. But as the cab approached the Palace of Art, her stomach lurched and she wanted to sink down below the door's window and stay there until the cab drove somewhere else. This had to be fear of rejection, she thought. Sometimes love could make you sick.

Jessie paid the driver and circled the little pond to the temple, violet stone columns shooting up to a dome. Hiawatha stood directly below the dome and listened to his own echo. He wore the same red bandana, the same stained jeans, the same blue T-shirt he'd worn through much of the trip west.

She leaned against a column and said his name.

"Hey," he said, and walked over and kissed her on the mouth. "Where are we going?"

The light had a queer fuzziness to it, and Jessie's face flushed. He seemed familiar, he seemed like a stranger, and at that moment she couldn't imagine going anywhere. She didn't answer him but instead kissed him again, hoping the fuzziness would dissolve. It only seemed to worsen.

"Something's wrong," she said. "I'm sick."

"You don't look sick," he said. He pushed her hair away from her eyes, ran his fingers very lightly over her temples and cheeks, kissed them. How lovely the sensations were; how queasy she felt. "I'm sorry," he said. "We'll sit down. Maybe you'll feel better."

And she did sit down, on the grass in the sun, and she let him stroke her hair and her face. She kissed him on the cheek and kissed him on the mouth. He was dusty and salty and warm, and Jessie felt trembly, as if she'd been up all night, as if she'd been to a funeral. She kissed him until she couldn't anymore, until she had to double up and lean against him.

"What's the matter?" he said. "I don't get it."

Then she pulled away. "I'm just shaky today. Not feeling so good."

He held her hand and wrapped an arm around her shoulder, hugging her against him, kissing her ear, her neck. He brushed the hair out of her eyes. "Are you coming down from something?" he said. "It'll get better."

"No," she said. "It isn't that."

She straightened up and squeezed his hand. "I missed you," she said. She meant it. The missing had been real, almost palpable, but now at the Palace, it seemed even worse, and that made no sense. She only knew that the longer she stayed, the sicker she would feel.

"You're a sweet one," Hiawatha said.

They stood and began to walk toward the street. One step, another step, her body off-balance, the dizziness in her legs.

"I think I should go back to the hotel," she said.

"Then let's go."

"No," she said. "Just help me find a taxi."

"A taxi, huh?" But he flagged one down, and before she climbed in she hugged him hard and kissed him and squeezed his hand again. "I'm sorry about today," she said. "I'll call you later. We'll make another plan."

"Sure," he said. "Call me."

———

It was a relief to ride up and down the St. Francis elevators with Emmy, who for once had kept a secret. It was a relief to order room service, to eat dinner in restaurants with candles and waiters who brought anything you asked for. It was a relief to sit beside her father in the hotel bar while he and Dr. Bloom, his college pal, relived the old days; to wander the art museum with her mother. In the phone book she found the address of an airline office to return her ticket, but she didn't copy it down. She pictured Abby's apartment, which seemed too crummy to return to, and her travel money wouldn't go much further. On the street, she continued to watch for Joey: she kept extra cash in her wallet in case she found him. She didn't know what else to do. She didn't once call Hiawatha. For the remainder of the week, Jessie spent every day with her family.

The day before Jessie's flight back to Boston, Abby showed up at the hotel and they sat at the bar and ordered drinks.

"What happened?" Abby said.

"I thought about what you said," Jessie said. "About poetry and not making too many compromises. I can't just give up everything to be near him. I just can't see it working for us."

"Sorry," Abby said.

"Yeah."

"You know you're right though, Jess."

"You think so?"

"Oh sure. You need your independence. You need to develop your art."

She wanted to ask if that was the truth. She wanted to ask how people figure out who they are, for real, how they could ever manage that without love. "My mother wanted to know if you'd join us for dinner," she said. "Some place fancy, I don't know where."

"Thanks anyway," Abby said. "It's my night with Shane."

———

At the gate for her flight back to Boston, Jessie hugged her mother for the fourth time.

"Jessie, sweetie," Elaine said. "It was a lovely vacation."

Jessie nodded and pushed her face against her mother's shoulder.

"You have a whole month before classes," Elaine said. She stroked Jessie's hair. "You can see your Boston friends."

Jessie pulled away and nodded and bit her lip. Her father stood at the window with Emmy, pointing and talking as the planes took off. They were holding hands. Jessie clutched her airline ticket, which she secretly wanted to exchange for a ticket to Buffalo. At that moment, she wanted only to be Emmy, to order Cokes on the plane and sleep in her parents' house and wake up to bowls of cereal and Mom in the backyard talking out loud to zinnias. To hold Dad's hand without being embarrassed.

When Jessie boarded the plane, it seemed that her insides had been scooped out. She buckled herself into the seat and rubbed her fingers over the shiny cover of *Women Speak! A Poetry Anthology* . A woman in a red linen suit took the next seat, nodded, and buried herself in the *Times of London*. From the plane, the terminal windows were opaque: maybe her parents and Emmy were still there. Maybe not. On the ground, luggage carts scooted back and forth like large insects. Men holding orange lights waved their arms and left for other gates. Other planes crossed the tarmac, and from the small oval window Jessie watched them rush down the runway and hover just above ground before angling up and out of sight.

FEEDING MARY E.

Dulcie Leimbach

Every day I wanted to quit. My infant daughter, Mary Eloise, had a suck that could pull a hubcap off a tire. When she latched on to my nipples, a sharp pain coursed from my breasts to my stomach and through my legs, making my toes curl.

Hormones, love, duty, guilt: they kept me going. But it had been difficult from the minute I was handed Mary E. in the birthing room. I never believed I could have a daughter so good looking. She stared at me intently, darkly, as if to say, You better take me. She had billowy cheeks, lips like rolling Vermont mountains, eyes the color of a frozen pond—deep blue shot with black. I had wanted another boy to wrestle with my four-year-old Paddy.

"Why don't you feed her?" the nurse said, and I slipped Mary E.'s mouth onto my right nipple. She sucked as if she had been waiting for this moment for months. I preferred to think the milk tasted like cream, although I knew it was like watery evaporated milk. Chas, my husband, had given it a taste-test in a cup soon after Paddy was born and never took another sip again.

The nurse had just given me Tylenol with codeine to relieve the postpartum contractions, and I felt slow and easy, like a river. I wracked my brain for something to complain about and for the first time in my life nothing came up.

Mary E. slept for the next twenty-four hours with only two wakings. I didn't sleep at all. The pain at her latching on crept up slowly, and I was so anxious to meet her one demand—to be fed—that I ignored my cracking nipples, the fissures and grooves where there had once been solid pink flesh. By the time we left the hospital forty-eight hours later, I was certain my nipples were going to drop off.

"Just get her mouth around the areola," Betty, my friend, said over the phone. Chas bought a portable phone for me to carry from the kitchen to the couch, my main living areas with the baby. "If you can get a part of it in her mouth and not so much on the nipple, you're going to live."

Betty knew about breast-feeding the way a stockbroker knew about puts and calls. She breast-fed her daughter, Holly, until she was four, when Holly stopped. (Betty could have continued.) She was also about to have her second child in a week or two. Even with Betty's reassurance, I knew that I wasn't going to be OK. I'd been through the same problems with Paddy. My areolas had swelled almost to the breaking point. Just as with my son, I couldn't possibly get Mary E.'s tiny mouth around anything but the tip of the nipple.

"Didn't you have these problems with Holly?" I asked Betty. The portable phone was propped in my neck so I could feed Mary E. and commiserate at the same time. "Wasn't it so painful that you felt like it was a bad joke?"

"I've forgotten," Betty said. "The way you forget about labor, supposedly. But I remember every second of that, the thrust, the sewing up, the feeling that Niagara Falls was coming out of me." She paused and I heard her slurp. "Chocolate milk shakes are the only thing that make me happy. When I was first breast-feeding Holly, I tied a string across my bedroom window so I wouldn't throw her out. Or I think I did. Maybe I did that in a dream."

I always felt better after talking to Betty.

My nipples acquired deep cracks, some of which were scabbing. When Mary E. latched on, the pain was like a dagger thrust, reminding me of a visit I'd had with a dentist who refused to numb me up enough during a root canal. I couldn't decide which pain was worse.

"I can't take it, Betty, I think I'm going to quit," I said, knowing that she would disapprove. The phone was in the crook of my neck. It was another Birmingham, England, kind of day: sooty and gritty. The sun, what you could see of it, was about to go down and National Public Radio was about to go on. I was thinking how I prayed not to have a girl, how I had been sure that she would fill me with loathing. All those pink, flouncy clothes.

"You can hang in there, Zollie, you're a Scorpio," Betty said. "We have claws, remember." Mary E. was also a Scorpio, and Betty was crossing her fingers that her baby would be a Sagittarius. Betty said it was bad to have so many Scorpios in one house but it was too late for Mary E. and me.

"When am I going to feel better?" I asked Betty, thinking of the days before motherhood, when my breasts had been slender and bouncy, high up instead of like misshapen bowling balls.

"Can you tell me?"

I had gone to disbelieving everything Betty said. I blamed it on the estrogen, or progesterone, I wasn't sure which. My breasts were fully engorged, like balloons about to pop, and it was only my third day home. I understood why our mothers—the ones from the 1950s—had popped pills, smoked Salems, had affairs, and drove their cars off cliffs. All my aunts were drunks, most were divorced. One killed herself in the garage by turning on the car and shutting the doors. My own mother had been in and out of rehabs. Everything about our mothers made sense when you thought about how they tried to cope but too much was working against them.

I talked to a lactation consultant over my trusty portable phone. "My breasts are like rotten grapefruits," I said, aiming for humor and sympathy. "When I walk they rumble like thunder." She stopped me, but in my head I went on: Whenever anyone comes near me—my son, my husband—I scream like a psycho.

"Have you tried warm washcloths?" she purred. I said I would give them a try. But the can of Enfamil on the kitchen counter was looking more and more like a life jacket. I thought if I fed Mary E. formula, it would miraculously alleviate the pain in my breasts. But if I quit breast-feeding, I would be giving up on Mary E. and motherhood. My own mother hadn't breast-fed, no one did then. It was my generation versus hers, good versus bad—a mental battle in which I was determined to win.

Before each feeding I iced my nipples, swallowed a Tylenol to cushion the pain and said one Our Father. I tried the football hold, the cradle hold, lying down like a cat with a kitten at her teats. I tried feeding Mary E. for a few minutes, and then for fifteen minutes, on each side. I drank cups of awful tasting fennel tea to keep the flow of milk up. But the pain stayed with me, like a friend you've grown to hate but don't have the heart to blow off.

"I understand you sent me a check." It was my mother on the phone, her first call since Mary E.'s birth.

I was still living on the couch, where I now sat with the phone cradled in my neck, the baby in my lap. When my mother called, it was for money. She lived in Greenwich, in a rich lady's mansion. She got by on Social Security and Medicaid and jobs that paid cash, like walking a neighbor's dog, watering someone's garden.

"I sent it," I said, waiting for her to ask how I was, how the baby was, to send warm, loving blips through the phone.

"What day of the week did you send it?"

"I don't know, things are kind of blurry right now," I said, starting to sweat profusely. "I just had a baby."

"She's OK, isn't she?"

"Yes, she's OK. I'm not. I don't get much sleep. Two hours a stretch. I'm so weak I can't walk to the store yet."

"Well, at least you're not in my boat. I can't pay the rent. Besides, you have Chas to help you."

"Chas works. Paddy goes to day care. I'm alone, except for the baby. It's dark at three o'clock. I'm having very bad thoughts."

"Don't be ridiculous. I thought you were going to name her something else, anyway. Mary Elizabeth."

"I wanted to have more fun, be more distinctive. Don't you like Mary Eloise?"

"Zollie," she said. Sometimes she'd beat around the bush, other times she was sharp and insistent, no time for chitchat. "I will get kicked out if I don't pay the rent."

If she got kicked out, where would she go—here with me? The threat, real or unreal, always loomed. I moved out on her the day after my high-school graduation. I couldn't be in a room with her without feeling a wave of depression hitting me. Her mother died when she was ten, her father touched her for years in the bathroom, in her bed, her husband disappeared—but I could never make any of that up to her, with or without money.

"I sent you $300," I said, waiting for her to say thank you. The last conversation with her, two weeks before Mary E. was born, she'd asked for money and I hung up on her. I sent the money anyway.

"I wouldn't ask you if I didn't have to," she said, her voice razory, as if I were the one being unkind. She used that tone when she knew she was being wicked, but pretended it was me. It worked: I often wondered who really was the nasty one—her or me?

"The postman is deliberately hanging on to it to torment you," I said and hung up.

I put Chopin etudes on and tears dropped onto Mary E.'s face but she didn't flinch. Would she be nasty to me? Would I manipulate her for money?

"I know you can keep going," Chas whispered as he kissed me. It was four in the morning, the baby's cries had awakened him. He came into the living room, where Mary E. and I slept on the couch. She was hungry, but I didn't want her near my breasts, which were still distended with milk. I was using a manual pump to keep the swelling down, to help her latch on to the A-R-E-O-L-A as Betty said it, slowly and deliberately. I longed to fill a bottle with formula, to never again feel the baby's tight gums clenching my nipples.

"You'll feel worse if you stop," Chas said, standing in the middle of the living room, the legs of his baggy flannel pajamas extending past his feet. I felt suddenly jealous of him, wishing I could sleep like him, hours of dreams lying ahead and no one to feed. He knew, though, that if I gave up, I would say to him for years, "Why did you let me do that?"

"And you'll never forgive yourself. You'll think that all of Mary E.'s problems stem from not being breast-fed."

"Oh, you're so objective about it," I said. "What kind of problems will she have anyway?"

But he was too smart, or too tired, to answer. "It's only been a week, not a long time in the history of breast-feeding women," he said, stepping into the kitchen and grabbing two Pepperidge Farm Milanos, one for me, the other for him. "Your hormones are whacked out, the pain is in your head."

"Don't belittle it. It's very real."

She latched on. My shoulders sprang up and my legs curved into an *S*, making me think of Paddy and how he loved to write that letter over and over with his magic markers. After a few seconds, the pain eased and her jaw moved like a locomotive, her eyes as alert as a traffic cop's. She was still not getting too much of the areola in her mouth, but she was doing an excellent job otherwise. Mary E. would be a good Girl Scout, a good daughter, a good mother. She would do it so much better than I, and I would still love her.

Chas kissed me again. He could afford to be cool and relaxed, I thought, he could sleep. "Do you want another one?" he asked, holding up the Pepperidge Farm bag.

Betty had her baby, Juliet. Betty's nipples were cracking after two days of breast-feeding.

"Vitamin E oil," I said. "And you don't have to wipe it off, the baby can ingest it." I was confident now that my own nipples were healing.

"But it's so painful. We go through nine months of getting fat and craving every food in sight, except for shrimp, and then there's labor, which makes you feel like you belong in the animal kingdom. And this. It's an insult. How much are we supposed to take?"

"Survival of the fittest," I said, knowing how useless that sounded.

"What does Darwin have to do with it? If that were the case, Juliet and I would be dead now," Betty said, her voice sounding corroded like rust. I knew she felt too tired to barely form sentences. "What did they do before formula?"

"Wet nurses, women who did this for a living, like in China."

"There you go," she whispered to Juliet, her voice like a slip in the breeze. "I'm moving to China. I've always liked bok choy."

"Take warm showers, put hot washcloths right on the old breastes," I said, giving the word two syllables, the way Paddy did. "Drink dark beer."

"Dark beer?"

"Old wive's tale. Supposedly keeps the milk flowing. But all it does is taste good, make you feel a little blurry. Which is good. You want that."

I had been drinking a Guinness every night at the same time the Million Dollar Movie used to go on when I was a child alone in our dark house, my mother not due home from work for an hour. I was so scared I wouldn't move an inch on the couch for fear of provoking the murderer I was sure was hiding in the hall closet.

Now when I drank Guinness, I didn't care if a murderer was in the house. I wondered if this was mental progress or deterioration. In fact, I hardly had any thoughts, which alarmed me. Was I losing it completely? The time was early December, with daylight disappearing at four o'clock, leaving a sudden blackness. I was keeping all the lights off in our loft until Chas and Paddy came home. Chas never asked why it was dark but would quickly turn a light on. In the middle of the night, say at 3:00 a.m., I'd turn all the lights on in the living room and focus on the dirt in our beige rug. One night I scrubbed it after feeding Mary E., spraying the rug cleaner and wiping the spots up with a sponge mop. The rug looked worse after that.

"I still haven't got the check." It was my mother a few days later. The thing about a portable phone was that everyone sounded as if they were calling ship-to-shore from, say, the ocean, where I wished my mother was. "Mrs. Forbes is about to kick me out. This is it, Elizabeth." She always called me by my full name when she thought she was about to die, or when she wanted me to think she was going to die.

Mary E. was asleep in my arms, hot as an electric blanket. We were sitting at the kitchen table, next to a coffee cake I'd been picking at, crumb by crumb. My right scapula was aching from holding her. I had a pinched nerve in my neck from feeding her on my side. Earlier that day I had seen a doctor to find out why I was still coughing: pneumonia. My left breast had a red spot on it, the first sign of mastitis. My crotch was still so sore that I had to put a down pillow on the chair.

"Are you there, Elizabeth?" my mother said, her voice blunt, as if she were the captain of a sinking ship. She was on tranquilizers. "Are you listening?"

I looked down at Mary E., thinking how lucky she was to be a baby and how fortunate she was that I loved her enough to breast-feed her. "I'll never ask you for money," I whispered in her ear.

I wondered if I turned the phone off whether my mother would sink. "Go look in your mailbox."

"How are you anyway?" she said, sheepishly.

"You don't want to know," I said.

"I'm interested. Just because I don't sound like it doesn't mean I'm not. I have a lot on my mind."

"Your world is very small. There's only you in it."

"You're a very lucky woman, Zollie. You don't know how lucky you are."

"I do, but that doesn't mean I don't need to hear a sympathetic voice once in a while. Especially after I've had a baby. AN IN-FANT!" I hung up and the phone emitted one final static blast, as if a whale had swallowed her.

The mastitis left me reeling with fever that night, and my temperature shot up to 103. The heat ran through my body and burned my limbs.

"Get me a washcloth, a cold one," I called to Chas. "I'm dying, you know."

"No, you're not," he said, smiling.

"How do you know? Will you be good to her? Raise the kids as Catholics?" He was a diehard agnostic.

"You're delirious." He took my temperature, then looked at me queerly. "I'm going to call the doctor."

The fever dropped after two Tylenols. The next night it returned, and by the third day I was at the doctor's again, leaving with powerful antibiotics. Meanwhile, I had to feed Mary E., as the La Leche woman ordered me.

"It's the only way to kill the mastitis," she had said, her voice scratchy like everyone else's. I held the phone from my ear as she lectured me, hoping she, too, would be eaten by a whale. I'd told her about my right nipple cracking again, the blood mixing up with the milk.

"A little blood won't hurt the baby," she said clinically. Then, in a long-awaited note of encouragement, she said, "You're doing great."

I woke in the middle of the night, my clothes hanging off me, wet with sweat. I drank gallons of water and pulled Mary E. close to feed her. Her hands pawed the air, getting in between the nipple and her mouth. She breathed heavily like a feral animal. She kicked and clawed as she sucked, as if she may never eat again.

"I love her so much," I said to Betty the next day, amazed that I was saying such intimate things. The portable phone made me do it. "I love the way she burrows in my chest, like she's in a blizzard, lost in a mountain range. She's Hans in *The Magic Mountain*. I love it when she acts wild, like she's got rabies, searching for the nipple. When I lay her sideways, she calms down, as if she knows she's about to get it."

"Yeah, yeah, yeah. You got any remedies for obstructed mammary ducts?" Betty sounded exhausted. I imagined her in a sailboat, trying to raise the sails in a ferocious wind, the canvas flapping uncontrollably. "Why do we do this? Remind me."

"Slug down that beer. It doesn't have to be Guinness. Try Dos Equis. Get through the day."

"But it's so dark out. It's like a shroud. I'm all alone. I'm going crazy. I am crazy. I'm afraid I'm going to do something."

I understood. There were moments when I looked down at Mary E. and I wanted to crush her head on the floor.

"Give Juliet a bath. Put her in the swing. Go for a drive."

"Nah, nah, nah. I need a tranquilizer. I need a mother."

Betty's mother was dead from breast cancer. The breast-feeding was important to Betty. She thought it would keep her from dying young.

"I can't help you with that," I said, ready to press the off button on my phone. Talking about mothers made my jaw tighten. "Listen to Mozart. It's brain food for the baby."

I hung up and popped open the lid on my Guinness, wondering if I could be as unsympathetic as my mother. Was it in the genes? The dark, thick liquid slid down my throat. It was how I imagined love from a mother might feel, consoling and kind.

It became easier to dress. My breasts still felt as if they were rockets at countdown, but Mary E. was working them—squish, squish—releasing the milk from the ducts and encouraging a silky flow. It was all so marvelous, so streamlined, so factory-like! Instead of heading against the wind, we were finally sailing with it.

We could even heel! I stroked her angel-thin hair. I thought of buying a new winter hat for myself, a pink-and-black floppy velour I'd seen in SoHo. I was sure the floppy part would make me happy. I studied Mary E.'s feet, which were like custard. I cradled her the way the La Leche woman told me to.

"Don't ever make the breast go to her," she had said. "She must come to the breast."

Mary E.'s belly was filling out, wide as a lake. She looked like a truck driver who had eaten too many jelly-filled doughnuts. I thought it might be a tumor, but Betty said her baby was the same way, so we decided nothing was wrong. Mary E. was looking better overall: her head was more shapely, no longer tangelo shaped but now like a navel orange. I had read that breast-fed babies were more intelligent and friendlier, that they got sick less, had clearer skin, closer relationships with their mother, sort of the way elephant mothers and daughters are, friends for fifty years.

"I can't stop eating chocolate," Betty said. "I stand over the sink and eat and eat and eat." It was five o'clock, two days before Christmas. Her voice was clear and resonant, like Christ must have looked pushed from Mary's womb. I could almost hear bells tolling. I longed to be in Bethlehem, to follow that star. I attributed my euphoria to the Entenmann's I'd just finished without moving from the couch.

"I think it's the carbos," I said, unwilling to admit my own eating habits, even to Betty. "They're filling in the gap left by you-know-who."

"Our mothers?"

"Well, certainly not our fathers." Mine was alive somewhere, I was sure of that. He'd disappeared when I was six. Betty's was dead. Cancer again. "We deserve the sugar."

"Yeah, sure. Breast-feeding is like boot camp. You can die before you even get to the war, which is of course raising them."

As she said this, I could feel my breasts growing hard making milk. Mary E. was sleeping in my lap, her breath short and shallow, then long and deep. I would have to wake her.

"I ate three chocolate cupcakes right now. Three," Betty said, hoping I would exonerate her.

"You need the serotonin, that chemical in the brain that makes you feel good. The way sex once did."

"Never again. Did your mother ever find her check?"

"I have no idea. I get this creepy feeling that she's like plankton in the waves, rolling in and out, minuscule but indestructible." I had said too much, even to Betty, high on sugar.

"Sometimes I'm actually jealous you have a mother. Even yours."

"You can rent her for a day. I'm sure she'll be glad to get the money."

"Zollie!"

"Oh, so what." It was true I could be worse than my mother.

"Maybe we should start a support group. No bottle-feeding mothers allowed," Betty said.

"Do you think I can have two Guinnesses tonight?" I asked.

"If we had a support group, you could ask them that."

Mary E. started squirming and the phone popped from my ear. I rescued it and she was quiet.

"Have a Peppermint Patty instead," Betty said. "I've been craving one for hours. I can't get to the store. Out here in the 'burbs, the roads are ice. Jim keeps forgetting to bring one home. Probably on purpose. He thinks I'm eating too much."

"You're producing milk, you need the calories, for Chrissake," I said. "Ever think about selling the milk?" I envisioned it in sparkling glass bottles. "Fresh-squeezed, free-range, only one-percent dioxin. $3.79 at Dean & DeLuca's."

"Put an Italian Madonna on the label," Betty said. "In Sweden, they pay the mothers to breast-feed. Or is it Canada?"

"Those socialists know how to treat mothers." I wanted to hang up. Cynical humor exhausted me. Besides, Mary E. was moving her legs bicycle fashion. Her arms were flailing. She was tense, whereas a second ago she had been as lax as a mop.

I got up to squirt milk in the sink, to make the breasts less full. As I lifted my T-shirt, I noticed my nipples were covered in bruises. Mary E. had given me bruises! With my right nipple in between my fingers, I squeezed the milk and it sprayed the faucet, the sink, the clean dishes in the drain. An errant spray even hit my nose.

She was now screaming. I sat down on the couch and waited a few seconds. I thought of my mother in her measly little room in Greenwich, bare and loveless. If only I could try to like her. But it would always be a struggle: how could I care for a person who gave me so little? I would never know the answer, it would never come to me in a neat, tiny package. The question would always loom ahead of me, like a storm I have to pass through.

I looked down at Mary E.'s face, a china doll's really, her eyes remarkably like my mother's, determined and willful, widely spaced and almond-shaped, brimming with herself. Then she smiled—her first—and I smiled back, a soft give and take, a subtle awareness of each other. I pulled her close to try and stave off the waves of anguish rushing toward me, an oceanful of wishes that my mother had been different. But I was determined not to let my ambivalence toward her get in the way of how I cared for Mary E. It was up to me to chart the course of our lives together, to navigate us through the inevitable troughs.

I held her fat, chunky body close and she, too, held me tight, her hands gripping my fleshy arms as if we were both being rescued. We generated a lot of heat between us, enough to fuel the world, I thought laughingly. She was now working hard at what she was doing—feeding—and I was doing pretty well myself, churning out the milk, murmuring and stroking her, encouraging her on her way. We were two machines operating in tandem, once lost in a flurry of uncertainty and hunger, of anxiety and misguided attempts. But now we finally had it right, and oh, how delicious we tasted.

C'EST LA VIE

Jim Nichols

Listen: I was a quarterback from the time I was twelve right up through my freshman year at college, the whole time living for that moment when you stroll up behind the center with the game on the line and the coaches watching and the spectators yelling and everybody waiting for you to set things in motion.

This was my life, *n'est-ce pas?*

All right.

But then I blow out a knee during summer practice. I'm done for the year and maybe for good, depending on how I recover from the surgery. I'm under the knife for four hours, and they do a number that will let me play again if it works, but if it doesn't I'll need another and my playing days will be over.

Nice.

Back at school, they take away my tutors because I'm inactive. And I've never been much with the books. I last a few weeks, crutching around campus, then quit because I can see what's coming: I'll flunk out for sure, which will make it harder to come back the next fall, when theoretically the knee will be recovered.

Okay.

I load up the Belair and head home. The old jalopy doesn't deal well with hills and when I get to the mountains it slows down to a crawl. It takes four hours, and when I finally pull in the driveway beside the old man's pickup, my knee, just out of the cast, is aching like a son of a bitch.

The old lady comes out onto the porch. She stands there in her curlers and pink corduroys, looking eager, wanting to hug and kiss, but I tell her I'm in no mood and besides I've got to unpack, and I start lugging things into the house, limping you know, and after a while she swallows her disappointment—she wanted me to cry on her shoulder—and pitches in and then the old man tears himself away from the TV long enough to clap me on the back and help, too.

Pretty soon I'm re-installed in my room. I look around at the pennants, pictures of teams, footballs with dates and scores. There are trophies all over the place, a bookcase with more awards than books. On my desk is a big album of clippings that my mother saved for me over the years, and I open the album to the last page, where the two most recent articles are waiting to be arranged inside the plastic.

One has the headline: JOEY CLOUTER SUFFERS KNEE INJURY.

The last one is a little stiffer, as if I'm already half-forgotten. CLOUTER LEAVES SCHOOL, it says.

———

So I'm home. I do the rehab exercises in the morning, working hard enough to make the room stink, even though I open the riverside window and let the cool breeze blow in. Then after lunch I have to get out of the house and I jump in the car and cruise up and down the streets. The town seems smaller than before, the houses shabbier. It's just a little French town. I cross the steel bridge over the river and ride around the country looking at the farms, and then come back. The Belair struggles along: there's no compression left and it stalls a lot, but keeps going. I know it should be looked at but I'd have to take it to Jerry's Sunoco out on Mast Road and sit around half the day waiting, and it's just too much to think of.

You know how it is.

Then one afternoon it won't move out of the driveway. It starts all right, but as soon as I put it in gear stalls. I sit there looking out at the dead leaves blowing around the yard, a little afraid to try it again, because this could be it with the old car, and I don't want to know that. But finally I try it again.

It stalls.

I keep trying, lurching a few feet toward the street each time. Eventually I'm so pissed I floor it until the engine is roaring. I'm beating on the steering wheel, daring it to stall again. Without letting up on the gas I throw it into drive, and there's a metallic screech and a bang loud enough to bring Mrs. Rioux to her door across the street. She looks out at me, shakes her head, then goes back inside and shuts the door. I sit there in the dead car.

Smoke's seeping up from the hood.

I'm fuming, too.

———

It was a stupid no-contact drill, the kind you have so you won't get injuries. No helmets, pads, nothing. I was rolling out and Jimmy Evans—a tight end filling in on defense for this drill, getting into the role, pretending to be a bad-ass—thought he'd be cute and chase me. I can see him running after me, dirt flying up from his spikes. He laughed and grabbed my shirt like he was going to slam-dunk me: big joke. Only my foot was caught in a field drain. When I screamed Jimmy lowered me to the ground. I pulled my knee up tight against my chest. I could smell the turf and hear Coach's feet thudding as he ran out from the bench.

He bent to look at me, then straightened and slapped Jimmy's face, hard. Jimmy stood there and took it, kept saying he was sorry. The trainer pushed him out of the way and knelt down to pry my hands loose; he manipulated the joint until I let out another holler. Then he looked up at Coach.

"Well?" Coach said.

"It's not good."

Coach swore and then he and the trainer carried me over to Coach's Town and Country and loaded me in and took me to the hospital. We drove around the track to get to the exit and all the kids stood on the field, watching, holding their helmets by the face-guards.

Let me tell you about knee surgery: it's to be avoided if at all possible.

———

The old man hauls the Belair to his brother's junkyard across the river and then gets me a job ironing shoes in the shoe shop. Just till I'm better, he says. I've never had to work there, unlike most of the people in town, but I know everybody anyway: it's Mike Cote, my favorite receiver during high school, who shows me how to iron.

"See these?" Mike says that first day, holding out his arm. "The iron gets slippery. You got to watch it."

I look out the grimy window at the rows of old cars, their windshields glinting in the sun. "I'll be careful," I say. But I've got welts, too, before the week is out. The problem is you have to concentrate, and I keep daydreaming. I think about my senior year, when they let the whole shoe shop out early, so nobody would have to miss the trip north for the state championship game. We had a caravan of townies following our bus. The cheerleaders rode with us and chanted the whole way. Debbie Wilkinson sat in my lap and kissed me and the coaches just laughed about it. I remember the thick feel of her sweater. All the townies were drinking beer in their pickups and by the time we got to Presque Isle half of them were shit-faced, and during the game there were fights in the stands. The next night, back in town, there was a parade down Main Street under the elms with me in the high seat on the lead fire truck. There were guys from the shop all along the street cheering, some of them with black eyes, the same guys I was working with now.

———

After a while I start bringing my football to work, and at lunch time Mike and I go outside and throw it back and forth. I can't move much because of the knee, but there's nothing wrong with my arm. I throw one, and Mike runs after it and catches it. He takes a couple of hops and stretches back and throws it hard. It lands short and skips sideways and I limp over to the railroad berm and bend like a stork to pick it up. It's dusty out there: the fall has been dry and warm this year.

"Hey, remember what they called us?" Mike says.

"The French Connection." I throw one as hard as I can. Mike laughs, sprints to reach up and make a nice catch. Then he runs in a leaning half-circle, nonchalant, dropping the football behind him, as if scoring yet another touchdown.

At quarter to one, we sit down in the shade of the south wing to eat lunch. Mike eats half of his sandwich in one bite and chews with his cheek sticking out and his mouth open. I'm a little embarrassed to be back where people eat like that.

"Look at the old man," I say. He's playing volleyball and his gut is bouncing under the T-shirt he always wears. Dust puffs up from his feet. He jumps and hits the ball with his fist; it goes into the net.

"They play evenings at the high school," Mike says.

"I heard." I make a furrow in the dirt with the heel of my sneaker.

"I'm thinking of helping them out."

I feel my knee. The clicking and rubbing has stopped, but it's still stiff as hell and sometimes when I move just right there's this tremendous pop. It's taking a long time to come around.

"Christ, I couldn't even play volleyball now," I say.

"Maybe when it's all better."

"Then I won't want to."

"How's it coming, anyway?"

"All right," I say.

"Well, I wish you luck." Mike washes down his sandwich with coffee.

The whistle on the roof blows, and my old man walks over, his face red as an apple, drops of sweat popping out on his forehead. He wipes his face on his T-shirt and I look away from his sweaty old gut.

"*Il f'chaud,*" he gasps. "Hooo!"

"It ain't hot," I say.

"Sure, not to stand there and throw-throw-throw. Why don't you play with us?"

"For one thing," I say, "I can't jump."

He can't quite believe in knee injuries, and he snorts a little. The whistle blows again and we all head for the enclosed stairway that's stuck to the side of the building. It's like a dark tunnel and we climb up to the third floor where it's hot as hell and the machines are just starting to clatter across the wide, open room.

Mike and I head off for the irons and my old man waves and crosses the floor to his tacker and switches it on. He slips right into the old piece-work dance. There are five of them in a row in their T-shirts and jeans, walking in place, moving all over, grabbing shoes off the racks and slapping them in the holders, turning them this way and that, moving at the same time, like a good backfield.

Mike and I are on the clock. We punch in by the foreman's office and walk past Denis Archambeau in his foul-weather gear, hobbling around and around the soaking tub, poking the shoes with a mop handle, rubbing his big hook-nose. He's got something wrong with him that makes him knock-kneed, but he gets around pretty well anyway. He's my old man's age and I can remember him since I was a kid. He's always been crazy. Nobody knows if it's from breathing the fumes or if he was born that way, but one sign of his craziness is you can't leave anything lying around or he'll steal it. He steals things and you never get them back. He stole Mike Cote's letter jacket out of the pool hall once and Mike and I followed him across the bridge to his house but his mother answered the door and wouldn't let us in. She jabbered French at us until we left. She had bright red spots on her cheeks. She was as crazy as Denis so maybe it ran in the family and wasn't the fumes.

As I'm watching Denis work, one of the embossers across the room throws a handful of tacks at him and the tacks rattle off his slicker onto the floor.

Denis tips his head back and laughs: "Ha-ha!"

"Listen to it," Mike says. He's never forgiven Denis for stealing that jacket.

We go to the irons and I take the left shoe of a pair off the slant-shelved rack and press it against the iron. The iron is shaped like an on-end prism. The shoe's just leather attached to a wooden mold at this point, and as I lean on it steam rises and the wrinkles begin to vanish. I have to be careful not to sear the leather. It's hot on the third floor and sweat drips off my nose and spatters on the iron.

I do the other shoe. When the rack is done I push it over to an embosser. It's hard to push straight because the casters are bent. I get another rack from Denis Archambeau and work it past Mike to my station.

Denis laughs at me and Mike shakes his head.

I'm thinking: What a strange place, and now here I am with them. But not for long, I hope. This is just a temporary situation. Meanwhile I'll try to hide how it makes me feel.

———

I try to hide it at home, too, because whenever the old lady thinks I'm down she wants me to pray with her.

"The hell with that," I say finally.

"Don't turn away from the Lord, Joey." She's just come back from the hairdresser's with a full, kinky perm, the kind you see on a diner waitress, which is what my mother is. She has to go in to work and she's wearing the blue uniform that makes her look like an old cheerleader.

"Spare me," I say. We're in the living room watching the tube. They're televising the school's games this year and every Saturday I sit there and watch the kid who replaced me get better and better, which doesn't improve my disposition. I've been crabbing and bitching about my injury, which is why the old lady started in.

"The Lord will help you," the old lady says. "But first you have to ask him."

"I'll help myself."

"He'll be fine when he's back in school," my old man says from the couch.

"You shut up," the old lady says.

"Throw the ball!" the old man yells.

"He didn't have anyone open," I say.

"He coulda thrown it away."

The old lady glares at both of us, then gives up and heads off to work.

We watch the whole game. It's tough to sit still, though, for that length of time, because I'm full of the old butterflies. Inside I still think I'm going to play, and I get all juiced up and then have nothing to do with it. I hit the rehab work extra hard on Saturdays and that helps a little. But by game time I'm antsy. I've always been that way. It used to start the night before, and got to be a town joke: every Friday night Joey Cloutier would have to go out and walk. I'd walk all over the damn town, down Water Street past the shop, across the open stretch beside the river, past Roland's Bar and Grill, up the hill to the Catholic Church and the cemetery and down the other side to where the river curves around to the south and where the downtown starts. There'd always be somebody in Roland's or downtown who would yell out at me: "Gonna beat 'em tomorrow?"

"Gonna try," I'd yell back. Then I'd keep on walking. Somebody else would wish me luck. They all knew I was gearing myself up.

———

Everybody still goes to Roland's after work on Fridays. Mike and I are usually the first ones there, though, because we don't take part in the crap games that run on each floor of the shop. Then when the gamblers show up we try to guess who's won or lost by looking at their faces. It's easy enough: the games are cut-throat and people lose big money. Denis Archambeau isn't allowed to play anymore, because one Friday he lost his whole paycheck and the next Monday his old *Memere* marched in and raised hell with the foreman until he took up a collection to pay Denis back. But then they banned him. He still stands around watching, rubbing his nose, banging his knees together.

Every Friday Mike and I laugh at him and go down the stairway and out into the sunshine, feeling virtuous, and we scuff through the chestnut leaves along the river, tossing the football back and forth, walking through the shadows of the frame houses and then across the open stretch beside the river where it's always windy. I'm walking better, although I still can't run. Mike does all the running. He makes one last cut and I hit him by the door to the

bar and he ducks through the doorway with both arms around the
ball, like he's pounding it in from the one.

———

So fall slips by. The days get colder, and as December comes the
snow holds off but I can feel it in the breeze that whips down off
the hills and across the river. It makes my knee ache where they
cut into it. It's cold enough that they stop playing volleyball, but
Mike and I still throw the football in the lee of the south wing. It
gets too cold finally on Water Street though, and one Friday on the
way to Roland's Mike says he's had enough, and we walk over
without throwing the ball, with our collars up and shoulders
hunched against the wind. We're the first to arrive, and take our
normal seats at the middle of the bar.

Rollie Pelletier comes over, looking sleepy. He likes to doze in a
chair by the wood stove when it's slow. I toss him the ball, he
catches it easily and flips it back: at the high school there's a whole
shelf of trophies from his era.

"What'll it be, boys?"

I set the football on the floor. Mike tells Rollie two draughts,
and he walks down to the taps, moving under the wall-mounted
TV. He brings the beer back.

I take a nice, cold drink, set the beer down and look at Mike.

"Good stuff." Mike pulls out his cigarette pack and offers it. I
take one and lean toward his lighter: I've begun smoking a little
but haven't taken up buying them yet.

Pop wipes down the bar and dries his hands on his apron. He
asks us how things are going at the shop. Then he says, "How's
that Archambeau?"

"Looney as ever."

"His mother," Rollie says. "She was a good-looking woman."
He says it in French: *"Sa Mere, elle etait une femme jolie."* Then he
gets this dreamy look on his face and keeps wiping his hands.

Mike winks at me. "Ever put the boots to her, Rollie?"

"I don't like that kind of talk," Rollie says, and stalks off to the
other end of the bar and looks up at the TV. We snicker, drink our
beers, wait for the rest of them to show, which they do before long:
some happy, others trying to figure how much money they have
left to drink on.

My old man marches in, waves a fistful of money at me.

"Joey!" he yells. "Want a drink? How about you, Mikey?"

"Sure, if you're buying," Mike says.

"Give the boys one," the old man tells Rollie. Then he puts his arm around me and kisses my cheek. He's been drinking already, and Rollie squints at him before he starts pouring. The old man's wearing a T-shirt under his biker's jacket and when he lifts his arms a smell comes off him.

"For chrissake, Pa," I say, and wipe my cheek with a sleeve.

The old man laughs, turns to Rollie and says, *"Ça va?"*

"Bien," Rollie grumps. He gives Mike and me a beer.

The old man slaps our backs and goes to join the rest of them around the pool table. Somebody pushes the coin slot in and the numbered balls roll through the machine, down to the vent, and are plucked out and racked.

"Your old man was winner," Mike notes.

I nod.

We take a few turns at the table, losing every time to the older guys who, like my father, keep their own two-piece cues in cases behind the bar. Denis Archambeau tries to play and when they won't let him he starts banging on a pinball machine and Rollie has to yell at him. Then Denis sits down at the bar to sulk.

Later on my old man asks Rollie to turn on the game.

Rollie walks down to the channel control and starts clicking through the stations. It's a Friday night game. He turns up the sound and you can hear the crowd noise. The announcer is talking about the first half, pretending he knows about football, although he looks more like a golfer. Anyway, he tells about all the scoring in the first half. Then the second half starts out the same way. The teams trade touchdowns. My replacement, this kid, is scrambling around, somehow keeping up with the other team's offense, which is smooth and efficient. Everybody in Roland's is watching. Every time we score there's a loud cheer.

It all comes down to a fourth-and-goal, and the kid walks up to the center like he knows he's going to do it, and then he does it, skipping away from a couple of tacklers and rifling a pass to Jimmy Evans in the end zone. Jimmy dives and catches it. He scrambles up, looks at the ref for the touchdown signal, holds the football up high in celebration. His teammates swarm over him. The kid quarterback jumps up and down, pumps his fist and runs past the other team's players, who are trudging off the field with their heads down.

In Roland's, everybody's going crazy.

The old man comes over and pats me on the back and says

something about it being my turn after my leg's all better—he talks fast and in French so I don't catch it all—and I just nod.

"You ain't had any luck," he says.

"*C'est la vie,*" I say, and drink off my beer.

On the screen, they're interviewing the kid. He's got black smudges under his eyes. Jimmy Evans is standing beside him, grinning, still holding the football. I slide off my stool and limp to the men's room. The old knee gives a pop when I step up to the urinal. I say, "That's enough out of you," and laugh, but I'm down. I know I'll never be able to run around like that again.

The rehab's not working.

I'm going to need that second operation.

I take a long time, come out to see everyone gathered around the pool table watching the old man run out a rack. I step up beside Mike to watch, too. The old man runs a hand through his hair, sights along the stick and banks the six into a corner pocket, leaving the cue ball close to the eight. He taps it in and cheers, punching the air.

Mike and I go back to the bar and I pull out my stool and look down at the bare floor.

"Hey," I say.

Mike looks. "It was right there."

Rollie points at the door. "I just saw that Archambeau sneaking out."

I move as fast as I can to the door and push it open.

It's dark out, windy, stiff leaves rattling over the ground. A car rolls by and turns toward the bridge and its lights fall on Denis Archambeau, knock-kneed as hell, hustling along with my football up against his chest.

"Look at it go," Mike says.

The car passes Denis and its tires hum as it crosses the river. Something snaps in me and I take off after him, so angry my knee doesn't even hurt at first, although it's clicking and popping like mad after the first few strides. By the time I reach the bridge it hurts, all right, but I just push harder. The more it hurts the more I force out of it. I've had it. I can hear Denis's feet making the metal of the bridge ring, and I start across after him.

What a sight we must be: Denis lurching along with his knees banging together, me following in a strange, one-sided gallop. I almost catch him, too. But then my knee locks up and I have to stop.

Denis keeps hobbling, crosses the river, heads off for home.

"Get back here!" I yell after him.

He ignores me. Pretty soon he's gone.

So all right.

I lean on the metal railing, look down at the water. The railing is cold. The water runs swiftly under the bridge and boils through a narrows to the curve that takes it out of town. There are big boulders in the bed of the river. I can't move and I stand there holding onto the railing until the old man's pickup stops, and then I hop to the door and climb in. He looks down at my leg, and for a moment I'm afraid he's going to try and make me feel better. But he doesn't say anything. He just puts it in gear and takes me home.

WHITEOUTS

Michael Blaine

Halfway between Grand Gorge and Accordia the snow starts falling in bursts. High up near Gaiter's Dairy Farm, where Route 23 coils in on itself like a spring, the road smokes with blow-off from the white fields. In the bursts of wind the car drifts sideways in small, heart-stopping skids. Capes of snow blind me in gusts, then tear away to reveal long views of fields skinned with ice. A moon-gray disk, the sun can't break through the clouds. It's the dangerous time, almost too warm to snow. Apparently damp pavement can hide black, hidden ice. Holding my breath, trying to fight the instinct to hit the brake, I let the car sail down the hill into Accordia, parachute down through the white storm.

All I can think about is keeping Lonnie safe, showing no fear. Staring mutely out the Lexus's window, he taps his finger against the glass to the vapid country and western on WBBG, the only station I can pull in this high up in the mountains.

"You reading anything?"

"Yeah, *Dr. Jekyll and Mr. Hyde.* It's kind of simplistic, but it's cool." I can hear Janet's tone in this remark. Lonnie is her protégé, her prodigy, even if he does have my Mediterranean skin, my hooded, Southern Italian eyes. "You think the trails'll be mobbed like last time?"

"Could be, the way this winter's been." For months the weather has imitated early fall, then a sudden storm dumped a foot and a half of snow on the northern Catskills. On its heels, a moody, shrouded thaw took hold. The skiers are like confused birds, unsure whether to stay or take flight.

In the middle of the car's soft, dreamy descent, a shiny red Blazer materializes at a dead stop in the middle of the road. Now there's no choice. My heart in my mouth, I feather the brake, but we seem to pick up speed. Below, the Blazer appears to be rushing backwards to collide with us. Now there's no alternative. I stomp

on the brake, preparing for the spin-out, my right arm flung across
Lonnie's bony chest, steeling my legs, getting ready to smash into
the guard rail. In the elongated moment before the crash, I think,
What a joke, I keep trying to give him everything, and I end up killing him.

Somehow, though, we glide gently to a halt, just kissing the
Blazer's high bumper. In a blur I'm out in the cascading storm,
ready to strangle somebody. Under the thick hush of the falling
snow, my own breathing is amplified with every sharp intake of
moist air. All around me the big wet flakes fall dense as a curtain.
Then I see the roadblock.

A pair of stone-faced troopers, their broad-brimmed hats
crowned with glistening crystals, talk quietly to a man in pink-and-
black ski pants. Maybe there's been an accident. It's strange how
these figures, so close, go soft around the edges in gusts of wind,
white mist boiling up from the road, twisting around their ankles.

A trooper is trying to calm the Blazer's driver.

"We advise you to turn back then, sir. We expect this to take
quite a while. Try Hunter Mountain."

"Shit!" he shouts. "I called in sick! I been driving for hours!
From Bayside!"

"Sir, we have a very serious situation on our hands. We've got
10 and 23 blocked off. If you want to get a bite to eat, if you want
to stay in town, that's up to you. The motel may be full up already,
though. And there's no way out of Accordia except the way you
came."

Edging in, I try to find out what's going on. "Officer, we live
here, can't we just get to our house? . . ." This isn't strictly true as
Lonnie lives with Janet in Hurley, but he visits me on weekends
when I can convince him. Skiing, though, he loves, and so do I,
the way you can go weightless when muscle and surface and slope
become one. Fearless, craving, Lonnie can really *lean into* a drop, a
look of mad excitement on his face.

In a flat, nasal tone, Dudley Doright calmly repeats himself.

"Not at liberty to say, sir. For your safety, though, we can't let
you beyond the town." That means I'm out of luck; my mangy
farmhouse is two miles up Redbone Road.

"Fuck! I spent all that money at Herman's!" the bald man mutters, gesturing to the skis on the roof of his 4 x 4.

Every table at the Hungry Heart is taken, the small cafe stinking of smoke and grease and mildew. We stand near the door,
stamping snow off our boots on a runner made of flattened cardboard boxes. Late on a Saturday afternoon the restaurant is usually

deserted, getting ready to close up shop. But this crowd is atypi-
cal, mostly stranded downstaters. You can tell by their expensive
clothes, by their fidgety impatience, by their unfinished meals.
They're not hardened to Hungry Heart fare.

I grab Kiki, the teenage waitress with the nose ring, before she
can scoop up another platter of Kilbassa, sauerkraut, and potato
chip specials. "What's going on, Kiki?"

"Nobody knows. Some kind of shooting over at the Colemans'.
All we got left is chicken grillas and Jello." Her upstate twang
makes no distinction between gunplay and the depleted menu.
Stabbed right through her nose's cartilage, the ring dangles, a tiny
silver trapeze.

For Lonnie's sake, I cover my terror with a bland tone. He
never knew about Sandra Coleman and me, nobody did. Anyway,
it was all over so fast, I barely knew it myself, except that I could
still smell that extra bedroom in her house where she worked with
piles of dried flowers, musty and faintly, faintly sweet. Hanging
upside down from the rafters were clutches of globe thistles and
hydrangeas. Through a dormer window in this room you could see
her ex-husband Nathan's converted barn, painted an alarming ma-
roon, where he lived with their son, Maurice. Sandra had kept Ali-
cia. On weekends the children crossed the road in opposite
directions, switching rooms and parents.

During their first years apart, she told me, Nathan spied on her
with a telescope. Strangely enough, she thought this was funny.

Their asses splayed on battered stools, the Hungry Heart regu-
lars exhale discount cigarettes, stir their bottomless cups of coffee.
A golf tournament from Hawaii plays silently on the twenty-four-
inch Mitsubishi TV behind the counter. Slightly off, the colors
render distant volcanoes turquoise, the golfer's faces ghosted with
magenta afterimages.

"Vincie, over here," O'Bannon calls to us from a rear booth.
"C'mon, we've got room." The town pharmacist, O'Bannon en-
deared himself to me years ago by dispensing discreetly wrapped
joints along with my usual medication. His pretty, gaunt wife,
Julia, moves over on the red leatherette seat.

"Julia, you know my son, Lonnie?"

"Hi," Lonnie says, pulling his dog-eared Robert Louis Steven-
son from his back pocket, quickly obscuring his face.

"The world's last thirteen-year-old reader," Julia says, gracefully
glossing over the kid's lack of social grace.

"Just the usual teenage, anti-social behavior," I joke. Lonnie shoots me a sour look from behind his novel, the kind of look that makes me cringe. Nothing I say seems to live up to his standards nowadays, a fact I can't help attributing to his mother's ironclad brief against me. And Janet can write one wicked brief. If you marry another lawyer, avoid experts in matrimonial. Of course, she does have some ammunition against me, the usual *flagrante delecto*, which she tried to use to get sole custody. I deserved everything else she dished out, but that one I fought tooth and nail.

To say I was a stupid, self-involved, arrogant asshole would be to merely state the obvious, but it's been years now, and I wish she'd let up. All I can do is focus on the main message to Lonnie: *I'll never desert you, no matter what.*

Glancing up and back at me and the kid, O'Bannon lowers his voice to a half-whisper and leans toward me. "There's some wild shit going on, Vincie. The troopers are all over the Colemans' place, their hunting camp."

"Sandra there?" is all I can manage. Piercing fear. I'm shocked at the intensity of my feelings.

I remember raising up from her boat of a bed and realizing that the floor sloped away at a good fifteen-degree angle. Across the room the dormer window seemed to tilt in the opposite direction.

From her cocoon under the down quilt, she waved her hand dismissively. "Oh, don't worry, the house is sinking, but I asked a friend of mine, and he said it won't collapse for another thirty or forty years. So let it sink!"

"We don't know who's there, all we know is that Harlan, you know, the guy who runs the B & B across the road from their camp, he called the troopers 'cause he heard some shooting or something."

"Nobody calls the troopers if they just hear gunfire. Shit, it's hunting season all year round at my place. D.E.P. catches 'em they say they were only shooting woodchucks."

"Well, maybe he saw something," O'Bannon says, turning over some dried scrambled eggs with his fork, dipping them absently into a blob of ketchup. There's something he doesn't want to say, at least not in front of Lonnie.

"Didn't you represent her a few years ago, Vincent?" Julia asks.

"Sure he did. That was when Sandra was robbing cemeteries," O'Bannon chuckles, his incipient jowls shaking. "Your dad ever tell you that one, Lonnie?"

"No. Not that one." Ever so subtly the kid manages to inject his weary contempt for my machinations. Can Jimmy and Julia pick up on it? What can I do? I pretend to ignore it for now.

Recalling the case, I can't help smiling. No doubt nothing is wrong with Sandra. She's indestructible. "This lady has a dried flower business, she also does those whatdoyoucallems?"

"Topiaries," Julia fills in.

"Yeah, anyway, she sells the flowers through some catalogues, and for years nobody knew where she got her stock till she got caught at the Protestant cemetery in Cobleskill stuffing some horse-show-sized wreaths into her van. As soon as some bigwig croaked, she'd follow up on their funerals figuring they're the ones with the dough to make the fancy displays. As soon as the mourners left, she'd scoop up the flowers. Then, if it was quiet, she'd loot the rest of the grounds. Anyway, the DA's got nothing to do, he tries to bring her up on some nineteenth century desecration statute, but I beat it down to a misdemeanor. Next thing I hear, she goes up to Schoharie County and gets busted in the Catholic cemetery near Cobleskill. I've got to bail her out again."

"You told me that," O'Bannon says, laughing in an odd, strained way. "You told me . . . What'd she say when you got her out?"

"'Low overhead! Low overhead!' She was singing that old Robert Hall jingle!" A warm, boozy cloud came off her when she took my arm and wished her jailers long life. A small woman with a wild shock of gray-streaked black hair, she had a ready laugh that shook her whole body. Once she had been a real beauty, and despite some extra weight, she still had that aura about her, the confident way she carried herself, her youthful face encased, unmarked, within the skin of middle-age.

"Vincie, can I talk to you?" O'Bannon nods his head to the front door. "Hey, Kiki, can you get the kid some ice cream?"

"No ice cream," she calls. "Just grillas and Jello. Green."

"Well, give the kid whatever he wants. Coffee. Cigarettes. Crack." This remark draws a wan smile from Lonnie, who has been reassuring me that he doesn't see the appeal of Kurt Cobaine or the romance of River Phoenix. What he likes is Bud Powell, Bartok, and bad Marilyn Monroe movies. On the ceiling over his bed he's tacked a black-and-white poster of Monroe in a teddy, and colored her lips with a ruby red paint.

"I'll have a Jello sandwich."

O'Bannon flicks a thumb the kid's way. "Whatever he wants." Raising vaudevillian eyebrows, he asks, "You like her nose ring, Lonnie?"

"It's just a clip-on," Lonnie replies knowingly.

"A hipster, huh?"

"If you ask me, it's just masochism," Julia puts in. She writes *These Old Times* in the local paper, and O'Bannon always says she'd be happier living in 1951. "They're piercing their bellybuttons. Uggghhh."

The pharmacist leads me out the front door of the cafe to stand under the Hungry Heart's plastic awning. In the Accordia Memorial Park, a triangle of land where local booze hounds finish their nightly sprees, stands the World War I gazebo, a peculiar structure that lists the town's casualties from the Great War in white plastic letters like the times for the next movie. On the other side of the park, Main Street is empty and still, an idealized painting— Massey's immaculate Queen Anne that's broken up into apartments, a Gothic concoction called the Autumn Leaves Rest Home, the square-towered Lutheran church with the frozen clock.

Through a veil of snow the mountains above the town blur, fade in and out of focus, blend with the swollen sky. In his shirt sleeves, O'Bannon hunches his big shoulders, stamps his feet like a horse. "It's bad, it's really bad. . . ."

"What the fuck's going on, Jimmy?"

"We're not sure, we don't know who was in the camp, but Maurice got out of the hospital, those fucking stupid psychiatrists . . ." He can't continue. To my shock the jocular, impervious O'Bannon with his inflamed Irish mug is crying, snorting up snot, rubbing his eyes with his shirt sleeve. "Gotta stop . . . Julia . . . You read about this stuff or you see this shit on the movie of the week . . . It's no fucking joke. Harlan saw the kid from the road. You know I had a thing with Sandy, a long thing . . . Almost left Julia, but Sandy didn't want me to . . . Sandy, didn't want . . ."

I'm seasick. Sandra sat up in bed, shook out her corona of dry, curly hair, extended her arms to me. The morning after, her face denuded of makeup, she looked pale, the energy drained out of her. One of her breasts flopped out over the quilt. I didn't know whether to plunge back into bed or head for the door. "You've got those almond eyes, like the boys on the frescos in Pompeii," she said.

"She dead?"

"Oh, yeah, she's dead. Kid blew his own mother to pieces . . . How does a certified lunatic get his hands on a semiautomatic? Know what? Yesterday she called Julia to work on this silly campaign, they were going to put these stone planters around the Park, all the way down to the Grand Union . . . Today, phhhttttt . . ."

The quiet invades me, the hush of snow getting under my skin, maddening. In all the years I lived in Manhattan I never witnessed a single act of violence. Then I move up here, to this retreat . . .

My mind shuts down. I make myself blind.

"Shit. What am I supposed to tell Lonnie? You think we're going to be trapped here all night?" I try desperately to think of some other entertainment I can offer him if we can't ski. Maybe the baseball museum in Cooperstown? No, he thought it was a bore the last time. Ice skating someplace, but where?

"Who knows? As fars I know, they haven't caught the little murdering sonofabitch. Schizophrenia, bullshit! At the store I'm giving out psycho-tropics like candy, nobody goes and . . . Yeah, he's still on the loose. You'd think those dumbassed troopers could catch one kid with a rifle, there must be thirty or forty of them up on Route 10."

"Yeah, but little Maurice knows the terrain . . . he's been hunting with his dad for years. . . ." Narrow-faced little Maurice with his sucked in cheeks, his hedge of black eyebrows, his black eyes, Jewish intensity.

At fifteen he got the idea that his father, the small town banker, was denying loans to starving peasants in Mexico and decided to stab him with a bread knife. Since then the shrinks have been putting his pieces back together again, but they never fit. He was a deceptive sight, a perfectly appointed young man in his khakis and pin-striped shirt and V-neck pullover rattling on about secret cul de sacs on the Internet that only he knew, terrorist bulletin boards he'd penetrated, speaking in such a rational way you started to believe him.

"I'm sorry, Jimmy. She was a nice woman." This sounds so empty I try to think of something else to say, but I'm numb.

"You know whose fault this is, don't you? It's that fucking Nathan's fault. First he insists on living across the road from her, and then he's spying on her all the time and filling the kid up with all his own poison. He's been telling that kid she's some kind of monster since he was five."

"Maybe I should take Lonnie back to Hurley."

"Fucking Nathan. The guy's an obsessive maniac. Probably put the kid up to it."

"C'mon, Jimmy, the kid's a schiz, it's chemical. You of all people should know that. . . . C'mon, I gotta go inside."

"Yeah, wait a sec, lemme wipe my face. Jesus H. Christ! Poor Sandy . . ." Without warning the big man lunges to the curb and starts retching, heaving, his broad back in visible spasms. It takes a while, but when he's finished I kick some snow over the virulent yellow bile.

Back in the Hungry Heart conversation is muted, but Lonnie, his novel at arm's length, suddenly lets go with a burst of laughter.

"Lemme guess. Mr. Hyde is pillaging and murdering," I inquire.

"He's a baaaad boy, that Mr. Hyde." Lonnie smirks. Under the wavering florescent light he looks very thin, his unblemished child's skin stretched, almost transparent along his jaw.

"I offered to feed him, but no luck," Julia says brightly.

"Know what, Lon? I think this thing's gonna drag on. Maybe we should head back to your mother's."

"That's OK, I can wait. I really want to do some downhill, Dad."

"Yeah, well, nobody's skiing this weekend. I think we ought to hit the road."

"Why can't we just wait? What's the big deal?"

"For one thing there's a storm coming. Lake effect snow, they said," I improvise, but the moment I say it the fear comes over me. Up in the Adirondacks I've driven through white-outs that sucked every sensation out of the world; in a burst of snow the windshield went dark, the wiper blades choked, the car lost contact with the road, an ice boat on the wind.

"My favorite, I like to ski downhill in that stuff blind."

Irritated, I toss down a few bucks, pat O'Bannon on the shoulder. "Thanks folks. Maybe I'll see you in a few days."

Sullenly, Lonnie follows in my wake. We're the only ones out on the street. "Hurry up, let's get in the car. Can't you see there's something wrong?"

"You always make such a big deal. You look like you're having a heart attack."

Unaware, I've broken out in a dank sweat; the nape of my neck is soaked, my armpits dripping. But getting into the plush sedan calms me, as if one of its luxury features were bullet-proof glass. In five minutes we can make Accordia disappear. In an imitation of composure, I turn the key and the car whispers to a start. Only a few blocks and we'll be back in the countryside, among the dairy farms, collapsed outbuildings, trailers, sweeping banked fields.

Though I know Lonnie thinks it's too staid, I slip Perlmann playing the Brahms Concerto for Violin into the deck. A shield of harmony, the music pours over us.

I'm driving a shade too fast, but under control, whipping past the abandoned Victorian Department Store, Accordia Liquors, Christian Notions, the Image Zone Tattoo Parlor, Harriet's Hairdos, Constantini's Truck Parts.

"I don't know why I bother," Lonnie mutters.

Without warning, I lose my cool. "There's a fucking lunatic loose with a gun, you want to hang around for the show?"

"Really? Why didn't you tell me?" For the first time all day, he sounds animated. "Who is it? Why didn't you tell me?"

Perversely, I'm happy for the moment. That flat affect of his drives me up the wall.

I'm almost going too fast to stop at the roadblock. In a neat bit of footwork, the trooper dances out of the way, but he's none too pleased. "Turn around! Nobody goes through!" he snaps. Hat slightly askew, he has a panicky look in his eye, and suddenly, despite his Marine-like demeanor, he looks like a child.

"You just told me I could go back this way an hour ago."

"No more. We've got police activity here. Get back into town. Now!" he barks.

As I struggle to turn around we hear the poppoppop of real gunshots, flat and matter of fact, muted behind auto glass. I keep backing up, turning the wheel, looking around wildly. Then I see the small black figures running in a chain along the ridge near Gaiter's dairy barn, dark blue shadows across the glinting snow.

"Don't look! Don't look!" I'm shouting, but of course Lonnie ignores me.

"EEEOOWWWW! EEEOOWWW!" he bellows, pounding the dashboard with a white fist. "You see that? You see that?"

All I can think about is jamming his head face down into the seat, but when I start spinning the wheel, I see it. By shouting, he has revealed it to me. Puffy and purple around the silver ring, the right side of his tongue looks like a piece of spoiled meat. Unbelievable. He's pierced his tongue. I'm fascinated by the sight of it, its livid reality.

Skidding around me, a van full of troopers disgorges five cops with rifles, telescopic sights. In a panic I try to maneuver the car into a U-turn, but my front tires start digging a trench in the icy shoulder. On the other side of the windshield, the kid trooper is shouting, waving his arms angrily as I spin my wheels. Finally, the car lurches forward, then I throw it in reverse. My heart roars in my ears as I skid back onto the road. At a crazy angle the white fields become the white sky, and for a moment I lose all orientation, white-blind. Surging forward, the car seizes the road. Half-melted, milky as a cataracted eye, Gaiter's pond swings into view.

Twisted around, Lonnie gapes at the distant, flickering figures. Far away, the gunfire seems to recede. Poppoppoppop, toy guns in a game of war. I slam the automatic into fourth gear, burning rubber back to town.

Once I'm safely out on the highway, I can't help looking over my shoulder too, but all I can see is Gaiter's silo, its washed-out yellow-and-blue dome a fixed, serene point in the landscape.

Without thinking, I head straight back to Accordia Memorial Park, with mechanical concentration aiming the car into a spot against an ancient, laid up dry wall. Silently, we sit there, the windshield fogging up, the hum of the fan filling the silence. Then I lose it. "You pierced your fucking tongue? What are you, nuts?"

"Yeah, I did it on a bet. Fifty bucks plus the price of the procedure."

"The procedure? The procedure? Who would do this to a thirteen-year-old kid?" Before the words get out of my mouth, I know I'm heading in the wrong direction. Too direct. Too self-righteous.

"I said I was sixteen. What about all the shit you did?"

"What are you talking about?"

"You oughta know, you're the big meat puppet. I used to watch the 'Dating Game' with Mom, that's what she called them, guys like you. You know the first memory I have of you? Really, honestly and truly? The day you packed up and left us. That's what I remember."

It's like getting kicked in the balls by the past; you can't kick back.

"Okay, I'm a meat puppet. I confess. So that's why you pierce your tongue?"

"Sure. Maybe." He shifts uncomfortably in his seat, looks away.

A cold anger seizes me. I'm beyond strategizing, maneuvering, keeping his tender sensibilities in mind.

"Well, listen to this. I'd cut my right arm off for you, whether you want me to or not. You want fifty bucks, you come here, you've got it. But I'll tell you one thing. Mister. You're going to get that thing taken out. It's not healthy. It's infected."

But he's not that easy to intimidate. Leaning back he appraises me with his black, almond eyes. "Do you realize something, Dad? We're sitting here talking about my TONGUE, and the cops are up on that hill killing somebody!"

"I know, it's weird, isn't it?"

Then we both start laughing, just for a second, but even then I'm afraid somebody'll see us.

Eagles

—

Sara Burnaby

There is a book at my sister's with an angel on the cover. A presence hovering so enormously it goes out of frame. You can't even see the ends of its wings. That's how hugely it fills Marysara's mind. Without room for discussion. As if she was already fixed between angel rib and wing. I watched her bedside table the entire week I visited and the book lay unmoved. Not a hair past the mark in the dust that I secretly made with my finger. When I got home I began to see the eagles differently. Watching them is as close as I can get to angels. Big winged birds, pinions cupped for landing. The whistling dive. The crack of air pumped at take off. In the right place at the right time, the stillest moment of the stillest day, you can hear them in flight. If I was going to have my own angel, I'd want it like an eagle. Powerful, ferocious; guide and protector. Every day, in the shadow of spanned wings, I talk to Marysara on the phone. It is where, most of all, we have gotten to know each other. Over hours and years of exchange, by breath and current matched. This morning the eagles are in the snag tree over the cove: two white heads facing one and other, conversing in high, short running notes that fall down the air like water. I hold the phone out the window for Marysara to hear. It is such a clear and tender sound. Not one you'd imagine from an eagle.

"Is it sunny, there?" she asks.

"Dark and clammy," I reply, wary even of differences in the weather. Of anything reminding her that I moved away and she stayed. About the only thing we have in common is the West Coast, one of us at either end of it. Marysara likes the south and warmth; she goes to Hawaii for Christmas. I have journeyed north with every change of address. But it is Marysara who likes change; I hate it. She is a great collector of what she calls *stuff*, anything to adorn her day, her house, her person. I keep stripping my life down to see what is left.

Right now, Marysara laughs, repeating, "Clammy." And reminds me of our childhood summers at the beach. On mutual impulse we recite Dad's "beach catechism."

How's the weather? he'd ask and put out his hand. Palm
cupped, we'd give him the clam handshake and shout, clammy.
Next he'd ask who screams loudest and we'd say, the eagle. And
who eats first? That was the last question and my little sister always tried to get the jump on me, yelling, THE EAGLE! Then she'd
run in to be first to dinner. I could out yell her though; starting
seconds later, I had more air. I prided myself that my yell followed
her around corners, through doors.

As we talk, I tuck the phone against my shoulder and take some
white curly down from the birds' molt that I collected last August.
It is against the law to remove eagle feathers from where you find
them; you're not even supposed to touch one. That's how the en-
vironmentalists show their reverence for a bird that has always
been holy. At potlatches the eagle dancers whirl and leap and nod
to make the down float from their headdresses for a blessing over
the guests. Which is why I am sending some to Marysara.

Against this thing that has been growing in her. She says it began when she was born, three years behind me. But I never noticed
Marysara behind me. In all our growing up together she was first, in
school, in sports, in piano. She had the most friends; she was class
president. Marysara was first in everything. Always. A thing I got
used to in order not to be overwhelmed by her. "You ignored me,"
she said, but how could I ignore a sister who went to the same
schools as me, from elementary to college, and then married my
husband's brother. What seemed to her like ignoring, I took as the
usual clockwork of our living, like being in the same house and getting our periods the same time of month. Invisible currents of tim-
ing and preference paired us. Our children bear that pairing on.
Double cousins, close in age, genetically the same as brothers and
sisters. Back and forth between our houses, almost interchangeable, they mirrored us, these children so brightly everywhere.

When I divorced, Marysara followed. Our decrees divorcing
spouses would have been better titled, sister vs. sister. We struggled like wild things in a net. Spent more passion against each
other than we ever did on husbands.

"You always hated moving over to give me room," she said.

"You mean you wanted to get divorced first?"

"I didn't want to get divorced at all. You've caused so much tur-
moil in this family. . . ."

This time I fought back and told her: "Take it to the chaplain."

Marysara wanted recognition, distinctions, definitions, and she had such readiness of hope. I would have killed for peace. I used to listen for the phone, her car as if all that was wrong between us could suddenly be made corporeal by her appearance. Or at least as substantial as it felt in spirit.

"I always wanted a sister," she told me the other day. Sorrowing over the resistance cumulative between us and time shortening in the gut, I wrote out the words for her to THERE IS A BALM IN GILEAD. Which carries a certain risk that she will think I am praying, even though it is an old hymn. Each day I try to find a blessing for Marysara in recognition of the fix she is in, and to acknowledge things out of control, because if I do there may be some chance of order. A different one, of course, but that would be fine. I'd take it and be glad. Meanwhile, I am careful not to pray for my sister. She would say I was putting on airs if I did. One upping. Acting holier than thou. But there can be no mistake over a song about making the wounded whole. That is something we both understand after years of war. Like good foot soldiers, our hearts crossed eighteenth century style by white bandoliers, we deliver the wounding salvo and weep at dark for the enemy. Except Marysara knows a lot more about grief and trying and discouragement by now than I ever will. What we agree on is silent. It occurs in practice, without words. The rule is never give an inch.

I gave just enough recently, to get reminded because one of the things that got us off on the wrong foot, finally occurred to me. That I wanted her opinion and she didn't want mine. When I said so, she replied, "I don't remember you ever asking."

When Marysara bristles, she makes the sound of taffeta. I used to think it was her hair or her clothes but in the hospital she wears a gown. Her hair is gone. "You never cared," she said, "what I thought."

My sister is an expert at hit and run. She is still at it, even dying. Maybe most of all dying, as I think on our conversations. She begins each one by asking how I am in a way and with a concern that absolutely warms my heart and brings up thoughts. It is impossible to answer only fine. I lose my balance. Plummet. Only later see how our talk got started. How are you? It is so easy to forget the way things are. How they have to be between us.

When Marysara went to the hospital for the surgery that was supposed to save what was looking like the very last of her life, I called from downstairs. "I'm here." I said. "In town."

"You're not."

Marysara never believes me. I don't trust you, she says, again and again in different ways.

"I'm downstairs." I used the obvious for proof.

"Well, I'm not dying!" She rustled in the bed and that day the taffeta sound was like pinions. I straightened even though it was only the house phone I was facing.

"I usually keep company with the living!"

She laughed then, tying her sound off at the end. She did the same thing when I said she was brave. With a little snort saying it isn't hard when your back is to the wall. Marysara takes her irony in small hits. She keeps it in reserve.

"We could have a fight," I urged. "No one out of character."

"We'll see," she said. I should have known better than to try to make her laugh again. And I did go up and sit there with her, on the bed, against the rules the nurses make you aware of, even if you aren't sure what all of them are.

"I want my two red dots back," Marysara said, patting her cheeks, the tubes in her arm shimmering like the bangles she wears on her wrists in the summer.

"Makeup?" I stalled, not wanting to bring a mirror. Under her look, I got up and rummaged in the drawers. The dots are OK on Marysara. They make her look French; she used to live in Paris. I played for time against the magnifying mirror with its harsh rim of lights, saying: "Who, at our age, needs a close up of wrinkles? Want an instant face lift? Just look in the mirror with your glasses off!"

"I don't wear glasses; I wear makeup!"

That's when I drew the line. It's not what you want but what you get that counts. Our mother said it a lot when we were little. Every time Marysara asked couldn't she be first, just once, before me. "Today you get earrings."

With a long glittering look my sister fitted the familiar gold hoops to her ears. Her shrewd eyes never faltering, nor her hands. Marysara is deft of glance and speech, and touch. Adroit at just about everything. The real grownup of the two of us, which is increasingly unnerving. She carries all of her makeup and jewelry in her purse when she travels. In case her luggage is lost or the plane goes down. "Worst time," she always says, "to be without!"

Sitting there beside Marysara, I thought how men loved her. After our brother-husbands I introduced her to my lover and when he and I parted, she fell in love with him, too. He used to say old habits die hard, but I only remembered it after things changed.

Then Marysara remarried—not the lover—but someone else, and she stayed married. The only of the two of us to do that!

From the look of Marysara in the hospital that day, you'd never have guessed she'd thrown the minister out of her room that very morning. Her book of angels was by the bed. There were the usual flowers everywhere; we voted on the worst arrangement. Marysara's scratchy voice was the only clue, but being used to the tubes they use in surgery I never gave her sound another thought. Until Mother mentioned in the waiting room that the morning had been a shambles. A real bell, book, and candle circus.

I met the minister five years ago, when he and my sister were friends. His name is Gabriel, but she calls him Gabe. They arranged a ritual of forgiveness and he came to pray over us in the church one afternoon. After he left, we talked and cried together awhile. And held arms all the way out onto the street to the car. The details are fixed in my memory probably because the moment was precious for its reconciliation and like so many others didn't last. Remembering how my sister trusted Gabe, I had mentioned to Mother that maybe someone ought to call him. Just to visit with Marysara like they used to was the idea. But he came to the hospital in his clerical collar, and in the middle of the prayers my sister stopped. Wouldn't utter another word. Wouldn't let him continue, either. "You are praying the last rites," she declared. "I can tell."

He didn't argue. Just mentioned that maybe she should reflect a bit on death. Maybe his gentleness was the last straw.

"No death prayers." Raising her voice, Marysara ordered him out. Yelled after him, "From now on, I do my own praying. My words for me. Nobody gets in the middle, understand. Nobody!"

That was my sister's official embargo on prayers and it's a good thing we are Protestants and mostly pray on our own anyway. As a Catholic, she'd be finished forever in Heaven. Listening to Mother's account, I remembered telling Marysara to take her troubles to the chaplain and just hoped no one would recall the minister's visit was my idea. Also Marysara's ban leaves me at a loss. As though I had given my word, and I have to be careful not to slip because this is her only way of having some say over what happens. And privacy. Both at a premium in hospitals. Instead, I call. Listen for the instant she answers, our breath and sound mingling. Each day, a litany for the living.

Right now, she sighs, says: "I get so little time to myself." She is telling me not to come there again. Unwilling to suffer the fate of the minister and get excommunicated according to the gospel of Marysara, I say, I'll stay put.

"Of course, I may croak." For the first time she mentions death. Hers. My caught breath acts on her like an interruption. She is not sharing, which goes way back. I used to think Marysara's thinness and tallness made her a terror at keep-away when we were little. She would drift toward the ball, all willowy, like she didn't know quite what to do if she got it. But once she touched the thing, she was a demon. And it wasn't height or her minimal body that gave her the power. It was the act of taking hold. Contact.

"Yes," I answer. "You could die. Anyone could die."

"Croak," she corrects. Peremptory. Still in the classroom, teacher of foreign languages.

I hurry past it to what is on my mind, "It is only important to be there while you're alive!"

After we hang up, I get to hating "croak." Dying is what people do and then they have funerals. Animals croak—fight for breath, clench jaws and talons, drool, pee, defecate, and resist. I've eased the death of animals by my presence, by touch. And sometimes they do go easily. I have never been with a person who is dying. In our family everyone lives forever or dies suddenly. But croak makes a zone of unexpectedness with Marysara at the center. Like a gyre, slow and indefinitely turning.

Look, I want to yell, croak doesn't go with angels. I consider calling back to lay claim to croak. Put it where it belongs. Slang is my thing, not hers. Marysara is out of character. And I'm not buying her embargo on prayers any longer either. There is no power in being the prayor, or lack of it as the prayee. It is the act itself that counts. That's what I have in mind to say as I phone back, and it is roaring so in my head that I can scarcely hear Marysara when she answers. "Is that you?" I ask.

"As far as I know," she says.

In a rush I tell her to lay off. And while she is at it to put that angel book in the trash. I am either coming to her right now or not at all.

"What's that supposed to mean?" Her voice is clear as a singer's. I almost have her back. A few hours south by plane.

"Either I come and be for you now or I'm not coming to your funeral!"

"Why!"

"You won't be there! It's no good without you."

"What?" she cries. "I came to everything for you. For your children. Everything!"

"That's what I meant; you've always been there. . . ."

"Of course. It will be my service, for me. My life!" Then without waiting for an answer she says, "I'll never, ever forgive you." And hangs up.

———

I've been sitting by the window all afternoon thinking of Marysara and me. What would we have been like, two old white-headed women sitting across from each other at tables? Our voices that people can't tell apart, still tumbling this story together. My sister who will never forgive me. And I at a loss for her. I wrap the white curly down, carefully, in my best heavy paper and seal it in an envelope.

When the time comes, everyone will say what a good fighter Marysara was and brave, adding judgments to Judgment. As if you could weigh things in favor of Heaven. Or against Hell. But Marysara isn't playing that game. She isn't playing the sister game, either, though until today, I thought she was planning to be born first out of her loss, and be finally free. But that's not it. Marysara is going to croak. She has a hold on death and the book by her bed isn't there to save her. It's a flight manual. She is going to solo. No phone, plane, letter, prayer, no angel-watch, or eagle-sighting will keep her now. I go back to the window unable in the early hours of evening to see anything on either side of the black glass.

FIRE NEXT DOOR

———

Steve Featherstone

Once, I thought I had special powers. I used them to kill Dave Spicer, the kid next door. He tormented us—my brother and sister and me—until he burned-up one morning in a fire. For a while I went around thinking that I had something to do with his death. The idea scared me, but I kind of liked it too. Soon enough I found out that there are some things you can't do a damn thing about, whether you're a kid with special powers or not.

"Cut his brake lines," I say. "That ought to work. Send the fucker right off one of those curvy mountain roads."

The car tumbles in slow motion, end over end, and crumples on its roof at the bottom of a canyon. Rocks bounce down into the cloud of settling dust. Then the car explodes—no, it doesn't explode. That's too good. The car burns slowly. A tire, still spinning, catches fire. Another tire flares. Black smoke boils up into the air. Inside the car, Sonny sits upside down, pinned against the seat, dazed. The last few minutes of his life come at him through a web of crushed glass. Hot oily fumes choke him. But Sonny hardly notices these things. No, it's all he can do to figure out why the ground is suddenly where the sky used to be.

I say to my brother, John, "What do you think? Baked beaner."

"Sonny doesn't live in the mountains," he says, dismissing the idea with a sneer. Hand-to-hand combat is more John's style. So far, his ideas have included busting Sonny's kneecaps with a baseball bat; cracking Sonny's head open with a tire iron. Crap like that. "Sonny lives in the city," he says. "It's nowhere near the mountains."

"How do you know?" I say. "You've never been there." I try to recall the postcards our sister Vicky had sent to us when she first got to Denver. There were mountains in them, huge ones, with snow on the peaks. The way it was pictured in the postcards, Denver was stacked high on top of these mountains, like a good wind might blow all the buildings away.

"Doesn't matter," John says. He pushes himself out of his chair and goes to the cupboard where he keeps his canister of super-protein supplement. The label on the canister advertises the stuff as "muscle building enzymes." Careful not to overdose, John levels off a scoop full of the brown powder with a knife, dumps it into a glass, then taps every last grain free from the scoop. Used to be that we argued over who ate all the Frosted Flakes. Not anymore. A few months ago John bought a weight set, installed it in his bedroom and declared that cereal rots your guts. Now it's all orange juice and enzyme milk shakes for him.

The baby whimpers in the next room. Earlier this morning we carried her crib downstairs so we could keep a close eye on her, but really it's just me doing the watching. John's too scared of her to do much beyond standing over her crib and making faces. I pretend to not hear anything to see what John will do. He sips from his milk shake like nothing's happening. Finally, I get up and check on her myself. Lying on her stomach, she sleeps with her face turned to the side, her hands curled into tiny pink fists next to her head. I draw the blanket down some and pat her sweaty back, gently, so as not to wake her. Then I lean down and whisper, "Just dreams little beaner, that's all."

Back in the kitchen I ask John whether he'd burped the baby like mom showed us. In the past week I've learned all I ever want to know about taking care of babies. "She's probably got gas," I say.

"I burped her," John says.

"Yeah, but did you do it right? I've seen you do it."

"I burped her," he says. "What the fuck—you do it then."

I say, "She's sleeping right now." And then, because I know he won't risk hitting me for fear of waking the baby, I say, "Dick wad."

John stares at me over the rim of his milk shake glass. He sets it down, wipes the foam from his lips. The refrigerator shudders and clicks off. "Don't forget," he warns, wagging his finger. "Mom isn't here to save your ass." He turns around and puts his glass in the sink. "When's she supposed to call, anyway?"

"She said she'd call when she landed."

"When's that?"

"Look at the ticket. I don't know. She had to stop in Cleveland first."

"That's stupid."

"The tickets are cheaper that way," I say.

"It's still stupid." John stands in front of the refrigerator, scanning the pieces of paper stuck to the door with plastic magnets:

our mother's travel itinerary, feeding instructions for Amelia, emergency phone numbers.

"Why don't you just go to work? I can watch Amelia fine."

"Oh yeah, right," John says, glaring at me over his shoulder. "Leave her here alone with you and your pot-head friends. That's a great idea."

"We worship Satan too, don't forget that."

"No fucking doubt," John says. He jabs his finger against the refrigerator door. "She's supposed to be eating right now. Look, right here it says eleven o'clock. That was twenty minutes ago."

"Ma said not to wake her up if she's sleeping," I say.

"This schedule says eleven o'clock feeding. That's now."

"I'm just telling you what she told me. Don't wake her up if she's sleeping. You can't wake her up just to shove food down her throat because the schedule says so."

"Whatever," John says. "You're the doctor, apparently. Doctor Mom."

"It's just what she said."

Sunlight streams in the window above the sink, glinting off the row of glass bottles and baby spoons and baby food jars lined up on the drain board. John goes to the window and looks out. It's a brisk, bright Friday morning in late October. The last leaves clinging to the trees twirl on bare branches. Somewhere high above the clouds between Cleveland and Denver, my mother wonders how she's going to persuade Vicky to leave Sonny, to leave Denver altogether and come back to Syracuse. Vicky's baby, Amelia, stays here with me and John. That's not how it was supposed to happen, but that's the way it is. For now she sleeps quietly in the next room where we can keep a close eye on her. Technically, I suppose you could say we're holding her hostage, but that wouldn't be right. We're not the terrorists here. We're baby-sitters. We're uncles. Brothers, we are.

———

The call comes later in the afternoon, around two o'clock. The first thing I hear when I pick up is the high-pitched screaming of jet engines. I can barely hear my mother's voice.

"Ma, I can't hear you!"

" . . . people . . ."

"Can you get to another phone!?"

The line goes dead. I hang up and wait. A moment later it rings again. This time the noise of the jet engines is only a muffled whine. "Ma?"

"I can't talk long," she says. "I can't even think straight with all these people walking around in here, bumping into me with their bags. Makes me claustrophobic. I just wanted to let you know I'm here. How's the baby doing? Are you and your brother following the schedule?"

"She's fine," I say. "She's sleeping right now. So, are they there to pick you up?"

"I didn't see them when I got off the plane," she says. "Of course, the plane was an hour late. They were probably here and gone already. It's better that way. I have their address. I'll call a cab driver."

"You're just going to show up at their door?"

"You don't think that's a good idea?"

"I don't know, Ma," I say. "I mean, you can't just show up without Amelia and expect them—or Sonny at least—to be understanding."

"Oh, Sonny doesn't scare me," she says. "I've learned a little bit over the years about dealing with men like him. You shouldn't be worrying about what I'm doing. You should be worrying about the baby. What's she doing right now?"

"I said she was sleeping."

"Well OK, I'll call later to let you know how everything goes. Remember, they're two hours behind here." She pauses for a moment. In the background I can hear what sounds like a room crowded with people and underneath that, the low roar of jets landing and taking off two thousand miles away. "The mountains are something else," my mother says. "They don't look quite real. I can see them right here from the pay phone."

"That sounds nice."

"I wouldn't want to live here though," she says. "Too many people. Too many Mexicans. Everything looks dirty."

"So what'd she say?" John says from the living room. "Did they meet her there? What's going on?"

"Nothing," I say, hanging up the phone. "She's going over to their house."

"By herself?"

"Unless I forgot somebody, she's not there with anyone else."

"Don't get wise."

"It's lunch time," I say. "She's probably hungry."

Brushing by me, John carries Amelia into the kitchen, holding her by the middle like she was a bomb. He sets her in the high chair and slides the chair to the edge of the table. In the refrigerator I find one of the bottles my mother had filled with formula before she left and set it next to the stove. As I run water into a pan, John checks the cupboard. The bottom shelf is stacked with baby food jars. John stares at them, then plucks one from the shelf and squints at the label. "Pears," he says. "Is this what she's supposed to have? Pears?"

"I think she's supposed to eat that like a dessert," I say, scanning the schedule on the refrigerator. "Pears are a dessert kind of thing. I'd go with the strained carrots."

John stands against the counter, watching the pan of water on the stove as I spoon the carrots into Amelia's mouth. In time, she eats the whole jar, and I switch to the pears. She looks at me without blinking, just opening and closing her mouth around the rubber-tipped spoon and staring at me in the funny way that she does. Her left eye is a little slow. When I bring the spoon to her mouth, her right eye focuses on it while the left drifts slowly away.

"She got that bad eye from Sonny," John says, waving his fingers in Amelia's face. "It's those spic genes of his."

"It's her eye muscles. They aren't developed enough yet."

"Listen to you! You really think you are a doctor! It's Sonny's beaner genes, I'm telling you. They're no good."

"She's only four months old," I say. "Give her a break. And don't let the water boil too long. The formula gets too hot for her to drink."

"Okay, Doc! The Doc is in the house! Better listen to the almighty Doc!"

The flame on the stove sputters and puffs out. John drops the bottle into the pan and jerks his hand away, swearing to himself. He leans against the counter as he had before, crossing his arms across his chest. With a damp dish rag, I clean up the food stuck to Amelia's face.

"You know," John says. "If Vicky had one iota of common sense, none of this would be happening. You'd think she'd learn. First there was Rick, now there's Sonny. And when she comes back—if she comes back, Christ!—it's going to be some other loser, you watch and see." John shakes his head. "I don't know what her problem is."

"You can't blame Vicky," I say.

"Well who can you blame?" John says, throwing his hands up in the air.

"I don't know," I say. But I do know it's not as easy as John makes it out to be. There's something about these guys, something you can't see on the surface. Like Rick—I used to buy pot from him before Vicky even knew who he was. I was in eighth grade and he was in his mid-twenties. He lived near the rez, in a little clapboard house surrounded by a perimeter of chain-link fence. The yard was packed earth. Other than the weeds that sprouted up around the fence, nothing grew there. And it always stunk like dog shit. Rick kept a few Redbones and Blueticks in plywood kennels at the back of the house. Except when he took them cooning in West Virginia, the dogs lounged around in the dusty shade of the yard's single maple tree, or sunned themselves on top of their kennels. Rick was kind of like those dogs, real low-key. If you knew him, he was nice to you. If not, he didn't pay you much mind.

But then there was Rooster, Rick's pit bull. Rooster didn't re-semble a pit bull so much as an alligator with fur. Rick's truck had a plywood and chicken-wire kennel bolted in the bed for the hound dogs, but Rooster always rode in the cab. When he had people over, Rick put Rooster in the cellar. He said Rooster was too high-strung to be around strangers. Locked behind the cellar door, Rooster would snort and snuffle and generally raise the hair on the back of my neck as I waited for Rick, who sat at the kitchen table, measuring out the pot on a little postal scale.

There were other times I didn't dare go past the front gate be-cause Rooster would be outside in the yard, his jaws clamped tight on the end of a knotted rope. The rope was tied to a tree limb, and hanging from the end of it like a side of beef was Rooster. He had this game where he'd scrabble around the tree trunk until he ran out of rope. Then he'd swing back the other way and do it all over again. As he did this, he'd growl from deep in his throat and roll his eyes into the back of his head. He did this for a long time. I'd come back an hour later, and he'd be there, still hanging from the rope by his mouth. If I was lucky, I had enough IOU's to my credit that I could rely on some friends to get me high until the next weekend.

Vicky got hooked up with Rick around the time she graduated high school. From there she went to the state Ranger School way up north in the Adirondacks. I was buying then from a black guy who lived on the south side of Syracuse. It was a drag because I had to take a bus into the city. But the black guy always had a sup-ply of premium island bud and no creepy dogs snorting at me from behind his cellar door. The whole year Vicky was at school, Rick drove back and forth to visit her. I don't think he liked the idea of Vicky being way up in the woods with the other forestry students, who were mostly guys.

The program only lasted a year. Near graduation time, she and Rick went cooning in West Virginia to celebrate. Vicky came back on a Sunday night with a black eye. I helped get her stuff out of Rick's truck while Rick sat there in silence, staring out the windshield until she had gone inside. Then he asked me why I hadn't been around, if I'd given up the weed. He clicked his headlights on and off and ran his hand over Rooster's fur as I made up a lie about joining the football team and drug testing and so on.

He said, "She hit my dog with a piece of fucking wood, you know."

Rick popped the clutch and the truck lurched backward into the street. In the cab Rooster scrambled to keep his balance, his fat muzzle squished flat against the window so that I could see his long yellow teeth. Later on I asked Vicky what the deal was but she didn't say much. The black eye, she said, came when she ran into a tree in the dark, chasing after the hound dogs. I don't know if she expected me to believe her. I don't think she cared. Her mind was on other matters. Central New York was dead. The people were dead, the place was dead. Things were really happening out West. They had huge forests out there. And jobs, too, working in the forests. The subject of Rick never came up again. In a subtle way, we blamed Vicky for what happened to her. We wanted her to leave and do good for herself, that's true; but we also wanted her to leave because she reminded us of things about ourselves we didn't like to look at. We wanted a new Vicky, and I think she did too. By the time she had her bags packed for Denver, her black eye had faded from blue to yellow and finally, to nothing at all. But she took with her a small, pale scar on her arm where Rooster had nipped her that night, coon hunting in the dark woods of West Virginia.

———

On the front porch steps I sit with Amelia riding my knee, waiting for the five o'clock late bus to go by. The sun hovers low over the hills to the west, its weak pink light lying flat against the sides of houses. John waits at the stop sign, on a mission to buy more baby food. Then he turns onto Route 11, dead leaves fluttering in his wake. Parked across the street, in front of the Murphy's old house, is a truck belonging to a landscape company. A man wearing a plaid hunting jacket rakes leaves in the yard.

"It's not your mom's fault," I say to Amelia, bouncing her on my knee. "Your dad's just a big loser, and we can't help that, can we?" I hold her close to my face and rub noses with her. "Loser, loser, loser."

She moves her arms around and gurgles, catching the ring of her pacifier with her finger and popping it out of her mouth. The pacifier tumbles down the steps. Holding her against my shoulder, I reach for the pacifier, put it in my mouth to get the dirt off, spit in the grass, then give it back to Amelia. The bus roars down Route 11.

"Time to go," I say, lowering Amelia into her stroller.

On the next block the bus rumbles past me, coughing up a cloud of diesel exhaust. I spread my jacket like a shield over Amelia's stroller. The bus rolls to a stop and Jesse gets off. I wave him over. "Hey, J. What up?"

"Where've you been?" He lights a cigarette and blows a thick plume of smoke into the air. "Take the day off?"

"Had to," I say. "I'm baby-sitting here, can't you see that? Say hi to Uncle J., Amelia."

"So this is her," he says, crouching down to look in the stroller. "Cute." He offers me a cigarette pinched between yellow-stained fingers. I take it and he lights it for me, cupping his hands around the end.

"I need to see Elvis."

"I just got some shit that'll make you be Elvis."

We stop first at Jesse's house. I stand in the living room, my hands on the push bar of Amelia's stroller and chat with Jesse's father. When Jesse comes out of his room, we leave. Outside, Jesse takes the baggy from his jacket pocket.

"The Mansion?" I say.

Giving the baggy a sniff, Jesse nods and stuffs it back in his pocket again.

The Mansion stands on the vacant corner lot of my street, abandoned since the fire. The county boarded up the windows and doors and was supposed to eventually tear the place down, but they haven't gotten around to it yet. The old people in the neighborhood complain to the county that the house is used by drug lords and Satan-worshippers, which would be, generally speaking, Jesse and me. Other than the odd Sheriff patrol, The Mansion is the perfect place for partying. It's also about ten yards from the back door of my house.

Jesse unhitches the chain and pushes the door open and we slip inside. With the door closed, it's dark and cool inside; and the air is tinged with the smoke of a fire six years gone. I push Amelia slowly through the shadows and patches of light, the rubber wheels of her stroller bumping over the charred floor boards. We sit on a ratty old mattress in one of the less damaged rooms, our backs against the wall. On the wall opposite us some lame-ass has spray-painted a lopsided pentagram and the numbers 666 in fluorescent orange. Torn condom wrappers and empty beer bottles litter the floor. I lift Amelia from her stroller and hold her close to my body where it's warm as Jesse packs the bowl. Then the lighter flicks and Jesse's face blinks on like a light bulb. He sucks in his cheeks. The flame bends like a snake into the bowl. Shadows spring up and shiver against the ceiling and then everything goes dark again.

"Loading torpedo bay number two," Jesse croaks.

I reach out and brush Jesse's hand, closing my fingers around the tiny red coal, blowing on it, bringing it to life. Against my body, I can feel the heat Amelia gives off, her quick little intakes of breath, her fluttering heart. I lift my chin and turn my head away from her.

"And . . . fire!"

———

They had to hose down our house. Flames broke through the windows, making a bridge of fire over the driveway. It blistered the paint on the roof of my mother's car. The firemen kept a steady stream of water pouring down on everything, the car, the burning house, our house. We watched from across the street, huddled beneath wool blankets on the Murphy's porch. Stunned and cold, we watched the Spicer's house burn until Bobby, the oldest one, dressed only in his underwear, jumped out of a rescue truck. He hopped over the tangle of hoses and pushed his way to the front door, dragging three firemen in heavy canvas jackets with him. And he was screaming.

David! David!

Our mother herded us inside, but we could still hear Bobby screaming. Waiting for us were steaming mugs of cocoa and a plate of sandwiches: perfect little triangles of bread and jam with the crusts cut off that I didn't eat because I was afraid to ruin them. Mrs. Murphy talked quietly with my mother in the living room. Mr. Murphy sat in silence at the kitchen table with us kids, sipping slowly from a coffee cup.

David! David!

A few years ago the Murphys died. First one went, then the other, like they were parts of the same person. Old Man Murphy had only one arm. He'd left the other one on a beach in the Pacific during World War II, but he didn't like to talk about it. For a guy with one arm, he was a champion horseshoe thrower. He tried to teach us the basics one afternoon. We stood in a row, clutching our rubber horseshoes, watching and waiting our turn. All in one fluid motion, his thin body unfolded from a crouch and the horseshoe floated from his outstretched fingertips, rising in a slow, graceful arc and looping end over end toward the metal stake. Then Vicky started to cry. Mr. Murphy put his good arm around her shoulders and guided her across the lawn as Vicky cried even harder and pulled loose strands of hair from her mouth. John dropped his horseshoe and started after them, but I stood where I was. I really wanted to throw that horseshoe. And I did, grasping it with both hands and heaving it as high and hard as I could into the brilliant blue sky.

———

The stroller jiggles over the cracked asphalt, making the little white pompom on Amelia's hat wobble back and forth. I think I might be pushing her too fast so I slow down when we hit Jesse's street. In front of his house we stop and Jesse says, "Later," and goes inside. On the way back to my street, I flap my jacket and run my fingers through my hair to get the smell of smoke out. I take long, deep breaths to air out my lungs.

The air has turned cold and brittle. Light retreats over the dark hills to the west, taking bits of ash and sparks with it. A blackened steel barrel burns in the Murphys' backyard. Standing next to it is the man in the plaid hunting jacket. I watch him from the street. He dumps leaves into the barrel and stokes the flames with a long black stick. Ashes and sparks swirl out of the barrel where they are immediately carried away on the breeze, sifting through bare tree limbs and rising up over roof tops.

———

It's already dark by the time John comes through the door, holding a bag of groceries against his chest. I'm kneeling on the floor, fastening the sticky tabs on Amelia's diaper. Then I lift her up on wobbly legs and zip her into a clean pair of cotton pajamas. In the kitchen, John sets the bag of groceries down and asks if our mother had called while he was out. No, I tell him. He mutters something under his breath.

"I'm sure everything's fine." The high is beginning to peak off now. I close my eyes and let myself slide with it. When I open them again, John is standing in the living room doorway, a jar of baby food in his hand.

"It isn't right," he says. "Vicky should just deal with her own shit. I don't see why Ma has to get involved."

"She can handle it," I say, wanting to believe it myself. I poke Amelia in her belly. She squirms and grasps for my finger. "She said on the phone that she could."

"What the fuck?" John says. "I thought you said no one called."

"Earlier I mean," I say, measuring my words carefully. "I meant earlier. She said she wasn't worried about Sonny."

"Yeah," John says, distracted by the jar of baby food in his hand. "Yeah, we'll see." He goes back into the kitchen. I play with Amelia for a while, then take her to her crib. She starts to cry when I leave the room.

"What's the problem?" John says, sneaking a look at her.

"She wants a bottle," I say. I put a pan of water on the stove and get a bottle of formula from the refrigerator. Next to the stove, I stand and watch as John puts the groceries away.

"Where do you think Dad is now?" I ask him.

"Why?" John says over his shoulder. "Who cares?"

"Nothing. I do. I was just thinking about the time he left. I only remember going over to the Murphys' house a lot."

"Well," John says, "you didn't miss anything."

"I don't know if I did or didn't." I must've been around six years old when my father left. I had just started school. That means Vicky was nine and John was eleven. All of us rode the school bus together. One afternoon, our father showed up. He waved to us from the parking lot. I was walking with Vicky because John was too cool to be seen with us. Vicky told me not to look and to keep walking toward the school bus. But I couldn't help myself. I twisted my arm and Vicky's hand fell away. I threaded my way through the lines of kids, passed between the idling buses, pulled forward as if a rope was attached to my waist. Vicky called after me. My father leaned across the seat and opened the door. As I climbed in something snagged my shirt and I turned to see that it was John. He took me by the shoulders and shoved me into the car. Then he got in too and closed the door.

The back seat of my father's car was crammed with boxes of and heaps of clothes. It was maybe a couple of months since he'd moved out. He seemed glad to see us. He smiled a lot and asked us what we were doing. A thin glaze of sweat shined on his face. Next to my leg, his fingers tapped nervously on the stick shift. I told him that I was going into the first grade and John slid his hand across the seat and pinched my thigh hard enough to make me jump.

Once we'd gotten on the road I said, "You look sick, Dad."

He looked at me and grinned, then glanced into the rear view mirror and gunned the car past a long yellow line of buses. When we were clear of them, my father wiped his face with the back of his hand and said, "I haven't been feeling too good these days, buddy." I watched that hand, so close to me, twitching and glistening with sweat from his face, pushing the car through its gears. He took the bus route through the rez and into town. He slowed as he passed our street, craning his neck around us to see out the window. I could feel his stale breath on my cheek. A few miles down the road, he turned into the Fay's Drugs parking lot. At the store entrance, he steadied himself against a bubble gum machine and said, "Go ahead. Get anything you want. I'll wait out here for you." He coughed into his hand and motioned toward the door. "Go ahead, I'll pay for it. Anything you want."

Inside the store, John pulled me close to him and said, "Don't get nothing." I asked him why and he pinched my arm and hissed, "Because." We wandered around the aisles long enough for the clerk to get suspicious. The store didn't have much to brag about. The toy aisle was the kind of toy aisle all crappy little drug stores have, its dusty shelves stacked with old car models and racks of faded coloring books. I grabbed the first thing that caught my eye: a parachute man. He was frozen behind a shield of clear plastic, crouching, waiting for the signal to jump. Cartoon explosions bloomed in bright reds and yellows on the cardboard behind him. Tiny black silhouettes of fellow paratroopers floated down amid the explosions.

"Put it back," John said.

"He told us to get something," I said, starting down the aisle.

John yanked me by the collar, tearing it almost completely free from my shirt. "Leave me alone!"

Our father appeared at the top of the aisle.

"What the *hell* is going on in here?"

Neither of us moved. John still held the ruined collar in his fist. Behind the register, the store clerk slowly counted out bills, pausing to lick his thumb. My father came down the aisle and squatted in front of me, his knees cracking. He'd taken his jacket off and slung it over his shoulder. I tried to look over his shoulder at the clerk. "You want that?" my father said, lowering his voice. He adjusted his jacket, draping it over his arm, then shuffled closer to me.

"No," I said.

"Aw, c'mon," he said, taking the package from me. "This is pretty neat, huh?"

I nodded.

"Sure, you can have a lot of fun with these things." With some effort, he stood up again. "Here, we'll get another one for your brother. John, grab another one of those and let's go. Your mother's probably wondering where you guys are."

Before he dropped us off at the corner of our street, he told us to have fun. "And remember your Dad, OK? Don't forget about your Dad." Vicky was sitting in the living room watching TV when we opened the door. She said we were in big trouble, that we were going to be arrested. Ma had already called the police from work, she said. A few minutes later our mother came home, followed by a Sheriff's deputy. The Sheriff scribbled the details as John told him what happened. Then we got a lecture we'd already heard a thousand times at school about taking rides from strangers. Our mother grounded us for a month, but other than that, nothing happened. She was more mad, I think, at John for leaving Vicky home by herself and ripping the collar off my shirt and revealing to the whole neighborhood that she ran the kind of house where police cars stopped. It was the last time any of us saw my father.

"Maybe I missed a lot," I say, holding my hand above the pan of water on the stove. Steam rises hot against my palm. "Who knows?"

"*I* know," John says, jabbing his finger into his chest. "If I didn't get into the car that time, *you'd* probably be living in a trailer right now and eating peanut butter and crackers for dinner. You owe me *big*."

"Maybe he won the lottery and he's living on the beach in Florida right now. Maybe if you let me go that time I'd be eating lobster for dinner every night. And all of you would be ancient history."

"Oh yeah—and maybe you'd have yourself a whole new family too," John says with an abrupt laugh. He looks at me and smiles. "With a cat and a big fluffy sheep dog."

I plop the bottle of formula into the water and turn the flame down. It's a joke, I know. The right thing to do is laugh at it, laugh at myself, laugh at the whole situation. Laugh at what we've come to. What else can you do? At the very least, we can be in on the joke together. I want to give my brother this, I do. But I can't laugh. I can't even look at him. Instead, I stare for a long time into the pan of water. Strings of bubbles rise from the bottom and curl around the bottle. Amelia cries out sharply, and for a moment, John and I turn our attention to the darkened entrance of the living room and we wait, John's smile fading from his face.

"Keep dreaming," he says flatly. "Dad's probably dead."

———

Sometime during the night the phone rings. It stops as I stumble half-asleep down the dark stairwell. I sit on the landing, waiting in the dead silence and wondering whether it was my mother calling from Denver. For another half hour I sit in the dark next to the phone, listening to the wind beat against the house. But the phone doesn't ring again. Upstairs, I lie in bed, unable to go back to sleep. The bars of Amelia's crib throw shadows against the wall. It's so quiet I can hear her tiny lungs expanding with air and gently pushing it out again. I listen to the rhythm of her sleep and stare out the window at the clear night sky, wishing I had some dope to mellow me out.

Amelia wakes me with a cry. I jump out of bed and stand over her crib and whisper to her that everything's going to be fine and it's OK and any other nonsense that comes to mind. It doesn't work, so I slip my hands underneath her back and shovel up the whole warm bundle of blankets and carry her into bed with me. There's a little formula left in her bottle, which I tip to her lips. She takes the rubber nipple, closes her eyes and immediately settles down. It's not long before she's asleep again. In fear of rolling over on her or shoving her off the bed, I don't dare sleep. I lie on my back and watch clouds creep up slowly on the moon and bury it. By morning, the sky is a dull gray sheet draped over the valley, no sign of sun or moon. The light is gray and watery, trapped in silver droplets against the window pane.

At seven o'clock John's alarm clock goes off. He gets up, takes a piss, flushes the toilet, and goes back into his room for his morning workout. Through the wall I hear him sweat and strain and push. The clink and clank of metal against metal. The gasps for air. In the silence between each repetition, I hold my breath with him and let it out slowly. In those moments, breath held tight in his chest, the heavy bar poised an arm's length above his gritted teeth,

I imagine that John thinks about all the Sonnies of the world and all the shit they get away with.

With Amelia propped against my shoulder, I go downstairs to eat. First, I rummage through the cupboards for Amelia's baby food and feed her. When it's my turn to eat she watches from her high chair, her head bobbing, her eyes trying to follow the movement of the spoon in my hand. After I've put the dirty dishes in the sink, I clean her up and take her into the living room to change her diaper. Kneeling over her, I study her face for features I might recognize as Vicky's. It's hard to tell. In a drawer, I dig out a stack of pictures Vicky had sent to us from Denver. There's one of Vicky standing in front of a giant pink rock. The picture is dark, Vicky only a vague outline eclipsed by the boulder's shadow. Written on the back of the picture is a description and a date: *Balanced Rock, Garden of the Gods, April '91.*

Flipping through the others, I find a blurry close-up of Vicky. I hold the picture next to Amelia's face, comparing eye color. But Amelia's eyes don't have a real color yet. They're sort of murky, like muddy water. The centers are black and in them I can see my reflection, a long hovering face. I set the picture on the floor and shuffle through the rest. Most of them are landscapes. Lots of rocks and trees and mountain ranges and names for all these things printed carefully on the back with the dates.

There's only one of Vicky with Sonny. At the point the picture was taken, we didn't know much about him. In the letter that the picture came with, Vicky mentioned that he specialized in skylight installations for malls and office buildings and the houses of rich people. His family was Mexican although they'd been in the United States for generations. He drove an old Jeep CJ-7, he didn't own a dog, and he was nice.

In the picture, they have their arms around each other's shoulders and they seem to be suspended in mid-air above a translucent blue sheet of ice. Purple mountain peaks, like the kind in the song, rise up majestically behind them. They squint into the camera and smile. In the foreground is the shadow of the person taking the picture. A tourist? A friend? I'd like to find the person who belongs to that shadow and ask them what they saw when they looked through the camera that day. Did they see what we see? Did they know that the moment the shutter clicked, they made a promise to us?

We had the negative of that picture blown-up and put it on the TV. We believed in it with something close to blind faith. Every bit of news we got from Vicky went into that picture. When Vicky said she was moving in with Sonny, that became part of what we saw in the picture. When she called to say that she was pregnant, the majestic purple mountains adjusted themselves in the background to make room for it. By the time she made arrangements to visit and to pick up the rest of her stuff, the picture had taken on a life of its own, in dimensions that went beyond its cheap gold frame. It was more real to us than Vicky herself.

The night they arrived we ate dinner together. Vicky sat next to Sonny, with Amelia squeezed between them. Sonny was charming. He spoke and ate quickly, scraping his plate with vigorous little strokes of his fork. In between bites he told stories about Amelia doing this or that, playing up the proud new father routine. Vicky just sort of leaned back in her chair and listened. Now and then she added some small detail to one of Sonny's stories, but other than that she seemed content to let him have the floor.

"Nothing gets past this one," Sonny said, patting Amelia on the head. "She watches everything. She's real curious, you know what I mean?"

"When John learned to crawl," my mother said, "he was always getting into things. I'd get up in the middle of the night and he'd be crawling across his room, going Lord knows where. He used to get stuck sometimes but he never cried. I'd find him in the morning, sleeping upside down with one leg caught in the rails of his crib." John, who was carving a thick slice of breast meat from the turkey, smiled at this.

"I guess we better watch out, then," Sonny said, turning to Vicky. "Looks like Amelia might have inherited the traveling-jones."

After the dishes were cleared away, my mother brought out a pie and I went to the bathroom. On the way back to the kitchen, John bumped into me. He grabbed my arm and whispered into my ear, "Did you see Vicky's goddam nose? You take a good look and tell me her nose hasn't been broken!" At the table, John raised his eyebrows and nodded toward Vicky. I didn't have to look. I knew it was true. But I did anyway. The tip of her nose was flattened slightly, as if she were leaning her forehead against a pane of glass. It was as plain as day, as if it'd always been there; somehow I had managed to look past it.

She ate a bite of pie, then went into the living room to nurse Amelia. Meanwhile, Sonny talked about his family, about the magnificent skylight installations he'd sold, about the West. I could hardly listen. I was angry and my anger was huge. I could feel it pushing underneath my skin, trying to get out. My arms and legs grew heavy and dense with it. If I wasn't careful, if I moved an inch the wrong way, I worried that I'd flip the whole table over. Glasses would shatter in my grip. Slowly, I lifted forkfuls of pie to my mouth and concentrated on chewing and swallowing, but there wasn't enough room in me for the pie. At one point, Sonny's voice softened as he talked about how his life had taken new directions with Vicky and Amelia. Then he paused and looked down at his plate, smiling to himself. When he looked up again he addressed my mother.

"I don't know how to say this, Mrs. Corcoran," he began to say.

As if on cue, the table went quiet. We knew what was coming. Forks hovering above our plates, we waited for him to say the words he'd come all this way to deliver. Sonny smiled bashfully and said, "But I think you'll be happy to know that we've been talking about getting married. Can't say when, yet. But it's definitely on the agenda."

"That's wonderful news," my mother said without missing a beat. "You'll have to give us more warning when the time comes."

"We've only been discussing it recently," Sonny said quickly, relieved that he'd gotten past the first hurdle. "We thought about mentioning it earlier, but, you know, it didn't seem right doing it over the phone. It's a serious thing."

"It sure is," John said, giving Sonny a tight-lipped smile. "Congratulations."

I didn't say anything at all.

They couldn't stay long because they were driving back in a rental van with Vicky's stuff. Amelia was to stay with us for a week, then my mother would fly out to Denver with her and see the new place. Now we've got this situation to deal with. My mother tried to talk to Vicky, alone, while she was here. But Vicky was always somewhere else, visiting friends and showing off Amelia. We saw more of Sonny than we did of her. John and I helped him load the van. The whole time he talked about how beautiful he was finding upstate New York to be, contrary to what Vicky had told him. Everything's so green and lush, he pointed out. I could see John sizing up Sonny as we carried boxes to the van, judging how strong he was, whether he could take him.

At one point he dropped a heavy box of books loudly onto the floor of the van and said, "Can't imagine you'd sell too many skylights in Syracuse." He gestured toward the sky. "There's not enough light to go around. People wouldn't pay money to look through a hole in their roof only to see a bunch of clouds."

Laughing, Sonny said, "You know, you'd be surprised at what people would pay money for. A good salesman could sell water to a drowning man."

Next thing I knew, they were gone. No fistfights, no accusations, nothing. We stood on the porch, waving good-bye to them through a gray mist of rain. The rental van turned onto Route 11, flashing yellow between the black trunks of trees as it headed toward the interstate; then, shivering, we turned to go inside.

"Here's a good one," John says and grins. Sweat rolls down his cheeks, collects above his brow. Red blotches bloom on his face and neck. He wipes his face on his shirt and says, "I just thought of this one. Booby trap one of his skylights, you know? Make it so the glass rains down on him when he walks underneath it. Shred him like paper with one of his own pretty skylights."

"That's a good one," I say. "A real stroke of genius."

"Better than anything you've come up with," he says.

I gather up the photographs from the floor and take them into the kitchen, cradling Amelia against my shoulder. John follows me. At the counter he mixes up his enzyme milk shake. I put Amelia in her high chair and tell John that I'm going out, that he can watch her for an hour or so. Before he can say anything I'm out the front door and headed toward Jesse's house to get good and high.

Since Jesse's father is home watching TV, we have to go somewhere else. Without giving it much thought, we cut through backyards and sneak up to the back door of The Mansion and slip inside. Five minutes later we're firing up the bowl and leaning our heads against the wall. We sit in silence for a while, letting the smoke thicken in our blood. Above us, gray light leaks through the cracked floorboards.

"I wonder what room it was," I say.

"What room?"

"The room he died in. Dave Spicer. I think it was upstairs. They said a bookcase fell on him and he got burned alive."

"That's messed *up*. You never told me that, man. That changes the whole thing. He died in this house? Right here?"

"Like a fucking hot dog."

"I thought he died on the way to the hospital or something. . . . That changes everything now. That's bad karma, man. That's like spitting on somebody's grave. All this time—I wish you would've said something before."

"I think it was upstairs. He was in bed, trapped under a book case or something."

"No wonder I'm failing classes. I got fucking Dave Spicer's ghost dogging me."

"I killed him. One day I told him he was going to die and then he did, just like I said. I wanted him to suffer, bad. Now *that's* bad karma."

"You shouldn't be saying shit like that. He's probably sitting in this room, right over there in the corner, and going, 'Uh-huh, keep talking, you'll get what's coming to you. I'm going to turn your ass into a dung beetle.'"

"*He* had it coming."

"Listen up, Dave! This is Jesse. I don't know this dude, man!"

We had these parachute men, the ones our father had given us. We were in the backyard, throwing them into the air. Dave came out and stood by the flimsy wire fence separating our yards and watched us. He was a few years older than John. He'd been kicked out of school for throwing a chair at a teacher. "If you put rocks in them, they go up higher," he said, pushing the fence down and stepping over it. I tried to move behind John but he wouldn't let me. Dave swept his long greasy hair back with a flip of his chin and said in an unusually nice voice, "Here, let me show you." I handed my parachute man to him and he knelt down on the driveway and unfolded the tissue paper chute. Then he scraped up a handful of pebbles and carefully folded them into the chute. He stood, brushed his knees off and handed it to me. "Now whip it as hard as you can," he said, pointing to the sky. I wanted to impress him, to show that I wasn't afraid of him. I took a step forward, arched my back and let it go with everything I had. The parachute man sailed higher than I imagined it could. There's this precise moment when the chute would pop out of the slot cut into the back of the soldier, unravel and open up, settling on the air with a puff. That was the point to the whole thing, waiting for that precise moment. It kept going up and up, further than we imagined it could, and we had to shield our eyes to see it. But when the parachute man hit his peak, he plummeted to the driveway and bounced. I ran over to find that the pebbles had torn the chute to shreds and I started screaming at Dave, who let out a short, loud laugh and stepped over the fence again and went into his house. I kept screaming at him until John put his hand over my mouth and told me to shut up, that it was only a toy, shut up! Thinking about it now, John was right, even though I hated him at the time for not doing anything. In the scope of things, it's not a big deal, definitely not worth a kid getting burned alive. But I can still remember that feeling of utter helplessness, the desperate wish for something bigger than me or John to step in and set things right. A week later, Dave Spicer was dead.

"He had it coming."

"He never did nothing to me. No, he did . . . he shot our dog in the ear with a BB gun. Then Pops went over and told him he was going to kick his ass."

"It's not the ghosts who can hurt you. Ghosts are ghosts. Hey Dave! Listen up—fuck you! See, nothing."

"No sense in getting the spirit world pissed off at you along with everyone else. Man, I wish you would've told me this before."

"What time is it?"

"I don't know. Noon?"

"Shit, I gotta get going. I'll talk to you later."

"Wait up man, don't leave me sitting here."

———

When I open the door John is standing there with Amelia crying against his shoulder. "Where the fuck have you been?" Ignoring him, I walk across the living room and into the kitchen. In the refrigerator I grab the carton of juice and bring it to my mouth. Behind me John stands holding Amelia. She cries louder.

"Getting stoned," I say, turning toward him. "And sacrificing animals to Satan."

Sucking in his lips, John looks around for some place to set down Amelia. He settles for lunging at me with his free hand, knocking the carton of orange juice on the floor.

"Nice going, dick wad."

"Don't get wise with me, little man," he says. He stands over me as I mop up the spilled juice with a dish rag. Amelia won't stop crying.

"Give the he-man shit a rest," I say. "You're upsetting her." Plopping the soaked dish rag in the sink, I go over to take Amelia from him but John won't let her go.

"I've been dealing with this shit all morning," he says, absently patting Amelia on the back. "While you've been out smoking dope. I haven't even been able to take a shower."

"Well, give her to me and go take one."

"Yeah, so you can drop her on her head—"

"That's not the way it works," I say. "You're doing it wrong.

You're supposed to sort of rub, not slap her." I press John's hand against Amelia's back and guide it in little circles, around and around, gently, like our mother showed us once. "Like that," I say. "And while you're doing it, you're supposed to say soothing things to hide the fact that you're absolutely fucking nuts."

Self-conscious at first, John whispers into Amelia's ear while looking at me from the tops of his eyes. Then he turns around and goes into the living room, making mechanically precise circles with his hand and whispering to her. After a few minutes, he wanders back into the kitchen, having quieted Amelia down. "Look at that," he says. "Uncle John's got the magic touch."

"Your magic touch isn't doing much good here," I say.

"What's that supposed to mean?" John says, trying to not to raise his voice.

"Why don't you take your magic touch on the road? Pull a couple of tricks in Denver."

John reaches out and grabs at my shirt but I dodge him.

"Whoops, be careful there. Don't want to wake the baby!"

I move toward the living room, keeping John in front of me.

"I've got a question for you, Mr. Weight Lifter. Do you think Ma is going to call and say, 'Hey, everything's squared away boys, I'm coming home with Vicky!' Why do think she hasn't called yet? Let me answer for you—"

"Shut up, you little dirt bag," John says through his teeth. He takes a swipe at me but I duck. On the way back up, his fist catches me on the side of the head and my ear starts ringing. Stumbling backward, I hold my hands up as John rushes at me, Amelia pinned to his shoulder. He kicks me in the knee and I fall on the floor, holding my head as John continues to kick me in the ribs with both feet. I roll over and scramble to my knees and pull the door open. Something lands hard on the back of my neck and I'm down again, crawling across the porch, Amelia wailing for all she's worth now and John swearing and hissing and flailing at me.

I get up and run. Halfway across the lawn I realize that I'm not wearing anything on my feet. The ground is cold and wet and soft, so I stand in the street where it's somewhat dry, my head buzzing and ringing, my body pulsing with a dull, distant ache. Behind me the door slams shut. I walk down the street and stop in front of the Murphy's old house and stand there. The For Sale sign in the front yard is plastered with fresh grass clippings.

Dead. The Murphys. Dave Spicer. My father. Everyone is dead. The wind blows through the torn screens on the Murphys' porch. Holding my arms, I sit on a cold steel chair and rock back and forth. Firemen swarm over the yard, dragging hoses behind them. Sirens howl and lights flash. People shuffle down the street in robes and slippers, stand gaping around the fire engines. David's older brother pounds on the door, screaming David's name, a sound as remote as singing birds to me. The firemen haul him away, but I don't care about him or David or the flames that lick the side of our house. Only one thing matters. And when I look at John, his face pressed to the screen, the lights and commotion reflected in his eyes, I know he's thinking the same thing: burn burn burn.

SOMETHING TO SAY

Andrea Foege

1.

The people Rachel hated most were the ones who forgot they were animals. Sometimes Bill would forget, which made her doubt she truly loved him, but she would remind him and he would remember, and then she could like him again.

One way she would remind him: a pinch when he was in the kitchen at the stove, or shaving with his back to her. A pinch on the side or the butt, hard, so he would flinch and say *ow*. She did it when he was talking too much and she had lost interest. "Why'd you do that?" he would say. When he said this Rachel knew from his face, a transparent shield across his blue eyes, curl in his lip, that he sometimes regretted being her husband.

"You felt that?" she would ask. "Just reminding you that you're an animal." She would say it mysteriously, coyly, so he would think about it but be afraid to ask her to explain. He would return to whatever he was doing, annoyed, but then think about it, she could tell, understanding on some level, and then remembering. They never talked about it, but thinking that he remembered pleased her.

Another way of reminding him: sex.

Bill did not like the goats she kept in the backyard. When Rachel would go out in the morning to feed them, the little blue bucket swinging at her side, heavy with the grain that tasted like sweet, salty cardboard (she had tasted it), their three year old, Gigi, trailing her, she knew he was sipping his coffee at the kitchen table behind her, gazing out the window, wondering how the woman he had married, the quiet and curious classmate always with her eyes wide open, had come to care for goats. Sometimes she could read his mind, although at other times this was impossible. Usually he made an effort to keep quiet about them, to let her have her hobby as long as he didn't have to be involved. He had

119

helped her build a sturdy pine shed for them in the backyard. She supposed she loved him for this.

Fred and Tasha were brother and sister, Saanen goats, white with short, upright ears. She bought them at the farm down the road where she used to take Gigi to pet the animals. Two springs in a row she watched Gigi gurgle and squirm away from her arms toward the tiny, wobbly kids who spoke her baby language. They nibbled at the edges of her jumpers, and Gigi buried her nose in their soft hair, clinging to them until she had to be pulled away, crying, to go home. Rachel started to love the goats. Unlike the baby, she was more interested in the adult goats, particularly the older ones. The younger ones would bound over as soon as she approached the fence, their mouths searching for something to gnaw on, although their jaws already worked endlessly, chewing, chewing. As they pleased, the older ones, their big round bellies hanging from thick spines, would meander toward her but stay at a slight distance, golden cat-eyes serene, mouths content with their own cud, ruminating. They looked like they had something to say.

She looked forward to the day when Tasha and Fred reached this stage in their lives, stopped needing, knew things.

Rachel had talked to the woman at the farm about breeding several times, as if it were a curiosity issue, not like she was going to do it, but just out of interest. But she and Bill had the room, four acres of cheap land behind their little two bedroom home, cheap fifty miles out of Worcester in a town with nothing, one blinking yellow traffic light in its center. The grass was lush in places, overgrown, and the two goats ate some of it, but more goats would eat more of the grass, and it would look better. And there would be milk, better for you than cow's milk, the woman had said, better for the baby, for everyone. This woman, someone Rachel admired for her strength and control, so many goats to be in charge of, told her the signs to look for when Tasha was ready, in heat. One day she saw them, the wagging tail, the crying out for something that wasn't there, that she couldn't have, Tasha's eyes searching, rubbing her head on the fence, trying to find an opening, an escape. Rachel had probably seen the signs before, but wasn't sensitive enough, didn't know what they meant. She felt now she should have known, or guessed.

She had to bring Tasha to be bred. There was a need there, she had to do it for Tasha because that's what she wanted. And so Rachel pushed her into the car, a Toyota, a small car, or actually pulled her into the car from the other side. Tasha didn't want to go, not knowing where the car would be going, not knowing what she wanted, what she was crying for, what the longing was. The next morning Rachel felt the pulled muscles across her back from the pulling. But the goat was eventually in the back seat, wedged in, unhappy with the situation, crying. Gigi, strapped into the passenger seat, cried too from the miserable noise, twisting against the seat belt to touch Tasha's nose, to make contact, not quite reaching, and Rachel almost started crying, but wouldn't everyone be happy later?

At the farm Tasha bounded out of the car. Rachel had to chase her, grab her, hold her. The woman came out of the farmhouse because she heard the car pull up, which would seem the case because the town was small, not many visitors to a goat farm in a small town with nothing else. The woman brought Tasha around to the back of the barn and there was a buck there, big and bearded, white, but really more like yellow, dirty, his eyes rolled to the back of his head, crying too, but more like a wail and a grunt combined, and with Tasha still crying the noise was horrific, almost unbearable. Rachel held Gigi, rubbed her back, shushed her, but she was also still crying, she was two then, but wouldn't she be happy when the new babies came? There was an electric fence at the farm, and the goats were very close to the wires, almost touching, one on each side needing to cross. The woman opened the gate and let Tasha in, holding her. She was strong, a real farm woman, brown skin, weathered hands.

The buck was on top of Tasha in no time, from behind, thrusting only four or five times, and then it was over. In one swift move, the farm woman opened the gate, pulled Tasha out, closed the gate behind her, all before the buck knew what was happening. Rachel turned to watch him, following the woman who led Tasha back around the barn, Gigi's crying turning into shrieking. The buck screamed, louder now, wanting more. Big and ugly, smelly and crazed, so different from Fred whom she had taken to the vet to be fixed shortly after taking him home. The woman had told her it was the only way to keep a buck as a pet.

Driving home, everyone still crying but running out of steam, Rachel had felt slightly nauseated, but exhilarated. She sang songs loudly, "Farmer in the Dell," "Three Blind Mice," until Gigi watched her, mouth open, tears streaking her blotched cheeks, but silent, watching. Tasha calmed, groaned, stopped kicking the back of the seat, finally.

2.

Tasha is bursting with unborn babies and Rachel is not sure how to tell Bill that she will give birth any day now, how to tell him about the trip to the farm to breed her six months ago, how to tell him why she didn't tell him then, because of course she doesn't know why. She could say she wanted it to be a surprise, but that somehow sounds cruel, like mocking him, taunting him. Keeping this, anything, from him seems wrong, but somehow necessary. The best she'll be able to do is tell him she doesn't know why she didn't tell him, which is the truth, she thinks. Holding Gigi atop Fred's broad back, Rachel feels bad for keeping so much from Bill, a little. He is at the university all day, never asks about the goats.

Art History is a full human field, Bill's field, and one that Rachel doesn't see much use for. She has never said this out loud because she doesn't want to hurt Bill's feelings, and she has to admit she feels a bit foolish now for having spent so much time studying it in college before realizing that it was useless. At one time she had enjoyed looking at paintings, mostly in books where she didn't have to stand around with other people and see a lot of them all at once, museums. She had liked to look at them in a book for a long time, alone, landscapes mostly. Her favorite was a painting called *Remembrance of Mortefontaine* by Camille Corot. In it a large tree reached across a ghostly lake toward the sky, the leaves thick, so soft. On the left bank of the lake a woman reached upward to the scant foliage of a smaller tree, it wasn't clear why. Rachel spent hours wondering what she was reaching for, what the other two figures in the painting were doing, one crouching at the foot of the small tree, another, a child it seemed, her arms outstretched. To receive something? The reaching woman seemed so familiar to her. A friend. Rachel dreamed that she herself was reaching for those leaves, that she was that woman, that her own child, Gigi, was beside her, her stumpy fingers outstretched. Brilliant sky dotted through sun-hazy leaves, spotting her vision. Even in the dream Rachel couldn't tell what she was reaching for. It was a beautiful dream though, vivid, more so even than the painting.

Corot was mentioned briefly in her Impressionism class, sophomore year, an influential predecessor to the period, but they didn't look at the painting in class, it wasn't that important. But wasn't it more important than blurry dabs of pastel, impressions, pretty but indistinct? It was important to Rachel, but for reasons she wouldn't have been able to explain in class, didn't try.

Bill gets excited about art in ways she can no longer fathom, says it "transcends reality," can talk about it endlessly. This is a good thing, that one can never understand why certain things excite the other. She thinks it's good, unsure what Bill thinks.

Gigi hardly ever talks. She sings all of her words, and gripping Fred's neck, Rachel thinks she hears her sing "Goats like apples, goats like apples," into his ear, but her lips are pressed against his skin and it's hard to tell. They never feed the goats apples. Gigi's little fists cling so tightly to him, and Fred turns his head back and nibbles on her Oshkoshes with an expression that looks like love, that could be mistaken for love, a dreamy half-smile, but it probably isn't. Rachel has to remind herself sometimes that it's possible to learn a lot about people from watching goats, but it doesn't work the other way around.

Her belly straining outward enormously, kicking her own bulging udders, Tasha saunters over to join in the gnawing, tugging on the bib of Gigi's overalls, almost yanking her off Fred. But Rachel has a firm grip on Gigi's arm and lifts her up and away, down to the ground, and through her delighted squeal Gigi really is singing that goats like apples, still.

Rachel likes her days of talking to no one but Gigi and the goats, listening to Gigi sing, to the goats hum and chew. When Bill was in school for his Ph.D. she had worked long hours as a waitress, listening all day to people, talking when she had to, but mostly just hearing human voices, nothing she felt the need to hear, wasted words. She doesn't usually miss hearing adult people talk, never misses working, although she knows Bill would like her to do something for money. It's hard to pay the bills, they save nothing for Gigi. But he doesn't say it because of the guilt. Without her waitressing he would not have been able to go to graduate school all those years, to be so young now and already a professor. She doesn't want him to feel a debt, but she doesn't want to work, so there is no choice. Gigi is hard work though, and the goats.

Usually when Bill comes home from school it's as if he is speaking a foreign language. She feels like gurgling to him, bleating, but he wants to talk about school, how the head of his department is sleeping with one of his colleagues, how he suspects one of the students in his Pre-Columbian class has plagiarized a paper. The day Tasha was bred, he came home, pulled off his shoes, and talked, but she surprised him, kissed away the words, and that made them stop.

"Otherwise I wouldn't have told him . . ." he was saying, a hand raised in the air, and she leaned down to him in his chair and pressed her mouth into his, running her tongue quickly over the edges of his teeth, under his tongue, across the insides of his cheeks, clearing all the words out. But then when it came to sex, moving to the bedroom, taking off their clothes, she wanted it to be slow, steady, human. She slowed him down, unzipped his pants herself, led him to the bed, laid him down, he let her, then drew him into her slowly and held him there. She held him tight, gripping him between her legs for a long time, it seemed like a very long time sitting on top of him, her muscles clenched. His eyes were closed, he was paralyzed, would seem dead if she hadn't felt him inside her, hadn't seen sweat beading under his nose. She willed it to last, willed him to wait, held him in time, but when she finally started moving, so slowly for a long while, and then he finally came she realized she had waited too long for herself, that she had been trying too hard for something, had ended up with less than she had hoped for, had lost something. She had stretched out on top of him, her head under his chin, still being careful to keep him in her a little, but he was finished, breathing now, his chest heaving, white with blond hairs so fine she could only ever see them when like this, her face against him. She wanted to stay that way, but he rolled from under her, finished, his breath slowing against the crook of her neck, his forehead cool and damp against her cheek.

"Talk," she said, wanting to hear his voice, his language, needing to feel human. All he would offer were even puffs of breath against her neck, a solid hand on her breast. He seemed frozen again, not conscious.

"Now I want to hear you talk." She liked the feel of forceful words on her tongue, savored the strangeness of it. "I'm ready to hear you talk now." She wanted to hear coherent sentences with discernible meaning, but he only kissed her softly under the chin, so softly she wasn't quite sure he had done it at all.

Her skin began to prickle, cold, and she gave up, nudging Bill away, pulling the quilt and sheet down from beneath them, struggling to get her legs underneath. Bill finally snapped out of his trance, helped her. They lay beneath the covers, his chest pressed against her back, and he finally whispered into the back of her head, "Do you think we should have another baby?"

They had never talked before about having another, only one, and that was Gigi, cozy in her pajamas in the next room. Rachel had suspected at times that he wanted another, even without enough money, the way he looked at Gigi when she wasn't close by, in the yard, like he wanted to give her something, something important.

Rachel had thought about this before, having another baby, but she doesn't know why she should want this and would like to know why before doing anything about it. Once Bill mentioned it, she wanted to know why he would want another, and she wanted their two reasons to be the same, but she knew the chances of this were very small. She saw the way he watched Gigi, the way he held her. He loved their baby very much, she knew, more than he loved her, but he looked at Gigi like a sculpture, held her as if she would break. When Gigi was born, in the delivery room, a slimy creature placed across Rachel's chest, Bill said she was perfect, a work of art, and right then Rachel wanted to tuck her away, to keep her from him. The feeling frightened her and she pushed it away, let Bill lift the baby from her, hold her in front of his face and cry. They both looked so beautiful, Rachel was exhausted, she forgot about that feeling.

Then at home, weeks later, he said it again over Gigi's crib. "She's perfect, a work of art."

"What do you mean, 'perfect'?" she asked, trying not to sound antagonistic, just curious, but failing a little, not sure why she felt like running, running far away with her baby. Rachel pointed out Gigi's tiny clenched fists, red, almost purple, her delicate veins visible beneath transparent skin, incredible, not perfect. Perfection seemed ugly, false.

"She's perfect in her imperfections," he countered, sure of his answer, sure she would see, but Rachel didn't, doesn't see it.

"What does that mean?" she asked and, when he didn't answer, she said it again. "What does that mean?"

He said a number of things, but all the same thing: something about transcending reality again, creating worlds, finding meaning in the meaningless. What did these things mean? Anything? All the phrases seemed to mean the same thing, and Rachel still couldn't understand that one thing they all meant. He said Gigi was beyond beauty, but Rachel didn't think she was beyond beauty, she *was* beauty. Reality, perfect in its imperfections, not art. But not really perfect at all. She couldn't resist the pull of her own logic, even knowing that it wasn't his, was probably no one's, she didn't want to argue, couldn't explain it anyway. Gigi was there and healthy and loved by them both, Rachel didn't need an explanation.

Gigi places a hand against Tasha's side. She seems to know what's inside.

3.

The kids will come in the evening, the first one's head peeking through, eyes closed, framed by two tiny hooves, soft as soap. Rachel will lead Tasha to the shed which Bill had made with no gaps between the planks, solid walls against the elements, containing animal warmth. She will lead her to the clean bed of straw she prepared for this moment. Crying, grunting, Tasha will push hard, still standing, Gigi by her side, singing to her, even while crying along with her, "Tasha babies, Tasha babies," louder and louder until Rachel can't help but sing along.

The hum of Bill's car coming up the driveway will only register as another background noise as the field grows darker, the crickets, the scrape of Fred scratching his head against the fence, as the baby finally dives out of Tasha in one wet rush, begins to cry, high and strong, Gigi too, leaping behind Rachel, her song and her crying silenced in the back of her mother's thigh. Rachel will clear the mucus away from the newborn's blunt nose and mouth, its eyes, but Tasha will turn and nudge her hand away, begin licking the baby clean, Gigi pulling Rachel back with all her weight.

"Where is everyone?" Bill will call into the half-darkness, knowing something is different, no one is home. "Where are you?" as the second baby emerges, quicker than the first, smaller, and the opening already stretched for it. So much easier than pushing Gigi into the world had been.

It will slip right out and Gigi will run to Bill, clutch his leg.

"Jesus Christ," is all Bill will say. He will stand at the fence in silence, watching Rachel work. She will wash Tasha's backside, caked with blood and slime, with warm water, bring her fresh water to drink, grain, dip the remains of the babies' umbilical cords, dangling withered from their bellies, in iodine. She will do all the things the woman at the farm told her to do, the things she has rehearsed in her mind over and over, and Bill will watch. Into Gigi's yellow beach pail Rachel will drop the gelatinous, purple afterbirth from the spoon of a rusty shovel. Gigi will leave the perch of her father's foot to follow Rachel far back in the field, her quiet stumbling heard through the grass from behind, not her voice. After digging a shallow hole in the rocky soil, Rachel will turn to find Gigi gazing into the pail, a finger extended to poke the afterbirth, but Rachel won't stop her, finding herself unable until Gigi looks up, extends a bloody hand, a crease embedded between her two small eyes. Rachel will snatch the pail, dump the placenta into the hole, toss the dust and stones over it, grab Gigi's doughy wrist, rub her hand over the thick grass, wipe it clean, and Gigi will not complain, just look at her mother, even when scooped beneath one arm, carried back to the shed, and placed beside the goats. There she will tentatively touch the new kids' damp fur, licked white, try to help them as they struggle to their feet, her tired eyelids fluttering like their unsure chests breathing first air.

Rachel will guide the kids to their mother's teats, leave them to nurse, bring Gigi to bed, where she will fall asleep while being undressed, that crease still planted firmly on her forehead. Pressing it gently with her thumb, Rachel will try to smooth it out, stop when Gigi stirs.

When Rachel returns to the goats Bill will still be there watching, peaceful, not asking for any explanations, but she will try to explain anyway.

"I wanted it to be a surprise," she will say, standing beside him, watching the goats too, and as she says it she will realize that it is true, that it was true all along, not a cruelty, but a gift. He will not question her, will not complain, only smile a smile she doesn't know, can't decipher, turn and walk back to the house.

Rachel will get the stainless steel bucket she bought the day before at the farm supply store in town from the garage, crouch beside Tasha in the dark, the babies full, tired, curled in the shed at her feet. Pressing her face against Tasha's empty belly, Rachel will breathe in hide and dung, listen to the fitful churning of perpetual digestion, and pinching and squeezing, pinching and squeezing, hear her thoughts rattle against steel, gaze in where they will float in warm milk.

HOW ALL THIS STARTED

Pete Fromm

Without a word of warning my sister Abilene jumped out of her crouch, shaking her gun at me. "Piss on this, Austin," she said. "What good's a gun if you can't shoot anything?" Then she was off.

I tore after her as best I could, holding my own gun out to keep the willow from lashing my face. I barely made the truck before she roared off. Holding on to the door handle with one hand and the fraying seat belt end with the other, I glanced over my shoulder at the red tornado we kicked up in our wake. That was always my favorite part of driving off road with Abilene—that furious rush of Texas dust and dirt.

"No moss on our backs!" she shouted.

I loosened my grip. "Where we going, Ab'lene?"

"The river," she said, bouncing us through a hole that launched me into the roof of the cab, driving the top button of my cap into my skull. I grabbed the door again, trying to hang on, and Abilene took a hand off the wheel and rubbed the sting away. "Sorry," she said, smiling.

I was never big on asking Abilene a lot of questions. I didn't say a word the day she cut the seat belts out of her truck, saying, "No moss," with each rip of her razor knife. But this time, maybe because of the way she was rubbing my head, I said, "How come the river?"

"What's the hardest thing you can think to shoot?"

"Doves," I said right away, picturing their herky-jerky flight, the teardrop-bullet shape of their whistling bodies. I'd picked up whole boxes of empty shells to carry home with only one, maybe two birds.

"Nope," she said, leaving me to guess.

"Quail?" I asked, "The popcorn kind?" That's what she called the ones that pop straight up and fly every which way.

She shook her head, snapping it back and forth. "Swallows!" She grabbed the wheel tight, slithering through the turn and bucking down the ruts to the river. "Think of trying to hit one of them."

Bodies the size of gnats, I thought, picturing them flitting up, down, left, right—wherever the bugs flew. The bets would come later, but until then I didn't think there could be anything harder than swallows. They lived all along the river, in mud nests stuck right to the cliffs. Now, at dusk, with the bugs coming out, there were swarms of them zinging around. They weren't afraid of us. Sometimes they'd come so close I'd duck.

Abilene said, "First one wins," and she fired before I thought she was serious. She missed and before long we were both blazing away, piles of empties growing around us.

When we took a break I rubbed at my shoulder, my ears buzzing. Abilene stared down at the empties, like all of a sudden this wasn't fun anymore. "Austin," she said, "do you think I'm crazy?"

"What?" I asked.

"This. Everything." She waved her arms around. "Do you think I'm crazy?"

I couldn't think of a way to answer so I didn't say anything, just stood there watching the smile grow across her face. "Thanks," she said, throwing her gun back up and firing, as if I had given her some sort of answer.

———

I hit the first swallow. Not the one I was aiming at, but the one flying behind and above mine. Zigged when he should have zagged. He crashed on the shore and I stared at him. "I win," I said, before I saw how Abilene was looking at me.

"You weren't aiming at that one," she said.

The way she said it I answered, "I know," as quick as I could. "Was just luck."

"No slop," she said. "Nobody's won anything yet."

"No slop" was what Abilene always said when we played pool in town on shopping day. I'd knock one in and if I didn't tell her beforehand where it was going she'd put one of her own balls down the hole to even it up. Then she'd take the next shot, saying I'd lost my turn. If Dad happened to be looking our way, he'd say, "Give him a chance, Abilene." She'd finish the game in just a few shots after that.

We kept shooting but I didn't aim anymore. I was afraid I might hit another by accident.

Finally it was too dark to see and the swallows were going back to their nests anyway. We stopped shooting, but Abilene loaded five more shells into her gun. "Want to know the secret?" she said. "The swallow killing secret?"

She didn't even lift the gun, but shot from the hip, straight across the river at the cliff crowded with mud nests—all five shots as fast as she could work the pump. I covered my face with my hands as the shots sang back around us. After the fifth shot I looked up and though it was dark I could see the big vacant holes where the nests used to be. The birds were in the air again, circling everywhere, back and forth, peep peeping.

Reflecting the last of the day, the river was glossy and as I turned to follow Abilene I saw the little dark spots on its surface, the floating bodies of the dead swallows that didn't reflect anything.

I hopped into the truck beside Abilene and as she spun it around to point back up the bluff, I said, "You got a pile of them, Ab'lene."

"I know," she said. "I win."

We started going out for swallows pretty often and after a while we got good enough we could hit them on the wing now and then, and Abilene never shot the nests again. She still didn't think we were hitting them often enough, but she said she had a plan for that.

Before we went out the next time she took my gun, which was really Dad's, and clamped it into the vise. "What are you going to do?" I whispered. She was rummaging around in the tool box and I moved so I was standing between her and the gun.

"Here," she said, pulling out the rusty hacksaw. "We're going to make the ultimate swallow gun."

"Don't, Ab'lene," I said, sliding out of her way when she kept coming. "Remember when you cut the stock?"

She'd done that when I was only ten, so the gun would fit into my shoulder. And though Dad hadn't used it in years he went through the roof when he saw it. Abilene shouted, "Gimme a break, Fatso! You'd have a heart attack just carrying it to the truck!"

That was the first time she ever called him Fatso. Dad stopped in the middle of what he was saying, his air leaking out. He stared at Abilene and his big, loose jowls trembled a little, not exactly the way they did when he was mad. Then he turned around and we almost didn't hear him say, "I wish I'd never seen Abilene."

He meant the city, not my sister. See, my dad's favorite story was about how we got our names. Not where we were born, but where we were conceived. "How all this started," he'd always say, waving his arms around him like he had a kingdom to show off.

He'd tell the story to anybody who asked, and some that didn't—
even then, with him probably going three hundred and Mom having all the figure of a razor blade. Made most people blush or
change the subject. The very thought grossed out Abilene and
me. After Abilene told me about The Facts, I could hardly believe
we'd been born in the first place.

At first, whenever he'd start, me and Abilene would leave the
room. Then, as Abilene got older, she's ask things to make him
look bad, things like, "What would've happened if Austin came
first? Would you have called him Abilene?"

He'd look at her, confused, then try to remember where he'd
been before she interrupted. If he couldn't remember, he'd just
start over. "We were young, newlyweds, and you know what that's
like. We were just in Abilene for the night." I could picture his
every smile and grin, always coming at the same parts. Abilene
said the whole story was so much lizard shit. She said, "I bet we
were adopted. God, I hope we were."

———

She sawed more than a foot off the barrel and we got tons of swallows, shooting down low along the river, where they cruised for
bugs hatching out of the water. The shot scattered all over out of
the short barrel and if you waited right you could knock down
three, four, five at a time. Nobody ever said Abilene didn't know
what she was doing.

One night we got so many she had me collect them. Wading out
in the warm water, I tossed them back to shore where Abilene gutted them. After bringing in the last of the birds, I sat down next to
her. The swallows were so tiny Abilene had to scoop with just her
pinky and I wondered if maybe she really was crazy. "What are we
going to do with them?" I asked.

"Have them for dinner. Deep fry them in olive oil. I read about
it. They do it all the time."

I looked at her. "Who?"

"Italians."

"Italians?" I said.

When she didn't answer, I asked, "Should we pluck them or
skin them?"

———

When we came into the house, Mom and Dad were in the kitchen and Abilene leaned both our guns against the wall in plain sight. I followed her in with my arms full of swallows. "Look," I said, hoping Dad wouldn't notice the sawed gun. Mom and Dad stared at all the tiny, naked birds, each one smaller than a golf ball. The meat was dark, dark red; almost purple. "I'm cooking tonight," Abilene announced.

When Mom started to say something, Abilene shushed her. "Austin," she said, "get me the fryer." To Mom and Dad she said, "Go into the living room and relax. This is going to be an experience. Most excitement for you guys since that night in Abilene, or maybe Austin." She gave me a whack when she said that, rolling her eyes to the ceiling.

Dad, I noticed, was looking at his old shotgun, at the hacked off barrel, even the splinters at the end of the stock still visible, though that sawing was a few years old by then. He looked over at Abilene and back at the gun. He must have felt Mom staring at him and he glanced her way before stepping to the guns, his shoulders sagging. He picked up Abilene's first and jacked out all the shells. Then he picked up his old gun and did the same. He put all the shells in the big pockets of his giant pants. Leaning the gun back against the wall, he said out loud, "I was so proud when I first got this," and Abilene snorted.

"Come on, Ruby," he said to Mom and they walked quietly to the living room. He breathed hard whenever he moved and even after they were gone I could hear his wheezing.

Abilene was getting old by then, nineteen, maybe twenty, and for a while now if Mom and Dad tried to get her to act any certain way she'd start screaming, calling Dad Fatso, or Tubby. She'd shout, "Please, please, please, tell me about Abilene again, Tubby. Tell me How All This Started!" She'd wave her arms to show what she wanted to know about—all of us, our whole lives. It'd been a while since Mom and Dad had done anything but glance at each other before lowering their eyes and walking away.

When Mom and Dad were safely in the living room, Abilene smiled and pulled a handful of shells from her pocket and reloaded the sawed-off gun. I was afraid of her then, even though she called me "Sidekick" and said we were a team.

We didn't have any olive oil so Abilene used Crisco. "There's not an Italian within a thousand miles of here anyway," she said. When the swallows were done, she loaded them onto plates, heaping Dad's so high they kept falling off. She called them to dinner

and we sat around the table staring at our swallows. Dad made the
first move, poking at one with his fork, trying to pull some meat
away from the tiny bones.

"No, Tubby," Abilene said, and I could see Dad's fat fingers
whiten around his fork. "Like this," she said when he looked at
her. She popped a whole bird into her mouth with a suddenness
that made me flinch. I could hear the crunching as she chewed,
then she swallowed and smiled. "Scrumptious."

I was next to try. It was kind of fun and the bones weren't much
more than sardines'. Abilene tossed one into the air, calling,
"Peep, peep," before catching it in her mouth. She winked at
Mom. Mom scraped her chair back and went to her room. Dad
stayed with us, though, and eventually he put a swallow in his
mouth and slowly bit down. He chewed and said, "These are
good, Abilene. Really."

Abilene winked at him too and he said, "Maybe we ought to do
more of this. Trying new things." His jowls trembled but even
with his downcast eyes he had a look of hope.

"Well," Abilene said, "with that new swallow slayer we'll be
steady on swallows for a while, but I think it's going to open a lot
of doors for us."

She was pointing right at the mutilated shotgun and I shrunk back
in my chair, but Dad just nodded and reached for another swallow.

———

Later that night, when I was in bed, another fight blew up downstairs. I couldn't make out many words, but when I crept out to
the top of the steps I heard Mom's voice, as thin and fragile as she
was, pleading, "But, Abilene, it's for your own good. We worry
about you."

Abilene laughed like crazy at that. Then she stopped, chopping
the laugh out of herself with a crash, something metal against
something wood. I could hear Mom suck in a startled breath. I pictured her standing there, her hand halfway to her mouth, trembling, even her bones thin, like the swallows', ready to crack and
crumble. Abilene shouted, "Don't ever call me that filthy name
again! Never! I'm Abby."

"That's fine, Abby, honey," Mom said and Abilene shrieked,
"My name is not Abby-honey!"

I wondered how Mom had gotten the word *Abby* out
so fast, so natural. It was the first time my sister had ever

mentioned it as her name.

Abilene thundered up the stairs then, carrying the gun she'd sawed off. I thought of the slam of wood against metal and figured she must have swatted the gun against the table to get their attention. I crouched against the hard, turned posts of the railing and though I was in plain sight, Abilene marched right past. The bang of her door made me wonder if she hadn't pulled the trigger.

I waited but Mom and Dad didn't come after her and pretty soon I went alone to her door and whispered, "Abby?" practicing the word in my head before I spoke. I said it again.

Her voice came muffled through the door. "You can still call me Ab'lene," she said. "That's totally different."

I said, "OK." Ab'lene's what I'd called her since I could first talk. I stared at her door, hoping that she'd open it and be all right and that she wouldn't open it at all. I waited as long as I could, then whispered, "Everything's all right, Ab'lene. It's a pretty name. I mean, what if it had been Amarillo or some place? Lubbock?"

I heard her laugh a little, and I could picture her in there, biting her red knuckles, trying not to laugh at all. I wondered where the gun was. "Good night, Sidekick," she said.

———

The bats were next, but they didn't last long. One evening we were getting set to go out for them—you had to wait till almost dark, of course—and Abilene came charging up the basement steps three at a time. I stepped out of her way as she started shouting, "Where are my guns?"

Mom and Dad were watching TV and when Abilene reached that door she shouted, "Where are they, Fatso?"

"Abby," Mom started and I heard a whack. Though I'd never heard it before, I knew right away it was the sound of a hand against a face and I backed up until both my shoulder blades were tight against the kitchen wall.

There was more shouting then, not words, just shouts, and in a second Dad came through the kitchen with Abilene pinched in his arms. She thrashed like a broken-backed snake but Dad was huge and she didn't have a chance, even though he was already breathing like he was having the heart attack Abilene always talked about.

Mom was right behind and she stopped long enough to say, "We're taking Abby to town, Austin." She apologized then, while I studied the bright pink outline of Abilene's fingers on her cheek.

Mom was out the door when she turned and said, "You tried so hard with her."

I watched from the door, Mom getting behind the wheel while Dad held Abilene down in the back seat. She shouted to me for help, but I couldn't do anything but let the screen door bang shut between us.

———

When I couldn't hear the car anymore, I went downstairs and found the gun rack empty, the same way Abilene had. I went through Mom and Dad's closet but our guns weren't there either.

They were in the attic, not hard to find, just behind some boxes. Both guns, Abilene's and the ruined sawed-off one, along with a whole garbage bag full of shells. It took two trips getting down the ladder. It was a dumb hiding spot. If Abilene hadn't blown up like she had, we'd be out right now, doing nothing more dangerous than pumping the night full of holes. Maybe a few bats too, at worst.

———

My parents had a long talk with me that first night, telling me about Abilene's illness. They kept saying I was great for her and I should try to keep being her friend. Mom did most of the talking while Dad stared at his hands.

I nodded and they said we'd all have to try to do everything we could. "You know what you could start with?" I said, looking at Dad. "Don't ever tell that story again, about the names. The How All This Started story."

Actually Dad hadn't told that story in a long, long time and he looked startled. I said, "We hate that."

I got up then, thinking of the two of them that first of all nights in Abilene. I couldn't keep from shaking my head, rolling my eyes. "I moved the guns," I said. "She would've found them there in a second."

———

Abilene didn't come home for almost two weeks. Then she was quiet for a long time, not shouting or calling anyone Fatso. She never asked about the guns and we never went out in her truck anymore. Sometimes I'd ask if she'd just like to go for a ride but she'd breathe slow and say, "I don't think so, Austin. Too hot."

I kept working at her though, being her friend, and when a Norther came through, chilling everything, I said, "Not too hot now, Ab'lene," till she finally said she'd come along. But she made me drive, saying she wasn't quite up to that. I wasn't old enough for a license yet, but Abilene had taught me how to drive years ago.

Even though Mom and Dad were up in town, one of the first times they'd left Abilene alone with me, I waited until we were out of sight of the house before goosing it and blowing off the road. Instantly we had a red Texas roostertail climbing the sky behind us. I pointed with my thumb and when Abilene looked back I shouted, "No moss growing on our backs!"

Abilene laughed at that, laughed a long time, and I slowed down just so I could hear. I was barely creeping along by the time she got over it. She wiped at her eyes and before I knew it she jerked her foot around the stick and hammered my foot down on the gas. I had a wild time just trying to steer.

When I lost it at last, ricocheting off the edge of the wash, grinding up the side of the truck and blowing a tire clean off its bead, Abilene finally let off the gas and we lurched to a stop in the center of the wash. It was a long time before we got our breaths back enough to talk.

"Ab'lene?" I said, and she answered back, "Austin?" teasing the way my voice shook.

We broke out laughing all over again until she stuck her hand under my nose. It was full of pills. "Want some?" she said. "Want to know how a voodoo zombie feels?"

I shook my head and she threw all the pills out her window. She'd been skipping them for a long time, she told me. She was biding her time. Until the perfect getaway opportunity presented itself.

"First," she said, "I was going to wait until you were old enough to come along." She punched my shoulder. "I mean, what good's an outlaw without a sidekick?"

"Outlaw?" I said.

"But can't wait that long, Sidekick," she said. "I'd never make it."

She punched my shoulder again and it hurt. She said, "But I'll be back for you. Count on that. I won't forget about Austin."

"Where are you going?" I asked, but she didn't answer.

———

It was closing on dusk by the time we got the tire changed and the truck going again and I didn't want Abilene to go away. I drove slow up the draw and said, "Want to get a few bats?"

She stared at me a second and then smiled. "Austin, Austin," she said. She looked straight ahead and crooked her finger like pulling a trigger. "Pow."

When I showed her where the guns were, safe in the old water tank, she shook her head and said, "Austin," again, smiling so wide it seemed her face might tear. She rubbed my head the way she had when I'd hurt it bounding into the top of the truck.

"Let's get us some bats," she said, though I would have stayed inside that old tank with her forever right then.

"Maybe swallows would be better," I said. "You can at least eat swallows."

"Nope. Bats. It's too late for swallows."

When we left with the guns, Abilene drove.

———

We were out late and Mom and Dad looked more at me than Abilene when we came home. "Did you two have a good time?" they both asked together. Dad, even with all his size, had the same nervous bird-look as Mom. Before I could answer, Abilene said, "Yes. Austin took me for a ride. It was pretty. The sun set."

How she lapsed back to her new quiet was startling. At sunset we'd been overlooking the river, blazing away at the shadowy traces of bats. I don't know if we hit any or not. We stayed out till after it was completely dark and Abilene kept shooting straight up into the night. "Look at the flame, Austin," she said every time she shot.

"I'm looking," I answered.

———

In the middle of that night I woke up scared, peering into the pitch black of my room, breathing hard, wondering what had woken me. I could hear the soft breathing of someone else in my room, someone standing close. Sweat popped out all over me. Then, quietly, out of the darkness, Abilene said, "You know, the only good part of the goddamn How All This Got Started story is the night in Austin."

"Ab'lene?" I said, and I listened to the floor creek beneath her as she walked out of my room and the gentle way she had closing the door, even turning the handle so the latch wouldn't bump over the catch.

———

In the morning Mom was shaking me, telling me I had to get up, I had to help. Abilene was gone, with her truck. I dressed as fast as I could, though I knew there was nothing I could do about anything. "She doesn't have a spare tire," I said, then shook my head when Mom asked, "What?"

Mom and Dad called Abilene's doctor. My job, they told me, was to stay home. "In case she calls," Dad said.

I said, "OK," though I knew there wasn't going to be any call. I said, "Good luck," to them anyway, and they raced off on their search.

Once their dust settled I set off walking, dodging through the cactus and creosote. At the water tank the sawed-off and the bag of shells were gone, but Abilene had left me her gun. I worked the pump and a live shell fell out. There were five of them, a full magazine. Last night, when we put them away, the guns hadn't been loaded.

I pictured Abilene loading up the sawed-off, dropping it onto the truck seat along with the bag of shells, then coming back into the black inside of the tank and working to slide these shells into the magazine, thinking about me, not stranding me helpless.

Loading my pockets with the other shells she left, I put the gun over my shoulder and stepped out of the tank, picturing Abilene thinking of me, while Mom and Dad and the doctors and who knows who all else were already chasing after her.

I walked back into the desert carrying her gun while she drove wherever she was going with the one we ruined. I pictured her white-knuckled grip on the wheel, just barely keeping from knocking herself out on the roof as she launched through the ditches; the red tornado that'd follow her everywhere. No matter how far anyone chased her.

I knew Abilene was gone for good. There was no way, otherwise, that she'd ever admit there was a single good thing about How All This Started. Even me.

I walked all day, getting dirtier and sweatier and thirstier every step. I went every place I could reach. And when at dark I lifted Abilene's shotgun and fired into the night, the gun slapped back against me and I worked the pump quick and hard the way she does, and I fired as fast as I could, straight into the darkness. It wasn't until I was out of shells, fumbling in my pockets to reload, my ears whining with the shock of sound, that I realized I was crying. I thunked in the next five shells and fired again, fast, watching the flame.

When I was out of shells, my shoulders and ears throbbing, I started home, wondering if I'd make it through the darkness and the cactus, the snakes and scorpions, everything out here Abilene had left me with.

––––––

The TV was off but Mom and Dad were home anyway. They popped up off the couch like Jack-in-the-boxes. I hadn't bothered wiping the tears and dirt off my face and they looked just as tired as me.

They started to shake their heads, letting me know they hadn't found Abilene, which, of course, I knew all along, but when they could really make me out in the dark doorway, still holding Abilene's gun, they stopped short. Dad sat back down so hard I don't know how the couch took it. He stared at the gun, then at my face, looking just as confused as he did the first time Abilene called him Fatso.

But Mom eased down beside him light as a bird. She sat close, her leg touching his, and they each put an arm around each other. For the first time they didn't look ridiculous, didn't look the way Abilene always made them look. I could almost picture them those nights Dad used to love to tell about.

I looked away from that. "She was wrong," I said. "About the best part of the story. It was the night in Abilene." I knew they wouldn't know what I was talking about.

I set the gun down, leaning it against the wall. There was nothing left for me to shoot. "Who knows," I said, feeling them watching me as I turned to leave them alone. "Maybe it was the two of you. *Before* All This Started. Maybe that was best."

The Girl and the Woman

Elisa Jenkins

There is a clammy, closed-in feel to the office; even the doorknob
is cool and damp to the girl's hand, the door itself cool and damp
as she leans back against it, clicking it shut. The girl squints; the
sudden, anemic light from fluorescent bulbs is painful, it requires
too much adjustment. Nevertheless, the girl forces herself to bring
blurred outlines and shapes into focus—and then is sure she has
made a mistake. She cannot imagine the woman working here. A
bewildering, gray network of walls stretches in front of the girl, not
quite meeting the ceiling—like the walls of public rest rooms, the
girl thinks, the walls of fitting rooms, those disquieting spaces of
air that must not be forgotten, privacy that must not be taken for
granted. There is a strong smell of mold, of air conditioning working hard. The girl shivers, presses her back tight against the damp
door, tries to breathe normally. Cavelike, she thinks, hunching her
shoulders. Dungeonlike. The girl shakes her head slowly. Can the
woman really be a part of this?

A reception desk, also gray, is nestled in a curve of wall; it is
empty. Lunch hour. The girl nods. She has planned this so she
may see the woman's desk, the woman's possessions, before she
sees the woman. The girl slides her purse strap higher on her
shoulder. She cannot have made a mistake, she decides, if things
are unfolding exactly as she has planned. But she must be careful,
someone must be here or the door would not be unlocked. So, the
girl makes certain the door does not click again as she pushes herself away from it; the girl places her feet as if on a balance beam,
soundlessly. The girl enters the labyrinth of walls. And is surprised
to find they are not true walls, not slabs of stone or plaster, but partitions, nothing more than gray upholstery stretched across metal
frames. Yet, somehow, the girl finds, that makes them all the more
disturbing. There is something sinister about a labyrinth of such
neatly seamed angles, such a civilized labyrinth.

The material gives gently under the girl's hand, springy and tight, like the sheets on the girl's bed, sheets always army-perfect as her mother has taught her to make them. The girl recognizes these partitions now, she has learned about them in the secretarial course she did not wish to take—the second major she was bribed into with the promise of this year, one year abroad with nothing but English Lit., no typing. If the girl's mother had her way, the girl would have three or four majors instead of the compromised two; the girl's mother fears unpreparedness. The girl's mother, when she was the girl's age, had nearly completed an Elementary Ed. major, only to discover that it was useless, she only liked children one at a time. The girl's mother had to go back to school, then, to learn business skills, had to spend twice as much time and twice as much money. This will not happen to the girl.

The girl often wonders how much the specter of the woman entered into the bribe of this year. The girl's mother knew that England would contain the woman, surely knew that the girl would try to find her, given the chance. The girl wonders if this year was her mother's way of granting permission, or her way of avoiding the possibility of the girl's asking permission.

The girl fingers the metal edge of a partition. Such partitions, the girl has learned, create the ideal office arrangement. They use space economically; they have a neat, clean, streamlined appearance; they snap together like Legos, conform and reform to the exact needs of any office staff.

This is terribly out of sync with the woman. At any rate, out of sync with the bits and pieces that have been read to the girl from the case study, the bits and pieces pried from the social worker's memory. "A bright bird," the social worker said, when asked to describe the woman at sixteen. A big, motherly woman, the social worker, perpetually flushed and perpetually amused; the girl could imagine the woman—the bright bird, the troubled teen—leaning on those big, motherly shoulders.

"Bright in every sense," the social worker added, "including the literal one. She did have a compulsive need to be different, that one did, some of the clothes she wore . . . well, I've never seen such color combinations." The memory made her chuckle—and the girl found herself suddenly jealous, she wanted to climb inside the social worker's mind, to see it.

"She was a clinker," the social worker added, "but obviously a good girl, obviously sensitive beneath her need to overwhelm. I don't know how you feel about heredity, dear, but I think anything you've gotten from her will stand you in good stead."

A clinker. The girl knows the words by heart, she copied them down exactly, desperately scrawled letters keeping time to the social worker's voice, she has typed them over and over on her portable when she should be typing an essay; the girl types far faster and better since visiting the social worker than she ever did in class. If she types the words often enough, the girl finds she can practically see the woman, can see the way she sat swinging her legs in the social worker's office, the way she snapped bubble gum—always, she was snapping gum, the social worker said. Very loudly.

Maggie, her name was—Margaret Dorning. Margaret Collins now. White-blonded, the social worker said, but the girl imagines her red-haired, with a name like Maggie. An Ann-Margret kind of teenager, the girl imagines, finger-snapping, volatile, afraid of nothing. Admired. Exactly the type of teenager the girl was not, is still not. Exactly the type of woman who could never hope to fit in here, in this frightening, gray place. But the girl has been thorough; this is the woman, this is where she works. So, the girl ventures deeper into the labyrinth, one hand trailing the curved wall to steady herself. It seems strange that her footsteps make no noise in the midst of such grayness, no deep, cavelike echo. But the carpet is thick and stiff; her feet do not even leave an impression.

The mold smell grows stronger. The girl shivers and knocks back the long strands of hair that pull at her arms like a spider web, shivers as the silk of her dress clings to her, fumbles about her like shy and clumsy hands. The dress is new, one of the girl's first purchases in London, unworn until today, and even the girl's pumps and pantyhose were bought for this occasion only; they have no connection to the girl's self before this day. The dress is an expensive one, overpriced, something the girl's mother would never have bought, but it is exactly the dress the girl needed for this day. It is a dusty blue silk, vaguely oriental in design, smooth and straight, with a soft gathering of ruffles at the back. In it, the girl is nothing in the extreme, everything vaguely—young, old, innocent, worldly, plain, exotic, pale, shimmering, pretty. The girl is all things at once so the woman may select the one quality she most wants to see and find it there. The girl is nervous.

She peers around corners, passes cubbyholes—work stations, as she has learned to call them—desks facing the wall to avoid distractions, chairs adjustable and curved to support the back, their seats and backrests a cranberry color, almost painful against the gray. All are deserted. The desks are like great collages: papers, books, pencils, unfolding reams of computer paper, all overlapping. These collages are so still that they almost seem arranged, the girl thinks, relics from some long-dead generation, on display. All have name plates that do not contain the woman's name. A clock on one of the desks shows ten minutes past twelve.

The girl knocks back her hair again, rubs her arms. The skin is growing damp and sensitive, and the strands cut into it, sharp as thin lengths of wire. The girl flinches, a sudden black shape startles her as she rounds a corner. She stops, allows the shape to come into focus—another name plate, tacked to one of the partitions at the level of her forehead. The girl stares at it dully. She realizes she is not ready for it, not ready to believe it is telling the truth. But its grooved letters are filled in with stark, white paint, so white it must be absolute truth. *Margaret Collins. Programme Development Specialist.*

Automatically, the girl reaches down to her purse, reaches her thumb into the half-snapped outer pocket to touch the folded square of birth certificate. She is still not sure why she has brought it, she does not need it, she can see it in her mind, always. Perhaps as a divining rod, to lead her to the woman? Or as proof, if proof is needed? "She may deny . . ." the social worker warned, " . . . you must be prepared . . ." But would she really, would she deny anything, that woman of the wild clothes and swinging legs? That woman of the signature, the bold, sprawling facsimile on the certificate, all outward curves, hiding nothing? The signature was the first thing the girl noticed when she reached across the counter to grasp the certificate; she felt a buzzing of excitement, a pulse beating all through her, as she saw how different it was from her own small, neat handwriting. Ten pounds, it cost, that handwriting. Ten pounds for the starting point, the name, the place of birth, the residence, the "Baby, female." The girl reaches up to trace the letters of the name plate, the *Margaret*, presses hard against the cloth wall, tracing and retracing the curve of the *g*.

Then she hears a noise from the other side of the partition—a swish of air, of rustling papers. She moves to the edge, eases her cheek against the rough material, listens hard. The sound continues, soft and rhythmic. And now the girl notices a faint perfume, a smell of raspberries, reminding her of the fat, raspberry-smelling roses on her mother's close-clipped bushes at home. Cautiously, the girl peers around the corner.

A woman is bent over a low file drawer in a sharp right angle, her fingers sorting swiftly through a line of hanging files. Her face is hidden by the desk; the girl can see only the beginning curve of a delicate chin. And a flash of blonde hair, sculpted by hair spray into a flawless whorl, yellow blonde and deeper gold swirled together. The woman slides a thick hanging-file folder out of the drawer and heaves it onto the desk, flinging open the cover; amazing, the girl thinks, such power in such a small body. Her, then?

"Oh, *Christ!*" The girl stiffens, the hard edge of the partition pressing a line down the side of her nose. The woman has caught sight of her.

"*Christ!*" the woman says again, small, dark eyes darting back and forth in panic. "It's not one o'clock already!" The woman's voice is jarring, like the girl's mother's voice; the girl wants to jump and do whatever the woman asks, just to make the voice stop.

But she cannot move; although the partition is becoming painful, cutting into her forehead, her breastbone, the girl can only press her body tighter against it. She is trying to look beyond the eyes, the sharp, all-seeing eyes, to search the face for some sign of resemblance. Everything about it is small and sharp, tiny nose, tiny, tense mouth, pointed chin. Nothing at all like the girl's own round face. The girl drops back from the partition. She feels surprising relief. This is not Margaret Collins, this is an assistant or secretary, working through lunch.

"Why, it's barely past *twelve!*" The woman snatches up a small digital clock from the desk and waves it accusingly. "You're *early* ."

The girl curls her hand around the cool metal frame, leans further into the room, wondering who she has been mistaken for, and how she can get this woman to leave so she can get at the woman's desk. Then she realizes the eyes are asking for some type of answer—eyes like Coca-Cola, the girl thinks, the way they snap. "Oh . . ." the girl stammers, trying to remember if there has been a question. The woman is a shield protecting the desk, hands on hips, feet planted firm as the spokes of a wheel. "Oh—no. No, I can come back—I'm sorry." The girl turns to leave. She will have to try her plan again during tomorrow's lunch.

But before the girl has passed the name plate, the woman is rushing after her, all fluttering hands and swishing silk—for this woman is wearing silk, too, the girl realizes, a dress of deep tan and mauve, full, flower-print skirt falling in cascades. "No—oh, no, wait—oh, dear, don't be frightened!" The woman seizes the girl's hand, grasps it hard, a brief pulse of pain. She smiles apologetically. "Yes, not a very good beginning, I'm afraid. I'm sorry. Actually, it's a good thing you're early. We're desperately short-handed and desperately in a hurry, so if you're at all qualified, I'll put you to work straight away. Come on, sit, sit." Hands on the girl's shoulders, the woman propels her back toward the office. The woman's perfume is now so heady that the girl feels a burning sensation in her chest; the smell is of wild raspberries now, warm in the sun and rich. The girl tries to ease herself away.

"Really, I—"

"No, it's all *right*." The woman steers the girl around the partition. "This interview is more important than anything else I have to do. Please, sit down—Elizabeth, is it?"

Elizabeth. Deposited in front of another painfully cranberry chair, the girl considers. If you're at all qualified, the woman said; the girl is halfway through a business degree, she ought to be able to at least sound qualified. Perhaps . . . and if she has a job here, if it is a part-time job that will fit around her classes, the girl will be able to examine Margaret Collins at length, perhaps take her phone messages, open her mail. Much better than her desperately thought-up role of student interviewer. And, the girl thinks quickly, if she can get the job before Elizabeth, if the woman does put her to work "straight away," perhaps she can be so brilliant at it that the woman will no longer want to see the real Elizabeth when she arrives. The girl smiles, her breath comes in a rush. She turns her smile on the woman.

"All right." The girl reaches out to claim the proffered chair.

"Good," the woman says, returning the smile. Her eyes are like a second set of eyebrows, they arch thin and curved as the tiny, plucked eyebrows above them. Elfin eyes to go with the elfin chin, the girl thinks. The woman seems younger now, perhaps a secretary, then, perhaps the girl will be this woman's assistant if she gets Elizabeth's job.

The woman moves around the desk. "You're American, aren't you?"

"Yes. But my ancestors were English," the girl answers automatically. She says this to everyone who asks—and some who don't. "I'm going to school here."

"And working your way through. Admirable girl."

The girl flushes, even though the compliment is undeserved.

"Good for you," the woman says, thrusting her hand out toward the girl. "By the way, my name is Mags."

"Mags . . ." The girl freezes, hand squeezing the prickly back of the chair. She stares at the woman's narrow face. "Maggie *Collins?*"

The woman raises one of the plucked eyebrows. "What, am I
not what you imagined? My God, it's true those temp people never
send me the same girl twice, but—they *didn't* tell you I was a
tyrant, did they, I mean, just because we're busy . . ." But the girl is
now unable to answer, unable to move any closer to the chair, unable even to continue staring at the woman; her eyes refuse to focus at any point above the woman's slim ankles—like carved
umbrella handles, the girl thinks, as she watches them blur in and
out of focus, exactly like the parrot-handled umbrella in *Mary Pop-
pins* the way they curve out of the woman's pointed pumps.

The woman, apparently thinking the girl is simply nervous
about the interview, stops asking questions and, smooth and efficient, propels her into the chair, hands cool through the silk of the
girl's dress, through the numbness the girl is experiencing. The
woman pats the girl's shoulders, whirls to a coffee maker on top of
a filing cabinet, turns up two clattering cups. The girl wonders if
she has agreed to a cup without knowing it; she does not like coffee. She did not think British people drank coffee. She can feel
the touch of the woman's hands as if they were still there, just
above her shoulder blades. The girl shivers. She tells herself that
she must take this opportunity to examine the woman's desk
while the woman's back is turned, she must learn something that
can help her relate to the woman now, the woman who is no longer
sixteen. But the desk is a blur of white mounds, the girl's eyes will
focus on nothing but the tremors of tan and mauve as the woman
pours coffee. Such delicate wrists the woman has, the girl thinks,
and elbows, birdlike bones. The girl's wrists are solid, like the rest
of her arms; bread-baking arms, the girl's mother calls them, saying
they remind her of the girl's grandmother's arms. The girl thinks
suddenly of the blank space on the certificate, the space for the father's name. An ugly boy, the woman told the social worker, blunt-
edged like a cave man. New money, ugly in restaurants, in parks
and pubs—less ugly behind the wheel of his Zephyr Zodiac. A
good argument against the Industrial Revolution, she said. And
would say no more. The girl is not ugly, she does not consider herself blunt-edged. Yet she must be like him somehow, she thinks.

"So." The woman sits down, clicks the coffee cup in front of
the girl. The girl looks up. The woman's eyes have softened to a
rich chestnut color. The color, yes, the color is similar now, the girl
realizes, dark and velvety. But brown eyes are in the majority, the
girl's adoptive parents both have brown eyes. The girl thinks of
how delighted her mother has always been when people, not

knowing, have told the girl she has her mother's eyes. The woman leans forward to look into the girl's face, smiles gently. "I did get your CV, I know it's Elizabeth, but I can't remember your last name. Something with a *W,* isn't it?"

The girl looks down, studies her wavering reflection in the coffee cup. She cannot pretend to be Elizabeth if Elizabeth has a curriculum vitae. But the woman will be angry if she tells her she is not Elizabeth now. And the girl is not sure at the moment whether she can remember her original story.

"Don't talk much, do you, love?" The woman takes a gulp of coffee and stretches across the desk toward one of the white mounds, the one closest to the girl; she begins flipping through it from the bottom up. "Duck if this falls, will you? Actually, that'll stand you in good stead round here. I'm afraid we've never much time for talk." The girl presses the small of her back hard against the chair; she is finding it difficult to breathe with the woman leaning over the desk so close to her, a certain heat seems to radiate from the woman, like the ghostly, watery heat waves that hover over highways in the very hot summer. This heat does not warm the girl, it makes her shiver. The papers make a slapping sound, which the girl finds suddenly intolerable. She is about to stumble up from the chair when, finally, the woman pulls a crisp sheet from the center of the pile, like the tablecloth trick. She holds it up, squints at it. "Yes." She nods, satisfied. "Elizabeth Wagner."

"No."

"What?"

"Well . . ." The girl presses her hands tight around the coffee cup. She lets herself wait until its heat becomes unbearable before she speaks. "Well, no, actually, my name is . . . you don't have my resume." The girl panics at the thought of giving the woman her name. "I mean, I'm not here for an interview. Or, well . . ." The girl tries to remember exactly what she has planned to say, but it will not come out the way she rehearsed, she could not predict what it would be like to be saying it to the woman. "I am here for an interview, or to set up an interview, if you'll let me, but . . . I'm sorry."

"No, no, don't be sorry." But the woman pushes at the corners of her eyes, drawing them tight; she looks suddenly tired. "To set up an interview?"

"Yes." The girl looks away from the woman, looks away until the words come back on track. "Yes, it's a thing I'm doing for school, a sort of career project. I'm supposed to survey three different careers, and I wanted to find out about yours."

"Mine?" The woman leans back in her chair. "Good God, *why?*"

"Well, it sounded interesting. . . ."

"How did you even know my career *existed?*"

"I saw it in a business directory." The girl eases her hands loosely around the coffee cup, balancing it by the rim. Her story is starting to come back. "I liked the sound of the title—Programme Development Specialist. I mean, it makes you wonder what it is."

The woman laughs, reaching for another gulp of coffee. "Yes, it makes me wonder the same thing. Every day. I'm in a business directory? Which one?"

The girl hasn't thought to give the business directory a name. She stands up shakily. "Look, I can see you're very busy. . . ." She sets the coffee down before it can spill. "And I know it's lunch time. I can come back another time—I mean, if it's all right—"

"My dear girl, I have not eaten lunch in years, unless it was part of a meeting. And sit down, you're making me nervous. If it's for a class, you've got to do it now, haven't you?"

"Well, not—"

"No, stop. And sit—please. I have an idea." The woman's eyes are snapping. The girl sits. "We are busy, because we've got this silly mass mailing to get out—that's why I want to hire that temp girl Elizabeth—but I'll tell you what." The woman disappears behind the desk—as if a trap door had opened beneath her chair, the girl thinks. She reappears in a moment on her knees, shoving a large box around the desk until it bumps against the girl's feet. "If you will take—sorry—if you will take these envelopes—" the woman hauls herself up and gives the box a kick "—and put these labels on them—" she rummages through another pile on the desk and yanks out a thick, milky ream of wax paper "—and let me sort through my handouts while we talk, I will give you an interview. All right?"

"Oh . . ." The girl wonders if she can remember the questions she planned to ask. The woman is standing directly above her, the shimmery heat is making the girl dizzy. "Oh, yes, thank you," she finally manages to say.

"Good." The woman drops the ream of labels into the girl's lap. It gives a soft, airy thud as the woman whishes around the desk and into her chair. The girl looks down at the thick sheets; they sit surprisingly heavy on her lap. Gingerly, she lifts the top one. She feels immediately blinded. The labels are relentless, row upon row of them, stark, black letters and numbers on brilliant white. They have a sickish, salty smell. Dropping the sheet, the girl reaches down to lift the lid on the box of envelopes. She is greeted by more rows of white, chaste and perfect as the dinner rolls the girl's mother makes on Sundays, lying all the same size and just touching in the pan. The girl looks in awe from one pristine row to the other, afraid to disturb either.

"What's in them?" she asks.

"Adverts for a conference on telecommunications. Nothing dirty, you're quite safe. Now." The woman reaches into the file she was getting out when the girl interrupted her; she lifts out a fat sheaf of papers and taps them on the desk. "What do you want to know about my career?"

"Well . . ." The girl balances a pile of envelopes on top of the sheets of labels. They tremble. "I suppose . . . what exactly do you do, to begin with?"

"Ah, yes, good question. Well." Moistening her fingers, the woman begins fanning out papers into piles, all lopsided on top of already existing piles. "I go into a company, or a business, or a school, or a university—any place that needs some sort of training program to update their services or generally to make their lives easier—and I figure out what exactly it is that they need, and then I go out and find people to train them. Or I do research and train them myself."

"You do all that?" The girl stops in the middle of peeling off a label to watch the woman, now flinging paper wildly; the girl is impressed. Perhaps this place is not out of sync with the woman after all, perhaps the grayness has been deceptive. As the girl glances around the office, eyes focusing now, she does begin to see splashes of color—a postcard pinned to the wall, showing a sparkling beach; a piece of jagged pink quartz pressing down a stack of papers; a canary yellow tablet peeking out from a leather notebook. The girl slowly unsticks the label from her trembling fingers. She smoothes it onto the envelope, still watching the woman's restless hands. Perhaps this is the same woman after all, Ann-Margret still. "It's pretty exciting work, then."

"Well, most often it's computer training, the way it is this afternoon, but yes, there have been a few more exciting ones—injection molding plastic, now that was a treat."

"Oh." The woman has not looked up, her eyes dart back and forth between piles, absorbed and impassive. The girl cannot tell if she is joking or not. "Do you like doing it, then?"

"Yes. Well, I like working with people and helping people, and that's mainly what I do, so yes. I never imagined I'd be doing this, of course."

"You didn't?"

"No, I absolutely fell into it. But that's true of most things in life, don't you find? Like some giant video game, you can never imagine what's round the corner. Oh, here, you can put the ones you've finished in this." The woman ducks behind the desk to wrestle out another cardboard box, this one empty; she tosses it over the desk to the girl. The girl jumps as it bangs the wall beside her, vibrating the tight-stretched upholstery. "I mean . . ." The woman struggles back up into her chair. "I was studying languages, I fully intended to be an interpreter. I wanted to travel the world."

"You did?" Reaching behind her where the box has landed, the girl can suddenly see the woman standing outside the doors of the UN, no longer in deep tan and mauve, but in bright turquoise or royal blue, a multi-colored silk scarf at her neck. The girl can see herself, too, equally colorful at the woman's side, and wearing a beret; educated in twenty different countries since kindergarten, she would be, and fluent in some thirty languages and dialects. The girl laughs at the silliness of this but cannot help saying, "Oh, why didn't you?"

The woman shrugs. "Well, you know, choices and all that. Priorities. And as I said, it's like a video game, you turn the corner and the road forks and the monster's behind you and you have to choose quickly."

"Are there—" But the girl has interrupted the woman, the woman was going on to say something else.

"I'm sorry?" The woman smiles politely.

"Oh, no . . ." The girl blushes, knowing she was meant to be interrupted, her question was not meant to be asked. But now she must ask it. "I was just going to say, are there any choices that you regret?" The girl bends her head further into the labels, further into the salty smell, forcing herself to inhale it, to punish herself.

But the woman laughs. "Heavens, you can't live past grammar school without making choices that you regret! But if you mean am I content with where I've ended up, I would say yes, everything has worked out as it should."

"Really?" The girl's head droops deeper into the labels, but she has been sufficiently punished for asking the question. And will be punished again when she tells the woman who she is, when the woman realizes what the question meant.

But the woman is dealing out papers, she notices nothing for now. "Anyway," she says, "I don't suppose I would have ever actually been an interpreter. To tell the truth, what I *really* wanted to be was a sort of foreign correspondent, you know, and be on the news, on television. Well, that was part of what I wanted. I thought I'd be a dancer till my legs wore out, then an actress, and I reckoned I could fit in some *National Geographic* assignments between movies. Then, once I'd caught the BBC's attention, I'd be a foreign correspondent."

The girl raises her head. She has heard this before. The girl's throat tightens, the girl presses a label hard to an envelope. This is the woman, this is the same story, this is clearly the same woman who sat and snapped gum in the social worker's office.

The woman lays down her last paper and grasps her coffee cup with both hands for a quick swallow. She makes a face. "Mm— cave drippings. You have to drink quick round here, I'll tell you." The girl stares. This is Ann-Margret, she tells herself carefully, this is the bright bird. There is no question. The girl shakes her head. It is possible, the girl thinks, to give birth without leaving a trace of yourself.

The woman scrapes open a drawer and pulls out three stacks of rubber-banded pamphlets, all jarring colors, orange, magenta, watermelon green. She flips off the rubber bands and begins flinging the pamphlets, all clashing, onto the piles she has made. "I didn't think I could do it, though, be a correspondent," she says, "because I never thought I could write. Of course, I write all the time now, constantly, proposals and proposals. Funny, isn't it?"

The girl cannot answer. The girl has reached across the desk to move her coffee cup out of the way of the flying pamphlets and has caught sight of a half-hidden photograph in a gold filigree frame. It is a photograph of a girl in a school uniform, a girl with blonde hair to her shoulders. A girl with the woman's face, the woman's face exactly, the same elfin chin, eyes, nose, smile.

The rhythmic slap of pamphlets stops; the woman follows the girl's stare. She smiles. "Oh. Yes, don't look much alike, do we?" The woman holds the picture up to admire it for a moment, then turns it to face the girl, the way the girl's mother might present a plate of chicken cacciatore, glowing. "My daughter. Speaking of priorities."

The girl is not ready for this, somehow she could never imagine the woman with another child, she completely dismissed the possibility when the social worker brought it up. Ann-Margret is a free spirit, she cannot be tied down by children. The girl swallows, manages to bring her voice down to only a slight tremor. "What do you mean . . ." She tries to lower her latest bunch of labeled envelopes carefully into the box, but they fall in with a clatter. She sits up slowly. "You mean, you gave up your career for *her?*"

The woman laughs. "Well, it wasn't exactly as dramatic as all that. And, of course, her father was a consideration too—"

"But—" The girl's knees are pressed painfully against the desk, but she cannot sit back, can only push harder, farther forward. "But you gave up your career completely, forever, because of her? And her father?"

"Well, one career. In a way. Indirectly. And I'm not sure 'forever' was in my mind at the time . . . though I suppose I am very single-minded." The woman smiles, twirling one of the pamphlets. Her eyes are velvet brown now, unfocused. "Anyway, when you have a baby, you don't really want to do anything else for the first bit. You're just too exhausted . . . and fascinated . . . and in love, really."

"In love!" Some envelopes spill from the girl's lap. The girl is losing control.

"Yes!" The woman leans forward teasingly. "What are you, a radical feminist?"

"No, I'm—" The label in the girl's hands rips in half. The girl freezes, stares down at the fragments, stares up at the woman. "I'm sorry," she whispers.

"Oh, no, don't worry." The woman reaches across the desk. "No, don't, it's easily fixed—look." The woman's hands move swiftly over the girl's, unsticking the pieces of label from the girl's fingers, pressing them quickly onto the envelope, overlapping them perfectly. "You see? No harm done. *Stop* it." She laughs, clutches the girl's hand, gives it a shake. "Don't look that way— you can see it's all right!"

Such kindness, the girl thinks, bending down to retrieve the spilled envelopes, but she knows that if she were the daughter, the one in the picture, the woman would not be so kind, she would say, "Honestly, darling, can't you be more careful?" would demand guilt, remorse, apologies, would take every opportunity to goad the girl into perfection. Such compassion, the girl knows, is reserved for strangers. The girl bends low over the labels, starts to peel off the next one, but her hand trembles, she is afraid to touch it. The daughter's picture fills the room, the girl has no choice but to stare at it.

"Does she appreciate—" But the girl's voice is still not right; she cannot allow herself to be this way.

The woman smiles helpfully. "Appreciate . . . what?"

Does she appreciate the miracle of calling you her mother, absolutely certain that no one will dispute her or be angry with her, does she appreciate the miracle of having you look at her picture so obviously loving her, does she . . .

"Appreciate . . . my career?"

"Yes!" The girl falls back in her chair. "Your career."

"Well . . . as much as girls her age do, I suppose. No . . ." The woman lays down a pamphlet slowly. "More. Yes, definitely more." She looks down, realizes she has filled all the piles, each has a complete set of blazing colors. "Oh, could you do me a huge favor, love, and hand me those folders off that shelf—yes, that one right above your head. You can just climb up like—yes—but be careful, I want no lawsuits brought against me, if you please. Oh, but yes, Jane really is very helpful, doing things about the house, getting dinner when I'm late. Of course, her younger sister really has no concept yet of—"

"*Her younger sister?*" An avalanche of glossy, white folders spills into the girl's arms; they fan out around her face, soft and slippery as bird wings.

"Oh, yes—Emma. She's right . . . well, she was right here . . ." The woman lowers her chin against the desk to peer between piles. "Ah . . . here!" She digs out another gilt frame from under an in/out tray. The fluorescent lights play dazzling patterns on and off its glass. "Emma."

The girl teeters on the chair, trying to keep from leaping to the floor like a leprechaun. Two daughters. It does not even matter that this younger daughter looks nearly as much like the woman as the older one does. The girl seems to float to the ground, the folders slide from her arms to the woman's, smooth as mother-of-pearl. Two daughters are not the same as one, not remotely the same, against two the girl remains a one, separate and undiluted.

The staticky sparks of the woman's voice continue . . . "no idea how much energy it takes, being in an office eight hours straight—well, usually nine or ten, as it turns out" . . . but the words skim over the girl like liquid. The silk of the girl's dress seems to have turned liquid, her smallest movement causes it to flow around her like bath water. The girl slides back into her chair, she scoops up the labels, the girl luxuriates. She realizes the woman is talking about her husband now. ". . . We made a deal that he would wash if I would iron, but . . ." The girl stops listening; she has, at the moment, no interest in this man who is not her father. And then she realizes it is not necessary for her to listen.

She finds she automatically knows when to nod and smile; the woman's voice, the woman's breathing, signals her. The girl peels off a label, smoothes it on, bends to drop the envelope in the box; each movement becomes a quick gust of air, each quicker than the last, carried along by the rhythm of the woman's voice, by the gusts of air the woman creates as she slips papers and pamphlets into folders and drops them to the floor. It is like a dance, the girl realizes, the woman leads, the girl smiles and follows, graceful, flawless, beautiful. The girl recognizes this beauty now, she has felt it when she has crossed the street while reading a book, when the breath of cars has signaled her that the light has changed. The girl glances up at the woman and is startled to see how much in focus she is, every detail of her sharp and exaggerated, every breath magnified. The girl stares, her fingers fly beneath her; she has no need to watch the labels now, only the woman's face. The woman's features seem carved out of glass, they are so precise.

I love you with all my heart; the girl's mind forms the words without warning. The girl nearly laughs, it is an expression out of an old movie, the kind of movie that, without fail, makes the girl's mother cry. But then the girl realizes that it is exactly right. All her heart. Like a love for a work of art, the girl thinks, as she studies the woman's glass-perfect features, a love completely pure, completely without obstruction. It spreads through the girl like melted butter, the girl begins to feel warm at last. Only her fingers are cold as they fly over the labels.

". . . scaring up funds, of course, is the main thing we . . ." The woman might be speaking another language, it is the sounds that matter, not the words. The sounds are comforting; they nest inside the steady rhythm like a jazz improvisation.

But as the rhythm continues, accelerates, the girl begins to feel frightened. She begins to wonder when she will have control of her movements, her breathing, again; it is hypnotic, this rhythm, the woman's voice is hypnotic, it is suffocating. And the girl suddenly wants it to matter who she is, she wants the woman to speak to *her;* knowing *her.* The girl opens her mouth to stop the rhythm, she opens her mouth to tell the woman who she is.

"Well, you're just putting on those labels so fast, my dear, you wouldn't consider coming back tomorrow, would you?" The girl jumps. The woman has broken the rhythm for her.

"I'm serious, I could ditch this temp girl and pay you instead. I don't suppose you can type as well?"

"Oh, yes." The girl smiles at the thought. She looks up to see if the woman is serious—then freezes. The woman has reached a hand up to her hair, has raked back a mass of it; she has left one earring exposed. The girl sits up, arched, as if a wire had been run through her and pulled. The earring is a rose leaf, a rose leaf dipped in gold, curved inward like a hand to cradle a small, domed crystal, exactly like a drop of water. *Exactly like the earrings the girl herself is wearing*—the earrings the girl chose herself, expensive earrings that the girl fell in love with and bought against her mother's wishes, earrings that, like the dress, the shoes, the stockings, belong completely to the girl.

The edge of a label slices across the pad of the girl's finger; it gives a quick whisper sound. The girl looks down, surprised. The skin has a strange, naked feeling; it opens into halves, a little mouth. The girl watches, fascinated, as a bead of blood forms and swells, a shining, red oval. Suddenly, the bead breaks, spills, splashes onto the label; like that, it has obliterated half the street number. The girl's eyes widen, the girl gasps silently. The girl quickly wipes at the spot, but she only smears it, sends it over the label and onto the envelope. The girl wets her finger, rubs at the stain. It thins to pink. Permanent. Helplessly, the girl looks up at the woman, the woman who has not noticed, who continues to talk, to carry the rhythm along without the girl. The girl can still see an edge of the woman's earring, just visible through the blonde waves, gleaming. Another drop of blood splashes, this time onto the wax paper, where it breaks into a dozen tiny beads. The girl begins to cry.

"Hey—" The woman looks up, squints at the girl. "What's wrong?"

The girl tries to stop, cannot.

"Honestly, what's *wrong?*" The woman pushes herself up on her elbows, peers over the desk, sees the label. "Oh. Oh, heavens, are you hurt, is that it?"

The girl shakes her head.

"Oh, are you worried about the label, then? Is that all? Because if that's all, honestly, that's nothing, heavens, one label, we can re-type that in a matter of seconds. I mean it, paper cuts are a professional hazard, they're *expected*—for heaven's sake, *stop*, honestly you don't need to . . ."

The girl cannot stop.

The woman pushes at the corners of her eyes. "Please, there's no need . . ." The woman's voice is high, soft, the girl can barely hear it. "It's not the label. What is it?"

The girl shakes her head. The girl is a mess, a snuffling, wet mess, the girl is disgracing herself, disgracing the woman, the woman she loves with all her heart. But the girl cannot stop. "I'm sorry," she gasps, "I'm sorry. I'm sorry."

"You don't need to be sorry, why are you sorry?" The woman reaches over the desk to touch the girl's hand.

The shimmery heat from the woman's touch only makes the sobs come harder, they bend the girl double, wrench her hand away from the woman's. "I'm sorry," she sobs, "I'm sorry." The girl is ugly, red, swollen, she can never tell the woman who she is now. The girl is sorry.

But the woman has somehow come to be standing beside the girl, the woman is pulling the girl up by the elbows, the raspberry perfume is engulfing them, almost painful in its richness. The girl is dizzy; if the woman were not supporting her, she would buckle, all limp.

The girl feels herself shift smoothly to the woman's left side; her cheek slides over the silk-covered shoulder pad to rest in a hollow just below the woman's collarbone. The girl's cheekbone fits like a puzzle piece. The point of the girl's earring is crushed into the soft flesh beneath her ear, but it does not hurt. The shimmery heat is gone now, only the warmth remains. This is the time to tell the woman who she is, the girl tells herself. But the girl's eyelids droop shut, the girl is so tired she cannot begin to form the words. And it is so nice to love the woman with all her heart; the girl understands the expression now, understands why, in old movies, it is so often spoken by new, young lovers. *All* her heart, undivided by familiarity, by memories of bad feelings. Mothers and daughters do not love this way, the girl thinks, friends do not, their love is clumsy, rough, ugly, they bump into one another, push, pull, hurt one another. Better to be Baby, female, the girl thinks, better not to have an identity.

But then the girl realizes, even this moment identities are forming, they cannot help but form. If the woman sees the girl again, she will remember her for this, the way she was this day.

The girl pulls back from the woman, looks at her very hard. The woman says softly, bewildered, "Look, are you . . ." The girl nods. She is all right, the sobs are just shudders now, just automatic response. But she must look at the woman's face hard, from every angle; even now it is beginning to blur, even now a film is inserting itself between the girl and the woman, an image of the woman which will solidify and impose itself over her, always, a double exposure moving as she moves. The girl closes her eyes, pushes herself more deeply into the curve of the woman's shoulder. Better not to watch.

"You're sure . . ." the woman whispers.

The girl hears a rumbling; it is faint at first, then separates into voices, laughter, feet brushing carpet. Lunch is over. And then sound eddies all around the girl and the woman, sound of paper being shifted, of computers booting up, of electric typewriters coming to life with a start. The girl holds her eyes tight shut. Somewhere in the distance a telephone rings, then another. And then the woman's phone rings, sharp and insistent. The girl feels the woman's body tense, feels a gap of air-conditioned air between herself and the woman. But after a moment the gap closes. The phone rings twice more, then stops. Over the woman's shoulder, the girl can see the clock; it is already past one. It is time for Elizabeth. The girl pushes her breath out as far as she can, pushes it over the shuddering sobs, pressing them out like lumps in dough. The girl reminds herself to pick up her purse from beside the chair. Tomorrow, she thinks, tomorrow she will come back. Tomorrow she will tell the woman who she is, will risk coldness, denial. Will risk friendship. Tomorrow she will destroy the purity of this love.

Today it is enough to have the same earrings. Today it is enough to love the woman—as strangers love—with all her heart.

THE SECOND MARRIAGE OF ALBERT LI WU

Zoe Keithley

Albert Li Wu trudged home to Twenty-sixth Street through the gloom of a late February afternoon in Chicago's Chinatown to tilt against his front window the sign he had made at Premiere Printing on the hand press. Wife wanted. Apply within.

He prepared his usual tomato soup, and grilled a cheese sandwich in the heavy wok his wife had favored. Then he sat with chopsticks at the kitchen table, dipping pieces of the sandwich into his bowl and scanning the Saturday sports page.

Tomorrow or Monday a widow would knock at his door. He would relate his circumstances: bereft these two years, in his early seventies, on a pension from Premiere Printing, but still making good money there from special jobs, and from his hand-carved chess sets. No close family. In excellent health: he would smile and show his teeth. He would look the women over closely before taking any telephone numbers.

He watched the news, a detective show, then a movie. Since his wife had passed, he didn't sleep well. At 1:00 a.m. he lit a stick of incense before the dust-covered Buddha.

In his dream, his dead wife K'uan Lai came to him wearing her wedding robe of red satin, with a white lotus in the topknot of her hair; the gold fan of her mother's bridal attire rose like a new sun in her hands.

"Why do you advertise for a wife? I am your wife." She spoke in the Chinese they had used together, spoke directly into his mind through the mask of her face in a voice so cold his scalp flocked.

"Since when do you speak so to your husband, or to any man? You are dead. Now I must cook. And clean. Take my own shirts to the laundry. I have no one to talk to." He drew himself up, scowling.

A wicked light scampered across her eyes, she, who for twenty-

158

seven years had never raised so much as an eyebrow over all his foolishness. She snapped her fan shut. "Since when do *you* talk?" She swept the closed blades across the half-formed knights and pawns where he sat in his dream, carving; then she dissolved like color washed from paper.

Albert Li awoke, enraged that she should tilt her head to look down at him, and, above all, scatter his carving.

But how his heart had blistered at the sight of her, so young, perhaps eighteen, and more beautiful than the day he married her. He had waited late, until his income could command a prize of traditional family, one his friends' eyes would catch at when they came around to smoke and play mahjong. Like any husband, he demanded excellent meals, a tended shrine, and at night the comfort of her breasts and thighs under his roaming hands.

Albert Li opened the door late the next morning to get his Sunday paper. The chatter of feminine voices ceased abruptly, and every pair of eyes flew to his hole-infested sweater, his pressman's hump, his outsized ears and wisps of hair. Younger females bolted from the queue and stomped up Twenty-sixth as though they had been bilked, leaving their scorn to crawl up his stoop, to glare at his flattened bedroom slippers, the filthy old bag of bones.

A neighbor walking his dog had telephoned the newspaper about the women, all doodied up, lining Twenty-sixth. A punk reporter in a wrinkled raincoat stepped up; he took in the sewing thread mustache and beard. "You Wu? *Sun Times.*" He tapped at the sign. "This for yourself, or are you starting up a business?" He leered around, his chest shaking. The man next door came huffing up, a video camera on his shoulder.

Albert Li slammed the door.

He had pictured one or two older Asian applicants drifting through the afternoon, drinking tea, admiring the bedroom, bath, kitchen, the porch overlooking the alley.

He slumped in his chair, angry all over again that K'uan Lai had not outlasted him. He had required of her only household duties a monkey could perform; they had had no children to wear her down. By now, the Buddhist priest should have found him a widow. What good was religion anyway, except to placate your ancestors as if they were landlords? He threw the sign in the wastebasket. Female eyes pried around the curtains; the chiming of the doorbell drove him from room to room.

After twenty-four hours the dragon returned to its lair. He could lift his shades, linger in his robe drinking tea from the oversized cup whose stains he did not know how to remove.

Now in her late twenties, K'uan Lai gazed serenely at him that night as she stripped the thread of black from the curled pink body pinched between her fingers. Her hair was done up in a large white napkin. "I knew you would never take another wife," she smiled sweetly, and pitched the shrimp into a vat of boiling water.

Since when did K'uan Lai know anything of a man's business? he bristled, as he spread ginger marmalade the next morning. When she was alive, he had to count the money into her hand or she would buy a lamp instead of a roast. He bit through the cool sticky sweetness. His father would have married if his mother had passed first. He snapped the newspaper open. If he wanted a wife, he would take one.

The next morning he heard an urgent rapping at the back door. A shadow filled the glass. Mr. Gillespie, the building manager. What day of the month was it?

"Mr. Wu?"

She was huge, with a plowed-field kind of face under wiry gray hair. A broad undergirth of chin sifted into the collar of her coat. She gave off odors of ironing and onions.

Her eyes scanned the scarred kitchen cabinets, outdated stove, and slumping refrigerator; took in the feathering linoleum, drooping curtains, the large, empty pantry.

She pressed a covered casserole toward him.

"No." He backed away. "No wife. A mistake."

"I seen you many a time at the Bumble Bee, Mr.—."

He shut the door, locked out the small brown eyes searching his kitchen. He waited an hour, then peered onto the back porch. There sat the covered dish.

Except for the sauce, it might have been Oriental food. It was his first home-cooked meal in over a year. He sighed and chewed, relishing the fantasy of someone in his kitchen tending to his needs. He washed the dish and set it back on the stoop. Under the lid he left a note: "Very good. No wife. A mistake. Albert Li Wu."

But each day she came again, at a different time, at the front door, at the back. When he didn't answer the bell she would leave something new and take away the washed dish. He would watch her retreat, her body rolling like a ship of trade, then snatch the meal inside.

The woman began to leave messages of her own. "I am not a wife, Mr. Wu." "I am a housekeeper, Mr. Wu." "I am looking for a live-in position, Mr. Wu."

At the kitchen table he picked at a pawn with the tip of his carving knife. An employee. No woman-minded silliness. But not from a good family. Not Chinese. With white-people smells and English words like rocks. A fat woman for everyone to see. He blew grains of ivory from an emerging eye.

After seven meals, K'uan Lai, in her fifties, came climbing through the shrouds of his sleep, lugging a scrub bucket, her face dark. "This woman will never leave while you eat her food—ox of a *how li* Irish. Pah!" She spat over her shoulder. "Do not bring her into my house."

Spitting like a peasant! he boiled, snapping on the bedside lamp. Speaking to him as if he were a street vendor. Why couldn't the ancestors control K'uan Lai? He had always found her perfectly easy to control. He rattled his pillow under his head. And how was this suddenly 'her house'? He rolled onto his side, staring, faintly aware of the distant chatter of the 3:00 a.m. elevated train to the Loop.

It was his wedding day. "This is yours now," he remembered his father saying, and taking the inlaid mahjong set of great-grandfather Chang from the mantle. "Keep your wife as you do your mahjong, and you will never have a sleepless night."

"What do you mean?" Albert Li opened and closed the shallow teak drawers, fingering the flat ivory pieces.

"Know everything she has, as you would count your tiles and sticks. In this way you way control your wife."

He had kept track of everything, down to the last spoon, to the underdrawers. He punched his pillow. He would show K'uan Lai he still gave the orders. He would see this woman.

Rose Malone was the name she gave out from under the black pie-pan hat. They sat in the front room, balancing tea cups. The porcelain dragon clock on the shelf dealt out the afternoon. A school bus coughed, then rumbled off to leave the footfalls and voices of children tattering the air.

"And I says to myself, 'They must mean that dignified Oriental gentleman comes in here for our stroganoff. Mr. Wu from Premiere Printing.' I seen you many a time from the kitchen. Everyone knows Mr. Wu, extra noodles. 'Now there would be a fine home to keep,' I says."

Albert Li felt his walls stretch, his furnishings modernize and gleam. He blew across his tea.

"I'm an honest woman, Mr. Wu," Rose Malone set her cup aside. "On my feet morning to night, cooking—it's getting to be too much. Oh, they won't see the likes of me again; and himself will be begging me to stay." She tucked a strand of gray hair behind her ear. "But don't you worry none, I got plenty of work left in me." She gave him a frank look. "Plenty of good meals for the right customer." She gave him a second look, a long look, and straightened her hat. "And I can do anything else a body might require."

His neck grew red. "Only one bedroom here. Where I put a housekeeper?"

"Why, your nice big pantry will be perfect." She waved toward the kitchen. "Have you got one of them cots?"

His eyes coursed the bulk of her. "You be—comfortable?"

"Once I fall asleep, twenty mules draggin' my bed through the door wouldn't wake me up."

He took in the dark shadow on her upper lip, the slough of neck skin, hams for arms, coal-hods for feet. Sex would be out of the question. He combed his fingers through his mustache. He could have a girlfriend. He showed his teeth.

"This room-board only. What you do for money?"

"Well, I have my poor dead husband's pension these twelve years. And Social Security. This will help out quite a bit—a woman my age—sixty-six—with no family, just wanting to live quiet and see Ireland again."

A professional cook. He couldn't believe his luck. He wrestled open the cot, then tacked a pillowcase over the pantry window while Rose Malone called to quit her job, did up the cups, then hurried off for her belongings.

That night his dead mother appeared in a peasant dress and paper hat. "Everyone will think you took her to your bed." Tears glistened down the crepe of her cheeks. She hunched over a mound of rice spread out on a cloth. He watched the familiar balls of his childhood emerge from the blur of her fingers. "And not even Chinese." Mountains rose behind her, black and white and green. "You have a wife. She is waiting for you." Her old eyes wavered and watered. "We are all waiting for you." The rice balls vanished last.

He awoke, popping his knuckles. What did his mother care anymore what people thought? And was he supposed to dry up here like a monk? He heard the woman thud against the pantry shelves. The yeasty smell of her body nosed about the apartment until it found his bedroom. He shuddered. All right; he would get rid of her and make everybody happy.

But in the morning the apartment smelled of buckwheat pancakes—paper-thin, wrapped over chopped cooked apples flecked with brown sugar—baking in the kitchen. His tea sat steaming and full-bodied on the table. A little tune from his childhood sprang into his head to carousel every unpleasant thought away. He breathed in. He had not felt so happy in years.

"Good morning, Mrs. Malone." He pulled his chair out.

"Mr. Wu." The spatula gleamed in her hand. The sun strode between the curtains, over the table top. "And isn't this a lovely day?" Her large, red face beamed.

In an afterglow of breakfast, he carried his taut belly to the bedroom to rummage in his bedside table, sliding the key to his bank box into a deck of playing cards while Mrs. Malone mopped around the stove.

"Shall I do up your bed with fresh linens, Mr. Wu?"

Albert Li startled. Big as she was, he had not heard her coming. He tried to find his feet.

"Don't have to be now," she held up her hand. "I'll be going out for a pork roast. We'll have fresh-made cherry pie for dinner too. I'll be using the back."

He fumbled on his bureau. "Back door." He held out the key, then dug into his top drawer for some bills. She peeled them apart, gave two back.

"We won't be spending all your money, now." She showed her teeth with their empty spaces. "A good housekeeper don't need that much money."

The early March snow turned to slush. When Rose Malone served meals, he came to the table; when she cleaned the house, he went to his old job or the movies; when she shopped or took "personal time," he worked at his carving; when she prepared their food, bellowing Irish ballads or cowboy songs, he turned up the television. Albert Li Wu almost forgot what life had been like before Rose Malone.

Might have forgotten altogether if, regular as the moon in all its phases, K'uan Lai had not appeared, now silently brushing the ebony fall of her hair, her night attire open; now bent to some humbling task from which she would train on him her eyes of steel.

One night, her hair buckled into a tortoise shell comb, she sat at a writing desk. Before her, like frozen lace, rose a multi-tiered pagoda intricately built of mahjong blocks.

"You give her all the money she likes, but you never gave me money." She positioned a tile at the top.

"You spent money like a child."

"I have a mind for more than money." She pivoted toward him, her face like a polished gemstone. "No one learns sitting in a corner, or finds out what she thinks with her tongue buttoned up." She opened her hands as if conjuring the pagoda. "If I made this, what else could I make?"

K'uan Lai pinched a brick from the bottom of the pagoda and the structure clattered over the desktop. "She will bring you down one day," she hissed, "I warn you."

Next morning, Albert Li combed through his mustache, admiring the arch of his eyebrows in the mirror, tickled that K'uan Lai should be jealous of the *how li* Irish.

But all week his dead wife's litany of injustices intruded on his thoughts. He shook them off. Wasn't that marriage? Didn't he take care of everything?

Now Rose Malone took care of everything. He gave over his household, like dropping stones from his pockets, and kept track only of what he withdrew from the bank each week.

He marveled at how he could live with a woman so large and loud. He had seen the huge presses at the *Sun Times* rolling newsprint back and forth across the pressroom in a wide ribbon like a cat's cradle. Just so, Rose Malone's sounds had come to swaddle his day; beneath them he discovered all the solitude and all the silence he needed.

After some weeks, the giant pillows of her bosoms pulling at the buttons of her house dress, the expanse of her hips rising and falling as she lumbered about the kitchen, the maternal belly shaping up like pudding when she sat paring vegetables began to stir in his flesh a deep yearning.

One night after a Perry Mason rerun, he remarked that it seemed a shame to use the pantry for a bedroom when they needed the extra space for supplies, now they were two.

Rose Malone dropped her eyes modestly. Her tatting needle winked.

"You be comfortable in my bed, Mrs. Malone? I small gentleman." He flashed his teeth.

"Call me Rose," she replied, and bit off the thread.

That night K'uan Lai, her face white with rage, parted boiling yellow clouds. She wore black silk edged with red; knots of eternity climbed the front. "You bring home *how li*. Now you take her to your bed."

"I was a faithful husband," he raised himself up, made his face stiff, "and this is not your business."

She pulled the wedding band from her finger. "You shame me before my parents, before my ancestors, before the gods and the hungry ghosts. I divorce you!" With a grunting sound, she pitched the ring at him, overhand.

He waited to feel it strike him; then, he opened one eye, then the other. In the grainy light he made out Rose Malone on her back, the landscape of her body rising and falling, unrolled toward the window, enjoying a healthy snore.

April rains came slanting across the lake, first cold, then warm. Cigar-shaped buds pushed aside the sodden earth to spread infant wings of pink and purple and white.

One evening Albert Li took from the top shelf of his closet the antique mahjong set and placed it on the coffee table. "From Emperor. My great-grandfather Chang his chief steward." He stretched his arms. "Handle everything."

Rose Malone thumbed the ivory and bamboo pieces, stacking them with a clicking sound in her hand.

"Is it worth a great deal, do you think?"

"Maybe five thousand, maybe more." His fingers caressed the case. "But I never sell."

"You should keep it in a bank." She passed the pieces under her nose to breathe in the scent of bamboo.

"No one think to look in old noodle box," he grinned.

Later that night, after his bath, in the steamed-up mirror he suddenly glimpsed an old man with large ears, fish-bone ribs, young-girl breasts, bones like clothes hangers, a curved spine. He stared, studying what had become of the body of his youth, worn away under the load he had, without a thought, piled onto it like shale.

You used it up, used it up just like a wife. He covered his head with a towel to rub up sound. Like a wife—the thought repeated anyway.

In his mind he saw her in the hospital, a corn husk, gray-skinned, so small, like something thrown away, her eyes pinched shut. Then she rose in that red wedding gown, in her perfect face, the whip of her tongue ready behind the bow of her lips. There had been girlfriends. Two; no, three. Free women who knew all about politics, merchandising, special sex practices. He had wanted the excitement of a younger body, a different smell; had wanted to show he could afford them, women whose arrogance drew married men like flies.

He turned with a groan to lean on the sink. If K'uan Lai had shown in life such fire as those women, such fire as she showed now, and such peculiar beauty, even with—and particularly with—that sharp tongue he had come to relish, oh, he would have worshipped her then—would worship her now, court her with jade, drape her in silk and fur, set her among lacquer, ebony, and mother of pearl.

He mopped the mirror, shut off the light, wondering if K'uan Lai had such a woman as that buried in her all along?

Sitting on his bed he buttoned his pajamas. How could he know, he had not let her speak, spend, move, had not wanted her opinions. He turned back the bedcovers. Now she was so alive, only too late. He felt the barbed irony. "All those years I never knew you." He spoke it through the walls of his mind, through the walls of the room, through the starry night to wherever she was roaming. In the bathroom, Rose Malone opened a faucet and dropped a cold cream jar. He shrank under the sheet, wishing to God he had the bed to himself tonight.

It was May. He and Rose Malone ate with windows open to the smells of back porch barbecues, the sounds of yapping dogs, and the pitch and drop of their neighbors' lingo.

"I'll be needing an extra fifty this week." Rose Malone stood over the spitting skillet.

"You need extra money last week too. What happening?"

"Money don't go so far these days," Rose Malone shook the pan, turned off the gas burner. "And we can't be always using fancy ingredients either, dear as they are. We have to eat more plain." She shoveled potato and polish slices onto his plate, then dumped the fry pan in the sink. She plopped down in a chair and took up her fork. "Them politicians puts a stranglehold on everything. It's always the poor what suffers. In Ireland them robbers 'ud be all be strung up over a tar pit and then the lines cut."

That afternoon at the bank, he withdrew three hundred fifty dollars, and stuck two twenties and a ten in her purse while she scrubbed the bathroom floor. His eyes picked up the gold trim of a savings book with "Rose Cullen" showing in the slotted window. Something cold knocked in his chest, and he slipped the book into his trouser pocket. When she left for the store, he sat on the couch and turned the pages, eyebrows high at the four months of climbing weekly figures. In April, deposits nearly matched the food budget.

"Who Rose Cullen?" he asked at dinner, and pushed the savings book across the table to her.

"Oh," she opened a wide smile, "Blessed Jesus, you found the book. My sister's savings. I been upset all day."

"Dates start at end of February; latest one this week," he set down his fork, frowning. "You never mention sister."

"In Ireland."

"Your sister named Rose too?" He took a bite and chewed, his eyes never leaving her face.

"Would you believe it, our dear Ma named us both Rose. Myself was Ellen Rose, her Mary Rose. After our Gram. When Ma died, we each wanted to drop our names we never liked and use Rose—me here and her there." She laughed, pouring milk into her tea, lacing it with sugar. "It's so comical writing to her. 'Dear Rose. Love, Rose.'" She stirred, raising her eyes.

"I never see you write any sister, or anyone. Why you have her bank book, make deposits?" He studied Rose Malone, wiping his mouth, leaning on his wrists.

"Lord love a duck," she tucked gray hair behind her ear, "they're poor as dirt in Ireland. She gets much better here. I made an arrangement with that Mr. Brownlee at the bank. He says, 'I wouldn't do this for everyone, Mrs. Malone.' The man's a saint, if he is black as midnight." She blew into a wad of Kleenex. "She shoots me the checks, I takes them in." She leaned to her cup and drew a loud draught.

"I never hear of arrangement like that." He laid his napkin on the table. "Why her deposits the same as money I give you for house?"

"Are they, now?" Rose Malone said, and looked surprised.

Albert Li scraped his chair from the table. "No wonder food bad now. You take money." He spoke through his teeth. Rose Malone glared. "The devil I did! Holy Mary, and I'd have a right to it too, the work *I* do around here."

Albert Li banged out the door into the night.

Before dawn he walked to the Bumble Bee. He would stay out of the house, think what to do. The idea of confronting Rose Malone—or Cullen or whoever she was—set loose a pack of hyenas howling behind his breastbone.

The girl brought a waffle, its yellow pat of butter oozing. His throat closed. He called the waitress back.

"Where manager?"

"Rose Malone?" The man had a black bow tie, bags under his eyes. "Nope. Been here ten year, never had nobody by that name." Years of restaurant cooking hung over his belt.

"How about Cullen?"

"Cullen?" He worked the toothpick in and out of his back teeth. "Nope." He sucked. "Wait a minute. Older?" He cupped his arms. "Real heavy? Yeah, two years ago. She lasted maybe six weeks. Great cook, but *slow*. Ran into her once at Zorba's, under the 'L', last year." He shook his head, "Sin to waste a good cook on the counter."

Albert Li stared away to the window. When he was young, he had hooted at stories about older men like himself, taken for a ride. Suddenly his fork slipped from his fingers. He lurched to his feet, twanging the silverware across the floor. The manager's eyes strayed up from his newspaper to the old man raking his pockets, leaving a ten on the table, banging out the door, his beard blowing back like a long wad of string.

Albert Li threw open the front door, then jerked at the bedroom closet. The vacant hangers on the left swayed. He saw the empty space where the noodle box had been. "No!" He slammed his fist into the closet wall. He rushed to the bedside table, rummaged and found the key to his savings box still in the pack of playing cards. But the tray on his dresser was cleared of coins and stamps. He stirred the socks and undershorts in his top drawer. The three hundred dollars was gone.

He flung himself into the street, walking, as if somehow his footfalls could make his disaster disappear. He passed the clock on the old red Dearborn Station. Hatred tore at his insides. He would set dogs on her. He strode north into the heart of the Loop, past Carson Pirie's, Marshall Field's. Rain fell now, turning the pavement dark. That mahjong set had been in his home since he was a boy. He remembered his father carrying it over on the freighter. Curious passersby stared from car windows at the bent old Chinaman, at the pants and jacket and whiskers, all plastered to his skin.

He followed LaSalle Street to Grand Avenue, and Grand to Navy Pier. He would contact Wong; one of his henchmen would take her in an alley; she would get a few lines in the *Sun Times* or *Tribune* and that would be that. No, he had eaten her food, had known her in his bed; he ground his teeth, had begun to think of her as a friend. He leaned against the cold railing. Anyway, it would be better to strap concrete to his back and jump into the water right now than to be in Wong's debt. The waves tugged at him: Who would miss an old Chinaman? He pushed on, climbing to Michigan Avenue, cursing her filthy Irish soul until he passed under the canopy of the Blackstone Hotel. He would file a report. What, and let those *how li* cops bleat about him in taverns all over town, shaming his father and all Chinese men? He spit in the gutter. Never.

At four o'clock, legs trembling violently, he let himself in at the back door. His sodden shoes chirped along the linoleum. He sat despairing. How could he have been such a fool, opening himself to a woman he didn't even know? The muscles in his buttocks thrummed. Thirty-seven years he had been with K'uan Lai and had never opened to her.

Rain beat at the window. Bitterly, he flung the mahjong set from his life. What good had it ever done to keep a wife like so many sticks? What comfort had he ever gotten from that? He peeled his wet things off. Too tired to make tea, he lit a stick of incense before the Buddha, crawled under his covers and lay there, his teeth chattering.

K'uan Lai came to him in a shining white gown cuffed with rabbit fur, her black hair rolled and seeded with pearls, carrying green leaves and a long lotus bud.

Albert Li waited for the tilted chin, the scalding look.

But a perfume of flowers filled the room.

"We should marry." K'uan Lai stepped closer, through gauzes of mist. "This courtship has gone on too long." She stretched out her hand.

"But you divorced me." He couldn't believe his ears.

"That was no marriage. My father saw your bank book; you thought you bought me. I was obedient. Both of us, blind."

"You were not much taller than a child," he murmured. She had been like a doll, a shadow. "So silent. Now I know you are fire."

"All women are fire; men must become tinder." The pearls gleamed. "You are thinking if I had been that way before, you would not have gone to other women."

His eyebrows flew up.

She drew nearer. "Every wife knows. Sometimes I called you Stone Man to my friends, waiting for you to become tinder—all those years, waiting, keeping my place. That was my blindness. You kept your place, not seeing me; that was yours. Now I would not hold my tongue for any man. When I came here," she gestured toward the mists, "I could watch and learn. When you put the sign in the window, my tongue was loosed; the words came like a storm. But I saw that behind your stiff face you had loved me, still loved me. I wanted you then even more than in life."

She stroked the lotus bud.

"An old man?" His face was wet.

"My chosen husband."

"I would not go to other women again."

"No," K'uan Lai smiled, "now you are tinder."

The wedding band, a circle of rubies, was there. He slipped it over her finger.

Radiant, she turned back the covers of his bed. For the briefest second, he saw the beauty of her naked form; then her breath was on his neck, in his beard; the warmth of her body stilled the shaking of his ribs; it came to rest light as a butterfly on his most private organ. A childlike happiness bubbled from beneath his breastbone.

Drifting off in this cocoon, he heard her voice. "In the morning, see Dr. Chow. You are about to get a cold."

Soothed under the nip of her tongue, he burrowed beneath the covers, smiling, drifting. Yes. In the morning. A cold.

In the morning he had a cold.

It came and went. The days came and went, and the weeks. One month, two months passed, and K'uan Lai, the band of rubies on her finger, appeared each night when sleep shut down his mortal sight. For a time Albert Li Wu was a man happy and lost in the arms of his wife.

But pure bliss ran out. His physical body, in a fever from the images in his mind, began to wrack him, to wake him to his solitary bed, his frantic member, and no one to do the soothing but himself. The mundane humiliation left him to face the luminous hands of the clock alone; disappointment piled up in his chest like rocks.

Mopping alley tracks from his kitchen floor, or dragging the bulging pillow slips to the laundromat, while women around him undid their hair rollers and put them in again and he watched his gymnastic underwear in the dryer, angry, he would try his own case: He would become spiritual when he was dead, but he now had a body. He had a marriage, yes; but no proper wife who tidied the bathroom and set out his clean shirt. And, sunup to sundown, the silence at home gnawed his bones. Lugging his folded laundry home, he would rescind: It wasn't K'uan Lai's fault, she was stuck on the other side.

September spilled into October, and he found now he rarely remembered K'uan Lai's coming—there was no perfumed air, no acerbic saying to savor—only sleep thick as pea soup out of which he would stagger, his eyelashes stuck together, to go to the toilet.

One evening he came up the back way from delivering a chess

set and there, jammed beneath the lopsided metal chair on the porch, battered and tied up with string, was his noodle box. Eyelids stinging, he lifted the mahjong set from its newspaper wrappings, then searched for the note of apology. Nothing. Probably the *how li* was afraid he might track her down with the police. Sliding the box onto the closet shelf, he struck the empty hangers on the left with his elbow; their plaintive notes wrenched his insides. He ground his teeth. He would set the cops on that woman if he knew where she was.

On his way to the green grocer a week later, her black pie-pan hat and square bulk came rolling toward him from the far end of the block. Fear pushed him into the elevated train station, and he peered, frozen to the spot, through the pebbled glass as she lumbered by. Then two teenage girls burst past him out the door, and he followed them onto the sidewalk. He hugged the buildings until she disappeared into Unique Dry Cleaners. After waiting ten minutes, he drew on a business face and rushed past the window to see her there, out of the corner of his eye, sorting clothes for a customer.

That night K'uan Lai surprised him in a housewife's dress, a pan in her lap, soybean pods at her feet.

"You followed her," her fingers moved like knives, opening the pods. "Our marriage is not enough?" Soybeans plinked.

Albert Li's face took fire. He pulled his eyebrows down.

"If you come at night, I do not see you, anymore."

"You see me now."

"You torment me—coming, not coming. Before I could feel you. Now I feel nothing; my house echoes like a cave."

K'uan Lai leveled the peas in the pot with her hand.

"You want what I cannot give. Your body keeps us apart."

"Maybe I run hose from stove to bedroom, so we can be together," Albert Li glowered. "Or, plastic bag work good."

K'un Lai shelled, saying nothing. When the last green pea fell gleaming from her fingers, she vanished.

Albert Li awoke in a temper, then thought he smelled pancakes and tea brewing; but it was only his old man's mind; the kitchen stood shadowed and empty as ever. He plucked a dish from the stack in the sink, passed it under the faucet, then fanned it four or five times at the end of his arm. He closed his eyes as he chewed his Raisin Bran and saw Rose Malone, could have reached out and touched her bosom, heard her bellow "Mamas, Don't Let Your Babies Grow Up To Be Cowboys," upper arms quivering and hips slipping about under her skirt; he opened his eyes and still she was there, piling hot food onto a plate, pressing it toward him. He slammed his fist on the table. He would *not* think of her.

November. People took to wearing scarves and gloves. Most nights now there were not even dreams, much less K'uan Lai. Albert Li would open his eyes at 6:00 a.m. and hurry to the Busy Bee to escape his empty kitchen.

One morning he looked up from his western omelet and there, three booths down, were the gray bun, thick neck, and black pie-pan hat of Rose Malone. How could he have missed her when he came in? His body began to shake. He fumbled in his pocket and threw a five down next to his half-eaten food. But his feet took him directly to her booth where her small eyes, progressively widening, traveled from his clenched fingers to his face.

"Why you steal from me?" He hurled the words at her. "Where my three hundred dollar, and the rest you put in your savings, and my stamps?" He stood glaring, ears out, chin out, sewing threads quivering.

Rose Malone, her eyes getting larger, gathered up her purse and clumsy coat, her feet paddling against the floor.

"No," he pressed his palm outward, "I call cops." He raised his voice. "What you got to say to me, Irish woman?"

She threw up her hands and let them fall on her lap. "I got nothing to say. What I done, I done."

"What you do not too nice," he shouted, ears bright red and face wild. The manager, a thin woman in her forties, looked over from the cash register. "Good thing you give back my box, or I get police on you! Why you do these things?"

Rose Malone pushed her plate away. "You be a woman. You be sixty-six. You be out of work with no health money, no savings, roaming the streets with young bastards ready to drag you into an alley and open your throat for a few dollars and a hair-pin." She stared out the window. "I'm sorry it had to be you; I got myself to think of."

"I give you bed, food, TV. You lie from get-go. Not even tell me real name."

Rose Malone raised her chin. "I told you my real name."

He blinked. "Malone your real name?"

She nodded. He wove his fingers in and out of his beard. "Malone your real name? You lie to bank?"

She lifted her chin higher, nodded again.

Albert Li slapped the table top. "You crazier than I thought." The deception tickled him, started his chest shaking. "You crazy woman!" He leaned on the booth. Rose Malone started to laugh too; they were both wiping tears from their eyes. Rose Malone waved him to sit down and he slumped onto the seat. They howled and howled. "Crazy woman" he would say, then slap the seat. Then he stopped abruptly.

"You steal from me every month."

"I needed a retirement fund, in case . . ." she looped her hands. "My Social Security's not much. With my legs, I can't work like I used to."

Three boys, nearly horizontal on bikes, bled across the window; at the same time they sped over the mirrors above the counter, jumping the door frame.

Albert Li's eyes narrowed. "You have husband's pension."

She lifted her gaze and looked him full in the face.

Albert Li raised his eyebrows far up.

"No husband either?"

"Died of drink before he was thirty. My last boyfriend cleaned me out, like the dirty Irishman he is. Got my pitiful money all tied up in fake antiques, then got busted."

"You figure you clean me out, then skip," he scowled. He pulled himself out of the booth, angry all over again. "You find foolish old Chinaman." He was shouting. The manager came over, worry crowding her mouth. Albert Li raised his hand. "Never mind. I leave, I leave."

He boiled down Clark and up Wentworth against a cold wind, his ears like ice; but once home and he had his rubbers off and the kettle on, he calmed down. He sipped some tea, then dropped oil on the stone and honed his carving tools one by one. Wiping away burrs, the thought came of Rose Malone fooling the bank. He started to laugh.

K'uan Lai stepped through the restless drapery of his sleep in a tunic of Jewish design, her black hair set free against the sheers which floated to either side of it.

"I must tell you, I have been in another place," she cradled her arms, "very small, with a woman holding me. More and more I am there." She dropped her eyes. "That is why you do not remember me; now I forget to come."

"You tell me we are married, and you forget me," he cried, jolting upright in his sleep.

She looked at him again. "You know what it is—what the priests told us. It is true."

He swallowed. K'uan Lai had begun an incarnation. "Can't

you wait for me?"

She shook her head. "I have finished my work."

"You trick me, seduce me, marry me to finish your work."

"Yes; but also I married you because I wanted you." The gold keystones of K'uan Lai's dress gleamed. "We have no karma now with each other. What is between us is forever. I learned to speak for myself." She held her index fingers side by side, "Learned to be one in a couple. What did you learn?"

He looked at his wife, the radiant spirit, who had already left him; this conversation like the train of her dress. "Nothing." He made his face stone to withhold from her, and to cover his terror of the dissolution he felt in his bowels to be coming. "I learn not to love."

"No, no." K'uan Lai threw her head back and opened her lips; her laugh tinkled like bells. "You learned more than that, something else. What is it?"

He scowled, shook his head. His head felt hollow, as if it were full of melon seeds. "I don't know."

"The ancestors tell me we have been together before. Perhaps we will be again. I hope so. I start a life; you finish a life. We carved our marriage like a chess piece. The ancestors say we have many lives and marriages. Perhaps you will carve with someone else." She folded her hands in the old salutation, bowed low to him, and vanished in rose light.

For weeks he thought he heard her move about the kitchen, or felt her brush against him in the bedroom. He pictured the plastic bag from the supermarket over his head. But how could he stop himself from ripping it open?

A few weeks later, carrying the garbage out, he found the covered casserole at his stoop. Inside was a note in plastic wrap. "Mr. Wu, Here's thirty. Will give you some every week until paid off. Them stamps too. I know you can use a good meal. Rose Malone."

He stripped away his jacket and sat turning the money in his hands, moved in spite of himself. He looked at the calendar. In a week she would come again. Maybe it was a trick to get into the house, to steal his clothes this time.

He took a few steps across the front room to the bed and threw himself on the spread. Finding the bank book had spoiled everything. Why couldn't he have left it in her purse; it would have been better not to know; at least he would have some company now. He stared at the ceiling, tracing the cracks in the plaster. All his life he had been a stiff old Chinaman like his father, shooting off like fireworks, then, blind, stumbling around in the smoke, never hearing anyone but himself. He was seventy-three. How could he change now? He threw his arm over his face. Something moved in him and he forgave K'uan Lai. What could she do against great spiritual forces? Such forces would scoop him up one day as well.

The next Wednesday he sat listening, watching the back door, and flung it open the moment he saw through the window Rose Malone's head and shoulders rising up the steps.

She hesitated at the door, her glance sweeping his face and the kitchen.

"Why you have to spoil everything?" He barked, leaning back, spewing words before she had gotten across the threshold. "I happy, you happy. Why you not leave things alone? We get along fine until you mess up."

She set the covered dish down hard on the table and made the cover rattle. "Sure. Fine for you, happy for you, with your pension. Some new chickie comes into Zorba's and I'm out on my tail. I promised myself that wasn't going to happen to me again. Listen, there's plenty of old women like me; we're a dime a dozen. I was buying myself protection, that's all."

He shook his head. "You not buy, you steal. You build up out of me. Why you not tell me?"

"Tell you what, sweet Jesus?" Rose Malone slapped her sides and dropped into a chair. "That I want to see Ireland before I die?" She took the lid off the covered dish to pick at the brown rim of potato crust.

The way she came right back at him with her sharp tongue stirred his blood. He smacked his palm with his fist. "When nobody talk, nobody know anything. My wife never talk." Before, when he was married, he had never wanted to know what was going on, what anyone was thinking. Now curiosity ate him. He puckered his forehead.

"You really *from* Ireland?"

She waved her hand. "Long, long time ago."

His face softened. "You have sister there?" He sat.

She snorted. "You know I got no sister. But I got a few cousins, where all the Byrnes come from." She stuck a potato bit in her mouth and chewed. "Malone's my married name. Other than that, I got nobody. Just like you." She looked at him straight on. "I figured here was a nice old China guy living all alone. What was he going to do with his money, leave it for the government? I figured you'd be better off having someone helping you spend it—someone like me, would cook good for you. I thought them things when I was at the Busy Bee and I seen you through the kitchen window. So when I heard about the sign—" She flung her hands out.

He looked at her a long minute, then shook his head. "It too bad I can't trust you. I start to like you. You too big and noisy, but I like you anyway."

Rose Malone stripped potato from the casserole edges and sucked her fingers, working in silence. "A person could make a mistake and learn something, Mr. Wu," she said in a low voice, not looking up. "I just couldn't sell that fancy box of yours. Would have set me up proud, too, but I just couldn't do it."

Albert Li put the tea kettle on so she wouldn't see the feeling flood his face. He offered her an empty cup, and when she nodded, set one down for himself as well. Outside someone laid on a car horn three or four times. The late afternoon sun fell softly through the curtains to warm the sugar bowl, the salt and pepper, and tired flowered cloth beneath them.

"If a person knew a person liked having her around, it could make a difference," Rose Malone went on when the horn stopped, leaning back and folding her arms, "in how they behaved, I mean."

Albert Li set the teapot between them. "You not know I like you around?"

Rose Malone shook her head no. She sniffed and ran her finger under her nose.

"Oh," he said.

Albert Li lifted the teapot's lid and peered past the steam. "Not ready," he said and chinked it back into place.

"I figured anybody who'd put me in the pantry and didn't want to offer no money was looking for cheap help, that's all. Big older woman like me, what else would it be? I was stuck, so I'd have to make it work. I figured I'd do you good, but get what I could for myself. Thought I might even drag you off to Florida one day, to warm our bones." She laughed, then sobered. "I got greedy. I'm not proud of it."

Albert Li picked up the pot and held it without pouring. "I get greedy, too," he said. "I want cook, housekeeper—" his neck got red, "other things, for nothing." He glued his eyes to the spout as he poured. "I treat my wife same way."

The tea rushed out dark and heady. He looked up at her. He blew and sipped, his eyes still on her face.

"You comfortable where you live now?"

Rose Malone set down her cup, pushed the casserole away. "You know, a few of them roaches. It's what I got money for."

Albert Li nodded. Amber beads of tea clung to the threads of his mustache and beard. He watched her top lip move delicately over the rim of the cup, saw her swallow. He took a draught himself. If she came with the money and her covered dish next week, he thought, what harm could there be if he asked her to stay to eat?

Losing Touch

Cynthia Kennison

When Bertha comes in from the post office, Leonard does not answer her. She has lugged home three large cartons addressed to him. Kevin, the postmaster, put string and a wooden handle onto the biggest, squarest one, so she could dangle it and carry the other ones under her arms. It has banged against her all the way. All the packages are from the Cannon Towel Company.

"Leonard—get down here. This time you've ordered towels." She uses her sternest, most resonating voice. It is the only one he reacts to some days. "We don't need towels."

She becomes more angry as she bellows. She feels herself swelling up, straining at her dress, at her own skin. She sits at the kitchen table. One end is piled with magazines Leonard has subscribed to, to increase his chances in the sweepstakes: *Golfer* (two copies of each issue), two years of *Connoisseur,* of *Chronic Pain, Polo World,* of *Guideposts, Electronic Musician, Gerbil Life,* of *Zookeeper,* of *Amateur Magician.* He never reads them, although he has looked through several issues of *Amateur Magician.* In her handbag, Bertha carries the latest of their multiple mailings from Publisher's Clearing House, and of personal letters from Ed McMahon. Months ago she filled out several post office forms requesting a stop to all unsolicited mail. But Leonard has solicited all this. His name is on all the mailing lists on earth.

She calls his name again and wonders if he is all right. She pictures herself checking through the house. He may be asleep on their bed, or in front of the television, or in his easy chair. He has done that a lot lately. He may have wet wherever he dozed off. He will deny it if she wakes him. He may be in the cellar trying to fix some pipe that doesn't need repairing. Or scratching the back of his neck, wondering why he went down there. The light will not be turned on. He will be angry if she asks what he's doing. He may have fallen, he may be flung out on the floor like a fallen scarecrow, his hair like a porcupine askew on his head. Wherever she finds him, he will not be the natty little pilot she finally accustomed herself to, or the painting contractor, intelligent, exasperated at anything that got in the way of his precise, well-planned day. He is a strange old man who messes up the house. She realizes she really doesn't want to find him today. But there is a funeral after lunch.

She looks at the boxes, and steps slowly into the living room. She stops. She has seen a movement halfway up the staircase. Leonard sits with a book open. He keeps his eyes on the book.

"This is a *good* story." He sounds happily surprised.

She is careful. "What is it?"

He closes it with his fingers inside and turns it to look at the binding. *"Treasure Island."*

It is his favorite book. He has read this very edition between every Christmas and New Year since he was ten.

"When did we get this?" He opens it again.

Bertha wants to say, "Open the front cover. See the inscription to you in 1932?—'Merry Christmas from Uncle Durwood Hatch.'" But no. She will be patient.

She doesn't know what to say. Oh Lord, Leonard has forgotten his lifelong enchantment with Long John Silver and Jim Hawkins. Last summer he read the story with Mikey, the grandson who comes east to spend his vacation with Young Lenny. Leonard made treasure maps, and he and Mikey buried them in the side yard. Here he sits today, the morning sun lighting his wild white wreath of hair, the book on his knees.

"You must be enjoying *Treasure Island*, Leonard." Is this the kindest thing to say? Is it going to make him angry? She thinks of the shipment of Cannon Towels, and her anger ignites in her belly, briefly. "You always liked Long John Silver."

Leonard looks at her. "Always liked who?"

———

Bertha is glad their son Lenny will come up from Florida for Easter. He will notice the changes in his father. He will make Bertha admit that something is wrong. Bertha won't admit it, not just yet. She has been telling herself it is because of Leonard's retirement, the loss of a regulated life, that his reaction is often vacant when she speaks to him, that he wets his pants and doesn't know it, that twice he has put the ice cream carton into the linen cupboard after he has served himself a spoonful or a fingerful. The first time he said he wouldn't have done such a thing. The second time, she watched him do it, and when she asked him why, he said, "Why do *you* think?" Then he said he couldn't quite remember where they keep the ice cream.

Every day Leonard does something new, and Bertha hasn't discussed it with anyone. She knows the people at the post office are waiting for her to make some comment: "Leonard is loosing touch." After church one Sunday, as she came down from the organ loft, she heard Harriet Crooks say that about Will Crooks: "Will is losing touch." Bertha thinks it is awful that Harriet would say that in public, right while Will was tearing open a tea bag and emptying it into his coffee for sugar. A week later, Will was in Winimissett Nursing Home, and now Harriet has shingles in the hospital. Shingles brought on by guilt. Bertha is willing to bet on it.

The thing to do is not talk about it, not give up. Find out what is wrong. Diet may be wrong. Leonard eats ice cream all day long. And peanut butter. Bertha finds spoons all over the house—on window sills, on side tables, as bookmarks—not quite licked clean. She thought for a while it might help if she could get him back onto apples. Until a year ago, Leonard ate seventeen apples a day. He ground his own apple juice in an Emperor JuiceKing that stood high on splayed nickel-plated legs on the pantry floor and vibrated with its electric motor straining while he rammed uncored apple halves into its hopper with a wooden pestle until the juice sluiced out its lip like water out of an old hand pump spout.

One afternoon, after "General Hospital," he said apples were too much work; ice cream from the Cumberland Farms store was easier. Ice cream and peanut butter. At that time, Bertha was relieved. The apples had been a mess. Now she would welcome that machine churning away, apple cores all over the house, the sweet almost vinegar smell. She thinks now that the change in Leonard's eating may be the cause of his losing touch. Or maybe it is the *result* of losing touch. And there is the question of the blood pressure medicine, Leonard's tantrum in the doctor's office. She doesn't want to remember the word Leonard called Doctor Ripple. Leonard would have whipped either of their boys silly for using such language. It must be the medicine. But they will have to change doctors. Bertha can't face Doctor Ripple.

Young Lenny will not hesitate.

In an old jewelry box—a rosewood apple that she pulls open like a jack-o'-lantern by its stem—Bertha finds a tangle of tarnishing chains wrapped around a darkened silver airplane. She unwraps the chains, picking at the knots, laying them straight on her side of the bed. The airplane is a brooch, but it can be worn as a locket; she used to wear it that way because it is too heavy to pin onto a blouse or a scarf without pulling the material down.

Leonard used to argue with her about whether the plane's nose should be diving down into her neckline or climbing up toward her chin. He didn't want other men's eyes following its downward flight into her bosom. The proper way was up. Going down was not the way Leonard wanted to see any airplane. The pin hung around her neck, against Bertha's chest day and night for three years, until she and Leonard were engaged and she could take it off. It is a very detailed airplane, pointy with straight-out wings, and Bertha liked to lie on her stomach and read *True to Life Girl's Romances* comics and eat Lorna Doone cookies. She had to be careful. Sometimes now, turning over in bed after all these years, she reaches for the airplane that isn't there, to pull it up over her shoulder out of the way.

The airplane is from Leonard's flight navigation school days, and he wanted it on Bertha. It was 1943, and he needed her to have it on all the time. She hasn't seen it for maybe thirty-five years. She thinks if she wears it now, it might take him back to the way he was.

Leonard is now so changed, so wrong. A petrified paintbrush left curling on the open paint bucket on the stairs is just one example. Forty years ago he would have raged—a year ago he would have raged—at the idea that someone might not have cleaned off the brush, had not saved it in turpentine and patiently stroked it back and forth on newspaper until the strokes came clear, had not wiped around the lip of the paint can and tapped the lid down gently, evenly. He would have lectured on and on about it—about the waste, the destruction, the carelessness, the ignorance spreading like a sinkhole underneath civilization, the sucking of civilization into the sinkhole. He would never have let that skin thicken on the surface of an open can of paint. He would never have responded to every envelope from Ed McMahon and Publisher's Clearing House by taking subscriptions to *Weight Lifting* and *Photography*, believing his number will have a better chance of winning twenty-six million dollars. Until last year, Leonard disapproved of door prizes at the Unitarian Church Fair. He called it gambling. And he always bathed and changed his underwear. Retiring from house painting two years ago started a change in him, hardly enough to notice at first, a relaxation of the order he imposed on himself. For a while she told herself it was good; he was taking his time, allowing himself to have fun, to be silly.

Bertha finds an unknotted chain, and slips the small end through the hook on the plane's belly so that the nose points up.

———

Does Leonard know this is a funeral? Bertha has explained to him that their friend the old Swedish cellist has died, but as they walk from the car into Lane's Funerals Leonard speaks to Clara Howe, who is backing herself out of her car. "Look at all these people, all dressed up in suits. You'd think they were going to somebody's funeral."

Clara laughs, glad of a joke, then stops, realizing that he may not be joking. She walks along with Bertha and Leonard, and none of them speaks again until Mrs. Lane, in the front hallway, says, "Sign the guest book. Sign right here."

Leonard chuckles. "Where did all these people come from? You having a big party, Annie?"

Mrs. Lane glances at Bertha and back at Leonard. She takes Leonard's elbow and leans down to his ear.

"It's for Sivard Andersen, and he's dead." Her voice is quiet and her message is shocking.

Leonard seems to understand somewhat. "It's old Andersen's party," he tells Bertha. "But don't expect him to say hello to us."

"Sign here." Bertha shows him where, and sees how slowly he writes.

Annie Lane speaks over Leonard to Bertha. "I want to talk to you. Call tonight."

She must need a pianist or organist for a funeral service coming up. Well, Bertha will mention that Lane's F above middle C doesn't sound, and then she will see what Annie offers.

For this service, Annie plays a tape on a radio-cassette player that she has placed in front of the coffin, on a stand between two floral arrangements. Bertha realizes they are hearing Sivard Andersen, Bertha herself, and Charlotte Angell doing a Mozart piano trio, years ago, in the days when they played in time and in tune. More or less. Sivard recorded it one night when they were rehearsing in Bertha's living room. He had brought a new cassette recorder to try out. The performance is wobbly, dusty-sounding. The sound of the tape recorder's own motor nearly drowns the music out. Not nearly enough.

Bertha hears Sivard Andersen's cello line move away from the piano and violin, and hears herself begin to count out loud. She knows what will happen unless Mr. Andersen edited the tape, and sure enough.

The music stops, and Mr. Andersen says, "By golly, that was a mess," and they talk it over and agree to start back at Letter D.

Leonard begins to laugh. Reverend Bensen steps away from the lectern where he is opening his Bible, and comes to where Leonard sits on the aisle. He reaches for Leonard's hand with his right hand. He puts his left hand on Leonard's shoulder. They shake hands, and Reverend Bensen pats Leonard's shoulder twice and goes back to his scripture.

Leonard sits quietly like a small boy, with his feet together and his hands clasped. Just before the Bible readings begin, he says to Bertha, "Is that an airplane you have around your neck?" and he is quiet the rest of the service.

The ones who sob the loudest are the West Indian couple who cared for Mr. Andersen the past year.

"Were you surprised to see her so aged?" Annie Lane asks on the phone. "It's the drinking, the living in New York, poor thing." She means Mr. Andersen's daughter. Then she gets right to Harry and Indiana. They took wonderful care of Mr. Andersen. The agency that brought them into the country has gone belly up. They can go to Indiana's sister in Far Rockaway, Long Island. But they like the people here in Massachusetts very much, and they don't get along with the sister. Harry is a younger husband. The sister doesn't like him.

Bertha listens to all this. She suspects Leonard is the reason for the call. She pictures Annie Lane talking to the daughter who is a teacher, or a guidance counselor on Long Island. Bertha doesn't like to think of a woman drinking on one of those jobs.

"Rose is alone, divorced." There is sadness in Annie's voice, the sadness that is there when she is arranging funerals, talking about music. She wants to help Rose with this couple. "They're young, from the West Indies. Intelligent. Hard workers. Not usual for people who speak Spanish. Or whatever they speak."

Does Annie want Bertha to be on the lookout for a place? Before Bertha can ask, Annie gets to the point.

"I got to thinking. You have your back el empty since Young Lenny went south."

"Oh. Well. Lenny's things are still in it." Bertha hears Leonard humming in the living room, not watching "Cheers." "Lenny's coming up for Easter."

"Those two loved looking after Mr. Andersen. They even had him teach them some Swedish. They didn't let him give up."

"He died."

"There you go, making one of your jokes. He died, yes. But he hadn't given up. I'll send Harry and Indiana over tomorrow afternoon."

———

Leonard chants: "Starting now, feel free. Abandon ship or lock a door. The nuclear plant is closed and locked, and water rises in the basement, as far as the eye can see. The eye can see the blank key, the blank page, the tiniest sound. The tiniest sound, the highest frequency, sets the stomach off in all directions. North and south, over and above, up and down, sink or swim. Live. Let live."

Bertha can hardly stand it. She calls him, but he repeats one line.

"The water rises in the basement, as far as the eye can see."

She hears him singing this as he unwinds the giant wheel of plastic hose from the sump pump up the outside cellar stairs, out onto the lawn to the roadside ditch that will carry the basement water into the culvert at the corner and under the road. He sings as he squishes back across the lawn to the side porch and into the kitchen. Rain has soaked the shoulders of his khaki jacket, the front of his green work pants, his shoes. His hair drips little streams down his ears and down his neck. He goes to the refrigerator and stands staring at it. He scratches at his head, stares at his wet hand, then back at the refrigerator. Now he stands in a puddle on the linoleum. Bertha watches him there, with the freezer compartment door open, the quart of Sealtest Rocky Road open, using all the fingers of his right hand to scoop out the ice cream.

"Did you start the pump?" She has learned that a question like this, instead of asking him what he is thinking, sometimes will get a reasonable answer from him.

"What pump?" He looks around at the sink, eating ice cream

off his hand. "Hey, look. Faucets where the pump used to be."

She breathes and holds her chest full. Finally she says, "The pump in the cellar. To pump out the water."

"Why would I want to do that?" It is his answer to so many questions.

Bertha looks out the window. "The cellar is filling up," she tells him, as she has told him all morning, hoping the ritual may be so ingrained that he will do it because it takes no thought. She knows how the cellar looks—bits of wood shavings, a folded grocery bag floating. The Caribbean couple will come and see this. "You've put the hose out. See it out there? But it's not shooting out cellar water. Go down and turn the pump on. Put your boots on."

———

Harry's English is fine, Indiana says. But he prefers her to do the talking.

Harry smiles, watching Leonard. "That's right. My wife talks."

"Hey," says Leonard, "that a gold tooth you've got there? I always wanted one of them."

Harry smiles energetically.

Bertha mostly watches Harry while Indiana answers her questions. Harry holds Indiana's brown hand between them on the roses of the slipcover. He watches Leonard very closely; he does not look around the room, does not case it for valuable things, does not even assess it.

"Any way you want." Indiana is talking. "We will pay rent, help with chores, find other work outside the home." Her speech is rhythmic, with a beat like a Vachel Lindsay poem. She uncrosses a shiny leg. "Harry's job at the wireworks—it is nine-to-five, home for his noonday meal. So if at night a problem arises . . ." She shrugs and pauses, looking for some response that Bertha doesn't give. "Or we can take over your household. Full-time."

Bertha suddenly takes a deep breath which comes out as a sigh. She realizes she wants this couple to come very much.

No I don't, she tells herself. We're all right.

"We've never had help." She knows she is turning them down. She thinks, *that's right.* Leonard would be humiliated to have a man doing his work. He has never let her call a plumber, a carpenter. He installed the furnace himself. He doesn't care for people with accents. Not Caribbean accents.

Leonard says, "You planning on moving in? That's a good idea.

Bertha can use some help." He leans toward Harry. "She's not so young as she used to be." He chuckles.

Harry smiles. Bertha feels herself grow warm. Indiana smiles, and Bertha thinks, *Oh my, she is gorgeous.* Leonard is watching her leg slightly swinging the gold sandal from its toe.

"This is fine. Oh, and Harry is trained in homeopathic medicine." Indiana's lovely foot in its sandal moves to the floor. "We can help here, most certainly."

Bertha wonders if the interview is to see if she and Leonard will provide work enough to suit Harry and Indiana. "I'm not sure yet," she tells them.

"With your consent. Only with your consent," Indiana says. "I will telephone tonight."

Harry is still watching Leonard. When he catches Leonard's eye, Harry makes a hideous face which passes in a flash. He and Leonard laugh together.

Well. Bertha doesn't approve of making faces. But Leonard is laughing. The bewildered look, the absence is gone from his eyes. His eyes watch something, watch Harry who is standing up, pulling his trouser legs into place before he steps over to Leonard.

"Very pleased to meet you, my dear," Harry says.

Indiana speaks to him in their language.

Harry reaches for Leonard's hand. "Not 'my dear.'" He shows the gold again. "My sir."

Leonard stands before Harry shakes his hand. "This has been a pleasure."

At the door, Indiana starts to speak, stops herself, and decides to go ahead. "Your house is quite lovely. So much sunlight, colors full of light. We can help you to find pleasure here."

After Harry and Indiana have driven away in their large old car, Bertha says, "Mr. Andersen was alone. He needed the help. That's the difference."

Leonard is looking down at the two edges of his cardigan, wondering what to do with a button. "We can use their help."

Bertha watches him very carefully. She speaks very carefully. "They would do things their way, use garlic, smell up the house, maybe slice the sandwiches on the diagonal. You hate that. You know you like things your own way, the way I do them."

He shrugs, watching the button he twists on its shaft while she goes on.

"You always said you'd never have another man change a light bulb in your own home. You always said that."

He looks directly at her.

"But then I was another person."

He takes her hand.

———

Leonard wants to drive when he and Bertha go to LaRue's Colonial Steak House with a coupon that came in the *Pennysaver.* While he is locking the side door, she says, as if she has just thought of it, "You know what? I'd like to drive. I feel like driving." She has the car keys in her hand. She will not go if he drives.

No. He says she will strip the gears, ride the clutch.

She isn't ready, doesn't expect how quickly he moves. He grabs the keys, pushes her aside, gets himself into the driver's seat, and she realizes she must get into the car, she must be there to keep him from making a mistake. As he roars the engine, she runs around the car's rear, knowing he may run her over, whichever way she circles the car. He mustn't drive. She is only partly into the passenger's seat when he begins to back out. The car has run partly over the curb before she gets her right foot inside and shuts the door. She wrestles with the seat belt without speaking.

Leonard has shaved, and she reminds herself to take the bits of toilet paper off his chin before he gets out of the car. This is nothing new; she has done this since before their wedding. And the toilet paper on his neck—why did Leonard shave his neck?

As the car heads for the shoulder and the pine woods beyond, she grabs the bottom of the steering wheel and turns it enough to put the car back onto the road, and enough to irritate Leonard. She knows he will yell, "Just let me drive! I'm capable."

He says, "You want to take over? I'm tired. I don't know where the hell I'm going."

———

By Tuesday afternoon Indiana is in the kitchen, and Harry is mowing the front lawn, even though it is still April and the raking isn't done. They have carried four large suitcases and six bulging grocery cartons into the el from their old car.

When Harry asked Leonard to show him how the lawn mower works, Leonard surprised Bertha by saying, "Oh, that's right. You're going to do that now. I guess you must mow by hand where you come from." Harry said he's not going to do all Leonard's lawn work, but he needs to know how Leonard likes it done.

Leonard walks ahead of Harry, picking up stones and twigs, sometimes pointing, directing Harry's path. Harry mows in smaller and smaller rectangles, overlapping each swath so there are no tufts left, no missed strips. Leonard walks sideways and sometimes backward along the latest swath, bent forward at the waist, almost bowing. Once he stands straight and looks at Harry. Bertha cannot see what Harry does; his back is to her. Maybe he smiles and shows that gold tooth. Leonard salutes.

She has seen this before, the ritual, the lesson with the mowing. She sees the connection. Leonard behaves with Harry the way he once behaved with the children—with Young Lenny, with Chip before Chip ran off for good. The salute. Well. She can live with that, as long as Harry lets Leonard be in control.

The problem is Indiana in the kitchen. Is she cooking for herself and Harry, or for the household? Bertha can't remember what was said over the phone about meals. The kitchen in the el—a tiny sink and range top built over a tiny cubic refrigerator—would not accommodate the smells or sounds that bulge from Bertha's kitchen right now.

It is five. Time for Bertha to start supper. She has meat loaf in mind, a meat loaf recipe that is very easy to make with Ritz crackers crumbled into a milk and egg mixture. Leonard likes it; he's apt to eat half at one meal. But in the excitement after lunch, when Harry and Indiana arrived, she forgot to take any ground beef out of the freezer compartment. What will they think?

Indiana will think Bertha isn't giving Leonard good meals, she isn't nourishing him, and that is why he is losing touch. She may think Bertha is losing touch, that Bertha forgets to cook. And that is not true. No matter how much Bertha dislikes cooking, she always plans a good solid meal.

Bertha will go right out into the kitchen and improvise. A can of tuna fish, a box of macaroni—standbys in the pantry always on hand—will show Indiana that Bertha intends to do the cooking.

———

Harry and Indiana go to see Indiana's sister on Long Island for Easter. Young Lenny's trip north turns out to be only for Easter weekend. He puts off speaking to his father until Sunday evening. After supper Bertha leaves Leonard and Young Lenny talking at the dining room table while she cleans up in the kitchen. When she goes back to scrape the crumbs off the tablecloth and put out the breakfast dishes, Leonard is alone, staring puzzled at the bluebells in a green glass jar. His head rests on his hand. He wears his winter overcoat and the nautical cap he bought to run his motor boat on the river in 1956 when the boys wanted to water ski.

"Lenny's gone?" She stands at the table, holding three cereal bowls.

Lenny is not doing his part. He's not talking to his father about several things that Leonard doesn't listen to when Bertha mentions them: giving up his driver's license, letting Bertha do the bills and taxes. Bertha has shown Lenny how Leonard puts the bills, the tax statements, everything, into his pockets, into the wrong desk drawers, yesterday into the freezer compartment of the refrigerator.

"Where's Lenny?"

"Right here." Leonard looks at her, alert for once. "I'm Lenny. My father will be along to take me home after my clarinet lesson. What are these flowers called?"

This is what she means. They are Scottish bluebells, which Leonard planted in the border by the driveway. His father brought them over from the farm in 1947, and Leonard has forced a few indoors every year since. She does not tell him this. It's the same as *Treasure Island;* he will look at her and say he has never seen them. This is what she needs Lenny to hear.

She says, "They're bluebells of Scotland," and hums the tune. Maybe the song will jog him.

"Bells." He smiles at them. "They are like little bells. They'd be nice in the garden." A little harrowing of lines radiates from between his eyebrows.

She turns at a step behind her. Young Lenny wears his navy uniform, medals on the blue chest. She has not seen him in uniform since he left for Vietnam. For a second she sees Leonard forty years ago, and it leaves her heart and head pounding and her arms weak.

Leonard half stands, and with his left hand on the table for balance, he salutes Young Lenny.

"Captain," Leonard says.

"At ease." Lenny salutes. "At ease, Captain." As much as he hated the service, he reached his father's rank. He watches his father sit. "We need to talk. Strategy."

Leonard nods wisely. "The African campaign. Where's the maps?" He looks at the walls and frowns.

"This is about you, Captain. Dad."

"I know. I'll be leaving the service soon. Someone else will be in charge here."

———

"Your son?" Indiana pushes the foods in the skillet, sides to middle, gracefully, gently, so the colors, especially reds and greens, mix and make Bertha realize how pretty the meal will be. "No wife for him? How sad. Sad for your grandchild."

"Two grandchildren." Bertha looks right at Indiana. "No wife. No wives."

Lenny did not marry either of the mothers. Mikey, who is twelve, lives in a trailer in Oregon with his mother and six little step-sisters. He is glad to come east for his summers with Young Lenny in the back el, and that is when Young Lenny leaves his fishing boat and his job in Florida and comes to be with both his children, Mikey and Aurelia. Aurelia is eight, and lives on West Street, over a garage with her mother the bartender and an older and a younger half-brother.

Bertha does not see eye-to-eye with Lenny and his women about marriage. Both Lenny and the bartender tell her, "You know you're going to get tired of each other pretty quickly, so why make it harder by getting lawyers involved?" They each use exactly those words, which says to Bertha they got this policy from somewhere, some influence.

"Easy come, easy go," Leonard said when Young Lenny told them that Aurelia's mother the bartender had met a new man in the Rustic Lounge, and Young Lenny would be moving back into the el. Bertha should have known something was happening with Leonard back them, that remark was so wide of his beliefs. ("You marry her now, hear?" he had yelled at Lenny about Mikey's mother twelve summers ago. "You do the right thing, or keep out of my sight!" Young Lenny and Brenda had gone to Oregon.)

Young Lenny moved to Florida and now works on boat engines in a marina. He fishes on the ocean for fun.

Easy come, easy go happened summer before last, when Leonard paid attention, when everything in the family still outraged him. And yet he said, "Easy come, easy go." Now he ignores the grandchildren, even when they come for supper and the evening. Even Aurelia has given up talking to him.

"Grampa isn't fun anymore," she said to Bertha today, after

Leonard asked her her name three times during dessert. She thought he was joking when he started asking everyone's name sometime during the winter, but now she knows he really wants to know. "He doesn't know us."

He will, Bertha told Aurelia. "He's just tired."

———

When Bertha asks Harry and Indiana how their work has been going, Indiana says, "We are quite pleased. Nice house, you are very kind. Mr. Hatch is a very fine man."

To Lenny in Florida, Bertha says, "They are nice people. I just don't like strangers in the house."

But Harry and Indiana—Harry especially—are less strangers to Leonard than she is. Leonard is more alert with them. How can that be, after forty-five years? They get him laughing and noticing what goes on around him. Leonard watches Harry and follows him, waves when Harry drives off to his new shift at three each afternoon. Harry says, "Hey, Mr. Hatch Sir, now don't wait up for me." Leonard laughs every time. "No chance of that, Harry." Harry flashes his golden smile.

———

When Bertha says, "Leonard, I'm on my way to play for the Ripple girl's wedding," he looks at her as if he has never seen her before.

"You play an instrument?" He speaks politely. "That's nice." She wants to cry.

"See?" She shows him her *Organist's Companion*. It was his mother's.

"*Organist's Companion*," he reads. "My mother played the organ. And the piano, for the Grange meetings. You may have heard of my mother. Leone Hatch?

At least he is talking to her, but not the way he talks to Harry. He calls Harry by name.

"Say, Harry. You ought to see what I have in the garage." Then he'll forget what he has in the garage. But he remembers Harry's name.

Forty-five years married.

"You relax, Mom." Young Lenny's voice in the phone is so adult, almost old. "Let this couple do what they can. You put your feet up."

Sure, Bertha thinks. *Thirty years ago I'd have wanted that.*

Indiana is chopping scallions. She tosses handfuls of the little green and white rings in with onions and mushrooms that snap and crackle in olive oil. Cooking wasn't in the agreement as Bertha remembered it. Indiana just seems to be in the kitchen, cooking unfamiliar and strangely delicious foods that Leonard, amazingly, likes.

Harry and Indiana are doing what they can. That is the trouble.

———

Harry follows Leonard into the garage.

"Something I want to show you in here." Leonard pushes his cap forward to scratch the back of his head. "What do you think it is?"

Harry looks around. A bird's nest on a beam above the hood of the Chevrolet? A bicycle hung straight up by its front wheel? "License plates!" There are license plates hung like shingles on nails, floor to roof on the back wall.

Leonard takes his cap off. "That must be it. License plates. Some of them go way back, don't they?"

Harry points to the highest in the left hand column. "1921, Massachusetts. Black with white numbers."

"It was on a green Nash touring car. Charlie Barr's. He gave me that for a day's work in his vegetable garden."

Harry smiles. "You worked bent over in a man's garden one entire day? For a license plate?"

Leonard smiles too. And then he frowns. "I don't know. Did I?"

"Ahh." Harry touches Leonard's arm. "That sounds like home."

———

"Please, Mrs. Hatch. Think of it as amusing." Indiana has found Bertha at the kitchen table looking through the latest box of mail. Offers, magazines, catalogs. Ed McMahon's smile on a dozen envelopes.

"They laugh at him in the post office." Bertha wonders if she feels relief at telling Indiana. Or is it that the knot inside her has finally pulled too tight and broken apart like an old shoelace? "Well, they don't really laugh. They don't say anything. They go quiet. Kevin hands over the mail—he pretends not to notice. It's the politeness." She is talking to Indiana as if Indiana is in the family, or as if she is a friend. She stops.

Indiana sits opposite and takes a little tube from her apron pocket. She squeezes aloe lotion onto the dark rusty backs of both hands. While she rubs the lotion into her hands, her voice rocks and relaxes with the rhythm.

"I know old people. I know many old people. Mr. Hatch is amusing himself. He looks around—he sees not much fun for him in the world anymore, so he makes his own entertainment." Indiana points to the mail. "This is not so bad. Less expensive than an institution for old folks." She tells Bertha that this afternoon she saw Leonard trying to show Harry who he was in family pictures in the photograph albums. "He needs people here, strangers, so he can explain to us."

Bertha put the two albums out in the sun room. She found them on the spare room shelves, and she put them out hoping that she and Leonard would look through them. She wants to point out to him that he has always done things without help. The pictures are labeled in his handwriting: "Caught this myself—only needed help lifting it." "Built single-handed to get the boys where they belong, in the trees." As recently as last fall he wouldn't let Lenny help with the storm windows. "Come back in twenty years," he told Lenny. "I'll still be doing this, but I may need help with the ladder."

Bertha thinks, *He looked at our pictures with Harry, not with me.*

To Indiana she says, "I would never think of an institution."

———

Bertha is angry. At least once a day she feels anger start in her mouth, feels it clamp her teeth against each other and spill down her gullet like sour water. She feels her stomach clench itself and reject whatever tries to eat its way inside. She swells up. There are strangers here.

She hasn't learned to deal with this—she knows she should because it is like an illness—but there is so much new to deal with on the outside. She takes a deep breath and holds it while Mavis Purvis tells her before choir that her cousin Sylvia cured her husband's Alzheimer's, enough so he could go back to work by feeding him only raw vegetables and taking away his blood pressure pills.

Bertha has seen Horace Purvis behind his meat counter, and he looks ready to explode. He is the color of one of his London broils. But he does say, "Keeping cool, Bert? How's Leonard? I don't see him coming in after his bag of apples anymore."

Holding her breath helps to loosen the knot in her throat while she gets the choir wobbling through this week's anthem, but the pain from the knot in her stomach doesn't relax until the church is empty and she has played *"Bist du bei mir"* only for herself. She cannot stop crying, but the pain is better.

———

"'O'er.' An abbreviation for 'over.'" Harry's gold tooth picks up whatever morning light is in the kitchen. It makes a twinkle in his smile. "Over. This explains many things."

Harry is reading poetry from a text for his ESL class at Sherman Wire. The word *o'er* has given him trouble.

"I knew you will identify this word. I spoke to Indiana in bed; I said, 'Mrs. Hatch will explain this word.' And you have explained it!" He reads slowly, holding the book close to his nose. "'By the stream and o'er the mead.'"

"Meadow," she says. "A pasture."

"I find this poem most beautiful." He reaches and shakes Bertha's hand across the table.

"That's from Blake's 'The Lamb.'" Bertha isn't sure why his exuberance pleases her so. She leafs through the book, points. "Have you come across 'e'er'? Like this?"

He frowns at the page. Then he snaps his fingers. "I see! 'Ever.' This man is no fool—Blake. When he has no *v*, he uses what he has. Whate'er he has."

———

An aerogramme has come for Indiana and Harry, not the weekly stuffed envelope, but a thin blue letter folded on itself until it is its own envelope.

"Our daughter." Indiana kisses the return address and slowly unsticks the three sealed edges. She looks at Bertha with tear-slicked eyes. "She learns to write—you see?—like your grand-daughter. This makes me so happy."

Indiana reads; her oiled hand over her mouth glistens. "My Harry will rejoice, he will dance with joy."

Harry and Indiana have left a child behind. Bertha does not re-member talk of a child. How can they do such a thing? Then she remembers a child she has seen in magazines, a dirty little bare-foot girl in a torn dress, hungry. She must beg on the streets to feed her little brothers, her sick mother. Fifteen dollars a month will help. Bertha hasn't wondered before what Harry and Indiana do with their pay. She hasn't thought that they may not plan to stay in this country.

———

She wakes up before she knows she was asleep, thinking, *I have to get my dolls out of the rain, they're out under the forsythia bush getting wet in the rain.*

Bertha sees them as she left them. Beatrice, the big cloth doll whose painted smile has been kissed away to the yellow buckram beneath, sits in her little rocking chair at the dolls' tea table. The red in her checked dress will run all over her silky knitted legs and arms. Her hair will lose its glue and loosen and fall onto the wet ground. Raggedy Ann will fall onto her face on the table and take days on the line to dry. Mary, with the hard baby doll arms and legs, will lie on her back in the dirt, and her head will have water in it and her eyes won't open and close anymore unless Bertha pulls up or down on her eyelashes. In the lightning, Bertha sees leafy shadows on the dolls, on their table with its little teacups, on their faces.

The dolls will be angry at Bertha for leaving them in the thunder and lightning, angry that they will be different from what they were, and no matter how she scrubs and rubs at them, they will suddenly look old and tired. Bertha tries to remember why she didn't bring them inside.

———

Indiana licks her index finger and tests Bertha's iron with the spit. Fzz. "Mr. Hatch—he knows what he is doing." She tells Bertha how Harry took Leonard to the Miss Sherman Diner on Saturday for coffee and a doughnut. This is where Harry goes for his break from the wire mill, to listen to the conversations. People sitting at the counter repeat everything twice or three times, and Harry repeats everything to himself. "In this way his English improves itself," Indiana says to Bertha.

On Saturday, Harry pointed to a stool for Leonard to sit on. Then Leonard turned to a man in a Red Sox cap who glanced up from his *Enquirer.* "So. This weather. It is warm enough for you?"

The man shrugged.

"The waitress leaned across to speak into Harry's ear. "Is your friend all right?"

Leonard stirred his coffee and poured sugar into it. He tipped the sugar container so it poured a cascade that he didn't stop.

Harry tapped Leonard's shoulder. "You need that much sugar?"

"I don't know. How do I stop it coming out?"

Harry told Indiana about this. Indiana said, "Time for me to speak to Mrs. Hatch."

"He knows what he is doing," she repeats.

Bertha doesn't want to hear this. Indiana has said it several times lately. She wants to tell Indiana not to press Harry's perma-pressed shirt on the high setting, that it will melt into the iron. But Indiana turns the dial back and quickly irons a large white cotton handkerchief before the iron cools.

He doesn't hear me, doesn't see me. Bertha almost says it. But she can't say that aloud, doesn't want to think it.

"You think Mr. Hatch does not hear you and he does not recognize you." Indiana has folded the handkerchief as she ironed, finally ironing a small square and putting it aside. "Not true. Not true." She smiles, holds the shirt by its collar on the ironing board. "My Harry tells me this: Mr. Hatch is simply getting you ready, you know."

She looks across at Bertha, and Bertha thinks of drawings of African queens.

"He gets himself ready, prepares himself. Many people do not have this opportunity. My own father—pneumonia—no getting ready." Her voice fills the kitchen like a deep sweet perfume. "It will possibly take a long time. Possibly not a long time."

Bertha says, "That's not true. Leonard is losing touch, that's all." She has said it. She puts her pencil down. The shopping list says *potatoes* twice. "Losing touch."

"No, Mrs. Hatch. He is not losing touch. He is leaving."

Suddenly Bertha knows. She knows what Indiana knows. Her life with Leonard is over—Harry and Indiana have taken him over. No, that isn't true. She has been angry at Leonard for something that is not his fault. She is a fat stubborn old woman. Her girdle is much too tight, and all she wants to do is go upstairs and take it off and lie down.

"You go upstairs. Undress. Lie down." Indiana turns the shirt around. The room fills with the steamy medicinal smell of the hot Dacron. Outside, Harry has Leonard playing bocci. Two balls hit each other. Bertha hears Leonard's new silly high laugh.

Indiana says, "Go." She hums deep down in her chest as she irons.

Climbing the stairs, Bertha thinks, *Maybe I can get her for the choir. Maybe after.*

CARPENTRY

William Luvaas

Sinclair asked if I knew carpentry.

"I've built a fence or two."

"Plumb and level carpentry?"

"Not much," I admitted. "Guess I can swing a hammer."

He looked me over as if he doubted it. At the time I was cutting shingle bolts in the woods. I knew checker wedge, froe and sledge, could drive a pickup anywhere loggers had been, come rain or shit salad. But business was slow. "No one's building houses," Mr. Angellino down at the mill said. "Pretty soon no one will be cutting trees either, what with this spotted owl monkey business."

The owl didn't trouble me; I just needed steady work.

"You have experience, I have the contact," I told Sinclair. "We could partner up." What I didn't tell him was I only saw the job advertised on the A & P bulletin board. He might as well think it was a friend of mine.

The notice asked for skilled carpenters. A man named Norton answered the phone, said he'd bought land and a couple of cabins out on the ridge. He planned to build workshops, barns, a shooting range, and he wanted estimates. That's where Sinclair came in; I've never estimated a carpenter job in my life.

Sinclair was a burly man. His forearms didn't taper one bit at the wrist, covered in a pelt of rusty fuzz. My guess is he was nappy that way chin to toe if you cared to look. Bald up top of his big billiard ball head. One hot day, straddling rafters with our shirts off, I suggested he might transplant chest hair up to his chrome dome. Sinclair had neat white teeth when he smiled, tiny bird's eggs in a beard's nest of orange scruff.

"You think so?"

"Just joking, Phil."

He stared off at the tree line a second. Then, quick for a man his size, yanked the framing hammer from his belt and slammed the rafter I was straddling. Vibration hit my testicles like electric shock. I glowed up there maybe five minutes and was still climbing ladders bowlegged next day. Sinclair wasn't your joking kind of man.

"I'm offering fifty-fifty partnership," I told him.

"Lopsided for a novice who doesn't know piss-all about carpentry."

"My business contact."

"Seventy-thirty, I'll teach you how to pound a nail."

What choice did I have? Slow economy and a wife and daughter to support. I look at her as my daughter anyhow, though technically Annie is Jack Nicholson's—Becky's first husband's—kid. She calls him Jack Nicholson anyway. "He kept playing joker, so I took a walk," is how she tells it. Joker is a role I don't want any part of.

We shook hands and I told Sinclair, "The economy's got me in a bad place." He grinned. I knew right then there would be trouble. But it generally comes from a direction you never expected.

———

It was Becky's idea to move to the ranch. Truth is she was bored in town, kept talking about finding a job. Norton said we could live in the main cabin rent-free in exchange for fixing it up. Something I could do in my spare time, chance to try my hand at finish work. There was no electricity. We used hurricane lamps and kerosene wickers. The cabin was cozy, paneled in redwood. One glance at the place—charred redwood stumps big enough to build a house atop—amid thickets of huckleberry, manzanita, and coyote bush—and you knew there had been one hell of a devastation back when. Ten trees to a city block. It pleased me fine to be out of the logging business. Besides, the cabin was romantic. Every marriage needs a booster shot now and then to keep its immunity. We were into three years already without one.

We began with the workshop: ninety feet long and thirty feet wide, shed roof, loft, concrete slab floor where Norton could park his vintage cars. He had a vision of the place. Regular redwood stump resort. Though, myself, I couldn't see it.

After a week, Sinclair asked to stay out there with us while his wife and daughter were south visiting her mother. "It's not the cooking," he said; "I do half the cooking myself anyway. But I can't stand sitting down to dinner alone."

Wasn't what I had in mind: ol' vulture dome sharing my second honeymoon. But Becky felt sorry for him. Motherly sort of thing. Or maybe she liked the idea of company. That's when I began seeing another side to Sinclair, something you wouldn't expect of a man his size. Type who talks easier to women than to his own sex.

I noticed right off he liked talking to Becky. I just counted it to him missing his wife. Jealousy didn't cross my mind. Though Becky began wearing cutoffs and halter tops about the house. Nothing out of her normal range of apparel, just to the outside edge.

I overheard them laughing in the kitchen one morning as I came in from the can, Becky in whooping hoots that sounded like a schoolgirl's imitation of a jay. Sinclair's hands waved clownish at his sides, while Becky swabbed soap suds from his beard with a towel and he eyeballed down her nightgown.

"Little give, little take, it all comes out even in the end," he was saying.

"Not everyone sees it that way," Becky said.

"You scrubbing plates with your whiskers again, Phil?"

He looked up, startled. Becky waved me off, taking a final dab with the rag and leaning forward to peck his forehead. "We're doing just fine."

Sinclair gave me a slice of his teeth. Morning light accentuated gaps between them; could have been a savage stepped out of the *National Geographic,* which lay in stacks about the place.

"Just like racism or nuclear energy, it takes time for stupidity to die out," Sinclair said. "Right, Ace?"

"Depends on what stupidity you mean," I said.

Becky laughed her careless laugh. "I never did expect to hear a man call it 'stupid.'"

"What's stupid?"

"Well, isn't it?" Sinclair ignored me. "Where's it written men fix cars and women clean house and watch the kids? The Ten Commandments of sexual behavior, right?"

"What's sex got to do with it?"

"How about carpentry? I don't see many women out on the job with you guys." She slid eyes at him in a teasing way.

"Come join us! Hey! I subscribe to a full and universal equality between the sexes."

Seemed a funny word to me, "subscribe," like you might receive it in the mail. It didn't phase Becky.

"That's two of us, then." She cut eyes at me. "Not like some I might mention."

"Guess I walked sideways into a conversation where I don't belong," I said.

"The original sideways man. You ready to do some serious damage this morning, Ace?" Sinclair stood over the sink with suds dripping from his big hands.

"Like I said, my name's Jimmy, Jim, James. You might call your dog Ace." Something in the way my wife regarded me put me off. "So what's the joke? I guess my daughter will wish me proper good morning, anyhow."

Annette wandered in from the living room in her white pee-jays with the bucking broncos. That was a mistaken diagnosis. The doctor had said Becky was carrying a boy, and her aunt who worked in children's discount clothing sent boxes full of little boy outfits. The compromise was she wore boy to bed and about the house, out in public she went girl. She was sleep-grouchy and slanty-eyed, reaching for me to pick her up.

"Mornin' Tex." I kissed behind a sticky ear. Her hair smelled shampoo sweet.

"There's a earwig in my slipper," Annie grumped, wearing only the one.

Sinclair's mouth fell open; he wide-eyed her in funny-paper horror. "Get out the Raid!" He stumped toward her bedroom, Lux bottle at the ready, his thumb over the cap. Annette giggled and squirmed in my arms, afraid he'd tickle her. He did that plenty, pinning her on the sofa while she screamed laughter. I wanted to put a stop to that but Becky told me to piss off. Annie likes him, she said. He claimed she reminded him of his own daughter, and Annie was no end of curiosity about the girl.

I stepped out in front of him. "I'll take care of it, Phil."

"Hey, I've faced some pretty mean earwigs in my time."

"I'll bet. But it's my cabin here."

"So that's how it is." He straightened to full height.

Becky frowned. "Is this a fucking earwig killing contest?"

"Pincers. They got pincers." Annie wiggled for me to let her down.

"They crawl into your brain and eat your thoughts," Sinclair hissed. "Then your eyeballs."

"You're sick," Becky laughed.

We were crowding into Annie's doorway—two men and a small girl between—eyeballing for that slipper. I decided he wouldn't get there first. But I no more than grabbed the slipper when Sinclair snatched it away in his teeth and went romping into the living room, Annie chasing behind. They squealed laughter, while I searched under the rug for earwigs.

When I came out, Becky sat at the table thumbing through a *National Geographic*. Sun rays lit her bare crossed legs and accentuated old acne scars that marred a German Madonna sort of pretty: sharp features, eyes deep set, seeming judgmental when she didn't intend it. Some women would curse her hair—limp, all-purpose brown (auburn with sunlight shining through)—but Becky didn't give a damn about your cover girl image. Some men read recklessness into that. Maybe Sinclair. Slim-hipped and large busted, an inch taller than me myself. Chin uptilted to suggest she'd rather be someplace else.

"Dubrovnik, that's a funny name," she said.

"Yugoslavia—on the coast," said Sinclair.

"We got ourselves a regular Mr. Know It All."

"I went there on my honeymoon. Blue water, white beaches . . . it's dreamland." He sat on the couch, flushed with exertion.

"I guess you miss your wife," Becky said.

"Now that's true, the way he mopes about this cabin every night. You ought to sit down and write her a letter some time."

He didn't react like I expected, just stared at the *Geographic*, eyes gone flat, the window reflected in miniature off his domed skull. "I'm the kind of person, out of sight, out of mind. When I'm there I'm all there. When I'm not I'm not."

Becky shrugged. "It's a philosophy, I guess."

"There's all kinds of philosophies in this world."

"But I like to think somebody is thinking about me." Becky tittered in her give-a-damn way, staring into the magazine.

"Guess you got it made, then. Right, Ace?"

"What I wonder is I wonder what your wife thinks about it."

"Hey, out of sight . . . Who knows?" He laughed.

"Or your little girl."

I glanced at Annie rocking on the couch, twin ponytails bobbing, cheeks so smooth the light shined off of them. You didn't imagine she would inherit her mother's gravelly complexion. She burped a giggle when Sinclair looked down at her. "My little girl? Guess who's my little girl now! He went for her; she shrieked delight.

"Hold on right there," I snapped. "There's things we got to get straight here."

"Don't be an asshole," Becky said. "He misses his kid."

"He just sat here telling us he don't miss nobody."

"People have their own ways of feeling."

"You want my opinion, he doesn't give a shit about anybody in this world. Not one soul."

"It's like a bug up your ass, isn't it, Jimmy? Like maybe we'd be out here at all without him."

"It's *my* job, you understand? *My* cabin—"

"Don't say *her!* Don't you say Annie." Becky stabbed a finger at her daughter perched on Sinclair's stomach (like they were on the far side of a one-way mirror and couldn't hear us). She's one thing isn't yours. Don't say *me* neither."

"Balls is what I say." I started for the kitchen. "You want some eggs, Annie babe?"

Becky dropped the magazine, eyes wide as a trucker's headlights out on the freeway. "Major moment in the history of Albion Ridge everybody. King James enters the kitchen."

My wife leaned around the partition to gawk at me—surrounded by the raw taco smell of cupboards I was building out of redwood quarter-inch ply. Beautiful work. Although Sinclair predicted they would warp. Fuck him. Fuck 'em all. I was trying to remember how to scramble eggs.

———

"Is there anything you know how to do?" Sinclair frowned, holding the chisel he had copped from my tool belt up to sunlight, which glinted from gouges where I'd snagged nails. Sinclair turned it over in his meaty hands. Grisly-chested sonabitch. All morning as we decked the roof, he had whistled that Beatles' song "Mr. Nowhere Man." I used to like that song.

"Anything at all, Ace?"

I glanced down at Norton, below, inspecting the slab we had poured the day before. He seemed to like the way it tapered toward the drain in the center. I was hoping he hadn't overheard.

"You do good work," he called up.

"Top notch." Sinclair grinned over my chisel.

Norton squinted. Maybe he saw the roof already on, clear stories up, gun lathe and workbench in place. He wore a fringed buckskin shirt, blond hair tied back in a ponytail: last of the Mohicans sort of thing. Early American features and a week's beard stubble, like he couldn't find hot water to shave that morning or he stepped off the cover of *Rolling Stone*. Norton built muzzle-loading rifles from scratch, what time he could spare from buying stocks and Bentley cars. Still, somehow, he reminded me of myself: piece from here, piece there, like clothes swirled together in a dryer. I liked the impression he had of me as a journeyman carpenter. We were already discussing other building projects on the ranch. I didn't need Sinclair mucking that up.

I reached for the chisel. "There's a sharp one in my tool box."

"Use it! Check this out," he called to Norton, shying the chisel end over end. It hit and skittered across clay-pack fifty feet below.

"Why'd you do that?" I whispered.

"A man ought to know who's working for him."

Norton picked it up and ran a thumb along the blade with the casual affection of a man who knows tools.

"Gouged it."

"Gouged already." Sinclair aimed his hammer butt at me.

Norton shrugged. "I have a grinding wheel in town. I'll re-edge it and bring it out next time I come."

"Appreciate that," I said.

There's two kinds of men. One takes what comes his way and figures, I can live with it. The other never finds enough fault to satisfy his craving. Norton was the first kind, Sinclair the second. Me, I fit somewhere between.

At noon Becky brought out sandwiches, her legs exposed X-ray fashion beneath a rayon see-through skirt. Me thinking: it's a morning done, I'll just finish up the sheet of ply I'm tacking down and eat lunch. Annette peeking at me over the top rung of the ladder across the decking already in place.

"Don't you fall," Becky warned her.

Maybe it was Norton and Becky looking on below made me nervous. Or the skirt. Or Sinclair grinning down from the sloping roof like a sailor on a rocking ship, one knee bent, the other leg extended, hands on hips. My first nail caught thin air beside a rafter. Sinclair saw the ply dimple but not pull down.

"Strike one," he shouted. "Clean miss."

He handed me a second nail.

I'll admit I was angry. What I had in mind: it's his chrome dome glinting in the sunlight, instead of an inferior 8d Japanese galvanized. I'd often fantasized that Easter egg cracking under impact of twenty ounces of case-hardened steel swung full bore. Nervous about fudging that second nail, I tapped it half-ass instead of bearing down.

"Bent it!" Sinclair flung his big head off toward the trees like an umpire. Plain gleeful. "How many times have I told you: drive a nail decisively or you'll bend it."

"Daddy bent the nail," Annette reported to them below.

"I know, honey. We saw."

"Federal fucking case."

I looked from ol' God in Heaven to Annie's worried face, settling finally on Norton. A vagueness to his eyes; like the family money, you didn't know what was behind it.

"Making him nervous," he mumbled.

I let the froth settle in my gut. "Hey, I guess I can drive a nail. OK! All right?"

Sinclair crossed his arms, lip pulling like cold putty away from teeth. "Lunch is waiting, Ace."

I didn't even see the hammer go. Just a quick snap off the wrist. What I saw was right off "The Simpsons" on TV. Sinclair's eyes widened, he staggered back, big moon head bunching on the neck then snapping forward as the hammer cracked off his forehead in an explosion of blood. His hands jerked upward trying to get there. But he went down before they could, slamming dead weight on decking with the dull terrible thud of a heavyweight going down on the canvas. The roof trembled for seconds after.

I can't say it surprised me. Although I never hit anyone with a hammer before. But surprises started coming in fast.

After a minute—Annette screaming bloody murder, me thinking him a goner with his skull broke and my whole sorry life flashing out ahead of me like it was me dying instead of him, and who knows what all happening below—Sinclair raised his head from the deck. His face red as a July Fourth raspberry down the roof angle.

"Mother of Jesus! I thought you killed me."

"Holy shit, Phil, I'm sorry. I didn't—"

"Don't worry about it." Closing his eyes, small teeth clenched together like a double string of costume pearls, he touched a hand to his forehead. It came away bloody.

I helped him sit up.

"Is he dead?" Becky asked in crackly voice below. I realized she couldn't see us. "Jimmy . . . you killed him?"

"He's dead, Mommy," Annette screamed. "Phil is all bloody. Daddy killed him with the hammer."

"Hushup," I snapped.

"I have a tendency to faint at the sight of blood," Sinclair mumbled, copper green creeping about his jawline. He wiped the bloody hand on his pants in a prissy way, not looking at it. I pulled my T-shirt off and pressed it to the wound to staunch the bleeding.

"Thanks." He seemed to mean it.

"Jimmy, what's happening up there?"

"Jim?" echoed Norton.

All the commotion seemed uncalled for: Annie shrieking he's dead over and over. While up top Sinclair and I had begun negotiations on how to get him down. He gritted his teeth and gripped my arm, beard clotted with jellied blood dribbling down his cheeks. There was power there, a small kernel of hate back in his eyes to tell me he could break my neck any time he's ready.

Surprise number two: Down at the hospital emergency where we took him to stitch the wound, we learned Sinclair's skull wasn't broke, just a mild concussion.

Number three. Norton didn't fire me. Only wanted a guarantee I'd stop throwing hammers. No problem.

———

Unable to negotiate ladders, Sinclair hung out below while I finished the roof—slipping me the good word on the q.t. when I fucked up so as not to embarrass me before Norton. Seems like we had reached an understanding. Blood will do that. Annie wouldn't let me touch her since the hammer business, but Becky assured me she would get over it. Nights when we put her to bed she asked, "Is Phil dead, Mommy?"

"Don't be silly. He's right out sitting in the living room," Becky told her. But Annette regarded me like she wasn't sure.

We were talking one evening over a beer, Phil and me, Becky making a cheery rattle of dishes in the sink and Annie in bed. Going over plans for the pole barn I intended to build, using redwood saplings growing on the property.

"For footers I'll dig holes and plant them in concrete."

"Termite resistant, dry rot resistant, rust resistant." Phil pointed to the south side of the stall area. "I'd do Dutch door for manure removal. Like the door to the tack room."

"Beautiful. I'm thinking cedar siding."

"It's cheaper. Unless Norton wants to take down trees."

"Let them stand. He's a rich man."

"Save a redwood, right?"

Sinclair no longer complained of headaches and dizzy spells. In their place had come a faraway gleam in his eye like he had travel on his mind.

Becky came in to sponge the table, leaning down far enough you could see she didn't wear a bra. Taunting is how it struck me.

Like there was something unsettled and she wanted to see it done. Sinclair watched her dark braid swing like a pendulum between beer bottles, gone quiet. Suddenly he reached out and imprisoned the scrubbing hand. All three of us stared at his sunburnt fingers, fat as sausages, atop Becky's pale slender ones. Me thinking: let him make his move, I made mine. Becky bug-eyeing flesh on Phil's forehead, puckered in a wicked "Y" held together by eight metal staples. Tittering as she does when she's nervous.

But it wasn't the hand Sinclair wanted, only the sponge. He extracted it across the web of her thumb and wiped the table himself.

"Male talk here," he said.

"B.F.D." Her eyes scalded him. Then me.

She turned up the radio. Throwing a hip into the music, skirt clinging to her legs in the lamplight. Bumps and grinds, halter strap slipped down one shoulder, lips miming words of a song. Phil watched sullenly, rolling the beer bottle in his hands.

"My old lady didn't go south to visit her mother," he said. "She left me. She's down in Frisco with her sister."

"Jesus, Phil! I didn't know. Your kid?"

"Your wife knows. I told her the morning you cold-cocked me."

"Really, I didn't."

"That's why I'm here. Trying to hold it together."

"Jes'christ, I nearly took you out. Nothing personal."

"Sure it was. Hey, I was an asshole. I watched it happening and told myself, 'Phil, you're an A-hole.' Didn't matter. I was trying to hit the pavement standing. You woke me up. I appreciate that." Touching the stapled Y on his forehead to make sure he was awake. In the lamp light, the deep-in-the-eye hatred had softened.

It all fell into place then: the way he'd been with Annie—everything. We fell silent then and watched Becky: slit-eyed, nostrils flaring like the gaping eye sockets of a trout caught in a weir. I wanted to call her a filthy name, wanted to slap her, let her know she had it wrong. *I'm right here*, she seemed to mock as she danced, *right out here in the open*.

"Sometimes you don't know what's living in your own house," Phil muttered, "until it stands up and announces itself." He leapt up like someone thumped him on the shoulder, stumbling over a chair toward her. For a moment I wasn't certain: his teeth clenched, Becky's eyes startled wide. Skirt frozen like ivy twining up her legs. Then he threw his pelvis at her in an awkward, slew-footed mock dance, swiveling on the ball joints of his hips like a fat man in an aerobics class. Clapping hands over his head and hooting, forehead staples reflecting lamp light. Becky boogieing around him. Me whooping. Like it had all gone and done and spent itself in us, leaving behind crackling glass underfoot, like a ballroom floor after revelers have gone home.

Coyote Comes Calling

Linda Watanabe McFerrin

Sam, a.k.a. Samantha Iphigenia Darwin, d.b.a. Sam's Wampum Wigwam, Main Street, Sedona, Arizona, was having a coyote week. She hadn't realized this yet. What she did know was this: certain things were going wrong.

It started when she dumped a bottle of the wrong color hair dye on her head. Her amber locks turned brassy blonde. Then she had a flat tire on the way back from Scottsdale, where she'd gone to her doctor. Her visit, precipitated by the sudden hyperextension of her abdomen, ended in her gynecologist's assessment that Sam had either a large fibrous tumor or she was pregnant. They'd know for sure in a couple of days. At the time of this pronouncement, Sam's legs were spread, her feet up in the pink pot holder-protected stirrups.

"I don't know, Sam," her doctor, Sally, observed, "I fear it's a fibroid tumor."

"What's that? Is it cancer?"

"Well, no. But, if it is a fibrous tumor, we'll have to remove it."

"Shit," Sam said, letting out a low whistle.

"On the other hand, you could be pregnant."

"What?" Sam asked, incredulous, fearing a pregnancy almost as much as a tumor. "What will I do with a baby? I'm not even married."

"You can still have a baby, Sam."

"That's not what I mean, Sally. It's just not in my reality. Besides, that would mean the baby was Daryl's."

"What's wrong with that?"

"Doc, Sally, we're talking Daryl. You know, Mr. Noncommitment. Fly Boy. Permanent Puer. It's like saying Peter Pan is the Dad. It's that serious."

"It's not that bad, Sam. Anyway, we'll know in two days."

"We'll know in two days." That's what Sam was thinking about when a piece of shrapnel jumped up off the road and speared her

209

sidewall. She heard the hissing first, like a snake. She rolled down the window and listened. The snake was following her. Naturally, she didn't have a jack, at least, not one that worked. It was that kind of week. She had a spare tire, but she'd broken the jack months ago, lost a part of it when she helped Cynthia, her best friend in the world, fix a flat tire in the Coffee Pot parking lot. She kept telling herself to replace it. She hadn't, and now she was "paying the price of procrastination," as her mother would have said.

Fortunately, she was close to Sedona and home when the tire started to go flat. It shouldn't have been hard to flag down some help. However, as luck would have it, her realization of the equipment shortfall corresponded with a certain unpleasant coincidence. At the exact moment that she realized that the jack was not going to work, a certain primer-brown pickup truck appeared on the shaky horizon. It quivered toward her, like a mirage. It was the worst thing that could have possibly happened. It was Daryl's truck.

"Your savior again," Daryl said with a wide grin as he swung his long legs out of the truck. Beau, his obedient hound, jumped out too.

Just what she did not want to hear. But, being in something of a bind, Sam let him change her tire. Sam hated herself for letting him do it. She was sullen when she arrived at her store, Sam's Wampum Wigwam, Main Street, Sedona, and listened to the messages on her machine.

Erly, her helper, had already been in that morning. She had stacked the packages neatly on the counter. Sam was grateful for Erly. Erly was her only support. She was a tough little woman, originally from New York. But, she was generous, dependable, and a darn hard worker.

You've got to see beyond the surface, Sam reminded herself, standing in the midst of the roomful of trading beads, prayer feathers, and amulets.

"Erly is a perfect example of squirrel energy," Sam thought, stringing totems.

Sam needed a little time with her thoughts. It had been a terrible morning. This baby. What in heaven's name was she going to do? An abortion, probably. Sam couldn't have a baby. She couldn't let an infant into her life. It was hard enough washing her own hair, feeding herself every day. Getting from one place to another was a perpetual challenge. She had trouble staying balanced and managing her own life. How could she do it for two?

The shop door opened. This was a great surprise. It was March, and Sam's Wampum Wigwam survived mainly on mail order at this time of the year. Sam immediately broke into a glossy cover model smile because it was David, her pal, and the man she'd recently decided she'd most like to go to bed with. The thought of her swollen belly ragged at her.

"Hey David," she said cheerfully. "I thought you were in Phoenix this week. What's going on?"

"Oh, I came back early," David said in his soft purr of a voice. David had the kind of voice that could coax eggs out of a rooster.

"Sam," David said, "I have a favor to ask."

"Sure," said Sam, "Anything. What'll it be?"

"Well," he said, suddenly shy (Sam found this endearing), "I wonder if I could get Cynthia's number from you. I'm thinking of asking her out."

Sam felt as though she'd been kicked by a mule in the solar plexus, right over that little tumor.

"Yeah, sure," she heard herself say quickly, to hide her surprise. "I'll give you her number. Here it is."

She wrote down the number and handed it to him.

She was amazed that her hands weren't shaking. She felt reasonable, even calm. She suspected she was in some kind of shock. Sam saw herself standing on top of Apache Leap. Below her, Cynthia and David were putting around on the green of the world's most obnoxiously situated golf course. It was built over an Indian burial ground. Sam hated that golf course. She, Sam, alias Wile E. Coyote, was rolling a boulder to the edge of the precipice. She was going to drop it on the spoony-eyed couple below. She imagined it squashing them both. Then a breeze came out of nowhere, ruffling her hair. It was the "Wind of Karma."

"That boulder," it said, "is going to bounce like a superball. It is going to hit the golf course lighter than angel food cake and bounce back on you with the force of a Peterbilt truck. Don't do it Sam."

"Thanks, Sam," David was saying. He'd completed his morning mission. He had Cynthia's phone number. He already had one leg out the door. "By the way, I don't know what you've done with your hair, but it looks great."

"Tasteless goon," Sam thought, as he left. But she knew that if he asked her to go out, she'd say "yes." Sam felt like she'd taken a ride in the spin cycle.

"What a rotten day," she thought miserably. "What else could go wrong?"

That's when she noticed the squashed package and opened it. She hadn't even seen it before. It was from Bella, the Italian bead

manufacturer. Her Venetian trading beads—she'd been waiting for
them for months. She needed them to fill one of her store's largest
orders. She had a very bad feeling about this. She opened the
package. It was filled with glittering powder—sea blue, gold, bottle green—beads ground to dust. On the package wrapper was a
note: "This package was damaged in transit. Please file a claim."

There are times when it all gets to be too much for you and you
just have to close up shop. This was one of those times. Sam could
feel a couple of big fat cow tears running down the sides of her nose.

"That does it," she said.

She turned out the lights and flipped over the sign on the door
to read "closed."

Sam didn't want to see anyone. Not Cynthia, Daryl, Erly or
David. She wanted to be alone. She jumped into her car and
headed for home. That's when she saw him, standing at the side
of the road. The mangy, yellow-eyed dog; the trickster; the hound
of the desert; her new pal—Wile E. Coyote. The coyote was
standing there, mouth pulled back in a panting grin. Its big yellow
eyes connected with hers—full of promise, full of mischief, full of
sorrow—and suddenly it let out a quick little yelp. Actually, it was
more like a greeting. That is when Sam realized that she was having a coyote week.

"OK, little brother," she said to the animal. "I get it. I'm out of
control. Nothing I can do."

Sam understood totems. She knew that an armadillo at the side
of the road meant that she wasn't watching her boundaries, that
when mountain lions appear it was time to take a leadership role.
She knew that a lynx meant secrets, a fox camouflage, and she
knew that the best posture during a coyote week was what she
called "baby in a car crash." You had to go limp and unresisting.
You had to relax or you'd really get hurt.

So, Sam took the cosmic advice. She drove to the bakery and
picked up a bag of warm chocolate chip cookies. Then, she
stopped by her house and picked up some tai stick to roll more
than a couple of joints and headed for Cathedral Rock, a powerful
feminine vortex, a place on the high red rocks of Sedona where
the energy collects and swirls. She climbed until she felt as though
she were sitting on top of the world. She could see the Coffee Pot
restaurant, HO-scaled in the canyon, like part of a train set. The
long line of hoodoos, spires, and minarets of sandstone that
crawled along the horizon made her think of the skyline of an eastern empire.

"Dr. Seuss," she thought. "It looks like a Dr. Seuss landscape."

Sam sat cross-legged on the ground. She could feel the earth humming up under her skirt. She meditated, smoked a joint, meditated some more, and ate all of the chocolate chip cookies. She was thinking of Daryl, of babies, of abortion.

"Everything is a risk," she thought. "None of us is ever really in control. It's all an illusion."

She imagined a cute little cherub that looked just like her—the same amber hair, Daryl's blue eyes. "How could I possibly prefer a tumor to that?" she wondered. "I must be out of my mind." It was true that a baby might send her over the edge, but she was a capable woman. She ran her own business. Daryl or not, she could make it work.

The day slipped out from under her. Evening bore down. It got dark and cold. Sam made an anthill of corn meal in front of her. She threw a pinch of it over her shoulder: corn meal offering. With a pocket knife, she ripped open one corner of her down vest: prayer feather offering. She lit the end of a smudge stick, a bundle of herbs tied together with string, and waved it around, letting the sage perfume the air. With the same match, she lit another one of the joints and took a long slow drag. The night snuggled in around her. The stars moved in a little bit closer.

"Daryl," she thought, "is not such a bad guy." Too bad he was constantly taking her out where the water was high or the road was too narrow. Careless Daryl generally found some way to expose the people around him to danger. But he did always seem to come through. "Her savior," he'd said. That was a laugh. He was more like her nemesis.

Sam took another drag from her joint, counting coup—the gains and the losses. The problems came tumbling in. The feather-light vest down was lifting and drifting around her in some kind of whirlpool of wind. It looked like snow flurries. She leaned back on her elbows and watched it. She watched the stars come sliding closer, between the down, like little souls settling on earth, filling angel-fluff—like babies.

The hard red Sedona rock was digging into the small of her back. The night air was kissing her cheeks. She was happy and sad at the same time. How weird the world was. How beautiful. How full of problems. At some point, you just had to relax. You had to trust someone, even if it was only yourself. That's exactly what she was thinking when the tumor kicked her. She swore that it did. It shocked her. It was a swift kick in her gut, that was certain. She even let out a moan. Somewhere in the cool desert night, the coyotes heard her moan and they answered. First one, then another, in a great chain of song until the night was filled with coyote music. Sam was almost moved to tears by the magic of it. Then the tumor kicked her again, and she let out a war hoop, a laugh and a big coyote howl.

"Praise the Lord. Hell's bells," Sam shouted in a spontaneous evangelistic frenzy, embracing the possibilities. This coyote week could turn into a coyote life.

Meantime, all around her, the dogs were singing.

Sybil and the Soft Red Rock

Dara Anastasia Moskowitz

A red round suitcase lay on the kitchen table, open, a vinyl oyster housing pearls of underwear and socks on a meaty belly of sweaters and denim. Young Sybil Carpenter and her mother Lillian sat alongside their breakfasts, enjoying the cozy space between sleep and the action of the day.

"Did you remember socks?" asked Lillian. She spoke through the fragrant bowl of her coffee cup, into which her face was sunk.

"Yes," said Sybil, stirring her cereal.

"An extra sweater?"

"Yes."

"Toothbrush?" Lillian gazed out at the yard and watched a sparrow, lit blue by the dawn twilight, dip into the birdbath. "Toothpaste?"

"Mom!" complained Sybil. "Yes. Yes twice."

"Pajamas?" asked Lillian.

"But of course," Sybil grimaced. "Pink terry ones. With feet. Yet I couldn't find any extra diapers—I scoured the nursery without success."

"Oh hush," said Lillian, and drank with deep attention from her cup. "I don't remember anyone mentioning subsidized debauchery in your curriculum. Why wasn't I informed?"

"You signed a permission slip weeks ago."

"Permission . . ." mused Lillian, to her cup.

"Did I tell you?" asked Sybil, crossing the kitchen to retrieve toast that had popped from a chrome toaster. "For our final project we spend a whole week in an opium den."

Lillian stood and massaged her neck with her long white hands. "Ha," she murmured. "'Drop her on her head in infancy,' they said. 'You'll never regret it,' they said. 'No,' said I. 'I want a smart one. She'll be a credit to me in my old age.'" Lillian left the kitchen, abandoning Sybil to her breakfast.

The first rays of sun ran through the old yew trees to the back-yard, dotting chairs and sparrows with a fine spray of light. Sybil's pale chin bobbed between upturned wings of perfectly curled hair. She had been up long before dawn, preparing; her wet plum fingernails gave her a volatile air. Sybil Carpenter was fourteen, had milk chocolate colored hair, eyes that were a hazel like moss growing on gold, cheeks doughy with the promise of another growth spurt, and a bedroom where half-finished books were stacked knee high.

Lillian returned, dressed in a brown suit, carrying a fist-sized cardboard box. "I want you to take these," she said, setting the box of condoms on the table beside her daughter.

Sybil blushed scarlet and dropped her spoon on the floor. It clattered off between the table's thick claw feet.

"Now I'm not saying you should use them," said Lillian, "far from it. But I know how hard it is for people your age to buy any-thing like this—"

"No," said Sybil shaking her head, her curls flopping like birds. "Absolutely not. Never."

"Syb, I'd feel much better if I knew that you and your friends at least had recourse to protection—"

Sybil recoiled from the table. "What if someone found it? I'd be humiliated. Mortified. Destroyed." She shuddered beside the rear window.

"A stitch in time, Syb," said Lillian, and poured herself fresh coffee.

"I'll feel like Hester Prynne," said Sybil, darkly, pressing her hands to her burning cheeks. She deeply felt the impossibility of both arguing with her mother and making it to school on time.

"We'll wrap it up in a paper bag," concluded Lillian. She took a bag from a drawer, placed the box of condoms in it, secured it with a piece of tape, and tucked the package into the heart of Sybil's suitcase.

"Talk about debauchery," protested Sybil, petulantly dumping the last of her cereal in the sink. "It's a geology field trip, not an orgy. No one has ever been so *inflicted* with parents."

———

At school, Sybil waited alone on the bus for the rest of her class. She was trusted by teachers, principals, and adults generally; she had answers for their questions, questions for their answers, and shored up their faith in youth. Sybil reapplied her lipstick, using the chrome of the window frame as a mirror, and tried to imagine the etiquette between fourteen year olds sent down to wait in buses and surly looking bus drivers. Her dilemma was relieved when the driver went outside to smoke.

Sybil held the bus while Ms. Thompson awaited the arrival of Tory Munro: dashing reprobate, habitual late comer, doe-eyed re-arranger of facts, and subject of many of Sybil's more earthy day-dreams. Sybil spied Ms. Thompson leading Tory down the hill to the bus, the rest of the class trailing behind them in a slow and staggering string. Tory walked beside Ms. Thompson: raven haired, bronze jawed, lean muscled, kicking up dust storms with his authority-mocking feet.

Sybil carefully smoothed the heaven-pointing wings of her hair, slipped her lipstick into her pocket, slumped in her seat, and assumed an expression of absolute indifference. Ms. Thompson entered the bus: determined, cheerful. Tory had somehow escaped her watch, and crouched on the school lawn with the bus driver, smoking.

"Well," Ms. Thompson announced. "All accounted for. Within fifteen minutes of scheduled departure. That's good enough for anybody." She deposited her luggage on a front seat. "Sybil, we have assigned partners for the trip, for the field project. You're with Tory."

Sybil's heart rose up in her chest. "Oh," she said, turned her head toward the peaceful street, and blushed. She had never spo-ken to Tory before.

The rest of the class filed through the bus, shuffling and whispering.

Sybil felt a pressure on the seat beside her, and turned to find a dusty, heart-stopping shoe. She traced it to a tall boy with slipping, brandy-colored eyes and a pout.

"Hi," he said, removing his baseball cap, his black hair a slightly damp tousle.

"Hi," squeaked Sybil. She returned to the window, bumped her shoulder against the windowpane, and shaded her eyes with one hand, overwhelmed with the smell of smoke that flowed from him.

———

The bus swooped through the bright rag pile of the prairie; yellow heaps of corn, gray ponds of water, and emerald patches of hopeful vegetation flew by as Sybil failed to find something clever to say. The sun had left the pale horizon for the blinding summit of the sky by the time Sybil removed her hands from her eyes, finding Tory fast asleep beside her. She spied on him using the rearview mirror above the driver. He looked like a faun, a tulip, a funnel to some unknown bliss. Sybil inventoried her lipstick and curls again and again as the farms slipped by, unnoticed by the dozing, fabulous boy beside her.

———

He awoke in the bleakest stretch of farmland, rolling his shoulders and shaking his head. Sybil watched this in the mirror, pretending to study the bleached strip of road. She was newly, strongly aware of air echoing in her ears; her head seemed to have changed into a giant whelk shell. She pressed one hand to her ear to see if that would stop the empty rushing. It didn't. She set her hand on the black denim arch of her lap, and was fascinated by the blue net of veins at her wrist, which stood out strongly, as they never had before.

"I really suck at science," whispered a husky voice in her ear.

Sybil turned to find Tory awake, languid and smiling, leaning toward her. She blushed passionately.

"I'm sorry," he said, leaning forward, a fountain of shining hair spilling over his knees. He peeked up through it. "I shouldn't say 'sucks.' I also suck at watching my language." He rustled his hands through his hair, exposing his bare neck.

"Oh no—" said Sybil, mesmerized by the glimpse of the hidden hills of vertebrae. She returned to the window, and dwelt on the black patches of newly turned fields she found through there. The fields were crested with empty, lacy corn cribs. She touched her ear, deafened by the rushing she heard.

"I was just daydreaming," she managed.

"About what?" he asked, leaning against the seat in front of them, fixing the pools of his eyes upon her.

"Nothing," said Sybil, still blushing, the freckles on her cheeks like gray ashes in a campfire. She returned to the window, which gave her green trees beside a dry creek.

"No, what? You can tell me," Tory said, nudging her knee with his. "You can tell me all your secrets. They'll be safe with me."

Sybil studied the scenery carefully and wiped her palm on her knee. "I don't think you're supposed to ask that of women who aren't your wife," she said, formally, to the glass. She peeked at him through his reflection in the chrome window frame.

"That's another thing I suck at, manners and everything. Etiquette." Tory smiled, shifting in his seat so his hair glinted. "Besides, I can't wait that long to find out what makes women turn so red."

"Great—" began Sybil, but stopped, cut off by the ocean in her ears.

"What?" he nudged her knee again with his.

"Great things come to those who wait," Sybil told the landscape.

"I suck at waiting too," said Tory. He put his baseball cap on, low over his eyes, and returned to sleep.

Sybil spent the duration of the trip marveling over Tory, recounting their exchange, and spying on him through the driver's mirror. The mottled landscape flashed by, like a quilt snapped and settling over a bed, but Sybil hardly saw it.

————

The morning lost, the class staggered free from the bus in front of the Pipestone Ranger Station, groggy, rubbing their eyes and coughing in the dry wind.

Ms. Thompson cleared her throat and stood on tip toes. "Welcome to the site of one of the richest veins of pipestone in the world! Also, one of the richest, starkest examples of cultural variation in land use!"

Ms. Thompson was a daydreaming young teacher who intended to touch her students with the ethics, politics, and soul of land composition and use. Unfortunately, she generally succeeded only in seeming eccentric and easily excitable. Her brown hair was bobbed, and flew around wildly in the Pipestone wind.

"You've read all about it, now here it is," she said.

The Cultural and Physical Geology class seemed unimpressed, hooking their arms over their heads to keep their hair from blowing. The class, which was a ghetto for bored senior girls who did badly in science, had Tory as its only boy and Sybil as its only freshman. She had been asked to take the class by her principal, as an experiment, and decided to stay when she found Tory there. Sybil listened to Ms. Thompson politely.

Tory sidled up behind Sybil. "Thrills," he whispered into her ear. "Wake me up when she gets to the part about lunch."

Sybil turned slowly toward him, and smiled, but quickly covered her smile with her hand, not wanting to seem rude to Ms. Thompson.

"I knew you could smile," Tory said. "Don't hide it. It's bad luck."

Sybil turned away, tilting her head so a sheet of hair hid her blush.

"You have half an hour free." Ms. Thompson held up her wristwatch. "Meet at twelve-thirty in the lecture room. It's through those doors—" she pointed, "the first door on the right. Twelve-thirty."

Tory disappeared, the rest of the class huddled off en masse to smoke, complain, squeal, lunch, and gossip, and Sybil retreated to have her lunch alone, daydreaming.

A tall, deeply tanned ranger delivered a lecture and distributed diagrams of rock strata, and showed the class a filmstrip about the legend of White Buffalo Calf Woman. Sybil looped "pipestone= ancestors' blood" in dizzy script in her notebook, and set mirrored sunglasses on her desk to try to catch sight of Tory, who slumped in the back of the room. Ms. Thompson sent the class off with sturdy cameras to photograph rock formations.

———

Sybil clutched her camera and handouts, and searched for Tory. Sioux quartzite broke through the flat prairie, in shelves and chimneys of red, glittering rock. The quartzite lay over clayey pipestone, a soft heart buried behind hard ribs.

She had given up on her carefully planned curls, and had tucked her hair under a floppy black cap. Tory did not appear. Sybil watched the other pairs of girls trail off into the belly of the park, and sat down, cross-legged, to wait. Finally, he came staggering around the corner of the building, his black hair devilish in the wind. He seemed a radiant, indifferent blade in the wind. Sybil touched her ear again, hearing nothing but the empty rushing shell.

"Heavens," she said quietly.

Tory approached her, smiling. "Howdy, partner. Done yet?"

"No," said Sybil, looking up at him, holding a hand cupped over her ear. Grass rippled in gold waves in the prairie, spirals eddying through the fields like the trace of a roving animal.

"Something wrong with your ear?" he asked.

She blushed and drew her hand away. "No. I can't hear very well today." She stood up.

"I hope you heard whatever they said in there," said Tory, jerking his head toward the park building. "Because I was definitely not listening."

"I did," said Sybil, squinting into the wind. "We're supposed to—"

Tory held up a hand in protest. "I didn't hear it on purpose. It bores me. I will parasite off your planning, intelligence, and talent. As is my talent." He executed a mocking half bow. "But I did notice that everyone went down there," he pointed toward the path, "so let's definitely not."

"All right," agreed Sybil. "We can go backwards. We'll start this way."

They headed toward the end of the path, through the high golden grasses. Sybil fell behind, her eyes wide, her heart racing. As they entered a patch of scrubby pine forest Sybil sprinted to catch up with Tory.

"My favorite parasite is the lamprey," she offered. "What's yours?"

"What?" He smoothed his sleek black hair away from his eyes.

"A lamprey. It's a sort of fish that sucks itself on to sharks and rides around with them. You would think that an orchid would be my favorite parasite, because they can be so beautiful, although they can be quite temperamental, and some orchids cost thousands of dollars." Sybil squinted up at him. "Of course, some orchids can be plain also. My grandmother collects orchids, but only the common sort of showy ones. I prefer lampreys."

They walked a dirt trail, buffeted by the wind.

"They ride on sharks? Sitting?" asked Torey.

"No. They have sharp teeth, and they bore into sharks, into their stomachs, I think, and drink their blood. Lampreys are quite brave, I think, to annoy something as menacing as a shark. They're also kind of voyeuristic, because they get right in the thick of things, bloody kills and feeding frenzies and all, and they see the murder and eat the fruit of the shark's violent labors. But they don't themselves risk anything. Like when you or I watch film footage from a war—" Sybil broke off, suddenly self-conscious. She checked the rim of her hat with her fingers, to see whether her hair was escaping. "I think the wind is making my cheeks blush," she said. "So what's your favorite parasite?"

"I don't know," said Tory. The wind bedeviled Sybil, making her eyes water, making her feel ungainly, but it seemed to only accentuate Tory's sleekness. He was like a seal in choppy seas, playful, narrow eyed, shining.

"Maybe fleas," he said.

"Why fleas?"

"I don't know. Because they go in circuses, I guess."

"I always wondered about that," said Sybil. "What do fleas in circuses eat? Do they go onto a dog at the end of the show, or onto their trainer, or what? I've never even seen a flea circus. I wonder if fleas are even parasites. They might be just carnivores. Or what's the difference anyway? Do cows consider us parasites?"

They passed through the park, Sybil prattling, Tory gliding, willowy in the high grass. Sybil photographed, and carefully annotated her handouts while Tory cut his eyes at Sybil, laughing easily, his lips curling. Hours sank away.

Sybil was crouched in a shadow at the top of the bluff, photographing orange and green lichen, while Tory stood at the edge of the bluff, his hand shading his eyes like an Indian scout surveying the land.

"Damn," he said.

"What?" Sybil stood up.

"Here comes Katrina." He kicked a rock off the bluff. "Katrina. My old girlfriend. She's a real pain lately." He jammed his hands into his pockets. "Come here a minute."

Sybil approached, squinting over the bluff toward Katrina's white form.

"She's going to want to have a scene." Tory kicked another rock for emphasis. "If it takes more than five minutes will you pretend to sprain your ankle or something?" He smiled at her, leaning close in.

"Sprain my ankle?" echoed Sybil.

"Or have a heart attack or see a snake. Something." He took her two arms in his hands, and pulled her toward him. "Katrina reminds me of a '62 Volvo I used to have. A beautiful ride, but a pain in the ass. Expensive and always in the shop. Took me years to get rid of that damn thing. Thank God the engine block cracked or I'd have it still."

Sybil hardly heard him through the ocean in her ears, stirred by his nearness and the pressure on her arms.

"Tor-ey!" A high voice split the air. "Tor-ey!"

Katrina stamped down the path, yelling, the pink O of her mouth a fiery knot on an otherwise icy silhouette. Katrina was a frosty girl: platinum hair, lake gray eyes, and petal thin, translucent skin. Sybil found her awesome. Every day she held court after school, leaning on her white convertible, surrounded by admirers, a diffident princess. Katrina wore a white cashmere sweater, white pants, and low, white suede heels. Tory released Sybil.

"Hi," he called down the bluff.

"Where have you been?" she yelled, her hands on her hips. "I've been looking everywhere for you."

"Rocks wait for no man," he called down to her. "There's great rocks up here."

"I need to talk to you," she demanded.

"Go ahead," he yelled.

"In private," she stamped her pretty foot on the dirt path.

"OK."

Tory turned to Sybil. "Five minutes, tops."

"I can't—"

"Hey," he put his hand on her arm. "A shark wouldn't abandon its lamprey, would it?"

Sybil watched his retreat in a daze, staggered away from the bluff edge, and sat suddenly on the ground where she tried to catch her breath. She held her hands up to her ears, wondering vaguely if the rushing sound wasn't the noise of her own blood. After a few minutes she scooted, still sitting, toward the edge of the bluff to see Tory and Katrina. They stood beneath the twisted boughs of a burr oak, Katrina talking quickly, gesturing, and pointing at the bluff. Tory stood impassive, staring off toward the horizon. He spoke, then walked away. Katrina turned on her heel and ran back the way she had come. Sybil scooted away from the edge, and shuffled through her notes, looking for something absorbing. Tory returned.

"Blondes," he said.

Sybil touched the cap covering her brown hair, and blushed.

"Your ear still bugging you?" he asked, extending his hand to her. She took it and was pulled to her feet.

"Yes," she said. "I don't know what it is. It's very strange."

They climbed down the path to the main trail, and set out in search of evidence of erosion. Sybil hopped along, happy, overwhelmed by the sky, which cupped them to the prairie as clearly as a bowl overturned on a table.

Tory turned to Sybil. "You were such a great talker before. What happened?"

Sybil examined the trail before her carefully.

"I don't know what it is," she said. "I've been feeling funny all day." She bent over a fuzzy caterpillar on the path, and transferred it to nearby grass. "Car-sick I suppose. Or, rather, bus-sick. My parents always say I talk too much. My father always says 'Sybil abhors a vacuum.' He means that as a double joke, because I talk so much and because my room's a mess. . . ."

They ventured along the path beside the blood-colored quartz bluffs, bent toward one another like dousing twigs to water.

———

At the hotel that night Sybil unpacked her suitcase, warily eyeing the brown-paper package tucked beneath her jeans. Ms. Thompson sat on one of the room's double beds, wearing plain flannel pajamas, reading a thick library book. Sybil slipped into the bathroom to change.

Through the door she heard music and squealing in the next room. She had overheard that everyone was meeting in Katrina's room, where vodka was hidden. Sybil was almost glad her rooming situation prevented her invitation.

In bed, she began a letter to her French pen pal.

> Dear Brigitte:
> Today's quote: Life is a terrifying admixture of delight and despair. What do you think? Too many D's?
> Today I am writing you from Pipestone, MN, on a geology field trip. You'll never believe who's here with me (well not here here, I'm in a dull, chilly room with my teacher.) Tory Munro! Of the raven hair and chocolate eyes! An admixture of d & d himself—things are going very, very well! Who would have thought? We spent all day together, we were inseparable. He is extremely affectionate toward me, and I feel as though we are very connected in an unspoken promising way, heart-string to heart-string. He calls me his little shark, isn't that, though I abhor the word, cute? (Though of course it's very difficult, never knowing what's real and what's hormones. Though I suppose hormones are real, so isn't what they inspire necessarily real? Whatever's real, the feelings he inspires in me are something like: I want to stick a spigot into him and tap out whatever it is he has that I want. I suppose, from some things he said today, that he feels mutually, although I don't want to be spigoted and tapped! So let's hope not. Or so, I don't know.) Here's wishing on stars anyway.
> Dinner was indescribably repellent. 1) Macaroni, ground meat, and oily cheese sauce. 2) Chicken wings baked in ketchup. 3) Shredded lettuce and grated cheese, with mayonnaise dressing. 4) Bread rolls that looked like toasted marshmal-

lows and tasted like old, old air. 5) Strawberry ice cream without visible strawberries but with an alien waxy texture. If this is the last letter you receive from me, you know why! The poison was evenly distributed throughout! (By the way, I'm the only person on this trip, besides my teacher, who is not currently guzzling vodka in one girl's, Katrina Rusokoff's, room. It's a special training session for future alcoholics. Isn't that mean? Forgive me.)

I suppose I shouldn't mail this, being a good example of counting my chickens before they are hatched.

I have new insight into Romeo & Juliet, they died not just for their love, but also because how embarrassing to go on after you've chattered on about your love *ad nauseam*, and who'd believe them next? If Romeo had said "Oh I love you too—more even," wouldn't his next girlfriend have laughed? So of course you have to promise to burn this if Tory and I don't work out— knock on wood. Listen to me! Knocking on wood, counting chickens, I'm Queen of Weird Old Superstitions of the Midwest! Speaking of which, I just found out this year that the whole center of the US used to be an ocean floor! Don't you think someone should have told me this earlier? It goes a long way to explaining a lot of things.

Thank you for the copy of *Le Monde*. I try to decipher it whenever I have free time.

As always I look forward to meeting you one day!

She signed her closings and name with a great flourish, and, listening to muffled scurrying and giggling in the hallway, fell asleep.

———

Sybil awoke at dawn, as a pink lace of sunlight pierced the net curtains, touching Ms. Thompson's sleeping, sexless, chenille-covered body. Sybil considered the moments of her yesterday like dolls, grouping them in possible families and arrangements. She rose quietly, showered, dressed, and crept from the room, her red suitcase banging against her knee like a damped drum. No one seemed to be awake in the hotel, so Sybil sat on the elegant front steps, her wet hair chilling on her shoulders, admiring the garbage skittering down the street in the wind.

Pipestone was a tiny town, five turn-of-the-century buildings on one side of the street facing five on the other, like soldiers at a cotillion, bearing their pilasters, arches, and cornices proudly. Sybil debated whether she would upset anyone by going for a walk, and, finding on a clock tower that it was only six o'clock, decided she would not. She left a note on her suitcase anyway.

She found a park laid out before a red stone courthouse. A squat green tank crouched in the middle of it, the barrel pointed menacingly at a ranch house across the street. Sybil circled the tank, running her thin fingers against its cold, dew-dotted metal skin, and read an inscription on a plaque at its base. She sat down, extracted a small pad and a yellow pencil from her pocket, and wrote: "Note: This tank is like me, because we are both in an unlikely place. However, I can leave. There is a monument to all of the men of Pipestone who fought in World War II, but no record of whether this tank killed people, and if so, how many, or where. This is intensely obvious, and cloyingly sentimental, I know. The observation is. But so is the tank."

This noted, Sybil replaced her pad in her pocket, rolled over onto her stomach and watched ants trail back and forth through the grass. Sybil had a great curiosity about ants, believing that there was some sort of wisdom to be gained from closely attending to their patterns. She had spent a good deal of time, the only child at a summer cabin full of adults, placing marbles and sugar cubes on ant hills and noting the results. She placed her pencil in their path, and daydreamed, watching their little brown bodies cross over the barrier, brave, unabashed. Somehow two hours had passed. The air had warmed considerably, and a wet blanket of dew coated the tank.

Sybil picked up her pencil, and shook two ants off on the ground. "That's fate, ants," she announced, standing. Then, on sudden impulse, she wrote: "T. M. loves S. C." in the dew with her finger. She quickly checked over her shoulder to see whether she had been observed, and skittered back to the hotel, feeling giddy and sheepish.

———

Sybil settled at a table alone, with a dish of runny scrambled eggs, damp toast, and a newspaper. Many green, ill-looking girls had assembled beneath the television. Sybil read newspapers not for news, but for a game she had played with her father when she was little, taking sentences from as many stories as possible, and putting them together into new stories. She had made a very dull story about a homecoming parade that caused a rig to jackknife, changing zoning laws to welcome a new drugstore, when she was confronted by a heart-stopping sight.

Katrina stood at the buffet, her white hair a radiant halo. She balanced one plate on her forearm, held another in her hand, and giggled as Tory whispered into her ear. He was wrapped around her waist, his hands hooked in the front pockets of her jeans.

Sybil studied the newspaper before her, blinking rapidly. She quietly patted her jacket pockets, found her sunglasses, and slipped them on.

"You were an early bird this morning!" exclaimed Ms. Thompson brightly, setting down her plate with a crash. "The fresh air does us a world of good. Is something wrong with your eyes? It's not like you to wear sunglasses indoors."

"Yes, they're all red," said Sybil darkly. "Fresh air does not agree with me."

———

Ms. Thompson's class sat greenly in the ranger station, slumped and nursing hangovers, lumpen ponytails sticking spiritlessly to bowed heads, pencils tracing disorganized notes slantwise across pages. Sybil hid behind her sunglasses, and took copious, meticulously organized notes. She had chosen a seat in the front row so that she could avoid the spectacle of Tory and Katrina, who hung on one another like monkeys.

Ms. Thompson conducted a lesson on Pipestone's cultural history, discussing railroads, quarries, treaties, churches, Indian schools, government, and trade in souvenirs. By the time modern architecture had abolished the popular use of quartz for building exteriors and the quarries were shut down, the class was fidgeting and rustling, all eyes glued to the clock, as the minute hand swept toward lunch.

"All right!" said Ms. Thompson finally, and notebooks snapped shut. "Now the announcement you've all been waiting for." Groans drowned out the rustle of notebooks reopening. "The term paper—I want to see all pens moving! I'm only going to say this once—ten pages, due on the last day of class. No extensions. None. The topic is 'How the physical geography of Pipestone has influenced its cultural developments.' That means architecture, art, the people who live here, businesses, everything. You must include specific scientific information when dealing with the geology, but you may include your own personal observations, experiences, and feelings. You'll have three hours of free time between lunch and when the bus leaves to gather information. Use your time well." Ms. Thompson arranged her papers. The class fled the classroom.

———

Sybil climbed the red rock bluff, grasping, grinding, loosing the fragile-rooted grass from its moorings. At the top, ragged-breathed and wild, she threw herself upon the ground, stared up at the sky, and thumped her head lightly on the ground, enjoying the futility and symbolism of the pain. Her humiliation and defeat were magnificent. A high clump of grass tricked with her face, bowing and rising in the wind. She yanked it out by its roots.

The sky was unmarked, depthless, a blue whole and endless. Sybil gazed into it until she became dizzy, and yellow stars flitted past her eyes. Her heart was a yawning monster in her chest; enraged, trapped, yearning. Yearning. She wanted to swallow the prairie, the sky, and the earth's red core; to ingest their secrets. She wanted to destroy herself, to join the anonymous universe of things she could not feel, and thus erase this oppressive desire.

A hawk soared by, its body still and peaceful as a guarded pool. It dropped from the sky like a stone.

"Oh," cried Sybil, and sat up. The hawk had plunged to earth, and emerged, flapping, a snake caught in its claws.

A current seemed to run from Sybil's grass-studded cap to her hot, distant toes. All her desires had merged, for an instant, annulling one another, leaving behind a sun-charged bliss.

She slid on her sunglasses, splashing sparks in the glare, and pressed her notebook flat on one knee, gouging her pen into the page as she wrote, like a tiny hoe turning up soil. The sun spun along, painting the country yellow. Sybil cut at the paper with her pen, until, well satisfied, she stood up and read a brief poem to the boulevard of golden grass. Gratified, she climbed down from her perch, her chin thrust in the air, and carried herself back to the bus, ignoring the burs that caught at her legs, and hopping over a red garter snake without seeing it.

———

At the bus she threaded through the clumps of girls directly to Ms. Thompson.

"Here's my term paper," she announced, thrusting forward her poem.

Ms. Thompson accepted it, raising her eyebrows. She glanced at it, and handed it back. "I think you had better reconsider, dear. I'm looking for a ten-page term paper, you know."

"I," said Sybil, drawing herself up to her not inconsiderable full height, "have lived three lifetimes in the shadow of these red rocks. One of sorrow, one of joy, one of knowledge. This is the truest work that you will receive about this desolate spot." She pushed the paper toward Ms. Thompson.

"Be that as it may, dear, I'm not going to accept this. I'm not looking for truth. I'm looking for term papers. You know that, Sybil."

"Fine," said Sybil grandly. "If all you seek is term papers, that is all you shall receive." She climbed into the bus and threw herself into her seat, languid, annoyed. She fell asleep, her cheek pressed against the window.

She awoke when Tory sat down beside her, his weight unsettling her balance.

"Howdy partner," he said, leaning toward her, his eyes steamy.

"Hi," said Sybil, sitting up, rubbing her cheek.

"Haven't seen you all day," he said, his knee resting against hers.

"I have lived an eon today," said Sybil. "I have learned why this is a sacred place."

"Why?" asked Tory, removing his baseball cap, leaning forward over his knees, and tousling his black hair.

"Because I thought I wanted something very badly, and then, on reflection I realized that it was something else that I wanted, and not the first thing at all."

She stared at the curve of his bare neck, a crescent acutely vulnerable, intimate, inviting.

"Oh, yeah," he said, sitting up, his hair falling like a shower of feathers behind him. "Like when you're really hungry and you think you want a whole bag of chips, but then, when you've had them, you're still hungry. So you should have had something good, like a sandwich or something."

"No, not like that at all," said Sybil crossly. "Like there's a heart of desire in all things. You can mistake it for hunger, or lust, or anything, but it's only the core of everything."

"Sure," said Tory, and he smiled at her, winking.

"Oh," said Sybil, as the ocean rose up again in her ears. "Yes."

I Lift Mine Eyes

C. Dawn O'Dell

EJ's mother pulls her robe as tight as the belt will hold and opens the door. Two white cops standing there leaning down to look at her through the doorway like the door is too small for humans. This door ain't too small, and this house bought and paid for, she wants to tell them. They say they got a search warrant for a gun EJ used to shoot at some sick pipe-head who tried to hold him up for a bottle. They head straight on by her, back to her son's room, leaving her with the sheet of paper. They stop outside the door. One of them reaches around and fumbles for the light while the other one tenses opposite as if EJ will come out shooting or swinging a bat at their heads.

They haven't surprised EJ. There's no surprising EJ. He is already dressed, or still dressed, sitting in the dark on the edge of the bed. The other bed doesn't hold a body, but it isn't made. He doesn't say anything. The cops would love it if he showed some anger. Cops got no respect for his rights. Rights are a game they play like some kid might say, "Ya wanna play 52 pick-up?" They are ignorant and fat-assed and got nothing to hold on him. He lets that attitude out though, he'll be in big trouble. Attitude alone will get you with these motherfuckers. They'd get in his face for forever. They arrest you for nothing if you show them any attitude, and he got some attitude. Attitude about all he got, and his attitude would melt them down to puddles of stink.

"You mind?" one of them asks before he starts in on EJ's socks and his boxers. EJ wouldn't grace them with an answer for nothing. The other one leans on the dresser and pretends to pick his teeth. He's going to be the talker. Cops always got a talker and a quiet one. "You a god-damned good for nothing nigger," he says congenially. "Half the black men on the street ain't niggers. Half the white men are." He's got this spiel memorized. They dig through a lot of black kids' stuff in a week. "But you a nigger, kid," the one

230

with the mouth goes on. He starts like he just remembers why he's there and goes rooting around in EJ's CD's, frisbeeing them aside one at a time. "You gonna end up dead on the street because you're getting desperate. That's pretty fucking stupid," he says. "Then even your mama won't cry. She'll be relieved."

When EJ was a kid his mama would come home from her college classes whirring past him through the living room with its trashed out furniture and into the bedroom, trying to shove her books under the bed and trying to get to the kitchen, saying, "Dinner won't be but a minute." Ignoring him, so he followed her. Just a kid, needed his mama. "I got big plans," she would say, talking all the while. Her body a nervous energy and a smell like sweet dirt. "I'm going to make us something that will turn ya'll's stomach to plain heaven." Hands flying, pans coming out.

But she wasn't quick enough. His father's face shone and his jaw wrapped around it like a vice. He would grab her from behind as she tried to get by, spin her around and hold her there like he was just checking did he remember what she looked like. She was dead silent while his hands were a vice on her throat until her eyes were wide; hit her, and hit her until he left her kneeling in front of him, holding her bruised stomach and sucking her bleeding teeth. Sometimes he grabbed her head then and shoved it into his crotch. EJ afraid she would die. EJ standing on his unstable baby legs, howling, and his father turning to give him his.

"Hey, is this a new shirt?" the cop asks. He holds up a new shirt. "I don't remember this one from last time, and, hey, where is your cousin?" He roots under the bed right at EJ's feet. EJ could kick him in the teeth. "He carry away the goods? Ain't he too young to be out this late? You turning him into your errand boy? You make him just like you? Or maybe he's just visiting his crack-head mama."

When EJ was a kid, he was out. He took up the games being played in the street. Running for a dealer when he was eight, getting it up on the world that was already telling what he was not. He was making more money than his father did working for the city all his life, coming home to the projects, threading back down the piss-stained stairs after dinner, making his way down to the Soul Palace to hang and rant some about how the white man held him down. Black man got no future. White man had, and had, and had, riding on black man's backs like monkeys on an elephant. Anger rolling under his skin, a river of molten hate. Sometimes he took the rent money and bought cheap liquor to go around, and cruised away in the fancy cars of his low friends.

One day one of those fancy cars squealed to the curb with the door already open and swinging a little with the movement, then his father fell out with a knife up under his ribs. The car drove off, door wobbling, banging shut. "Shit," his father said. "Ain't no way to treat a man." Squinting up into the sun at his boy standing over him where he had been squashing ants on the sidewalk with a stick, reaching his arm up for him, "Come here, boy. Help your old man up. Come here, boy," his arm fading to the sidewalk, his eyes drying up, his lips drying up. The man a chalk mark on the side-walk the next day when the rain came. His mother cried, he told her to shut up.

The police had gone through it all. The quiet one even ripped the inner soles out of his sneakers and threw the guts back in the closet. They left looking disgusted and having said the same old things: "You better get wise before you die out there."

EJ's mother is leaning in his doorway in her old bathrobe, got a paper in her hand. "Where your cousin?" she asks him.

———

His cousin, Marky, right at that moment, is walking down the street. There was rain, and the streets shine under the street lights, but it is still hot, South Carolina hot, mist rising from the pave-ment. Marky has a hitch in his walk that he is cultivating. Someday he's going to be just like his older cousin—that's what he hopes. EJ is cool, nothing much bothers him. Plus, he's got morals—loves his mama, respects women, does pretty good in school. Morals are im-portant. That's what EJ's always harping at Marky about: that's what is wrong with all these assholes out here who think they're so cool. They ain't nothing cause they got no compunction. Marky ac-cepts this without thinking. He doesn't think about much. He is failing school, but then he's been failing school all his life and they keep passing him, so it doesn't much matter.

Marky has his friend with him, Little Joe. Joe and Marky are thir-teen but Joe is about six foot tall, and Marky figures he's going to be a huge motherfucker. He likes having Little Joe with him, even though he can't play basketball for shit. He's too slow. That's where they think they're going. The courts always got something going on even late at night. He especially likes to play then. The lights at the court are weak. Everyone has a shadow that dances across the backs of everyone else, and beyond that there is just the black night. The street lights around are all busted. Marky makes sure they stay that way. He flings rocks at them. The dark world beyond the lighted court makes it like playing on the moon, and sometimes he feels like he loses gravity and flies across the court and up toward the glare of light and the basket. Then he has escaped.

There are little bits of wet trash in the gutters. When they enter the park they see an old bum sleeping on a bench. "Hey," says Marky, "look here." He walks to the bum and looks down at him. "What a piece of shit," he says. He scoops up some wet trash and leaves from the ground and rains it down on the old man, but the old guy doesn't move. This isn't satisfactory, so Marky goes over to the garbage can overflowing its wire cage and yanks the lid off its wire tether. It takes a couple of good yanks and Little Joe helps. Then Marky scoops the lid into a dank puddle and comes up with rain and mud, and the rain and mud rain down on the old man. "Keep you cool, man," says Marky. The mud runs across the grizzly face and under the stinking collar of the filthy, striped shirt but there isn't any movement still. "Shit," says Marky. "He dead." and Marky takes some firecrackers out of his pocket. He always carries them because he likes to catch cats and stick firecrackers in their mouths and ears and asses. "Shit, watch this fucker," he says and he slips two of the noisemakers off their string and lights them, then he grins at his oafish friend and sticks the firecrackers in the man's ears. He stands right over him looking down at his smelly face, watching. The firecrackers explode and so does the man. He surges off the bench, a thick gurgling scream gushing from him, then running, shuffling, and hopping in his lopsided, too big shoes and holding his ears and screaming.

Little Joe starts to laugh. He sits down on the bench and his fat belly spits out a huh, huh, huh panting laugh. Marky stands with his hands straight down in the pockets of his pants, bustin' the slack, looking at Joe. "It ain't that funny," he says, but Little Joe is falling out. Marky turns and looks up at the brothers playing in the fishbowl. He can see them flying away from their shadows. He doesn't feel like playing anymore.

———

EJ got the shadow of his father hanging on his back. He got the shadow of every black man. It's those cops' fault, made him think all that shit. He can't even see himself in his own mirror. He don't look like nothing. Thought he had the right to make himself something else. He's looking himself in the eye and it looks like he was wrong. Cops just come to remind him again. He brushes his hair and he walks out. Doesn't say a word to his ma. She is in the kitchen just standing there hypnotized by the hissing of the kettle. That's the way she was. Sometimes she gets in your face, sometimes she turns to stone.

The brothers are behind the Soul Palace doing nothing. Doing nothing at all, all the time. A street light glares across the bright blue front. The cars rotting in the back are covered with leaning bodies. He'd like to go over there and tell them they were all born dead men. Stand him on one of the cars and preach. Black man got no future. White man a monkey on their backs. Black man got no future. He'd like to take a bat and crunch all their bones to rice. Their cigarettes glow up and down in the dark, and the little bit of blue neon from a back window beer ad glints on the bottles as they make their slow go round.

There is Godfrey, bouncing at his elbow, up out of the dark from around those cars. "My man. I just about be looking for you." He is a nervous little scarred-up motherfucker. Nobody could mind half the shit he said. He rants so much it fogged up your hearing. He was like someone's retarded little brother hanging around the pool hall waiting for someone to hate him enough to beat the shit out of him. Only the little retard always managed to keep the games going. EJ wouldn't let kids deal the streets for him. He had a couple of Godfreys who did it. But now Godfrey had a killer connection of his own, and EJ was using him for that too. He had his arm sloppily around EJ's neck. "You gotta come hang with me, man. We gots to take us a ride. We gonna pick up some of the best shit you ever tasted. You gon' be able to stomp this shit, man." He jabbed his skinny finger into EJ's chest. "You gon' be rich. I gon' be rich. I deserves to be rich so I can spend it before the world end. You ever hear 'bout that shit, man? That shit is serious." EJ shrugs his arm off. "Ain't none of that Nostradamus or Revelations. None of that shit. It the Chinese."

"What the fuck you want?" EJ asks him.

"Woo, ain't we testy. Ain't we just steaming in our own puddle. What you need is something to take your mind off your troubles. You needs you a parrot. I had me a parrot one time. Tomorrow night, right? Same place, man. Why change around when you got a good thang to count on? You know what I'm saying."

"Get me at nine."

Godfrey was talking at someone else, already sucked back into the shadows before EJ had gone two steps.

EJ walks on blindly. He's practically at the strip before he realizes. All the money is down there, bunch of restaurants and bars where tourists and rich whites hang out. His funk hangs on his face like hate. Even if it didn't they'd be keeping an eye on him like they are, stepping off the sidewalk, cutting a wide circle like they would to walk around a snake. When he was a kid some of his friends and him used to jump out from behind bushes and listen to the squeals. Those folks would walk backward in terror, their hands held in front of them warding off a bunch of twelve-year-old pranksters. A few times they even fumbled out their wallets, throwing them and running. Once someone begged them not to kill him. They all thought it was proof of the omnipotent power they were practicing. It wasn't anything but the color of their skins. One time one of their victims pulled a gun and held it on them and said, "Come on, nigger." They didn't do it anymore after that.

He makes it to the river, down to the black up under the bridge. Black on black, ain't nobody gonna see him down there. There isn't any way to see the other side. Not in the dark. But there it is, something waiting out there for him. He strains his eyes after it. He's sick of it. Sick of everything. There isn't any sense or good. No way it'll get any better. On and on and fucking on. On the edge. He wants to jump. He wants to wash up somewhere else, wants to be alive somewhere else, someone else, but he can't swim. The dark comes right up in his face to stare him down. It knows it can eat him whole. Holding him right there like he already caught guilty, with the gun in his hand, with all the other shit he had to do in his life. Some day he thought he was going to walk away and be someone else, that's what he thought. A college man, a lawn man. Everyone but him probably knew that was shit. Impossible. He never could see it anyway. All he ever could see was what was all around him and he became it. So now he was shit—a dope dealer who wouldn't sell to no kids or pregnant women. How is that for shit? He could see that. The dark, it don't listen to his explanations, it just goes on breathing down his neck.

The next day is Wednesday. Wednesdays EJ's mother goes to church, so he plays Pied Piper, though he still got that evil on him. When he leaves his high school, the kids are waiting for him. They toss their cigarettes into the street and crowd around him. He reaches out and pushes their tight heads. They play football. First thing they have to do once they get to the elementary school yard is pick up all the trash. Every one of them so much jive in their walk that they look like puppets jerking around peeling candy wrappers, potato chip bags, and condoms off the bottom of the fence and out of the puddles under the swings. Those kids, they look in the mirror they see a great big future grinning back at them. EJ remembers. But that future is going to come right out of the mirror and suck them up to nothing—ones that live that long.

EJ sees two brothers he kind of knows hop the fence and start across the yard. They both wear baggy jeans and they have crue colors hanging from their back pockets.

"What up, EJ!"

EJ nods.

"What you got these kids doing, man?" "You get paid for being a Cub Scout leader?" They laugh. "No man. I respect that, man. You good. I mean it." They laugh more. They keep on walking across the hot sand yard and right up on some kid—kid been coming for a few weeks now, followed EJ around last week. Wanted to talk about rap all the time. Called all the girls in his fifth grade class ho's and bitches.

The two gang members shove the kid off his feet. The kid gets up and shoves them both back, one hand on each. The world has gone bad on EJ. He could try to chill the situation. *Hey brother, you need to give the little man a chance. Whatever he done, he do whatever it takes to make it right. Ain't that right, little brother?*

He'd just be in the middle of it. Some kid getting killed and there he'd be standing right there in the middle of it holding his hands out like some Bermuda fucking traffic cop, Cub Scout. What's he going to do? *Go on, man, this ain't your corner; this my corner.* Yeah, he could do that. *Go on, you messing with my turf now, and round here we love each other.* He could just picture that worthless shit. Same worthless shit he was looking at in the dark up under that bridge.

One of them grabs the kid. He can't hear anything but the clenching rumble of their threats. All the other kids come stand around EJ because they think they're safe there. They think of him same as those guys who are spoiling that kid. They think they're safe because they're with one of the bad guys.

The one holding the kid lets go and takes a step back. As soon as the kid's feet hit the ground the other one takes a swing at him. The kid spins around and drops to his knees, holding his face where blood is gushing through his jerking fingers. The other one slams his heel into the kid's back a couple of times. The kid wrenches around on his knees, still holding his face. He screams something up at them, his voice stuffed full. They laugh down at him.

One of the gang members picks the kid up from behind by the elbows, and the other punches his stomach five or six times—full cocked-back man punches. The kid folds around the fist over and over. He screams, his voice stringing across the distance like the hollow screeching whine of train brakes. And then the kid starts to vomit. The puke rolling from him in two great heaves onto his own thighs and the shoes of one of his attackers. They let him go, jumping back, but then start punching his head over so far it looks like it is hanging by a string. The kid is on the ground hunched over like he'll never get up. The gang members pace back across the lot. One hitches up his pants. "See ya, bro," to EJ.

The kids all run to the downed one. He is on his side, his hands clutching up his shirt over and over. His face is bleeding badly and some blood is coming out of his mouth and the one ear.

"Fuck," the kids say.

"They wouldn't do that shit to me."

"You ain't fighting no whole crue, you fucking weenie head."

"I get me a gun and kill them."

"Shit, I'd blow away they mother. Right EJ?"

EJ left already.

———

When Marky leaves his school it's with Vanessa because she has on some red jeans that wrap around her butt and that is seriously having an effect on his thinking. He never fucked a girl before, but he sure got imagination and need. "Come over my house," she said to Marky. "You EJ's cousin. You be cool to it." He knows what she's talking about; he knows she uses. EJ gets right up in Marky's face every chance he can get, his face so serious balled up with the pressure of what he is trying to say that it looks like his eyeballs are going to bust out. "I ever hear about you touching that shit, you'll have one whooped down ass." EJ wasn't everywhere anyway. EJ would never know what ticket he used to get hisself all wet inside those red jeans.

There were lots of problems with Marky's plan, though. Lots of problems. Like he is walking along behind that red butt and sweating the devil. And Vanessa, she got tits that point out from her like speed bumps. He ready to take her for a drive every time he sees her. Walking like that is not comfortable. And they're walking down the middle of the road toward his old neighborhood.

Nothing but about ten houses and a store that's so dirty and dark inside you can't read what it says on the grimy cans. That man in there is so mean that Marky stole a whole carton of cigarettes from him once, then stood right in front of his store and sold them pack by pack.

It makes him remember his Mama, when he remembers that neighborhood, remembers her lying on her bed with a man tucked up between her legs and an old cooked-up spoon and a lighter on the bed table, yelling at Marky to get her a cigarette when there ain't one in the house and she knows it. It wasn't only smokes she sent him out to beg. Usually, though, she was on that corner right by the store with her back against that wall, leaning. All the men know her. Some want it, and some spit at the sidewalk right in front of her like they couldn't hold it another minute until they get past. He hasn't been around here for a couple of years.

"Come on," says Vanessa. "You shuffling like you got a load in your pants." She walks backward, watching him walking. Her feet chop down behind her like the ground is supposed to be farther away. She grabs both Marky's hands, and jerks him along with her. Her tits float around in her shirt like little animals stuck in there trying real hard to hang on. Marky sticks his fingers into her belt loops and pulls her hard right into him. "Shit," she says and shoves him off. "You nasty." Then she laughs and turns around, walking fast.

She turns down the alley right before the store. Looks like that store hasn't been open for fifty years. Ain't no one gonna bother to spit there anymore. The alley is nothing but a dirt track, some mud holes and a grassy hump. Vanessa walks up to an old crooked garage and Marky sees someone leaning against it. Vanessa goes right up to this guy. She says, "Give me two." But the guy isn't looking at her, he's looking at Marky, then he's out of the garage and out into the bright afternoon light. He flings his arm around Marky's neck dragging him over sideways with the weight. "Yo, Marky," Godfrey says, "brother come all this way to find me must have him a job he doing, cause you ain't never visited me before. You holding something for me? About time that cousin of yours got smart, start using his kin to do the business. Now that's smart business. Sure as the sun come up every day on this same stinking world, family business a good thing. You can tell EJ I done said that. I said it to him before, but ain't till now he ever listen." The scars on Godfrey's face make it look chewed up.

"Come on," says Vanessa. She is standing half in the shade of the garage, half in the sun. Godfrey loosens his head squeeze on

Marky just enough so he can see the sidewalk going from the garage up to its old house with its shit green shingles.

"Well, well, well, who this pretty little thing you brought with you?" says Godfrey. "This a friend of yours, brother? You bring her here without you telling her we don't do business with no little girls. Not even if they special friends. You know what I mean? Real close friends. That what EJ say, and he still mainly the boss."

"What you talking about?" Vanessa asked him. "You always be selling to me. You know I ain't but thirteen."

Godfrey takes his arm off Marky and starts toward Vanessa, backing her into the shadows. "Now, you listen real good to Uncle Godfrey. Uncle Godfrey gon' be like Mr. Rogers, with some real nice advice. You shouldn't be coming around here, girl, or no place like it. You start hanging around here and you get yourself in trouble. That a fact." He keeps looking back at Marky.

"What the fuck you talking like that for?" asks Vanessa. She squints past Godfrey at Marky like he's the police.

Marky knows now he don't have to worry about facing EJ after he done run up Vanessa. He don't have to worry about going deeper in this neighborhood and maybe seeing his ma. He wipes the sweat from his forehead and pulls his stuck shirt away from his chest, fanning himself, takes one last look at that place where the red jeans cut up a crease between her legs.

———

EJ has been in his bed since he left the playground. He'd like to stay right there for days, forever, but Marky is standing in the doorway barking at him, "Wake up, EJ. Wake up, EJ." Then stands there and watches while he's trying to get his head up off that pillow. And that's about all the time Marky'll give him before he starts in with this usual whine. Can he go and he won't get out of the car and just for the ride. Marky never did listen very well. EJ was always telling him, talk himself hoarse-headed, but Marky still seemed to think it was glamorous. Now EJ didn't know why he thought it would matter. Like anything did. He rests the heaviness in his head in his hands. "Come on if you want," EJ tells him. So, Marky scoots out of the house behind him, slams the door so hard it bounces and he has to go back, peel it off the house wall, shut it right.

Godfrey is sitting with his wrists draped over the steering wheel of some brand-new looking fast car. "This car easy as licking a whore, sitting down in that neighborhood Marky Mama live in, but Marky, he don't go down there no more." Godfrey's blabbering is grating EJ even worse than usual. On and on. EJ stares out the open window at the scrubby pine slinging past—the dark against the lighter dark of the moonlit sky. He stares without moving his eyes, dragging them across the sky, so it all turns into a blur like on a carnival ride. His life is nothing but a rinky-dink carnival ride about to fly off the tracks. Godfrey goes on and on about fuckin' this and fuckin' that, stealing cars and tits and the Chinese, until they turn into the yard of the house squatting right on the highway like a boil—same rusty junk cars in front, same kids playing on the sagging porch. Their mother comes to the door in stretchy black pants and the usual mean look like she done learned not to take any shit from anything. Toaster don't work she'd probably stab it. "Get on in the house," she yells at the kids. She looks out at them. Her eyes look as blank as cement on a sunny day. She yells back over her shoulder into the house, "Romaine, you got some company out here."

Marky pulls the handle to make the seat go forward.

"You ain't getting out," says EJ.

Nothing Marky can do but just watch them disappear inside. It was uncool, him sitting out here in the yard. It made him burn. He yanks back and forth on the front seat. He watches the kids get yelled at some more by their mean-looking mama. She comes back out and smacks both kids on the head real hard. "You hear me calling you. Who you think you is? You best get your ass in that house when I call you." She swats again at one of them as they dodge for the house. Marky wished the kid'd shoot her the finger at least, stand there and maybe pull his little bitty dick out and wave it at her. Kid reminded him of himself.

Neither EJ nor Godfrey holds anything when they come out, but when they get in the car EJ slips a little brown lunch sack out of his pants and slides it under his seat. Godfrey starts laughing, just giggling to himself as he starts the car, adjusts the mirror around.

Marky wants to at least ask some things, but EJ has an evil look on his face like he saw something in there made him feel ill. EJ been looking kind of ill all day, so Marky is trying to keep his mouth shut. He slaps a rhythm on the back of the seat as he bounces up and down. He wanted to make some money, have anything he wanted. He didn't understand why EJ didn't have him a car like this one. Didn't understand what EJ had to sit there and look sour gone bad for. If he was EJ, made his money, he'd have three cars, give them away on the street to some fine chick. First one would speak to him who had one of them butts like a little shelf, he give her a car. "How fast this car go?" he asks.

"Shit," says Godfrey, "This car can fly. This car take you wherever you goin' without touching down. Shit." He floors it. The trees start slipping by so fast the moon is just a blue beating between them. Marky is scared shitless, but he isn't about to say anything to Godfrey. Godfrey'd just keep going faster. Marky can feel the exhaust under his feet trying hard to leave the car. He wishes EJ would say something. Usually EJ was the boss of wherever he was, acted like he was the boss of everyone, so how come he was just sitting there? The tires scream along the pavement trying to keep hold. EJ just staring out the window again like he was used to this.

"Fuck," was all Marky could think after the first endless minute or two. "Fuck. Fuck." Marky's stomach rises when they launch in the air way out past where they should be. Road gone behind them somewhere, useless. This is some ride for about a second. He slams down, something slams into him from the side. It yanks his whole body, jerks his head like it's going to snap off. The sound is terrible. He hears it like it's crushing him, like a skyscraper falling down. He is slammed into something else. Maybe the door will open and fling him out, maybe his shoulder is broken. He waves his hands out, blind man trying to hold onto something. Things are flying around inside the car, glass and pieces of trees. He starts to think he can see trees blur past, thinks he can see their bunched needles like silver blades aiming down at him. Things are falling on him. He is falling again. The air grinds with creasing and folding metal. The car goes over, skidding, crushing the ground, slamming into something else. Then there is silence like the world stopped breathing.

The car is on its side, curled up. Marky is on the ground where the window would have been. He's got his seat rising in front of him and the front seat's a wall beside him, a window right over his head, nothing but a ring of frizzled glass left hanging to the edges. He asked Godrey how fast was this car, then they are just sitting here in the woods. Hasn't been any time. He can hear someone shuffling up along the front seats. Must be Godfrey, must have fallen on top of EJ and trying to push himself off, but there isn't anywhere for him to go, not like he can just hop his ass over in his own seat. His seat is stuck up in the air. EJ grunting and panting like he stuck in a nightmare. Marky thinks he is working himself up to scream. EJ's scream would be a terrible thing. "Get the fuck off him."

"What you think I'm trying to do?"

"You hurting him." Marky can see the black blot of Godfrey crouching only inches from him on the other side of the seat.

"I think I the one bleeding here. I think I got me a cut on my head. Damn. My favorite shirt. Damn."

"You don't get the fuck off him I give you some real blood."

"You a real fucking comedian, man."

EJ makes a sound. That scream starting to come up.

"Get the fuck off him. Get the fuck out."

Godfrey plants his feet, and EJ's new groan chokes in his throat, breaks itself, and dies. "Sorry, man," says Godfrey. Then he reaches, gets hold of the window frame and pulls himself up, his feet scrabbling at the front window and the seats trying to find a push. Marky hears him fall from the top of the upturned door to the ground with a grunt like he landed flat on his back.

"I hope that asshole don't get a breath for a month. Come on, EJ. Let's get out of here." He reaches over the seat to where EJ is still hunched against the ground. EJ isn't answering. Marky shoves at him a couple of times. Seems like he got his arms around himself, seems like he's holding himself. That fucking asshole Godfrey. EJ won't answer, no grunts, no moving, sure as hell no talking. "Come on, EJ. Come on, EJ. Come on, EJ," like he's trying to wake him for school until he realizes he's not making any sense. EJ must be out. Must have hit his head or something. "We got to get EJ," he yells up into the dark. It's going to be hard to lift him. His cousin is a lot bigger than him.

"What you talkin' about, man. I'm dying out here."

"He hurt," Marky yells. "He hurt." EJ just a black hump, he doesn't feel anything coming off him. Not like he's not there. He's there. He's there like the weight of nothing. Marky feels like he is swimming up through the thick dark trying to find some air, but he just sits there, quiet closed around him black as his insides.

"Shit," says Godfrey. "Get the package first."

The dark focuses around Marky. He reaches over his own legs and along the floor of the car that is like a wall in front of him, reaches up under the front seat. "Come on, man," Godfrey begs. "Hurry up. We got to get that junk out of here before the cops show up. We got to go." Godfrey is dancing out there, about to piss his pants. "Come on. Your mama faster than you."

The package isn't there. Marky has to get onto his knees on

that little patch of ground, and feel all around up under EJ's seat, his hands scraping past springs and metal bars, in and out, until he finds where it is jammed. When he pulls it out he hears a rip. "I got it," he says into the air.

"Throw it here, man," he hears from outside. He throws it up. He couldn't get any power in the cramped space, his elbows knock against the seat beside him, but it sailed on up, out past the window. A fine sifting rained down on him.

"I'm out a here."

"Got to get EJ out," Marky yells. "Come on, we got to get EJ," panic ripping him.

"Naw, man. We got to get out of here. We gon' be charged with possession and stolen vehicle. We got to get out of here."

Marky reaches over and pulls on EJ's arm from the squat he has managed, but the arm weighs a million pounds, its muscles bunched under the skin like lead. He can see the outline of EJ's head curled up on itself. He can hear his own panting in the dark like some animal close by, waiting.

"Come on, my man." Godfrey was saying. "I ain't waiting for your ass. The police be here. They get him. They be here any minute."

"We can't leave him," Marky says. "We can't fucking leave him. We ain't fucking leaving him. He my cousin." He feels that animal down there with them, crawling on its belly. He feels the hair on his back go up. He's looking at EJ, trying to see him, but his face is gone in the dark. He wants to see his eyes like they shine. Ain't no eyes to see and he knows it.

He uses the heel of his hand to push the bits of glass out of the window frame, gets hold of the window frame, pushes himself off and catches it under his belly, teeters there. The air down there is sucking in around him, pulling on him, but letting him go. Bursting right out to go. He pulls himself up so he is sitting on the door that's flat to the moon. He's got his ass out now. He is tired. The dark pulls.

"What you gon' do for him?" Godfrey been talking all this time? "You his doctor? Since when you his fucking doctor? The police get him. There ain't no sense in no three niggers going to jail."

"I ain't leaving him," says Marky, but he pulls one leg free, then, slowly, the other. He is let go. He is out of it. He jumps down to where Godfrey is standing clutching the brown package like a baby.

"You a fool, man. He leave you. He ain't stupid. Ambulance come a lot faster than you trying to pull him out, man. You hurt him, you try to pull him out." Godfrey turns into the dark, walking away.

There is the car behind Marky, the roof shining like skin wherever the moon can find it. It's got a weight heavier than a boulder. "This car dead," he says, and he can hear Godfrey, not too far away yet.

"Fucking good thing it was free."

"Nothing is free," thinks Marky. EJ told him that: "Don't matter what job you got, nothing is free. It all work. Some work just pay better. But then you had to pay the work." He can see EJ's face in front of him like it's broad daylight, like it was the day he actually said it. "Go on," EJ says, and shoves at Marky's head. "Go on. Get out of here. You ain't going with me. You don't need this shit. You going to college or something. Go play some ball." And Marky turns away. Pissed off. Pissed at EJ. What EJ want? Like he gonna be something else. Pissed off. Son of a bitch, always leaving him. He can feel EJ far away in the dead quiet. "Fuck you," he says to EJ, then adds, "They be here to get you in a minute."

Godfrey was way off. He was just a dark head deep in the scar the car made.

Marky follows.

THE MOVEMENT OF STONE

Liz Severn

Gwen propped the wine bottle against David's hip as he leaned against the trunk of an oak. Thin shadows lay across his thighs. "I found something in the attic," Gwen said. She opened a black case and set it on the blanket. She hoped the breeze carried the scent of her rose talcum powder to him, stirred him in some way, like the memory of a favorite song.

"Checkers?" He touched the board, zigzagging from black to red squares.

"Fire before smoke." She tilted a cardboard box and spilled the checkers into a pile by David's hand.

David examined a black checker. "It's a sock." He lifted another. "Underwear?" He flipped the checker into the air and laughed. "Strip checkers! Set them up."

She placed her checkers on the squares. "I'm going to win," she said.

"I'll have you naked before the sun sets," David said. He repositioned the wine bottle to rest against her thigh. His hand moved along her skin for a moment, just a trace. The touch reminded her of fringe on his old suede jacket, the way it had swayed with his agile gait, tickled when he put his arm around her shoulder as they walked through parks. From the bog to the south of them, bullfrogs croaked "Jug-a-rum," and the heat of early evening lingered to warm their skin. Dragonfly nymphs climbed the stems of cattails, and new buds glowed golden in the sun.

David finished setting up his checkers. "Ready." He put the bottle between his legs and pulled out the cork. Gwen moved closer to him, sat on something hard, then tilted sideways and searched beneath the blanket until she found several stones. She tossed them aside. One landed at the blanket's edge. She moved closer to David and ran her hand through his hair, so thick and wavy, like wool sheared from the sheep they once kept so she

could spin her own yarn. He surprised her when he leaned over
and kissed her. She remained silent, letting the springtime sounds
of their land—hairy woodpeckers drilling into a dead oak and
squirrels arguing among themselves—remind him of what they
had together. It had been such a long winter, and weather had
nothing to do with it. The land was coming alive, and he needed
to feel that energy, *take notice*, as he used to say, when pointing out
wild strawberry blossoms and wild violets growing on the path
they walked.

David steadied a wineglass between his knees and poured.
Gwen took the glass, then held out the other, which he filled. He
placed the bottle down and accepted his glass. Their fingers
touched in the exchange, and she remembered a time when all
ten of his fingers massaged her, soothing and exciting the muscles
in her buttocks. Working her hips until she said *ahhh* and the ache
disappeared.

There were many tasks David could no longer do since the accident took his left arm. For every moment of frustration, she
mourned with him. But she never told him how sorry she was that
he could no longer twiddle his thumbs. How silly he might think
her. Why mourn a useless gesture when there were so many substantial tasks to consider? But in the movement of that simple gesture, she understood how thumb against thumb helped settle his
mind, brought perspective. At night while she knitted, he'd sit
nearby and twiddle his thumbs, letting them wrestle with worry
about the soy bean crop flooding or the corn dying out from the
drought. The movement of his thumbs had joined the clicking of
her needles and she had felt there was a pattern and purpose to
their synchronized movement, just as surely as there was pattern
and purpose in their fingerprints.

Since the accident, David took to the rocking chair in the corner
of their living room and held onto its arm, tensed up like someone
gripping a dental chair, waiting for the Novocain. She thought of
the Demerol he had taken for months after the accident to numb
the pain.

Tonight, his hand wrapped gently around his wineglass. "It's
warmer out here than I thought," Gwen said, and removed her
sweater and draped it across her shoulders.

"Shouldn't you wait to be jumped for that?"

Go ahead and jump me now, she wanted to say, wanted to
spread her legs and arms wide open to him, but why hurry? The
pile of leaves beneath the burr oaks was damp from the recent

rain, and the breeze stirred the scent of the decomposing woods floor. Gwen imagined the smell tangling in her long hair, scenting it, leaving the red tinted with gold. Not long after the accident, she had said she needed to help David learn to live with one hand in a two-handed world, and she didn't have time to take care of long hair. After all, if he talked about selling their land, why shouldn't she find ways to lessen their life, too? But David had cried that night, the first time since the accident. He begged her to leave it be, buried his face into her chest, and asked her to be patient. Don't punish him for his carelessness in causing the accident. And she had said he shouldn't punish himself either with talk about selling their land.

David poured more wine for himself, held the bottle up to Gwen, who downed her wine and accepted more. "You move first," he said.

"My pleasure," she said.

In the west the sun reflected light off the windshield of David's car, a 1969 Volvo. He had driven it cross-country before they met, but three weeks after they bought the farm the engine blew and he had it towed to the edge of their woods. It sat half in meadow and half in leafy shadow. Through the years, its shell came to seem less of an eyesore, like a slightly irritating but endearing habit of his, such as the way he sucked air through his teeth when he paused in conversation. She had come to understand that the car meant as much to him as her photo albums meant to her. On evening walks, he'd get very quiet and stop by the car, run his hand over the upholstery as though he could remember the smooth skin of a young woman he had once made love to there. The car had been freedom, driving from town to town, stopping to find work to earn enough money to travel again. There was always someone who needed shelves built, cabinets made, and decks added, always a contractor in need of a good finishing man.

He had been in his workshop the night of the accident. She had sat alone knitting, waiting for him to come in, sit and talk, work out his worry about the proposed property tax hike. But that night he had wanted to finish cutting the boards for the oak flooring he had planned to put down in the dining room. She had gone out to check on him, found him stumbling out the door holding what was left of one arm above his head. She wrapped an old blanket around him, guided him to the car, and placed the severed forearm, in wet towels, on his lap. She remembered David holding the wound up as she drove, how he leaned his head against the frosted window, melting it clear like a halo around him. Gwen had stared as much at the damaged arm as she had at the road, grateful that the tourniquet held during the ten-minute ride to the community hospital.

She shuddered, drank wine, and thought back to the image of David traveling the highways in his Volvo listening to Arlo Guthrie and Pete Seeger songs.

"What are you daydreaming about?" David asked.

"When's the last time we made love in the Volvo?"

David turned and looked at the old car. "The night you helped me push it there." He lay on his back and looked at the overhang of tree limbs, the low-hanging limb that he called a widow maker.

"Think we're still agile enough?"

"What's on your mind?"

"You are." She rubbed his thigh, moved across his hip to his waist.

"And if I fail you again?" The crease of his folded shirt sleeve dragged along the blanket.

Gnats hung in a cluster behind his head. Gwen whisked them away and touched his cheek. "You've never failed me."

He raised his eyebrows. "So you say."

"OK, my move," she said and placed a fingertip on her shoe checker. The breeze blew strands of hair across her face. She looked up to find him staring at her.

"Cigar eyes," he said, a name he hadn't called her in years, a name he gave her the night she smoked a Tipparillo and he said the cigar matched the color of her eyes.

Four weeks after the accident, his bandages were removed. Gwen wanted to celebrate with lovemaking. David sat on the bed, taking off one shoe, then the other. Gwen sat next to him, wearing her half-slip and bra. He had leaned over and kissed her shoulder, moved to her spine, then stopped as though someone had called out to him. He then picked up his shoe and threw it across the room. "I can't even remove your damn bra." He had left her to smoke a cigarette, a habit he had taken up again to satisfy some need that Gwen believed the twiddling of his thumbs once filled.

"Are you ever going to move?" David asked.

Gwen slid her shoe checker forward. David moved his shoe checker. Gwen moved her sock checker. David did the same. Instead of moving the next shoe, Gwen moved her pants forward. David pushed his glasses checker forward. Gwen moved her bra checker. David moved his shirt checker then leaned away from the tree and pulled at the end of her silk scarf draped loosely around her shoulders. "I remember how you used to tie these around your forehead."

She took his hand and kissed the palm. "It's yours as soon as you jump me for it." She held his palm to her cheek a moment longer. The sun was setting in layers of orange, and dusk took hold where the day had been. She lit the kerosene lamp and placed it to the side of the blanket. It cast light on the gold imprinted illustrations on each checker.

After that night of failed seduction when David left her lying on the bed, she had bought bras that clasped in front. She had slept naked. The more she disrobed, the more skin she revealed, the more David seemed determined to add another T-shirt, sleep on the edge of the bed. He could pull shirts down in one quick move over his head and zip his fly with such force that he seemed to believe he had locked what was behind it away from her, as though he could make her forget that he had lost his arm when he checked the belt to his circular saw without turning off the power. The dismemberment did not come by way of an even cut, but instead a ripping off of the arm so that the veins, nerves, and tissue were too badly destroyed to have what she carried to the car that night reattached.

"Do you still want to play?" she asked. He nodded, smiled, and drank wine.

She wanted to touch the healed bone and muscle where the artificial arm was supposed to attach. David wouldn't wear it, said the damn thing was too heavy. It made him feel more like an invalid to have a useless prop hanging by his side. He leaned it in the corner of their bedroom and slipped his wedding band on it. He had always removed his band when he worked on machinery. She left the ring where he put it. She had fixed all the long-sleeved shirts in his closet so that the sleeve didn't hang down. She said she'd remove the slip stitches any time he wanted her to. And if he didn't want his short-sleeved shirts anymore, she'd donate them to the Salvation Army.

She folded her sweater, got up, and tucked it between David's back and the tree trunk. He had helped her dye the wool the pale and creamy color of the camomile buds from which she made the dye. She let her breast brush against his shoulder, then moved away. She wanted to take off his shirt, let the last of the sun warm his skin, move her hand through the hair across his chest and down his belly.

When the saw belt had caught and twisted off his arm, he said it had jerked him so violently that his glasses flew from his face. She did not think to find them, to put them with his arm as they fled to the car. The next day, David said he felt he could live without his glasses. What was left to see? Afterward, she returned to his workshop and found them speckled with sawdust and blood.

David moved his pants checker forward. Was the move sloppy or purposeful? With the next move of Gwen's shoe checker, no matter what he did, she'd get his pants. He moved his sock checker as though she might go for it, but it was his pants she wanted, and his pants were what she got. She held up the checker and bit its edge. "Hand them over," she said. David unbuttoned them, pulled down the zipper, and tugged at the waistband while lying on his back. She forced herself to refrain from entering his one-handed struggle. Once he had them past his buttocks, he sat up and pulled down each leg in turn.

"Can I take off my shoes, too? Or do I have to sit here looking damn silly with my pants around my ankles?"

She poured wine. "Suit yourself, but when it comes time for me to jump your shoes, what will you have to offer?" She leaned a palm on the blanket and felt another stone beneath her.

He removed his shoes. "I'm taking my socks off, too."

"That's four items in debt to me," she said.

He pushed his shoes, socks, and pants over to the side and leaned against the tree. The slit in his boxer shorts opened. She placed a hand on his inner thigh. "Are you teasing me?" He looked down.

"Hey, you're not there yet." He covered his crotch, removed her hand, and drank more wine. Gwen wanted to lose her shirt, feel the night air settle on her breasts, position herself so the light from the lantern would flutter on her pale skin, make the freckles seem like stars David could touch. She moved the shirt checker near his shoe checker, then hit her forehead as though it was a dumb move.

"Smart move," David said.

Gwen unbuttoned the cuffs, then the row of buttons down her chest. She slipped the shirt off her shoulders, arched her back, released her arms from the material and heard David take a deep breath.

"No bra?"

Gwen looked down at her breasts. "Guess I forgot." She let the scarf drape loosely around her shoulders. The tips played with her breasts.

"Your bra checker is as worthless as my shoes and socks checkers."

She wanted his glasses. She wanted him closer. She moved her shoe checker so he could move his glasses checker. He jumped her shoe checker. "Give it here," he said. He untied the lace, pulled off her shoe, and placed her heel on his lap. She felt his nest of pubic hair against her heel. She jumped his glasses checker. He leaned toward her. She held his face, touched his temples, tickling his eyebrows, and removed the glasses, first the stems behind his ears, then the frames off the bridge of his nose, which she kissed. She placed the glasses on top of her yellow blouse near the lantern, and its flame reflected from a lens. She moved for the wine bottle, bending over so that her breasts swung freely. David brushed his fingertips against one of her nipples. She wanted to grab him, lay him flat on the ground and take him, but she felt around instead for her wineglass and brushed against his lap. The bottle tipped and David's boxer shorts absorbed most of the spill.

"I'm going to attract ants," he said.

"Not at this picnic." She tugged and he lifted his buttocks. Her mouth was down on him before he had time to shy away. She moved her hair to tickle around his waist and thighs while she took as much of him as she could. His hips moved and the breeze rustled the grass. She dug her fingertips into his hips, squeezed, and sucked. He said her name. Then he stopped moving, reached down, and tugged at her, guided her. "Take off my shirt," he said. She fumbled with the top button but soon had them all opened. She freed his right arm, then gripped the fold of material below his wound and pulled. The arm came free from the material and hung by his side. She touched it, traced the shoulder, felt the bicep, made her way to the folded flap of skin where an elbow once was. The purple, red marks reminded her of the grape and beet dyes they made last summer, of the wool they had dipped into the colored liquids. He lay flat on his back. She removed her shoe, her shorts, her underwear, then straddled him and brought her face close to his. "Take your time," she whispered. "Listen to the frogs."

But he came too soon to satisfy her, closed his eyes, and turned away.

Several minutes passed. The frogs continued to croak. She could see that his mouth was slightly open.

"David?" She pulled at his arm and nestled it around her waist to keep away the chill air of dusk.

He moved his hand to the small of her back. What she felt was not his hand against her skin, but movement close to her skin. Puzzled, she lifted his arm. Between his fingers he rubbed a flat stone, moved it around and around, working the stone as though it had a familiar shape. When she turned to him, he didn't look away but continued to stare, whether at her, at the stone, or into the darkness where his car waited for him in a clutch of woods and weeds was impossible for her to say.

THE RIDDLE OF FLESH AND BLOOD

Rachel Simon

It was time to get my daughter Tina the surgery that would leave her unable to have children. This conviction sprang upon me without inner debate, without my wife Sadie at my side, whispering her wisdom in that quiet way we'd had between us, lips courageously forming the word I'd never let myself utter: "sterilize." The decision came as I sat, white haired and ailing, in my retarded daughter's room, and found myself gaping at an obscene Polaroid of her sweetheart. I peered up at my Tina, whose slender thirty-year-old body contained an eight-year-old mind, and I thought to myself that while hope is stained by so much in life, the cruelest stains of all come from love.

This was the scene: I was sitting in Tina's upholstered rocker, shaking with my Parkinson's tremors. Before me, on her bed, sat my daughter, chewing grape gum, wearing the latest teenage fashion. Across the room crouched her stocky beau Freddie, tightening the spokes on his ten-speed. The room was silent, except for the distant sound of Tina's houseparent, who was in the living room discussing the day's television schedule with the three disabled ladies who shared Tina's apartment.

Tina had asked during our call last night that I come over to meet Freddie. Not pick her up to attend a matinee or get soft ice cream, as we usually did on Sundays. But meet her boyfriend, as she put it. This had not concerned me greatly; as she had never mentioned him, or any boy, before, I imagined that Freddie was little more than a companion with whom she enjoyed watching her *Three Men and a Baby* video. But I was disavowed of this shortly after I had arrived in the autumn chill in a freshly pressed woolen suit, new cane in hand, and been introduced. As Tina was telling me the story of how they met—only the week before—she deposited her photo album into my lap, and performed her usual ritual of identifying each photograph. "And then, well that's when we came to my room," she said, and there was the picture of Freddie, posing buck naked for my daughter, prominently flaunting what, in days long ago, my more tactful students would have called his "scepter of seduction."

Until last spring, Tina could not even accurately describe the basics of reproduction, let alone photograph them. Sex was something other people had, like a driver's license or an interest in politics. If the PG rating at our matinees proved misguided, and we were treated to some Babylonian display of passion, Tina would sigh, "I'm bored." Then my Parkinson's had accelerated, and I, a widower, seventy-two years old, had to place my daughter in this group home, and shortly after that she had stopped being bored at the movies. And now here we were, the moment I had wished off the calendar since Sadie had pointed out that our little girl would someday, in spite of her mental age, develop a woman's body— "And then, Theo," Sadie would say, "and then a woman's desires."

I flipped to the next page in the photo album.

"Wait, Daddy," Tina said, turning back. "You didn't say what you thought of these."

I laid my trembling fingers on the laminate. "Oh," I said, pointing to an adjacent photograph of a pumpkin. "These must be from the Halloween party last week."

"Yup. That was the night I met Freddie."

Freddie called across the room, "Not *met*. I only live upstairs, Mr. Klingerman. It was when we—"

"What a pretty dress you were wearing." I indicated another photo. "Had you told me you were masquerading as an angel?"

Tina shook her head. "Sharon Stone," she said.

"And I was Arnold Sortsagegger," Freddie added, revealing the speech impediment that his own retardation had bestowed upon him. He added, "Arnold can go pow to anyone he wants."

"Freddie pumps iron," Tina said. "See?" She touched the biceps on the pornographic picture.

"This is . . . unseemly," I managed to say.

Freddie turned from his bicycle, perplexed. I acknowledged him: the scar on his temple, the Hulk Hogan sweatshirt, his congenital grin. "What's unseemey mean?" he asked.

"It's just junk my dad says," Tina replied, and my spine gave a barely audible crack. "He don't use words like we do."

"Doesn't," I corrected what she already knew.

"Then," Freddie went on, "how do you know what he's saying?"

"You guess," Tina said, snatching the photo album away from me, leaving my hands to tumble like broken eggshells into my lap. "Sometimes you get it. But sometimes you're wrong."

———

Kay Frances was waiting in the van when we stepped outside. She gave a quick wave. "Senior Transit Co-op," was written on the van in script, which meant my daughter, who was proficient with print yet lost with cursive writing, could not read the name of the company that conveyed her father from his house to hers. Most of Tina's skills were similarly inconsistent. She had never crawled; she went directly from crib to walking, then didn't graduate from diapers until she was five. "We understand very little about retardation," the doctor had told Sadie and me at the diagnosis. "Expect what you'd never expect. Then you stand a chance of coping."

I descended the steps slowly. Freddie had carried his bike down in front of us, and Tina had spent the staircase journey filling me in on the sheltered workshop where she earned money. "A new guy there crawls around on his stomach. He chews on your shoes when you're standing up." She told me about her boss's puppy, and the latest addition to her own seashell collection.

For twenty-seven steps this went on, and with each thud of my cane my decision about her sterilization fixed itself more firmly in my mind. It was not the boy himself. Freddie could have been anyone. It was just the only option for Tina.

"Kay Frances lowered her window. "Need help, Mr. Klingerman?"

"Thank you, but I can manage by myself."

"Take your time." She held up a red pen, as if to show she had something to do. Kay Frances never minded a wait; she was perpetually occupied with ghostwriting her son's college papers.

I turned to Tina. "We need to speak about the repercussions of romance," I said. "That is, accidents can happen."

"I *know*, Daddy."

"I'll call to talk about this tonight at my ordinary time."

"I won't know when that'll be. Kim ran the vacuum cleaner into the living room clock and it got a crack. And then today I took off Mom's watch to do dishes and put it up safe but by mistake I knocked it into the water. It stopped."

I glanced to her wrist. A strip of white encircled the skin where her watch—the one she'd inherited from Sadie—had previously blocked the sun. "I didn't want to let you know and get you upset," she said.

Breath caught in my windpipe, though the watch was only a plastic timepiece to which Sadie hadn't even been attached. Cheap. Insignificant. I cleared my throat. "That's OK," I said, and I reached inside my overcoat and unhooked my pocket watch from my vest. "You can use this."

Unlike my wife, I had never accepted digital displays. "Do you remember how to read this?" I asked.

"As long as the big hand is on the twelve."

I fastened the chain and slipped it over her head. Then I explained how to tell when it was eight o'clock, so she could be ready for my call.

Tina admired this gift she could barely use. Her hair was blowing in the November breeze. It was a cascade of walnut, the color of Sadie's eyes. The color of my sweetest daydreams every morning, when I wished with all the healthy cells left in my body that I could see my wife again, coming into our room in the sepia tint of the dawn light, touching my shoulder and sitting down on the bed beside me, her clear brown eyes locked just one more time onto mine.

"Tell me," I said. "How much do you like Freddie?"

"I like him."

"I know. But how much?"

"A lot."

Across the street, Freddie was, to use Tina's terminology, popping a wheelie. They seldom know why retardation happens—if it's from a flash of fever, or born fully sculpted into the genes. We used to wish she had been mongoloid, so we would know which. But Tina looked as normal as anyone, with the exception of the increasing disparity between her age and her attire. She just acted like a child.

I kissed Tina good-bye and climbed into the van. Mabel Stein had left me the front seat so she could sit in the back with Polly Schultz. They both sported party hats. We exchanged greetings as they chuckled over the endearing habits of their grandchildren, one of whom had evidently just celebrated a birthday.

I leaned toward the window, and through the glass I could see her, my grown-up child, squealing and applauding her thirty-five-year-old suitor as he braked to make artful skids in the street.

―――――

Sadie had warned me about love. Before any of the pregnancies or my tenure, when it was still just us and a rented apartment and hope as untarnished as gold. "Someday, Theo," she'd said, hands in oven mitts, auburn strands popping free of her barrette, "we'll have children, and they'll want everything we've wanted."

I thought she meant what we wanted then—carpets instead of throw rugs, a house we'd know as well as our own bones. "You mean a settled life?" I asked. "No," she said with a grin. "I mean what we do now." And she had shaken the oven mitts in the direction of the sofa, where we made love almost every night.

Sadie was a prescient woman; this was well before the days of prophylactics in the schools. But our success came slow, Tina not being conceived at the beginning of our marriage, when television still spared innuendo while telling its tales in black and white. Tina did not arrive until television dipped its tales in color and served them overly spiced with crude. By then, we were almost middled-aged, and libido had been massaged into every corner of the culture. But we did not care about the character of the epoch in which our child would be raised.

Tina lived at home. She attended special education classes in the public schools, then went to the county-sponsored work center. We recognized that, instead of Prince and Pearl Jam, she played recordings of New Kids On The Block and Barney. That at twenty she preferred receiving celebrity magazines in the mail to receiving boys at the door. But these things didn't matter. We believed our parenting would prove mightier than the handicap. So we played dominoes, glued collages. Sadie rode bicycles with her around town. I read to her from folk tales and Greek mythology, and then, in her twenties, the American Girls books. Tina always knew she was wanted, and whenever she sat beside me in the movie theater, asking me to explain what the big words meant, relishing the buttered popcorn we balanced on the armrest between us, turning to me for my hanky at the sadder moments, I knew then that I was wanted, too.

Then last year, on Sadie's sixty-sixth birthday, after the cake and presents, my wife pulled me into the sun parlor. "We need to make plans," she said. "We won't be here forever."

"Come on, Sade. We're healthy."

"We're *senior citizens*. And look. Tina took five years to handle her period without mussing herself. Even this afternoon, I had to clasp her bra for her. How do you think she'll do at the Shop-Rite once we're gone? Handling a broken water heater?"

I had turned my thoughts to this problem from time to time, but always with an averted eye.

Sadie said, "Maybe we can get some information on these group homes. I'll look into it tomorrow."

Sadie always took charge of our milestones. It was she who knew it was time to house hunt. It was she who knew it was time for a child. My thoughts always skimmed past such possibilities, occupied as I was with lectures, or exams. Days folded one into the next for me; appropriate enough for an historian, I could not see the future. That was Sadie's job. It was she who insisted we try again after the first miscarriage, and the second. Who cut back on her volunteer work at a local school so she would be better rested, and said we had to try once more.

Tina's arrival was a terrible birth, Sadie bleeding onto the kitchen floor, thrashing about in the ambulance; me beside her, helplessly stroking her head. Two days of agony, and when they finally went in to find our Tina, they also found a tumor lurking on my wife's ovaries. "There's the culprit for all those miscarriages," the doctor said, tapping the x-ray with his fountain pen. "I'm afraid it will all have to come out now."

And so our first child was our last. Through her fear and sorrow, Sadie managed to teach me how to heat formula and to diaper, and while I cared for our child, my wife lay in a hospital, her reproductive organs lost, her hair falling out. She came home around the time Tina learned to smile, but remained bedridden until teething. I brought Parcheesi into our room and we played on the bed. I bought the indigo velvet dress she had coveted for months; hooked up speakers in the bath so she could listen to balalaika records. Night and day, I attended to her. I couldn't see straight in my classes, stumbled to the library and committee meetings. But I didn't care; in a year she tested clean. Her hair grew back thick and lustrous, and together we watched our daughter grow. I would look at my family during meals, and even after we knew Tina would never, figuratively speaking, make it out of her high chair, I would take a deep breath, and think: the world is a fine place, and I am a lucky man. My history persists in front of me. I have no complaints.

———

The agency referred to me to a doctor. He said I needed to ascertain that Tina understood the consequences of sexual activity. "Does she want children?"

"She fantasizes. In the mall she says hi to every passing infant. But she has no sense of what parenthood means."

So we decided on a real-life experiment. I'd tell Tina I wanted her to play a game. "Take one of your conch shells off your shelf, wrap it in a towel, and pretend it's a baby," I proposed on the phone that night. "Since it's a baby, you can't leave it alone. You have to carry it all the time."

"That sounds stupid."

"Just as a game, all right?"

She tried it. The next night when I called, she said, "It's too hard. Besides, I dropped it, and it broke."

"That's what having a baby will be like. Only harder."

"She let out a long sigh.

"Do you know," I asked, "what you can do to make it easy?"

"I can not have a baby?"

"That's right. And do you know how to do that?"

"You put these . . . *things* on."

I grimaced. "Who puts what on?"

"I don't know. I think Freddie."

The grimace became a cringe. I imagined them fumbling. A finger punctures the latex, or Freddie says, "Ah, forget it." The phone call one month hence. A child he will not want and she cannot care for; a child I am unable to take. "There is another way," I said, and I told her about the tubal ligation. "And when it's over, you won't have to worry."

"Forever?"

"Yes."

There was a pause. I said, "How about if you consider this for a few days?"

"All right."

"And bear in mind what we discussed about accidents."

"But will it hurt?"

"Just at first. And then never again."

"That's good. I don't like it when I hurt."

"I don't like it when you hurt, either," I said.

Tina and Freddie were watching "Power Rangers" on the waiting room television when I arrived at the hospital. Earlier in the morning a houseparent had brought them in, making certain Tina was registered, and then had left my daughter to fend for herself among the reruns of "Scooby Doo" and copies of *Smithsonian*. I had coordinated my arrival with Kay Frances, but after my bath my fingers had misbehaved while knotting my tie. Finally I grabbed a clip-on bow tie Sadie had once purchased for a joke, and then I got in the van, annoyed and unforgivably late.

"Daddy!" Tina said, jumping up from her chair.

I wrapped my arms around her. "It'll be over soon."

"That's what I been telling her," Freddie said.

"I brought you something." I handed Tina a greeting card. "You look at it up close and it has a picture hidden in the colors." She looked and made out a horse which I myself had been unable to detect.

"Thanks," Tina said. "I'll put it with the others."

"Others?"

"I have five cards like this. Freddie likes Magic Eye cards."

"Is that so?" Tina collected many items—seashells, Ninja Turtle mugs, shiny stickers—but this was the first I had heard of cards. "What kinds of other pictures are in the cards, Freddie?"

"Birds and fish and stuff I don't know what to call. They're nothing I know too good."

Before I could react, a nurse emerged to lead us to pre-op. We walked three abreast, and all the way I reassured Tina that, after she recovered, we would go to Ponderosa, her favorite restaurant, and then afterwards, if she wanted, I would take her for ice cream, too.

In pre-op, the nurse instructed Tina to go behind a curtain and disrobe. Freddie, waiting, removed a bicycle chain from his pocket and poured it like small waterfalls of tension, first into one fist and then the other, his eyes riveted on the curtain.

I excused myself and stepped into the corridor. At the far end was a nursing station where, I reasoned, I could learn the number of the room in which Tina would convalesce later in the day. A row of windows lined the hall, and as I plodded toward my destination, I glanced outside. This was a shock, a mistake, though not because of the scenery—a group of women huddling on a veranda near the side door, enjoying a cigarette break—but because of the memory. I had been on that same veranda myself, not so long ago. It had been raining, and I had staggered out into the wetness and begun to weep. The smokers had turned away, and I had fished out my handkerchief but forgotten to use it. I'd had no idea what I was doing.

Tina was lying on the bed when I returned from the nursing station. Her hair was in a green cap, her body in a hospital gown.

Soon the doctor would enter her navel to alter her insides, and then it would all be over.

Freddie said, "They just gave her a shot."

"Did he watch?" I asked my daughter.

She nodded.

I tried to remember what I had done with Sadie that last time, when she had been in a similar room. It was a little less than a year ago, for surgery she had dismissed as "silly." Tina still lived at home, and my Parkinson's had not yet come into full bloom. We had been told it would be a short procedure. It was elective surgery, after all; just a few hours in to remove an old cyst from her back. Nothing important. I had not watched her get the shot. They were to deliver it in surgery—local anesthesia, that's all it was. They hadn't planned to inject it into a blood vessel. But they did. They aimed wrong, and the simple turned tragic, and then the doctor came to find me much too quickly, I had barely even opened my waiting room book, and his face ashen, he knelt beside me and said she hadn't made it. I could not fathom the concept. Sadie—over. Lost. History had gone wrong. Even a year after the fact, I could not believe it.

I stood beside our daughter in her hospital bed, holding her hand as she waited to enter her own surgery. Sadie, my Sadie. In those moments we had not known were our last, what had we done? Your eyes were soft, I remember, your face more wanting than usual. And we had spoken. Yes. I had tossed out some riddles from ancient Egypt, and you had tried to solve them, which was difficult—actually, impossible. No one, not even the greatest scholars, had ever figured out those answers. How you laughed when I told you that fact, and how your laugh had made me laugh. It was a good moment. Contagious pleasure. Every night since, when I listened hard, I could almost hear you laughing still.

"We're ready," a nurse said.

I tightened my hand around my daughter's. "What would you like me to do?" I asked.

"Wait out there," she said, pointing to the hall.

I'm sure my face twitched, but I caught myself with a nod, and muttered, "All right, then." I bent close and kissed her, and for a second I had the sensation of falling. Not physically, but inside my heart. "Daddy will be right outside," I told her. "He'll be here waiting when you get out."

———

My book seemed a swirl beneath my eyes, the characters on the television screen glowed with inanity. Freddie sat beside me, watching the TV, waiting for the surgery to end.

Strangers populated the waiting room. Flocks of families, all chatter and shuffling playing cards and shared cups of coffee. Bodies moving, consoling hand in hand, and in each face I could see the genes of others.

I was outside before I knew I had left. Doors were closing behind me, the December wind was pricking at my lips, and I was on a walkway, heading toward a fountain, its water turned off because of the cold.

The air seemed a tonic on my cheeks, and I realized I had been breathing too quickly. As I tried to still myself I saw a shadow approaching, and turned. Freddie was ambling toward me.

"Go back inside," I said.

He hesitated.

"I'd prefer to be by myself."

I scanned the walkway. A few yards ahead was a bench. I started toward it and he came up beside me. I expected him to speak but he remained silent. He simply progressed at my side, so close I could hear his breath and feel the heat from his body.

At the bench we sat. I smoothed my overcoat, rested my hands on my cane. He was not wearing a jacket, and he was shivering.

"You don't need to be here," I said.

"It's OK," he said, wiping his nose with his sleeve. "Tina said to stay with you."

The lady smokers near the door guffawed with camaraderie, and here I was, groping for small talk.

I said, "So, where does your family live?"

"Next town over."

"And what do they think of all this?"

"They don't know nothing."

I looked down at my hands.

He went on. "I don't tell them nothing. They want me to live at home and give them all the money I make. But I won't."

"Is that why you live at the group home—because your family is so demanding?"

"Because my dad likes to smack me. That's why."

I started, suddenly comprehending his facial scar, his appreciation for going pow to anyone he wants. The thought occurred that I should reach for his arm, or pat him on the shoulder. But that seemed inappropriate, so for several moments I wrestled with in-action until finally I opted for the simplest solution. "Freddie," I said, "I'm sorry to hear that."

The smokers finished and went inside. A car then pulled up to the veranda, and a young pregnant woman climbed out. Pregnancy and anti-pregnancy, side by side. It didn't seem fair.

Freddie observed the woman too, and then he shook as if reject-ing the idea of a chill, and said, "I need to go in. Want to come?"

"No. I'll stay here for awhile."

He gave me a look I couldn't understand. "See you inside," he said. Then he shoved his hands in his pockets and got up.

I wrapped my coat tighter and leaned back on the bench. In an hour my daughter would get out of surgery, and I would be wait-ing. I would come into her hospital room and sit beside her, the way I used to at home when she was an infant. Every night I had done it, after both my girls had fallen asleep and I finished mark-ing papers. I would pad into Tina's room and gaze into her crib. We knew something was wrong already, though we thought it might be treatable, as Sadie's cancer had been—rich in youth, I was at the time, and still possessed of the purest of hope. And I would look at my daughter in the moonlight and remember the evening she was conceived, my beautiful wife beside me, her arms around my back. That night we found a touch that seeped inside us and melted something we'd never realized was frozen. We couldn't remember later where the touch had come from—our fin-gers? Cheeks? We'd laughed about it, but whenever I gazed at my baby asleep, her story as yet unwritten, I thought of that touch and I could still feel it, melting that same place inside me. It happened many times over the years, when I saw Tina in a certain light. The angle of her head, the shadows on her face; they never stopped do-ing this to me. A flash of the moment, my wife's eyes wide open, our sweat, and a something deep inside me I could never lose yet never know.

I watched the back of my daughter's lover as he strolled into the building, thinking of all the party hats I would never wear, the birthdays that would never be, and as I cradled my hands over my cane in the cold, I believed I felt my wife sitting beside me. Yes. Right there. Not old as in these last years, but young, wearing the indigo velvet dress, her long auburn hair twining wild and free of pins in the winter air.

Sadie, I said.

She reached over to me, laid her fingers on my knotted knuckles, her hand shielding my skin from the breeze.

What did you do, Theo? she asked. She nodded toward the hospital, then fixed her dark gaze upon my eyes.

I gave our daughter a gift, I replied. The final gift we could give her.

But the bow, Sadie said. It can't be untied.

That's the point.

But our daughter can never open it.

It's what you wanted, Sadie. It was the right thing to do.

Was it?

Yes. It was the only choice.

Are you sure?

I parted my lips to respond, but instead of words my mouth filled only with emptiness.

My wife removed her touch from my hands, blinked the future away from her eyes. Now, Theo, she said, now I'm really gone.

We are gone, I cried. I gripped my cane to my chest, and then I could feel her no more.

WHIR OF SATISFACTION

Lara J. K. Wilson

My Uncle Reed and I were laid off during the same week. He was a machinist for GM. I worked in advertising in the brownstone-brimmed Back Bay. He had a wife and two kids. I had charge cards at Lord & Taylor and Filene's. He asked my dad for help. I asked my dad for help. Dad sent him two thousand dollars. Dad sent me three hundred and a note which said, "You're young. Waitress."

Frankly, I was pissed. Who would think that a twenty-four-year-old woman with a college degree and two years of real job experience could be laid off? I was an account executive at a Boston ad agency which won an average of five Hatch awards each year. I had my own cubicle with a window and a contour desk chair. I ate lunch on Newbury Street, dinner in Cambridge, midnight cannolis from the North End. My hair stylist, Jorge (he spelled it "Whorehey!" on the receipt), decided I should grow out my bob, and as soon as my hair passed my shoulders I bought silk pony tail scrunchies and sterling silver barrettes. I had jazz brunch with my boyfriend on Sundays, and sex with condoms coated with Nonoxynol-9. I sold my old Prelude so I could afford to live alone in a first floor apartment on a slim, wobbly Beacon Hill street whose shape made me think of my grandmother's legs. There was more than just a couch in my tiny living room. My debt exceeded my income, for godsake!

Sondra had actually been embarrassed when she called me into her office and gave me the news.

"You're not serious," I said, glaring at the foot-tall copy of Michaelangelo's *David* on her window sill. A naked man should not have been witnessing my demise, no matter how small he was.

"I'm afraid so, Amanda. In the last two months we've lost Just Juice and The Wingdingery. I know it's not much of a consolation, but you're not the only one we have to let go."

"Wonderful." Obviously, I was not the singular corporate peon,

I thought, but one of several bottom-rungers who are first to be canned.

"This is so difficult." Sondra played with the small Waterford clock on her desk. "The situation is grave for all of us. You know we all took a ten percent pay cut. The economy is . . ."

"A bituminous shitcake." I had recently read an article about coal mining in my dentist's waiting room before he gave me the root canal I was paying for with the sale of my mountain bike. Bituminous stuck in my mind and I had been waiting for the right moment to use it. It had a great vulgar ring, better than shitcake.

"Listen, Sondra, I don't mean to be contemptuous. I appreciate your sympathy." Tears were damned up by my lower eyelashes. My voice sounded like I was riding over the grate bridge near the Science Museum. "I guess I should go home to look over last Sunday's *Globe* and eat a large Alden Merrill cheesecake."

"Call me," Sondra said, coming around the desk to hug me. "You worked hard here. I'll try to help you out."

As I hurried to the coat closet to get my London Fog, my heels sunk into the plush carpet, denying me the chance to hear them quickly click away and leave an echo. The darkly paneled elevator doors opened and swallowed me, then spit me out in the empty lobby next to the directory, which was a jumble of last names stuck together, commaless.

"Evenin'," the doorman said without looking up from his portable TV.

"It's afternoon, you idiot!" I slammed my hand on the counter. The doorman's face turned into a caricature: bulbous nose, bushy crew cut, beady black eyes. I glared at the white socks sticking out from between his dark pant leg and black vinyl shoes, then noticed his eyes were really the same color green as my Aunt Velda's, who had taught me how to bake sourdough bread on rainy days.

"Sorry," I mumbled. "I just lost my job."

"Hard times," he said, turning back to an "Andy Griffith Show" rerun. I hurried for the door so he wouldn't see me cry. Out in the open, the frantic crowd rushed for the T, and I pushed my way down the dark hole that reeked of urine despite the cellophaned bundles of flowers shoved into plastic buckets at the bottom of the worn, sticky stairs.

———

After I lost my job, making Jello became a ritual. When the refrigerator was nearly empty, I filled the small glass bowls I bought at Crate n' Barrel with colored liquid and arranged them in rows on the three shelves beneath a pint of cottage cheese and the ever-present generic spring water poured into an Evian bottle. Every morning I opened the cold, white door and saw the frigid insides full of lemon, orange, raspberry and lime lines glistening like sorcerous gems.

I was out of raspberry (why have we been conditioned to go for red first?), so I grabbed one of the two-dozen blue boxes from the pantry shelf. When I was a kid I used to eat the sugared granules out of the box with the smallest measuring spoon, 1/8 I think. My dad used to cringe. Why do you do that, Amanda? he'd ask, and I'd just smile and stick out my green tongue. I poured the colored dust into a mixing bowl, a magic powder that could turn an iguana into a Hollywood starlet.

The incredulity of my situation surfaced once again while I waited for the water to boil in my teapot with the train whistle. I threw some ice cubes into a measuring cup, then went into the living room to turn on the stereo and sulk, listening to Diabolically Thematic Musings, a new band from Ireland. Outside through the swirling wrought iron bars covering my front windows two men in black trench coats stood next to my stairs holding hands. The one with long auburn hair had perfectly shaped lips much like Paul's.

Zoe had introduced me to Paul several months before the layoff, at an art exhibit at the ICA. He was wearing Doc Marten's and faded Girbaud jeans with a black T-shirt that said "Do you know how many doughnuts I can fit on my dick?" on the front, "How many can you eat?" on the back. His thin gold nose ring glinted under the track lighting. He was definitely not my type. Zoe told me Paul was one of the exhibiting artists, a grad student in art history at Harvard. "He's not gay," she whispered when he turned around to grab a passing hors d'oeuvre. I regarded the canvases surrounding us with as much acuity as I could muster after a four-hour client meeting in which we discussed the relationship between feminine hygiene products and the *hikaya* of Japanese flower arrangements. Paul's work was full of oblique faces and trees whirling down spiral gutters, wispy bodies floating over spheres of water only to be sucked into what looked like a gigantic paper shredder or composter. The dissolution of social structure. Or ecological cataclysm, I couldn't decide which. I did notice the paint specks on Paul's clothes and the way his firm lips slid over his straight, white teeth. If he was HIV negative, I wanted to sleep with him. He was. I did. Several times. Even the day after the lay-off, which struck me as a great irony.

Paul stayed around during my initial stage of unemployment. We didn't talk much, but at least he was there, alive and breathing the scent of spring potpourri next to me. I knew from the beginning that our relationship was not about communication, in the literal sense. Zoe had said I should go with it if we both felt the same way, but as soon as it seemed like see-sawing with sandbags, cut loose. When things bottomed out, I ignored her advice. Paul could have been a dozen sash weights on his end of the plank and I still would have wanted him to be there with the Kleenex and classic movies. He listened. He brought Italian chocolates.

Soon enough, Paul resorted to veracity. He pointed out that something positive had come out of my unemployment: I had increased my volunteer hours at the family crisis center to console myself. I had to admit, I enjoyed going to the dark little counseling room and answering the hot line, even if I had to dress down and couldn't wear jewelry in that neighborhood. Often I would wear things that didn't match or were outrageous—a plaid mini-kilt with a polka-dot blouse and cowboy boots, for instance—and I felt cool, like the change in my attire made my narrow face with its pointed features look less ordinary.

When I started at the center almost a year earlier, I had been told I'd do a little counseling, since I had experience. But most of my time was spent on the phone, and although I couldn't see the people on the other end, it was nice to know that for several minutes a complete stranger needed me. On my way home after my shift the city looked still and safe, and I felt my whole body was enveloped in a private, liquid goodness. I'd circle the Common, stroll up and down Charles Street looking in the glowing second floor windows until my feet cramped inside my tight shoes. Then, as I entered my apartment and saw the bills in my mailbox and the 00 on my answering machine, the memory of that warmth disappeared like dew on hot pavement. If Zoe wasn't home, I'd call Paul to relieve my emptiness, recounting the day to get some sympathy. But after a while my strategy backfired. He knew I hadn't received a single reply to the resumes I had sent out in weeks, and when I was supposedly at an interview the previous Tuesday, he saw me buying piña colada jelly beans at the candy store in Copley Place. Paul soon thought the volunteer work was admirable, because it was tough and I wasn't being paid, and ridiculous, because it was tough and I wasn't being paid. He felt I should focus on my career, stop being so goddamn apathetic. Then he'd grow silent and complain about the ramifications of his focusing on my life, how stirring up certain emotions affected his art, caused him to use too much magenta.

Soon everything about me got on Paul's nerves. My shredded cuticles, new French underwear, the stack of untouched newspapers next to the bed—then the Jello. He would slam the refrigerator door shut so the bowls would crash together and I'd shrug into anticipated humiliation in the living room. "I'm going out to get some food," he'd shout from the hall closet. His keys jingled as Paul jumped down the stairs and I'd watch his tall, thin frame crumple into his roommate's rusty Jetta before he sped off to the sub shop. Even though he was frustrated, he'd bring back a veggie pita pocket for me. Then one day we were making love on the white cotton bath mat I found in Euro Trash and Paul noticed the ends of my yellow hair were coated with red streaks of gelatin. I had briefly steamed my face over a pan of Jello squares I was making without putting my hair in a pony tail. Paul raised his voice. He couldn't stand my sulking and Jello-making any more. His chest heaved like a moonwalk with kids jumping on it. I was wallowing in self-pity, he said. I let him become furious without interrupting because I knew he would leave. He did. That day. I ate six bowls of Jello (one red, two green, and three yellow) while picking the flowers off the delphinium on my kitchen table and arranging them in a wavy river on the glass. Paul's leaving was inevitable. Sex can't keep you together in times of strife. The touching matters more than the climax for one, and the other actually minds.

––––––––

Two weeks after Paul took off, I spent the last of my dad's money on an ivory linen vest with sheer palazzo pants and was getting nervous about paying my rent. The family crisis center posted an opening in PR that would barely cover my bills, but a day after I applied someone called to say they hired a woman my mother's age who had a master's in counseling. I tried pestering a few contacts from my former job, including Sondra. The story was status quo: no one had any openings. Zoe suggested I hand model.

"You have nice, long fingers," she said as we walked from her agency to Piazza for lunch. "And you don't have these chicken feet tendons like I do on the backs of my hands. You wouldn't believe how much they pay you." Two men rolled down the windows of a BMW and tried to get Zoe's attention. She tossed the remainder of her Häagen Dazs shake across the front fender. It oozed down the chrome hubcap.

"Okay, what's the down side?"

"Well, you have to put your hand over your head for a few hours before the shoot so all the blood rushes out, and then you have to hold something in your completely numb hand for an entire afternoon. But the pay. It's criminal!" Zoe held the door for me and we walked down the slick black steps together.

"And . . ." She was famous for leaving essential details out. Once she asked me to watch her cat for the weekend and neglected to tell me it was in heat and had developed an ankle fetish. I couldn't wear boots for a week.

"And, let's see. You can't garden, wash dishes, do laundry, bathe without gloves. . . ." The hostess showed us to our table next to a group of women wearing blouses with puffy bows at the neck. They scowled at Zoe in her catsuit and she told them their mothers must be proud of their celibacy.

"So basically, you can't use your hands for any practical reasons."

"More or less," she said, chomping on a bread stick. "But the pay is unreal."

We shared arugula chicken salad and pesto pizza, then spent the afternoon at the State Street Clothiers sale. Zoe bought a pair of white platform shoes and a red sequined bra with matching blue and white striped hip hugger shorts for her date at The Rock. I passed up a thirty-percent-off slightly damaged Coach handbag so I could replace my empty sloughing cream at Clinique.

We walked back to my place along Newbury Street, looking at the store displays instead of each other. Zoe pointed to a pair of shoes at Otto Aradian, thick-soled and black with chunky silver buckles. Zowie, she said. My reflection refused to be superimposed over the mannequin in the window. I stared at Zoe's body shimmying to imaginary Pearl Jam as she described the Seattle Grunge runway show she did the previous week, and it hit me. Finding an opening in advertising was futile. And I didn't have the qualifications nor the lifestyle for social work. Yet I couldn't bear the thought of wearing a black-and-white uniform every night, waiting on people who were sitting in my former life. There was no alternative: I'd have to stall. I'd have to temp.

———

I chose SunnySide. (We had done a radio spot for them that embarrassed me every time I thought of it: "SunnySide's Up Before You Take Out the Pup.") At the interview, Ms. Barbara Baddish twirled her pearl earrings and squinted through her rose-tinted Christian Dior's at me. I was irked about having to take a typing exam, and told Babs I had had an executive position and used seven different kinds of software for Macs and IBMs. I could open my own print shop, I said. Well, since you haven't and you're at SunnySide, you'll have to take the test, she said. It was policy. I was shut in a dimly lit room with a typewriter and a test booklet, the page open to an essay on the benefits of colostomy. Babs said I could practice for one minute and the test would be two minutes long. She returned to tell me to begin, and chimed "time's up" what seemed like ten minutes later. In her office, she whisked a red pen over two of the dozen mistakes I caught, did some calculation in the margin, and pronounced that I had typed ninety-five words a minute. I raised my eyebrows, thinking about the delete key that had to be replaced on my computer at work.

"Well, I see by your resume that you have some wonderful experience, Amanda."

"Yes, I . . ."

"And you graduated with honors," she continued. "Now, Amanda, we can offer you our executive wage of $10.00 an hour for secretarial and $8.50 for reception."

"Is that . . ." She held up her hand as if it were protocol to do so rather than rude.

"We hope to place you at an extended services locale, but one may not be available at this time. However, we have some regular clients who might have openings that will suit your skills." I checked the wall next to me for the cue card she may have been reading. "In any case, you will be called by the end of the week with an assignment which you can accept or refuse. If you accept, you will be required to fill out time cards for each day of work and mail or drop the cards here. Let me introduce you to your manager, Marilyn."

I glanced at my file on her desk as we left her mauve office. In red letters on the top right hand corner it said "A; blond/blue; priority." Sticking out from the file beneath mine were the words "D-; fat, acne" in thick black ink.

———

I swished my hair under the bath water in a seaweed-ish motion. Yellow kelp in a bathtub with feet. My nose, mouth, and chin poked above the surface like an island where little people who used my nostrils as cave-dwellings lived. Somehow this thought did not make me sit up abruptly. Yet it kept coming back, tiny, naked beings dancing across my upper lip.

The muted sound of the dryer thumped around in the rhythm of the Orange Line, dah-DUM, dah-DUM, dah-DUM. But it was Sunday, and I didn't have to go to my temporary job where I sat in a temporary uncomfortable chair at a temporary oak veneer desk next to permanent administrative assistants still wearing socks and Reeboks with flowered dresses at three p.m. I didn't have to muster up scarf confidence to make one of my five basic suits feel like a new outfit. There was no need to stuff my hips into hosiery dotted with nail polish where runs might shoot down my legs. I could stay in this tub all day, notice that my nipples were too large for my small breasts, that the moles on my legs would make a great slalom course, that the toenails on my pinky toes are almost nonexistent. I could imagine Lilliputian families picnicking on my face all day. My favorite brushed cotton underwear were crumpled in my lingerie drawer, I had half-and-half for my tea instead of two-percent milk, and if I shut out the dim balls of lights shining around the mirror, I could even imagine a man lounging in my bed, waiting: someone who sweat when he worked out and ate organic vegetables, someone who knew how to communicate without Post-it Notes, someone who had perfect moons under his thumbnails.

I finally drained the tub. I had refilled it three times, the last with blue bath gel from Crabtree & Evelyn. My mother sent it to me in a big basket with a loofa mitt, raspberry bramble tea, hyacinth and peach foot powder, clean pore lotion, real Scotch shortbread, and a natural bristle toothbrush that I was afraid to put in my mouth because it looked like something that happened on a pig's back when it got mad. Themes were never my mother's strong suit. She hadn't ever shopped for separates until I came home from college and insisted she fill her closets with mix-and-match items. I explained that these days a "shift" should only refer to change or work hours, never to clothing.

Mom was a bit disgraced about my temping.

"Mom, there is nothing out there," I explained. "I've had informational interviews with every ad agency in town. My former boss even tried to set up some interviews for me, but the agencies are letting people go rather than hiring. They all say I should move to New York, but I don't have the money."

I heard Mom sip something. Black coffee, I was sure. She drank two pots of decaf a day. She said I had gone beyond the introductory job stage. That I didn't need information.

"It's employment you're after, Amanda."

"Unfortunately, Mom, that's the only way I can get in to see people."

"Well, I wasn't going to bring this up, but your Uncle Reed has already gotten into Ford, making pistons or something." She rushed on before I could tell her that our situations were hardly comparable, that I'd have an easier time getting a job doing oil changes at Lube Land than working in advertising again. "And New York is filthy. I hope you're not really entertaining ideas of moving there. Crime up the wazoo. Why, people are shot down just waiting for the subway. Young tennis players, even. And terrorists love it there. . . ."

Of course, she wouldn't understand. She was born and raised in Omaha, and had only been on Lake Okoboji vacations and to visit me at college twice.

". . . Boston is so quaint. Those bumpy brick sidewalks and rows of stairs. You love it there."

Mom also was convinced I loved brussels sprouts, wool long johns, and lavender eye shadow.

"Maybe a different business would suit you better, honey," she went on. "Advertising is so, so, well, you know. Jingles and that sort of thing. Flashes of skin and loud, crazy music. They even have bras on TV now, for heaven's sake. Your brother is in the room sometimes and I can barely change the channel fast enough."

I didn't mention that I had found the *Joy of Sex* in her nightstand when I was twelve with the corners of the oriental position pages folded back. Mom continued her diatribe while I struggled to push a vision of "hovering butterflies" out of my mind.

"Actually, Mom, a lot of people my age are going back to school. I was thinking about counseling. Remember when I worked at the rehab hospital the summer after college? I really liked those kids." I raced on before she could jam her foot in the door of the conversation and shove it open. "And I've been volunteering for the family crisis center here for over a year." I took a deep breath. "But I need to get an advanced degree, and, well, I thought you and Dad might help."

Mom gulped coffee. "Now why would you want to surround yourself with drug addicts? I know how much you always liked helping the less fortunate, but you have enough problems right now, honey. You don't need to waste energy telling other people how to get their act together. Besides, Daddy is not too enthused about giving you cash for things after that last stint with the designer bedroom furniture."

I took the risk. She had to bring it up, even though I had paid back half of the furniture debt within six months. That was Mom, the eternal pessimist. I made a mental note to recommend some Sylvia Plath the next time we spoke.

"Mom, it's for school." A whine crept in from some childish place.

"Well, get yourself a loan. We paid for your college, the whole nine yards." I could hear my mother filing her nails. "You have a degree, Amanda. It's time to quit fooling around and apply yourself. If it's advertising you hate, try something else. Reporting or selling clothes or maybe newscasting. You have a pretty face, and with the right make-up, you'd look great on television."

The bathtub drain gurgled and sucked. I put the towel back on its rack, grabbed the clean pore lotion. It smelled like cough medicine. The thing was, Mom was pretty intuitive. I hated the ad biz. I never used to care about the tag in my nightgowns. We shopped at Target when I lived in Omaha. Kinney shoes were fine before I was wooed by the world of slogans. And then every day in the office, John O'Malley would ask if I liked his new suspenders from ChiChi. People from other agencies called to ask if Felicia Green, the vice president of the firm, had an original Paul Klee in her office (it was an authentic copy). Was it just a coincidence that I was promoted to account executive the day after I bought a Coach briefcase to replace the Shreve, Crump and Low bag I had been using to carry paperwork? At the time I had thought, hell, it's from Shreve's. And it wasn't just my co-workers; the creative process itself was predicated on things. Things to have—such as white teeth and low cholesterol. Things to not have—foot odor and termites. Things to invent needs for, like designer toilet paper, so both client and agency make millions while duped consumers flush their money down the hopper, satisfied to have wiped with style.

I should have quit early on, but I couldn't. I had to stay with it because I always wanted to be in advertising. Then the college specialization. I had been groomed to do one thing. To force myself to think about the target market for *Thigh-O-Sizer* before I fell asleep at night. To sell flowery language printed in a maximum of three type faces per ad. To conduct focus groups in which people are paid to eat gourmet muffins and talk about the kind of person who puts deodorant on before going to bed. If I left, I would have to admit that those essential years of learning had been a waste, and I couldn't repeat them. I would feel cheated. I'd have nightmares in which a big cartoon anvil was tied above my head with dental floss (to fight plaque build-up), the giant German-made scissors poised above that would click shut when I gave in and repudiated every last *thing*.

The bathtub faucet dripped, plink, plinkplink, plink. I pushed the door open to let the steam out, the cold in. I was out of Q-Tips, so I cleaned my ears with a twisted piece of toilet paper. My skin was blotchy. I smiled at the fogged mirror, glad I didn't have to face myself.

Advertising was at least better than temping. You didn't really feel needed, but you felt less needy. It could be construed as a career, whereas temping was an act of desperation. I had always considered that advertising really didn't contribute to society. In a positive way, that is. I felt I should do something more profound than providing post-purchase reassurance to the man whose wife left him because she "Felt the Feeling" in her new mini-van. Maybe Mom was right, I could get a loan. Zoe told me there are agencies that you can pay to clean up your credit history (she had borrowed money from her mother to do it twice). Or I could find a work-study job. Would it pay enough? There might be a counseling center on campus that pays interns. Could I live on that income? I had experience, the volunteer job. And I had worked with troubled kids in the Boston area.

It had started as an undergraduate psychology experiment to "expand my horizons in ways previously implausible." I took a part-time position in the referral office at Friends in Far Away Places, a teen counseling group and outreach program. When the semester ended, they offered me a slot in Touchbase, and I stayed on as a volunteer until I graduated. Julius Reardon had been my first client. His father had broken Julius's right arm so many times he had to become left-handed. He was a street musician in a four-man *a cappella* group that sang in Harvard Square. Zee Bop, they called themselves. I used to watch the way the crowd would bob their heads as they stood around Out-of-Town News, listening. An elderly gentleman in a Brooks Brothers suit and a Ve-ri-tas tie once stood next to me, snapping his fingers with the same beat of

Julius's left hand. When the group wrapped it up, I took Zee Bop to Balizzi's for lunch. They ate four pizzas with every kind of meat on the menu. Then they sang the Harry Connick, Jr., song about the man in the moon for me because Julius knew I liked it. I managed to get them a chance at the Black Crow, but a day before the gig was scheduled, Julius's friend Ray died of a heroin overdose. I hadn't even known he was an addict. Julius stuck a card in the door of my building before he disappeared. The blue envelope was dirty, but the card was fine. It had a picture of a half moon on the front, glowing like a crooked smile. Inside Julius had written, "Thanks to the girl in the world."

The underwear were there, soft and white. I pulled a pair of teal Liz Claiborne sweats over them. Although the volunteer work was fulfilling, I wasn't convinced that I could adapt to the life of a social worker. Not now. I'd have to give up my apartment, move to Somerville, live on hummus and carrot juice, and sell my suits at a thrift store where I'd buy a new wardrobe of plaid flannel shirts and rust-colored corduroys. It was too late. It wasn't me. The scary thing was, I realized that I didn't know what to do with my life. I was another pawn of the big X, the unnamed, undistinguished, uncertain generation that waits for change to flow through the atmosphere like clean air, hoping that, like so many others, I could just inhale and feel I was part of the movement. Actually, it couldn't even be considered a generation, but more a melange of previous ones, as Zoe had said when we had our "State of Life" talk last week. We made statements with all kinds of clothes—corporate chic, neo-retro, grunge—then said what you wear is immaterial. We avoided choosing an identity because being self-reflective was frightening; our shortcomings and obstacles would gag us like last month's egg salad. Parents feared our ambivalence, academics analyzed our ambiguity, teenagers revered our independence. Yet no one considered the individual, full of unique emotion, wanting to be included somewhere since personal desires couldn't be forced into action. The rules had dissolved. There was no previously paved path, and the light at the end of the tunnel was too dim to recognize. Go back to school. *Travel. We'd love to hire you, but there are two hundred over-thirty applicants with ten years of experience who need to feed their babies.* And although it was other people who could help us, society encouraged us separate ourselves from each other, to watch real-life drama on the VCR while eating take-out homecooking. Humanitarianism won't put gelatin in the fridge, said the devil on the left shoulder;

but it may be the only answer, said the angel on the right. Your head was in the middle, about to explode like a frazzled computer searching for the proper sequence. It had to be there, somewhere, behind the whir of satisfaction.

———

On Thursday Zoe came over. She liked herself—her hair was down, her lipstick more pale than usual. She was wearing flats. I had worked at a vet clinic and was soaking my hands in baking soda and water at the sink when she walked in. Cats suck, I muttered.

Zoe was a model, which sounded glamorous, but wasn't in Boston. Most of the time she did fittings for athletic wear companies and the occasional slutty-look photo shoot for an editorial in the *Herald*. I knew Zoe would like to leave Boston, but since her father's stroke, she had been supporting her mother, living at home in Woburn. Zoe told me about her brother's new house in Milton, its white picket fence and thirty-year mortgage fixed at 7.9 percent. We talked about the world, our world. How it was supposed to be but actually was. I had dreams of New York and she of Paris. I temped at funeral homes. She had straight pins stuck in her ass.

"You know what I heard at work today?" She poured herself some pinot blanc. "Some runner came in and had pulled a butt muscle, and he said he had to sit on frozen vegetables two hours a day."

"What?" I howled. Zoe laughed and her hands flailed about her wildly. She knocked over the bowl of pistachios I put too close to the edge of the table.

"Seriously. He said ice cubes were uncomfortable, but frozen peas conformed to the shape of his cheeks!" Her rear end stuck in the air as she reached under the table to scoop up the scattered red nuts.

I loved Zoe. She made me remember how Kool Aid had tasted as a kid, how it felt to rollerblade down a steep hill for the first time. Her only problem was men. Or, her only men were problems. Last year she had been engaged for two months, but broke it off. She admitted later that the only reason she had said yes was because she felt pressured to be married, not because it was trendy, but so she could stop obsessing about all the times she was stupid enough to have unsafe sex.

"So, what's his name?" I asked.

"Who?"

"The latest."

"How do you . . . ?"

"You're wearing the pink sweater. You always wear that after you get laid by a new man."

"Joey Farelli." Zoe opened the fridge. "Jesus. More Jello. Your nails must be great." She took out a jar of Kalamata olives and put two in her mouth at once. "Italian and kinda thupid. Workth in a fruit market." She spit the pits into the garbage. "Nice body, though."

"I admire you, Zo." I pulled the rubber sink stopper, dried my hands on a semi-clean dish towel and sat down at the small glass table. I was out of hand lotion. "I wouldn't have anything to say to someone like that."

"I never said I was in it for the conversation. Anyway, you would. You're just a snob." Her head was in the fridge again. "We talked about the Flintstones. Remember, Fred, Barney?"

"Oh yeah. They used them in that cereal commercial."

"Cut the shit, Amanda. You did watch the cartoon at one time." She turned to the table with a hunk of dill havarti and a knife. "I shouldn't eat this, but what the hell." She shook her finger at me, imitating her mother: "Spread it right on your thighs, honey."

"So what's this Joey guy like?" I asked. "Are you interested?"

"In a fruit man?"

"Who's the snob?" I ate the piece of cheese she handed me.

"OK. He has a hot bod and makes great marinara 'gravy,' as he calls it. What else could you ask for?" Zoe took the slice of cheese from the knife blade with her teeth.

"Diamonds, trips to Tahiti, an intellectual conversation once a month . . ."

"You've been in advertising too long, my friend." I winced and got up to get some Triscuits. "Sorry. Anyway, he knows the deal. I'm not looking for a soul mate. What do you want me to tell you? He's a great lay and he makes me laugh."

"Sex and shallow conversation. It's like watching television." I bent down in front of Zoe to pick up a stray pistachio. She wrapped her fingers in my hair.

"You need a new look, Manda. To go with your new lifestyle."

"Are you kidding? This is my 'forever foolish' look." I stood and pushed my hair from my face. It felt heavy and damp. "It is perfect for my 'forever floundering' life."

"Then I guess it fits you," she said, walking to the bathroom. I sat back down, leaned my elbows on the table and held my chin in my hands. The small piece of sky I could see through the kitchen window clouded then cleared.

"But you're not floundering." Zoe's voice floated through the open bathroom door like a conscience. "You're on the verge of something, and you're free to do it when it dawns on you."

"What's that?"

"I said on *you*, not on *me*," she yelled over the flushing toilet. She returned zipping the fly of her oversized jeans and pulled her chair closer to me.

"Forget regrets, Amanda." The sink faucet gurgled and dribbled. I looked my best friend in the eye, knowing she understood without being told a thing. That she'd watch Merchant Ivory films with me while I cried, and she'd have a lotion in her purse that got rid of under-eye bags overnight.

"It's your life. I mean, only you can change it, can do what you really want to do." Zoe rubbed my arm. "The only constant is that you are who you are *inside*. Close your eyes. Look." She lightly pressed her fingertips on my eyelids. "There's no label attached to that."

―――――

I was going against the flow of commuters, from the city to Brookline. Old women blocked the stairwell at every stop. An Indian man with a plastic bag of God-knows-what-but-it-smells-like-a-rancid-E.-coli-burger squished into the orange plastic seat next to me. The curry evaporated from his skin and left the inside of the train in a pungent, yellow fog. Monday.

It was my first day working for an environmental clean-up company which was secretly decontaminating a toxic waste site that produces enough Radon gas to make four-tongued mutants out of the next five generations of Framingham-ians. I didn't know that, I was just guessing. My role would be to answer the phones for Dr. Schlockman (from MIT, of course), and to report to Mrs. Callis, whose butt-cheek impression had probably been bronzed into her office chair. That guess was more accurate; after I had accepted the job, Marilyn told me Mrs. Callis hadn't been late in her twenty-seven years at Clean Earth.

I got off near The Bagelry on Beacon Street, ran in for a toasted sesame with pineapple cream cheese and cranberry juice, and walked upbound, eating. When I had to work at 7:00 a.m., I never drank coffee. Public bathroom paranoia.

It was sunny. I flipped on my Ray Bans as I passed an Italian market where a middled-aged man was sweeping the stoop in filthy white pants, shirt, and apron. A dark brown stain ran down the left pant leg. He glanced up and whistled before yelling to me.

"Che bella!"

I pointed to his pants. "K-opectate," I said without stopping. He actually laughed and for some reason it saddened me.

The office building was a beige brick '70s nightmare. I pushed the red button next to the shiny aqua elevator doors. After five minutes, nothing. An elderly woman with a slightly crooked, curly red wig wiggled down the hall.

"It's outta awdda, deeya." She stuck her ladies room key into the door behind me and disappeeyad.

Climbing eight flights of stairs while swooshing sesame seeds out of my teeth with cranberry juice was a challenge at 7:00 a.m. I could barely open the fire door by the time I made it to my floor. Maybe I'd join Zoe for aerobics or jog along the Esplanade later in the week, wear the Lycra biking shorts I bought just before selling my bike.

There was only one fluorescent light flickering in the hallway. Suite 806, finally. Mrs. Callis zipped out to meet me as I tripped over the gold, industrial-grade carpet in the waiting area. She had the greatest beehive hairdo I had ever seen, but by the look of her gray tweed suit and painful-looking pince-nez, I could tell she wasn't into retro. Her lips were painted hot pink and their shape indicated she had chosen an alum shake instead of coffee.

"Good morning, Amanda. May I take your coat?"

I juggled the empty bagel bag, juice container, and my briefcase. The office smelled of pine incense and turkey gravy.

"If you can lead me to a trash can, I'd appreciate it." I thought, "I'm going to be sick" should follow but didn't.

Mrs. Callis told me that Dr. Schlockman would be out on a project all day as I hung my coat in the coat closet. I followed her down the short hallway to an office where two women my age squinted at computer screens.

"Girls, this is Amanda. Amanda, this is Rita . . . ," Rita chewed gum with an open mouth and had a vulture beak-shaped nose. "And Sue." Sue was painting her nails. Her hair was as big as the dryer she must have sat under after getting her perm. "Sue, why don't you show Amanda around before you give her the documents." Mrs. Callis patted me on the back and walked to the door, duck-footed. "You'll be typing instead of phones today, dear. If you have any questions, please ask."

Sue looked me up and down before she got up to flap her burgundy fingernailed hands around.

"So, where are you from, Amanda?" I expected her to jut one

hip out, rest her hand on it, and glare at me. She just stood there, waving at no one.

"I live on Beacon Hill. Small, roach-infested, leaky pipes. Just charming."

She snorted a laugh. "Yeah. I have the South Shore variety."

Sue showed me Dr. Schlockman's office, which was more like stacks of papers with a desk underneath. We visited the chief engineer's office, the supply closet, the kitchen (smaller than the supply closet), the ladies room, and the utility room—which Sue called the scary wire room—where copies were made.

My job was to type the recently edited procedural manuals for Clean Earth's EPA reports, tax exemptions and government proposals to the beat of Rita's gum popping. Rita and Sue left for lunch at 11:45. They both needed purse discipline: their handbags were the size of small children. I called SunnySide as the smell of their Aquanet faded.

"What happened to the law firms and the financial district office assignments?"

"Is there a problem?" Marilyn asked.

"It's not your fault. I guess I didn't define what I thought would be a step up from admitting family pets for euthanasia." Mrs. Callis poked her head in to say toodles and to warn me about personal calls. I told her it was my gynecologist's office with the results of my herpes culture, and turned back to Marilyn.

"I'll finish the day out," I told her, "but from now on, please don't send me out of the city."

I hung up and sighed. In my jewelry box at home were two gold rings I had never worn that my great aunt Melda left me. I was sure I could hock them for about eight hundred bucks. This is pathetic, I said aloud on my way to the rest room. Just who was I kidding? A temp was one step above the primary stage of life. I looked in mirror over the bathroom sink and pretended to be holding a cigarette. "I used to be an amoeba," I half-closed my eyes vampishly, "but now I'm a temp."

When Mrs. Callis returned, I went to the deli across the street for a tuna sandwich. Since I was eating alone I ordered a huge garlic pickle. The bar at the window was greasy. There were no stools. I watched a bag lady roll a shopping cart full of cans and bottles past a group of school children in navy uniforms. She wore men's shoes and a dirty Red Sox cap. One little boy squirted his juice box at her humped back and ran off with his friends, giggling.

On my way back to the office, I noticed a girl with buzzed white hair sitting under the window of the dry cleaners. The sign next to her said, *Work. Anything. Please.* She was picking her fingernails, but as I approached she looked up at me. Our face was the same shape, and for a minute I thought I was looking at my reflection in a puddle. The grainy sidewalk beneath her was dry and cracked. A dozen small silver hoop earrings lined her ear. The girl's eyes were so light green they were almost yellow, and looking into them, I wondered what they had seen that made them so shockingly bright. Her lashes were little thorns, stuck together as they do after you cry for hours. She smiled and pointed at my feet. "Nice shoes," she said. Her voice was barely louder than a whisper. "When I was in retail I had some like that." She tilted her head as if to look into my open mouth. "Do you have any extra food in that bag?"

The street was like a long line of monotonous brick and stone and glass with a dot of an intersection at the horizon. There was no point in looking back. I squatted down, opened the bag. Mrs. Callis could manage; temps were as interchangeable as the fuses in the scary wire room.

The girl said her name was Melissa as I handed her the two oatmeal cookies. She gave one back to me. "Hate to eat alone," she told me, smiling with raisins stuck in her teeth. I pointed to her sign, told her that she had very artistic handwriting. She touched my hand like a child trying to befriend a strange animal. Patchouli oil from her coat whirled around me. The cookie was gone. I offered to buy her lunch at the deli and we walked in together. The waitress said, "Back again?" to me and I put my arm around Melissa's shoulders, saying that I brought a friend. Melissa laughed a bit too loud. I ordered tea and she got a cheeseburger plate. When the waitress went into the kitchen, Melissa told me she usually stayed in the city or Harvard Square, but had been visiting a friend. Drinking her second Coke, she slipped that the friend was a counselor at the teen hostel where she used to live. The dam behind her voice broke free. She was a runaway from Worcester. Melissa's father had molested her when she was thirteen. She had taken off soon after, lived in people's garages or restaurant basements, then got a job in Urban Outfitters which she soon lost after she stole a coat for a street friend. The hostel—hostile, she called it—kicked her out when she arrived there the morning after she was fired. She had missed curfew. Lately she had been trying to convince them to let her back in.

"I was hoping I could scrape up some change today to get back to the square," she said. I opened my purse, passed her my token.

The food arrived while I called Zoe to ask her to meet me for a manicure. Melissa checked the clock behind the counter as she talked about her old job and shoved french fries into her mouth. As we got up to leave, she searched her pockets and handed me a plastic medallion, the kind from Cracker Jack boxes. "I don't have any money to pay you back," she explained, "but this is lucky." We rode the T to Copely in silence. At our stop, Melissa hugged me after I gave her all the money in my wallet and my phone number. She told me I was the only person who had cared about her for days.

"You're real nice, Amanda," she said. "Pass it on."

I stood on the filthy platform and watched her walk away, imagining the rest of her day: eating a bite-marked sandwich from a dumpster; lying in a hollow doorway, pulling a rank wool blanket over her curled up body; waking to screaming, realizing it was her own voice as she fought off a shadowy man who was trying to put his grubby hand in her pants. Starting all over again in the hushed, empty morning. I felt something burn my face, hot, like a slap. I moved toward Melissa, pushing the crowd around me, and tripped, almost throwing myself onto the tracks where a rat made its way into a hole. Lights from the tunnel glared, and I regained my balance, still searching for the white crew cut in the stream of commuters. Thick, stale wind blew around me as the train screeched and lurched by my side. I could barely see her now. She didn't turn around to see my tiny wave.

―――――

The guy behind the desk at admissions was bobbing his head, reading Camus. A little cross dangled from his right earlobe. If I hadn't been completely over Paul, it might have bothered me that their chins had a similar squareness. He put the book down and stared at the top of the desk, passing his palms over his slicked-back hair. I cleared my throat. After the third cough he looked up.

"Do you have an appointment?" He didn't ask for my name.

"Yes, with Ms. Jenkins." I sat in a rocking chair near the coffee table covered with old *Atlantic* magazines. Ms. Jenkins appeared as he reached for the intercom.

"Here she is." He returned to the novel.

"Are you Amanda?"

"Yes." She must live on rice cakes and seltzer water, I thought as Ms. Jenkins shook my hand. Her neck seemed thinner than a baseball bat, and her green dress draped her petite form as if her shoulders were a hanger. But she was smiling and her eyes were calm and shiny brown, like the skin on warm chocolate pudding.

The mismatched vinyl furniture glowed in the sun in Ms. Jenkins' office. I sat on the edge of an olive green chair. Ms. Jenkins offered me spring water and I said no thank you. We discussed the nice weather, living downtown, the new Moroccan restaurant near her apartment.

"So, Amanda," Ms. Jenkins took a sip of water, "why are you interested in pursuing a degree in social work?"

I opened my mouth to reply, but realized I didn't have a spit-polished response. Yet there were words flowing out; they sounded familiar but tentative, like long-lost friends. The fact was, I didn't just want a change, I wanted to change. I didn't want my life to be measured in decorative pottery and hand washables. The questions everyone asks were mine: Can I do it? How? Who am I, who will I become? Where do I go from here? Answers didn't follow, couldn't follow. I imagined a dog with its head out the car window, squinting, streamlined, not knowing where the road would lead but glad to be traveling.

The sun started its descent, shining gold right into my eyes from across the Charles. I didn't lean out of the way, though I could have, but sat up straight, trying to focus on Ms. Jenkins. I talked about reality as I was struggling to see it. Ms. Jenkins was a shadow listening and nodding, and I strained to see her clearly, squinting enough to notice the curve of my eyelashes. With the light in my eyes, I saw colors running down the white wall behind Ms. Jenkins, and I envisioned a liquid rainbow, red and green and yellow swirling beneath a burst of hot water, splashing down the drain in my sink full of clear glass bowls.

This Time of Night

Bonnie ZoBell

We're sitting on plastic picnic chairs in the backyard as the sun sets. Willy is grilling swordfish for dinner, and we're planning a camping trip to San Onofre State Park, nineteen miles from home. We're going on our maiden voyage in the twenty-three-foot trailer we just bought.

"Is the campsite right next to those two big cement things?" I ask Willy. The evening is as close as it can be to darkness while still being light. A lingering red strip of sun hangs over the trees and roofs in the neighborhood, and our dog tries to align himself with us humans as much as possible, thinking he might get a bite of something.

"The boobs?" Willy says.

Everyone in Southern California calls the big cement mounds on the San Onofre Nuclear Plant near Camp Pendelton the boobs. It is as if a giant woman is lying face up on the beach, exposing herself to the elements. I shake my head. "Wouldn't be so funny if something went wrong up there. Wouldn't be so funny if there was an accident."

"Okay, OK," Willy says, "'the containments,' then. What's with you, anyway?"

I know this isn't really what's wrong, and it makes me even more mad that he knows too. "So what do they contain, anyway?"

"If there's a nuclear accident," Willy explains patiently, nudging the potatoes with a poker, turning the swordfish, "they're supposed to keep radioactivity from escaping into the atmosphere."

"So what are those cement nipples at the top?"

He shrugs.

"Great place to go camping," I say, "right under some radioactive boobs."

"When it happens, it won't matter how far away you are. No one will escape."

I tell him, sighing, "They just caught that serial killer up there, too, what's his name. We're going camping in a place where serial killers get caught."

Willy's eyes roll up toward the moon, and he shakes his head so slowly I finally smile. I love it when he makes dinner for the two of us.

"You've got to stop focusing on things like that, honey," he says, standing and taking the fish off the fire.

"What else is there to focus on?"

He retreats quickly into the house with the food, without even looking at me.

A trailer is for when you need to get out of your own life for a while and experience something else. Just buying one is a huge act of faith on our part since Willy's health has already begun to deteriorate.

———

When he heard the price of the trailer, Willy knew something was wrong. "People don't sell 1990 trailers for that price," he said. We'd been hoping to find an '82 or an '83.

And it seemed funny that there were still vacancies at the San Onofre campground when we called a week ago. Funny because it's right on the beach, a haven for summertime campers.

"Maybe," I suggested to Willy, "it's because of that serial killer. People don't want to be so exposed. They want to be somewhere they can lock the windows against a person like that, bolt the doors."

"Who's going to be afraid if the guy's already been caught?"

"I am. About all the other ones still out there doing it."

We drove down to a friend of Willy's dad's to look at the trailer. We took Willy's dad, whom we call the Chief, along with us.

When we got to Stu's mobile home, he and his wife Cissy were sitting in a room they'd cordoned off to trap the air conditioning. The lights were off and there were "Roadrunner" cartoons playing on a large TV console. Even though they were standing to answer the door, you could see the spots where Stu and Cissy usually sat, where they'd been sitting before we got there. On top of the television were at least fifteen framed photographs of various grandchildren, nieces, and nephews. Most of the frames had brass curlicues looping around their perimeters. The small dark room was filled with home-made doilies, boxes of Kleenex, Cissy's knitting needles and Stu's fishing lures. This is where they'd decided to grow old together.

We were sitting there at the dinette. Before stopping by, we'd been all over the trailer Stu had up for sale. It was parked a few blocks away. We'd tried all the switches, got the AC going, pulled the blinds up and let them slide down again. We'd seen that you had to run the appliances with gas when you couldn't hitch up to a 110-volt outlet. We'd turned the pump on, flushed the toilet.

"Why is there water on the carpet?" Willy was now asking Stu.

"Well," Stu said, then crossed his arms over his chest, preparing to tell the story. When you're in your twilight years, you make the most out of everything, even a small story. Willy and I understand this better than Stu suspected.

Stu is almost square, he's so short and fat. Like Willy's dad, he prefers not to wear his teeth because they're uncomfortable. Sitting there in Stu's mobile home, just down the way from Willy's dad's mobile home, neither man was wearing his teeth. Cissy sat across from us in the mobile home's living room. Both her La-Z-Boy and Stu's had bath towels on the seats, hand towels on the backs, wash-cloths on the arm rests to prevent the chairs from wearing out too quickly. They would like the chairs to outlive them.

The Chief was on his third beer of the six-pack he asked us to buy him when we were getting sodas at the 7-11. He'd already had a little something before we picked him up.

The Chief has been known to cut a deal now and then, especially since he is living on virtually nothing but Social Security these days. Social Security off a social security number based on a card he got when he joined the navy underage over fifty years ago. He knows something is wrong with Willy's health, that my health is fine; he knows Willy is terminally ill, but Willy won't tell him exactly what it is.

The Chief was so excited that Willy and I might buy the trailer that we were perplexed. Maybe it was the beer talking. Or he wants Willy and me to have at least a brief taste of the happiness he and his late wife shared for decades in trailers before our life to-gether is over.

Maybe Stu was giving the Chief a kickback.

"Well," Stu finally said again, after thinking things over, "the reason there's water on the floor is because we had the trailer over to the beach." Now Stu tamped another cigarette on the dinette, lighted it. "Had to warsh the carpet. Still a little damp."

"Something's funny about the way the paneling's attached," Willy said. "It's all flimsy. You can see daylight everywhere."

"Boy hasn't spent enough time in trailers," Chief told Stu. "Don't know how they're rigged." The beer had made him frisky. At six foot three and two hundred twenty-five pounds, this is a lot of friskiness. You could land a fighter plane on the Chief's gray flat top.

Stu was taking everything under consideration. He listened to Willy patiently, then the Chief. He nodded for a second or two. Now that he is retired, now that he and his wife have their spots, he's not in any hurry. "There was a fire in the trailer. Gutted it. Rebuilt it myself."

"I knew something was funny," Willy said. "That explains everything. The price . . ."

"First I heard of it," Chief said, his thick arms up in the air, Scout's honor. While they were up there, he cracked a fourth beer. "Ain't heard a word about it till now." Then he turned to me, said, "Don't know why I'm doing this, Babe," meaning drinking the beer, "haven't had a drop in six months."

I asked Cissy if I could use the bathroom. It was Cissy's job to make guests comfortable, Stu's to tend to the finances.

"Oh, here—let me get rid of some of these," she said. She walked ahead of me to the bathroom, picking up damp towels left to dry on doorknobs.

"Don't know what we'd do around here without doorknobs," she said.

In the outer room I could hear Stu and Willy still talking. Willy said, "Can we go over and take another look at the trailer so I can ask a few questions?"

Thirty seconds went by, and I imagined Stu nodding his head. "So you think it's the type of thing you might want to buy?"

"I might," Willy said.

"Well, then, I *might* go over with you to look at it."

Stu and the Chief erupted in guffaws, knee slaps.

In the bathroom was a collection of porcelain figurines. My favorite was an elderly basset and schnauzer couple. She was wearing a poodle skirt and a bow, he a top hat and trousers. Like Stu and his wife, this couple had been together for an awfully long time. They knew each other's imperfections and accepted them. They knew each other inside out. Willy and I will hardly have a chance.

———

So then Stu, the Chief, Willy, and I went over to inspect the trailer together. I suspect Cissy rarely leaves their mobile home. Stu and the Chief rode in one truck, Willy and I in another. Maybe Stu and the Chief talked about the length of Willy's sandy-blond hair during the ride; Willy's grown it out shoulder length, the longest it's been since the sixties, a time in his life when he didn't have a care in the world. Or maybe the Chief and Stu listened to the C.B. Except for Willy, everyone in his family has a C.B. Willy has a car phone instead that chimes when he starts the engine. I sat right next to Willy on the way over, our thighs touching. Later, I don't want to remember times we could have been closer, things I should have said, that somehow our life got away from us and I never let him know how much I loved him.

Willy said several times in different ways: "I *knew* there was something funny about that trailer. A fire . . . that explains some things. . . ."

We got down on our hands and knees outside of the trailer. First Stu's knees cracked like cap guns when he lowered himself to the floor. Then his gut was so big he could hardly show us how you light the gas for the hot water, the refrigerator. "You hear that?" he said when he'd lit the pilot and we heard a steady hissing. Willy and I nodded.

Down on the floor in front of the twin beds, Stu lifted a panel, showed us how to light the heater. He showed us how to dump our gray water, our black water, how to make sure we were level, how to hitch the truck.

"You kids'll have so much fun," the Chief said. "Now lookit this here, Babe," he said to me. His arm was looped over my shoulder and he opened the trailer's bathroom door with the other. Inside there was wallpaper covering the particle board so it looked like wood paneling. He waved his arm inside as if it were door number three and a grand prize and not a three-foot-by-three-foot toilet and shower stall that smelled a little funky. "Ain't that something?" he said. He didn't know that it was Willy and not me, the woman, who wanted, needed, the bathroom. Either because of Willy's clothes or because of not being able to bear knowing, the Chief doesn't see that Willy is losing weight as a dozen smaller maladies and a few larger ones converge on his body.

I just know Stu must have thought us a couple of whippersnapper young kids to be buying a trailer for ourselves in the first place, whippersnapper young kids who could afford to lose a little money on the deal. Even though we are family to Chief, I'm sure it was very clear to Stu and Cissy that they would never see us again.

On the drive home Willy pulled me toward him, our thighs again aligned, said, "I wish I was going to be around to see your hair when it's gray and up in a little bun like Cissy's."

"Maybe you will be." My eyes filled, and I couldn't stand to look at him.

"I wish I was going to see you in bifocals and stretch pants and with Kleenex tucked in your watchband."

———

Willy is backing the trailer onto the side of our house. Stu drove it up to Vista, to a mobile home service center down the street from us. He left it there earlier today. The serviceman attached a tow package to Willy's truck so he could drive the trailer home.

"You know what Stu did?" Willy asked me on the phone a while ago. "Switched batteries on us. There was a perfectly good RV battery in it the other day. Now there's only a dead car battery."

At least we know the Chief hasn't been gossiping about Willy. Nobody, not even Stu, wants to think of himself as someone who cheats a sick person.

I'm standing in the street. Willy wants me to watch cars coming from the west as he backs into the driveway. He wants me to watch cars coming from the east. He wants me to tell him which way to turn the wheel so he'll back in straight. He wants me to watch the trailer hitch and ball to make sure it doesn't hit the truck. He wants me to watch the tires so they don't run over the curb.

"I can't do all these things at the same time!" I shriek at him. My voice resonates in the air between us. I hear it over and over again. I'm sure I'll hear it later, too, when this is all over. Why do I have to be so loud? What's the matter with me?

"Try to be patient," he calls from the cab of the truck.

"But you're asking me to do something that's impossible." Of course I should be patient. Of course I should try.

"Just help me. Please."

And then he's holding me in his arms right out there on the curb. I look over his shoulder at the trailer, freshly painted blue and white. Maybe the trailer will be good for us, like it seems to have been for Stu and Cissy.

———

"Call Rosemary. See if she wants to go," Willy says. "It'll be fun."

I leave a message on Rosemary's phone machine. Rosemary is an old friend of mine, now a friend of ours, who was my roommate when I met Willy.

"So did you call her, hon?" Willy asks later. "It'll be fun if someone else comes too." He messes up my hair, gives me a kiss. Tall and lanky, he has on his most recent pair of shockingly expensive tennis shoes, which he bought over a year ago and which are now held together with silver electrician's tape. He doesn't mind spending money occasionally, but he hates shopping—staying still long enough to try things on.

"You call her. It'll mean more to her if you leave a message," I tell him.

So Willy, too, leaves a message. "She *begged* me to call," he says into Rosemary's machine. We're laughing and he's staving off my hands, which are trying to grab the receiver. "She begged me and is twisting my arm behind me at this very moment. Oh, it will be so much fun if you come, Rosemary. You're always so joyful to be around. We're going all the way up to San Onofre," he says before hanging up, "just to try everything out."

Later Rosemary calls back. Unlike the Chief, Rosemary knows exactly what is wrong. She knows because I told her. She and Willy have never discussed the issue outright, although he knows she knows and she knows he knows she knows. Willy doesn't want people to know he's sick. Then they'll feel sorry for him and be careful around him and so his life will be over even sooner. It's one of the things Willy and I clash on: the dangers of telling too many people versus the dangers of keeping it all inside.

"So, what, did you pin him against the wall or something?" Rosemary asks. "Did you make Willy call me?" I can tell from the tone of her voice that aside from wanting to come, she thinks she *should* come, and always present in her voice now is the worry that if she doesn't come there may not be a next time. I'd like to tell her he's going to live a lot longer, but the fact is no one can say. He could live six months; he could live three years.

"He begged me, really," I tell her, feeling a little desperate for her to come along.

But Rosemary already has plans with her new boyfriend. "Steve and I'll drive down in the morning, though. We'll go for a walk on the beach with you."

"Good," I say. "Great."

———

Willy backs his truck up to the trailer the morning of our trip and I yell instructions. This time we hook up right the first time.

We're on the road. Nineteen miles from Vista to San Onofre. The dog is in the back seat. The trailer and the car seem to be going up and down over invisible bubbles; we shimmy from side to side. Every time a semi goes by the force of the air in its wake makes us lose control, veer to the left.

"Are we almost there yet?" I ask.

"Only fifteen more miles."

Both of us adore the dog. Each of us sneaks him treats when the other isn't looking. We call him sickening sweet love names. The other night I found the two of them hugging in the pantry, our baby's big red tail thumping against the washing machine. "You're going to outlive me, old boy," Willy said into the fluffy red ear while the dog eagerly licked at his neck. Then Willy stood up and said, "The two of you will have to look out for each other." I leaned against him for a minute, promised him we would, then got back to the dishes before I broke down.

"There's the boobs," I say now, soon spotting them on the horizon.

We pull off the freeway onto the San Onofre exit. The ranger Willy talked to on the phone said there was a one-mile walk to the beach, that dogs were allowed, that we'd be staying in the San Mateo section of the campground. All of it sounds perfect.

We're gazing over the Pacific as we take our turn driving up to the ranger's booth. A sign reads: "San Onofre is booked solid. There are *no* vacancies."

We tell the ranger our name.

"Don't see it here," she says.

"I've got a receipt," says Willy, reaching into his back pocket.

"You must be staying over in the San Mateo area or something," she says.

"Yeah, that's it."

She shakes her head, points down the road we just came in on. "You gotta go back, get on the freeway again, exit at Cristianitos and take a right, go onto the Camp Pendelton Marine Base, and you'll see it a half a mile up."

"Aw, shit," Willy says, slamming his hand on the dashboard. "You mean it's not on the beach?"

"We'll have fun anyway, honey," I tell him. "It'll be OK."

"I just can't believe it," Willy says. "No wonder there were campsites available in the summer. Who'd want to stay there?"

"It's better if you don't stress out, Willy. You want me to drive?" I shake my head and look away from him. "Just our luck," I say.

The ranger is a big woman. She adjusts the belt on her uniform, says, "Sorry, sir—go ahead and write a letter complaining. There's nothing I can do about it. We're all full up."

We manage to get the trailer turned around, follow the ranger's directions. There is no discussion of going home; our life seems fated at this point, our destiny out of our hands. The radioactive boobs loom over everything we do.

Soon we're exiting the freeway at the other off ramp, heading onto the military base. I look down to the bottom of a dry, dusty canyon, see dozens and dozens of campers wedged compactly together—no trees, no lakes, no streams, nothing but dust.

"Can that really be it?" I say to Willy. "Would somebody stay here on purpose?"

I make a face when Willy looks at me, and somehow we both manage to laugh.

"I can't understand why they'd let people on a military base."

We pull in. The place is swarming with teenagers wearing lots of makeup, college couples who rarely peek out of tents. There are toddlers riding bikes everywhere.

"We're only here for one night, sweetheart," I say, laughing and patting Willy's leg.

At this ranger's window, there is a handwritten sign reading: "Mountain Lion seen in the area. Watch your children and pets."

"Great," Willy says, laughing, "that'll just make our vacation complete."

I ask the ranger whether there are really mountain lions around here, while he looks on a chart for our reservation.

"A little girl got killed in June, but it was further up in the hills, near a different campground."

"Great," I say.

"There aren't mountain lions here," Willy says. "Too many people."

The ranger shakes his head. "Somebody reported one."

"One person?" Willy says.

Now the ranger nods. "*I* haven't seen a mountain lion, and I'm here everyday. It was probably just a bobcat."

"Great," I say.

There is a crop of tomatoes or some other low-to-the-ground vegetable further down the dusty valley and covered with plastic. From a distance you can see the reflection off the plastic, pretend it is a lake that you are camping nearby. We drive up and down the campground lanes, amazed at how many people have been pushed together in one small area.

"Who would intentionally camp here?" I ask Willy.

Willy shrugs. "It's cheap and near the beach."

I nod as we go down another lane, this one full of loud rock music.

"Great," Willy says.

When we find lot 81, we back the trailer in like old pros. Not only are we not at the beach, but we are in a handicapped spot adjoining the public rest rooms. Men, women, and children from all over the grounds cut the corners of our lot walking through to use the john, rinse their dirty dishes, brush their teeth.

"Great," Willy and I say at different times. We pat each other's knees.

I let the dog out of the truck. Immediately he runs to the campground two feet from ours. I watch as a family of five all pet him, say how pretty he is. Then the dog runs into their tent, comes out with a package of Oreos.

"I'm so sorry," I say. Even at home our house is further from our neighbors'. It's as if everyone has decided to pitch a tent on the freeway. The only thing to do at the bottom of this mostly barren, unlandscaped canyon is observe one another.

I tie the dog up. He gets more room in our backyard.

"The refrigerator won't light," Willy says. We can't use electrical here since there aren't any hookups. Willy rushes to one side of the trailer, then to the other. Wherever I go, whatever I try to do, I am in his way. Soon he will have our whole trip planned out: hiking, singing by the fire, fishing if there is any. Like with Stu and Cissy, our duties are clearly delineated: mine is to explode occasionally, let some of the steam off; Willy's is to keep us busy.

"I'm going to walk the dog up to the ranger's and make sure we can take him on the beach," I tell Willy, who is completely preoccupied with the trailer.

The dog and I walk the half mile up. Everywhere there are tents, so close they're almost touching. Is this what my life would have been like if I'd had children? Squalid living conditions, no privacy, husbands with buzz cuts who squash beer cans in their fists?

There is one cement bathroom after another all the way up the hill. You have to figure that a hundred people must be assigned to each one. A serial killer could easily pretend he's taking a stroll at 3:00 a.m. when momentarily you're the only one using the toilet. Or he could hide in one of the stalls and wait. Or camp next door and conceal the bodies in his tent.

The ranger tells me there are two trails I can take the dog on.

He pets the dog, says he's a good boy.

"I think the refrigerator's broken," Willy says when I get back.

He can't fix things like refrigerators at home. I don't know why he thinks he can fix one here. "Give it a little time," I tell him. "Stu said you had to give it some time."

"Stu said he was selling us a new battery."

"It's just a battery, honey," I say, but I'm wondering if buying the trailer might have been a mistake. Maybe we're in over our heads. Maybe we shouldn't have spent the money.

I look up at a tall cement post on our campsite. There seem to be speakers coming out of the top. "What's this?" I ask Willy.

"Sirens."

"What do you mean?"

"Nuclear plants are required to install sirens within so many miles in all directions in case there's a meltdown."

"Wonderful."

I'm following Willy around the outside of the trailer as he listens to the different pilot lights, but now I can't stop glancing at the siren and wondering why it has to be on our lot, why it has to be us.

Inside the trailer I try again to put things away, to retrieve chairs to sit on, but as soon as I do, Willy's on his knees in front of the refrigerator again, feeling the racks for coolness, blocking the way.

I tell him, "I'm going to find a pay phone and call Rosemary so she doesn't go to the wrong campground."

"Use the one in the truck."

But when we try it we discover we're between cells, there's not enough juice. "I'll find a phone," I tell Willy again.

Once I've walked back to the station, the ranger explains there are no pay phones on the campgrounds; the closest one is at a Carl's Jr., about a two-hour walk. "Good boy," he says to my dog, who loves everybody.

"Two hours round trip," Willy asks when I reach our site again, "or two hours each way?"

I shrug, tell him I could walk back and ask, but he shakes his head. "Let's just unhook the trailer and drive the truck over."

"You don't want to do all that, Willy. You'll be exhausted."

Willy's hands are on his hips, and he's perspiring. He's lost weight, he's tired, he's shrinking before my very eyes. It's no longer a question of just being infected; he's got the whole thing, the full-blown version. Yes, maybe we should never have bought the trailer. It was silly to believe the trips it took us on could somehow help us have some of the life Stu and Cissy did. We've just thrown away money we're going to need for more important things—the medications, the hospitals, after that.

It's hard to imagine now how important a link the Chief might be for me when these things start happening; the Chief, who has certainly been known to get on my nerves, and I on his. Of course his enthusiasm over the trailer must simply have been his shared excitement over future camping trips. Since the beginning, the three of us have camped together—before we got married, before this disease. We'd fish, throw sticks into the lake for the dog, sing along with Willy's guitar in the evening. Later, after I'd crawled into the tent to sleep, the two of them would get into the apricot brandy and sing "Jack Was a Lonesome Cowboy" and "It Was Only an Old Beer Bottle" and "They Had to Carry Harry to the Ferry." This was back when their bodies could afford pints of apricot brandy, when I had a day to throw away for pouting over their keeping me awake.

Willy looks away from our campsite, says, "Well, after dinner we'll walk a little ways, see how far the Carl's Jr. is. How do you get there?"

"He said you take the dirt path by the regular road," I say pointing.

"We'll have to be careful—I just heard what sounded like the marines practicing artillery up there."

"Great."

Willy laughs, then shakes his head again. "Damn refrigerator," he says.

"It's only a refrigerator. You can ask John about it when we get back."

Willy won't tell John, his brother, specifically what it is either. Willy won't tell anyone. Only my father, whom I was going to tell anyway, because Willy was afraid if he himself didn't tell, my father might hate him. It was the time I had to be admitted to a hospital. I, of all people, ended up in a hospital because I couldn't stand the thoughts in my head anymore, because I can't stand to think of what it will be like afterward. In my mind there is a black hole.

"How can you not think about it?" I finally asked him when I was in the hospital.

"I'm always thinking about it. It's always on my mind."

Only I have told people, have had to tell people. Otherwise I can't seem to function. So, no, John, a little on the old country boy side like the Chief, hasn't been told exactly what his brother Willy has. But, of course, because of the very fact that Willy won't say, what else can it be?

We're eating the steaks Willy has barbecued. It's getting dark. The trailer is between where we're sitting by a fire and the public rest rooms. Occasionally people walk through our lot, toilet paper and mess kits in tow. Across the lane are two families with two adult couples, two teenage girls wearing lots of lipstick and eye shadow and interested in the college boys on the other side of the rest rooms, and next to us is the family with the cookies. Every once in a while one of them calls our dog's name and throws another Oreo. Willy and I can't figure out how the five of them fit all their stuff into one car, what with a large tent, clothes, sleeping bags, and a surfboard.

I do the dishes after dinner, straighten things up. The car phone still doesn't work.

We're walking up the hill toward the Carl's Jr. Willy has brought his phone. Maybe it will perk up at the top of the hill with fewer obstructions, he thinks. I have a flashlight in one pocket, my address book in the other. The dog is on a leash.

Willy laughs at me. "Come on," he says as we climb the paved hill. Cars shoot past us, spraying gravel, blinding us with their brights because they can't figure out who would be out on such a busy highway at this time of night. He puts his arm around me, points out the dirt path only twenty or so feet away. We both know it's there. "Let's walk on the dirt. There aren't any mountain lions."

"I'm sorry, Willy. You just have to accept this about me. I can't do it. I won't walk there. I'm positive there are ten or twenty mountain lions just waiting for us to step off the road." Partly I'm laughing, partly I'm not.

Willy hits his forehead with the palm of his hand. "Honey, there hasn't been a mountain lion here in thirty years. You heard the ranger."

"What's the difference between a mountain lion and a bobcat?"

"If a bobcat saw us, he'd run *away* from us. They only weigh thirty pounds. A mountain lion weighs a hundred and forty, and he'd run *for* us."

"Please, Willy, I can't."

"Fine." He throws his arms up in the air.

I lean over to the dog, say, "I don't want my little sweetie to get eaten." Every time I talk baby talk, the dog wags his tail. A civilized animal, he's more terrified by the headlights than we are. He wouldn't do well with a bobcat.

Above us the radioactive boobs flicker with red lights telling airplanes and everyone else to stay away.

We're leaning against a guard rail trying again to call Rosemary. Not only does the rail not seem like a safe place to be, but it's such a thin piece of metal to do such a big job. And what I don't mention to Willy is how afraid I am of who's inside those cars. All those serial killers who haven't yet gotten caught have to get around somehow; they have to drive cars too. Who's to say they don't travel on this road, that a serial killer doesn't live in the neighborhood? They have to live somewhere. There's nothing ridiculous about this, I want to tell Willy. Just watch the news at night. What he doesn't understand is how it all builds up inside me, takes on a life of its own, how I can't sleep at night with all this danger going on.

We can see black bars denoting there is enough power on the lit green screen of the cellular phone. We're receiving a dial tone, but then all we get is a busy signal.

More cars come flying around the corner and then swerve, not knowing who or what we are, sitting here with a cellular phone with green lights and me holding a flashlight above, a frightened dog on our leash on the shoulder of a busy highway. I ask Willy: "Is that a tract development?"

We look out across the valley where the campground is, over to another hill. Willy nods. The usual Friday night traffic has picked up on Interstate 5 between San Diego and Los Angeles, making so much noise it's hard to do much else besides nod. While most of the hills and mountains in the area are barren, this one across the way is densely populated with what looks like near-identical houses and street lamps a near-identical number of yards apart from each other.

A car comes over the hill so fast it almost loses control, so I agree to take the dirt path back to our campsite, despite the mountain lions. When we arrive at the trailer, Willy says, "There's water on the carpet exactly where it was that first day."

"You're kidding." We're on our hands and knees again, touching it, smelling it. "It must be from when I did the dishes," I say. "It must have come through the floor."

"Great," Willy says, shaking his head. "Can you believe it? Stu out and out lied."

Now we're sitting in our chairs outside by the fire. I scoot mine over, right next to Willy's, pat his knee. "It's only a trailer," I tell him. "Just a trailer."

I think about Stu and Cissy watching cartoons on their bath

towels, Stu and Cissy with whom we have more in common than any of the young families camping or in the tracts above us, and I wonder how they're able to rationalize such things. They must think a little lie is OK because they are the ones in their twilight years, because they are the ones who have put in hard lives and now deserve to relax as they creep closer to whatever they believe happens afterward. And then I feel sorry for them because they don't know Willy like I do, because they don't know what a horrible waste this is. They can't possibly comprehend what's really happening. And who knows what happens next? Maybe eventually, in some other life, they will discover the truth, after all. And maybe the truth will seem like nothing in the bigger picture.

We're sitting by our siren and looking up at the stars above the valley. It's a clear night, and there are stars everywhere. I gaze at them, then over at Willy looking at them, then back to the stars. He has questions about destiny, about what happens next, whether there really are such places as heaven and hell—things a thirty-nine-year-old man should still be able to laugh off. And I can't help him. Heaven and hell are as real to me as a man sitting on a cloud and calling himself God. There isn't anything I can do, even imagine what he must think about tomorrow or the next day.

I hold his hand, and we peer over at the campsite next to us. "Are they all sleeping in the one tent?" Willy whispers. I shrug, but we figure they must be. How do they all fit?

We watch the kids playing across the lane, kids we will never have. They ride their bikes, push the brakes on as hard as they will go. They're competing to see who can leave the longest skid mark. One of the fathers comes out. All the adults have been playing poker. This dad says, "I told you not to ride those bikes anymore. That's it. Wash your faces and then you're in the camper. Got it? No bikes tomorrow."

"*Dad.*"

"We'll see . . . if you get in bed *now.*"

The boys scurry across our lot with their toothbrushes as fast as they can to the public sink. We smile as we listen to them whispering to each other to hurry up, hurry up or they'll have to walk to the beach tomorrow. "So you think they'll ever really use them?" I ask Willy, patting the cement base that leads up to the nuclear siren.

"Sure," he says. "We're using more and more of that energy."

"Soon?"

"It's inevitable."

Families in the subdivision above us are settling down to relax for the evening. Homely blue and white lights flicker across their windows and down into the valley, onto us. I wish we could keep some of it.

I tell Willy, "I bet Rosemary's sorry she's missing this—nestled in on the military base on our relaxing camping trip . . ."

". . . with our cellular phone that doesn't work," he adds.

". . . or we'd be calling Stu and telling him a thing or two." Not to mention feeling reassured we could phone out if we ran into a mountain lion, or the next serial killer.

That's when we hear what sounds like a piece of metal clanking loudly behind us—a shrill, piercing sound, it whines, crashes, clangs. It reverberates throughout the whole trailer, onto the pavement, through our feet, screaming in the air around us.

"*What!*" I shriek. "*What?*" I jump to my feet, knock over my chair.

The Oreo family unzips and peaks out of their tent. The boys across the way, finally in bed, crack the curtains of the camper.

"It's the siren!" I shout. "*Oh my god, it's the siren!*"

My hands are on my face and I can hardly believe it—is everyone running out of their campsites, toward us? Are we really having a catastrophe?

Stunned, Willy finally reacts. He moves close, one of my shoulders in each of his hands. "I think it's just the water pump, honey," he says, though he too looks scared. "It's just the trailer."

"It's just a trailer," I say, but now I can't stop crying.

The dog barks and runs into the tent next door, as Willy and I turn to face the rest of the world. We gaze up at the siren, beyond.

Crickets are somehow cricking, though there's hardly any ground cover in this place for them to hide in. The stars are so thick and full, twinkling, throbbing, falling—all at the same time—so beautiful over all of us, this ugly and overfull population, that they make you think there must be some reason we're here, wedged in together; they make you focus out there, project yourself, airborne, slithering with the comets, the constellations, the galaxies, somewhere out there where we all come from, where I have to believe we'll see each other again.

Biographical Notes

Editors

Alan Davis has published an acclaimed collection of short stories, *Rumors from the Lost World* (New Rivers Press, 1993). His fiction and nonfiction appear in such newspapers as the *Chicago Sun Times, Cleveland Plain Dealer, New York Times*, and *San Francisco Chronicle;* and in such journals as *Ascent, Hudson Review, Quarterly*, and *South Dakota Review*. He has received a Loft-McKnight Award of Distinction in Creative Prose, two Fulbrights, and a Minnesota State Arts Board Fellowship. He teaches at Moorhead State University in Minnesota, where he chairs English and co-directs Creative Writing.

Michael White is the author of *A Brother's Blood*, published by Harper Collins (1996) in the United States and Viking/Penguin in Great Britain (1997). His fiction appears in numerous magazines and journals ranging from *Redbook* and *American Way* to *Nebraska Review* and *New Letters*. He teaches at Springfield College in Massachusetts.

Assistant Editors

Kassie Fleisher grew up in the Philadelphia area, received her masters from the University of North Dakota and her Ph.D. at SUNY-Binghamton. She is now based in Chicago, where both she and her husband, Joe Amato, split time between writing and teaching. She has written two novels and is currently gathering her short fiction in a collection called *Powdered Bones*.

Debra Marquart's work has received numerous prizes, among them the Dorothy Churchill Cappon Essay Award from *New Letters* (twice) and the Guy Owen Poetry Prize from *Southern Poetry Review*. Her first book, *Everything's a Verb*, (New Rivers Press), won the Minnesota Voices Project Award. She teaches creative writing at Iowa State University and sings and writes for The Bone People, who have released two CDs.

David Pink has published fiction, nonfiction, and poetry in many magazines, including *American Literary Review*, *The North American Review*, *Salmagundi*, and *Nimrod*. He has received grants and awards from the Loft-McKnight Foundation, the Edelstein-Keller Fund, and the North Dakota Humanities Council.

Maggie Risk has received scholarships from the Bread Loaf Writers Conference, the Sewanee Writers Conference, and the Ropewalk Writers Retreat. A graduate of the master's program in creative writing at the University of Denver, she has published stories in various magazines (one was a finalist for the Katherine Anne Porter Prize) and has taught writing at the University of Cincinnati. She is currently working on a novel.

Authors

Michael Blaine's short fiction has appeared in many magazines and journals, including *The New England Review*, *The North American Review*, *Shenandoah*, and *New Letters*. His story "Suits" was published in *American Fiction 88*, edited by Raymond Carver. Mr. Blaine lives in rural upstate New York with his wife, the artist Rose Mackiewicz, in a Civil War vintage farmhouse balanced on a boulder. Authorities in his county warn that he will steal anecdotes or even entire life stories if they're not nailed down.

Sara Burnaby's first fiction, "Bears," was published in *Story*, nominated for a Pushcart Prize, and included in the anthology *The Company of Animals*, edited by Michael Rosen and published by Doubleday. She has also written a biography, *The Practice of Mountains*, about Olympic skier Andrea Lawrence, published by Seaview Press in 1981. She lives in Bellingham, Washington, after living for years in the high desert country of the Eastern Sierra.

Steve Featherstone has an MFA from Syracuse and has published creative nonfiction in *The Gettysburg Review* and elsewhere. He lives in Nedrow, NY.

Andrea Foege won the 1996 Frank Waters Fiction Lectureship at New Mexico State University. She lives in Las Cruces.

Pete Fromm is the author of the collections *The Tall Uncut*, *King of the Mountain, Dry Rains*, the novel *Monkey Tag*, as well as *Indian Creek Chronicles*, winner of the Pacific Northwest Booksellers Association 1994 Book Award. His work has been published in such magazines as *Glimmer Train, Good Housekeeping, Manoa*, and *Sports Afield*. He lives in Montana.

Elizabeth Graver won the 1991 Drue Heinz Literature Prize for *Have You Seen Me?* (Ecco, 1993), and is the author of *Unravelling* (Hyperion, 1997). Her stories have been anthologized twice in the O. Henry Awards anthology and also in *Best American Short Stories 1991*. Her work has been published in *Story, Antaeus, Ploughshares, Glimmer Train*, and elsewhere. She teaches at Boston College.

Elisa Jenkins won First Prize in the 1994 Hemingway Short Story Competition and Third Prize in the 1995 Literal Latte Fiction Awards Competition. She lives in Muncie, Indiana.

Zoe Keithley, of Chicago, has had her work in *North American Review*, and other magazines, and has received two Chicago Artists Assistance Program grants. She teaches in Chicago's public schools for Northeastern Illinois University and at Columbia College.

Cynthia Kennison lives in New Braintree, Massachusetts. Her short stories and plays have received several awards and her work has appeared in literary journals as well as in *Seventeen* Magazine. She co-directs the Worcester Writers Workshop.

Dulcie Leimbach lives in New York. Her work appears in *The New York Times* as well as in *Elle, Family Life, Parenting, Ms.*, and *The Washington Post*. She has an MFA from Warren Wilson College.

William Luvaas, of San Marcos, California, published *Going Under*, a novel, in 1994, and, earlier, *The Seductions of Natalie Bach*. His stories have appeared in numerous journals, and he teaches fiction at San Diego State University.

Linda Watanabe McFerrin lives in San Francisco.

Dara Anastasia Moskowitz lives in Minneapolis. She has won the Tamarack Award, sponsored by *Minnesota Monthly*.

Jim Nichols lives in Thomaston, Maine, with wife Anne and

sons Aaron and Andrew. He has published fiction in *Esquire, River City,* and elsewhere.

C. Dawn O'Dell, who lives in Georgia, is a graduate of the MFA program at Warren Wilson College. She is a mother of one, a teacher of emotionally disturbed children, and the owner of a ramshackle house and garden.

Margo Rabb lives in Tucson. She has received a PEN Syndicated Fiction Award for "Shanah Tovah," which was broadcast on National Public Radio. She has also written for *Poets & Writers Magazine.*

Nancy Reisman's fiction has appeared in various magazines, including *Glimmer Train.* She has received an MFA from the University of Massachusetts at Amherst and has taught at the Rhode Island School of Design.

Liz Severn lives in North Dakota. She has worked as a writer for years and is completing a novel.

Rachel Simon lives in Pennsylvania. She has published *The Magic Touch* with Viking in 1994 and a collection of short stories, *Little Nightmares, Little Dreams,* in 1990 with Houghton Mifflin.

Lara J. K. Wilson, who lives in New Hampshire, has published fiction in *Indiana Review.*

Bonnie ZoBell lives in Oceanside, California. She won a 1995 NEA Creative Writing Fellowship and her work has appeared in several magazines.